GIFTED

KORA GREENWOOD

Cover: Kora Greenwood
Editor: Katie Evelyn
Interior Formatting: Nonon Tech & Design

ISBN: 978-1-7377254-0-4 (Paperback)
ISBN: 978-1-7377254-1-1 (Hardback)

For Kyran and Eli
You are braver than you know.

CHAPTER

"When the ancients saw the looming war,
They buried deep, down to Earth's core,
And from that place, our founders bore-Paramus,
the eternal cure."

- The Chronicles of Discord

It's time. I can feel the seconds ticking by as I stand outside of door numbered eleven in an otherwise empty hallway, the only sound in my ears--my unsteady breathing. Fourteen, fifteen, sixteen, I'm counting the seconds now, an old trick I learned to keep myself calm. A cool bead of sweat snakes down the back of my neck as I glance once more at the cameras overhead, a painful reminder that I've already hesitated too long.

It's just a door, I remind myself, feeling all of the eyes watching me. It's more than that, the little voice in my head argues, and I glare at the door, willing myself to just do something. I force myself to swallow and reach for the doorknob. It turns easily in my hand and so, with one last deep breath, I step inside of a dark room. The door shuts behind me, motion sensored lights flickering on overhead to reveal a rather disorienting room.

My footsteps are loud against the shiny black glass underfoot and echo back to me off of the identical black walls glistening around me. Twenty-one, twenty-two, twenty-three, I breathe, my eyes landing on a single table and chair at the center of the room.

"Arin Wells, take a seat please and we can get started." A voice sounds in my ears as clear as if he is standing right beside me, carried by my skin coms, the threads of artificial wiring that run beneath my skin. I cross the room in exactly twelve paces and pull out the chair, the scraping sound the legs make against the glass floor sending goosebumps down my arms. "Very good," the instructor continues as I take a seat and get a good first look at the desk laid out for me. The sleek empty surface glistens, and I recognize the touch screen desk module before me from school. "Go ahead and place your hands on the desk to activate the software," the voice instructs, and I assume the familiar position of resting my hands just inches above the glassy surface. The system blinks to life, displaying a series of applications. "We are going to be running the Criterion test." I hear his voice in my ear as the secondary screen projects in front of me, its holographic lines glimmering. "This program will take you through a series of exercises, each more difficult than the last. Your overall speed and accuracy throughout the course will determine your Criterion score. Good luck." My heart pounds against my rib cage as I wait for the test to begin. Thirty-one, thirty-two, thirty-three. Everyone in my graduating class will be taking the exact same test today. It is meant to quantify our intelligence with a score between 1-1,000. Whoever gets the highest score will be allowed to come work at Cortex. I swallow. I have to do well, my family is depending on it.

Start program? The screen blinks. I lift my right hand, fingers spread wide. My hand hangs in the air in a brief moment of hesitation and then, with a deep breath, I slam it down on the start icon below.

"Your time begins now," the interviewer informs me. The first question appears, a complex math problem, consisting of lines of letters, numbers, and symbols. I smirk, I've been completing these kinds of equations since year seven. I input the correct answer and move on to the next question about electric fields and their relation to magnetic fields. I apply Maxwell's first equation without hesitation and wait for the next one. As more and more questions come, I find myself relaxing into the rhythmic dance of problem solving. Letters and numbers swirl before me, a dizzying waltz with which I am comfortable. I know the steps, I've moved through this exact routine before. Look for the patterns, I chant to myself quietly, my fingers switching from problem to problem as easily as changing between partners. Find the eye.

I lose contact with the outside world. My senses, sight, sound, touch, all become laser-focused on the algorithms swirling in front of me. Tiny droplets of sweat form on the back of my neck as my hands fly from one edge of the hologram to another, chasing solutions, twisting and turning, dodging false solutions and untangling complexity. The familiar choreography makes me feel so alive, so myself. Before I know it, the screen in front of me cuts to black.

Simulation complete. I'm left staring at the glass wall in front of me, breathless.

Nothing happens.

The sound of my breathing echoes in the empty room and I shiver as the sweat on the back of my neck starts to cool. Still, nothing happens. I suddenly wonder if I have done something horribly wrong; if I somehow broke a rule.

"Thank you, Miss Wells, you may go now." The voice in my skin coms startles me and I glance around the room for any sign of movement, any indication of how I did, but the glass walls remain motionless. I dip my head in parting, and walk, in a daze, back down the hallway, joining the rest of the students in the waiting room. A few of them look up at me expectantly, as if they are waiting for me to deliver some kind of news, but I don't have any more answers than they do. In one corner of the room, a girl is softly sobbing. I was the last student to go, and now that we're finished, we line up once again and file out of the waiting room.

Myself, a blond haired boy named Thiago, a short haired girl named Trix, and a freckle faced boy named Leander step into the glass elevator when it's our turn, and even though they've been my classmates for the past four years, we ride in a silence so heavy that it presses down on my shoulders. I understand why. There are more important things to be focused on right now than making small talk. We all have families whose livelihoods are on the line, and our own destinies to worry about. My peers are no longer my peers. Today they are my competition.

The elevator stops at the Cortex lobby and we join the rest of our classmates inside. The room around us is breathtaking, a dizzying combination of high ceilings, polished white floors, and gigantic glass doors. When all of the students reach the lobby, we walk in a single file line through the gigantic glass doors. The girl in front of me is taller than I am, which is not hard to be since I only measure at five feet and five inches and I have to strain to get a good look as we walk back to the hover-bus that brought us into the city. But it's worth it. The hedges along the lawn are cut into crisp, clean lines and almost impossible shades of green surround us on all sides. Perfectly placed fountains sparkle with crystal clear water, their showering displays timed in synchronicity down to the second, a breathtaking display of the rich opulence that comes with success. Of course, it's perfect. I would expect nothing less of a city whose motto is "Excellence and Innovation".

Once I'm back on the bus, I press my forehead against the cool glass window, replaying the puzzles over and over again in my mind, and a little pang of disappointment runs through me.

The questions were challenging, sure, but not as challenging as I'd thought they would be. What does that mean exactly? Was I looking at them all wrong? Does that mean I failed? I go over each obstacle again and again, but in my mind's eye, I can't find a mistake. As the bus comes to a stop on my street and as I climb down the steps into the brisk evening air, I can't shake the feeling that I've somehow done something terribly wrong.

The vibrant rays of the sinking sun bathe the identical rooftops along my street in a blood-red glow and the wind whips wayward leaves across my face, stinging my cheeks. From this spot outside the house, I can see the yellow glow from inside the windows shining in the quickly approaching evening, and I can practically smell the delicious aroma of dinner on the table. Usually, I'd rush inside, eager to warm myself and cozy up in my favorite chair. But tonight, the image before me sends a pang through my chest. If I wake up tomorrow and learn that I've failed the Criterion test, then all of this will go away. There is no way that my mom, dad, and I can earn enough coin on labor assignments to keep this house. My eyes dart to the west side of the city, the area closest to the massive white wall that surrounds Paramus. If we are lucky, we might end up there, in the poorest of the five districts. But as the wind whips harder against the thin fabric of my blouse, causing me to shiver, I know that isn't the only possibility. If I've failed, then there's a good chance that my parents and I will be thrown out of Paramus forever. There's nothing left to do now but wait.

Gifted

CHAPTER

"Good things only come to those who work to be the best."

- Articles of Axiom. Section VII, Part B.

"Mom, Dad, I'm home!" I let myself in through the front door and force myself to put on a much more confident face than I truly feel inside.

"Arin!" My mother's smile is wide, but I can see the lines of worry around the corner of her eyes as she wraps me in a warm embrace. I brace myself for questions about the test but they don't come. "Come in, I've just put dinner on the table." My shoulders relax with relief and my stomach grumbles in response. I haven't eaten all day. I follow her gratefully into the dining room.

"Hey kiddo." My dad looks up at me over the glass of tea in his hands, eyes twinkling. "How was it?" My mother shoots him a look as I sink into the chair directly across from him.

"Timothy, give the girl a chance to eat!" she warns him, setting a steaming plate of food in front of me, causing my mouth to water. "There will be plenty of time for questions after dinner."

"Yes ma'am," he concedes and shoots me a wink. I grin back and then busy myself with eating everything on my plate. Now that I'm not attending school anymore, I know that soon our rations will be less. Also, a low score today will mean fewer rations from this point forward. No sense in wasting what could be my last good meal. My mother joins us at the table and the three of us eat in tense silence. When we are through, I start to help my mother clear the table but she shoos me away.

"I think you've worked hard enough for one day." I glance at the woman before me, who, although changed out of her labor assignment clothing, still wears the lines of exhaustion on her face. "Go on in the den with your father, I'll be in in a minute." I think about protesting, because even though the Criterion test was difficult, I wouldn't mind just one more night working in the kitchen with my mother but I decide against it.

"Alright, but don't be long. You know Dad can't wait to talk about it much longer," I warn and she laughs, honey-brown eyes dancing. My father is in the den already, and he glances up at me from the fire.

"There she is. How are you feeling, kiddo?" His question makes my stomach sink further. I busy myself with settling in comfortably on my favorite chair, the big brown one with the soft cover and pillows.

"I'm feeling alright, everything considered." I glance up at him and he nods, concern furrowing his brow.

"Sometimes I wish I could change the way Paramus works. All of this pressure on you—"

"Dad," I chide, and he holds up his hands in surrender. My parents remember a time from life outside of the wall, where things were done differently. But that life was difficult.

"I know, I know. The Criterion test is the only way to maintain excellence." He sighs and leans back in his chair. "What was it like? Was it as hard as you thought?" I feel my pulse pounding in my ears. I don't want to give any indication about the fears brewing just beneath the surface. I smooth the fabric of my slacks.

"It was actually easier than I thought." That part is true. I decide to not share that I'm afraid the reason it was easy was because I completely misunderstood the test somehow and have doomed us all to a life of poverty.

"Now why doesn't that surprise me at all?" My mom joins us after finishing cleaning up dinner. She snuggles up next to my dad on the couch, tucking her feet beneath her.

"Because Arin has always been amazing," he answers, planting a kiss on the top of my mom's head, his eyes somewhere far away. "I still remember the day that we found you like it was yesterday." He turns his attention to me, and I roll my eyes playfully, trying to ignore the pang in my chest. I've heard this story a thousand times, and though I would never tell my father this, the story always makes me a little sad. It stands as a painful reminder that I wasn't good enough for someone out there. My true mother left me, thrown away like garbage in a dumpster outside of the wall.

"You were this big." He continues, holding his hands a foot apart. "Just THIS big and absolutely perfect. We couldn't believe our luck." He shares a look with my mother. "But you know Lara, always looking for treasures in unexpected places." My mom giggles and he joins in, his hearty laughter bringing me back to the present. I soak up the sound. It's just as familiar to me as breathing

"Good thing I did too!" she says. He nods and gestures to the room around us.

"And you brought us here." I join him in glancing around the plush family room, the place we have gathered nightly for the last four years, and the pang in my chest returns. How many more nights will we have together here by the fire? My mother watches me, her warm brown eyes full of knowing.

"Arin, whatever happens with the Criterion, no matter what your score, we are still very proud of you—"

"So proud, in fact, that we have something for you," my father interjects and reaches into his pocket, retrieving a small black drawstring bag, and extends it out to me. I take the bag carefully, noting the soft velvet fabric. Inside, I find a single diamond, suspended on a delicate silver chain. I gasp in surprise and glance up to find both parents beaming back at me.

"Where did you get this? The house doesn't make diamonds." I cradle the gem in my hand, watching its multi-faceted surface sparkle in the firelight. Our home may be equipped with a printer, but it doesn't have access to any kind of organic materials.

"I made it," my father answers simply, and I shake my head in disbelief. What a truly beautiful gift.

"Here, let me help you with that." My mother rises from her perch on the couch and retrieves the necklace from me, her touch light on the back of my neck as she fastens it. Then she steps back, hands clasped in front of her, admiring her work. My fingers go to the pendant, the diamond's surface smooth against my fingertips. I love it. When I glance back up, my mom looks nervous. "I just wanted to say," she begins, "that even though I didn't give birth to you, to me you *are* my daughter, in every sense of the word."

"And you're my mom," I assure her. "There's never been any doubt about that." We talk well into the evening, and I soak up every moment, watching my parents as they joke back and forth lovingly, unable to keep my hands from touching the precious diamond around my neck. We talk about many things late into the evening, but the one thing we don't talk about is the one thing on all of our minds—how this could be our last night together like this.

After wishing my parents goodnight and ascending the stairs to my room, I collapse onto my bed, exhausted. The events of today have worn me down, but try as I may, I can't seem to fall asleep. I just keep playing the test over and over in my mind, trying to guess which problems I might have gotten wrong and what my score might be. The truth is, I realize, as I stare up at the familiar white ceiling above my bed, that it doesn't matter whether I got a good score or a terrible score today. Either way, my life is going to change. If, by some miracle, I become the next Cortex employee, I'll have to move there. My mind flashes back to the boy who won last year, Linc Mattox. He hasn't been back since last Criterion day. I wonder if his parents miss him. I barely knew him, since he was a year ahead of me at school, but I do remember there being something striking about him. In fact, I can remember most of the faces from last years' graduating class and I don't see any of them anymore. The lucky ones were given labor assignments like my parents, and the rest cast outside of the wall. None of them ever came back here, to this neighborhood, and neither will I. I wonder how many days I have left. One? Two? It can't be much longer than that.

Eighteen, Nineteen, Twenty. I count for what feels like hours, trying to calm my racing heart until eventually I drift off into a fitful sleep, numbers flashing through my mind, unsure which one will determine my fate.

The next day I'm awoken by the sound of shouting. I hurry to the window and my stomach drops at the sight of armed guards pulling my neighbor Hana's family out of their home. I swallow, knuckles turning white against my windowsill. Hana's results must have come in this morning. A shudder travels down my spine. They didn't waste any time removing her from her home. I stay glued to the windows all day, watching as guards go to the door of family after family, extracting them from their homes of the last four years. Some families fight, some of them cry, but most are silent. They knew the outcome that comes from not getting into Cortex. One by one they file onto hoverbuses, taken to the outer lying districts in the city, if they're allowed to stay within the city at all.

When night comes, the guards leave, and I breathe a sigh of relief. We are at least safe for one more night. While my parents prepare dinner, I keep myself busy with the task of reprogramming the house's interface. Since we'll be leaving it soon, I need to remove the real wood texture that I custom created and set it back to the default stone appearance. I'll also need to disconnect the house's brain from my skin coms. I don't know if my new house is going to even have a brain. I try not to think about how foreign that would feel. I have a lot of love for this place; after all I fell in love with hacking in this house, and now one of my greatest passions. Out of habit I flex my right hand and feel the house give me access to all the cameras on its feed. I scan them lazily, not really looking for anything in particular. The one thing I want, the answer to my fate, won't be found within these four walls.

By the fifth day after the Criterion exam, the neighborhood is practically empty, but no answer has come and I find myself avoiding my parents. In the mornings before they leave for their labor assignments, and in the evenings when we gather together at dinnertime, I can feel them watching me, waiting for any sign of news. I don't blame them, I'm just as anxious for any news, to just get the waiting over with. But I'm doing a good job of keeping myself distracted as much as I can. Seeing the tapping of my father's foot as he sits and watches the evening broadcast is too much of a reminder for me that we are all just in limbo, waiting. Instead of enduring another evening of light small talk and someone jumping with each new notification, I decide that tonight it would be best for me to get out of the house for a little while, some fresh air might do me some good. Staying here in the house won't change anything, I remind myself, as I pull on my running shoes and move through a set of stretches.

"I'm going out!" I call on my way out the door, and I shut it behind me before I can get a reply. I start out at a comfortable pace, letting my muscles get warm. My feet carry me down the street of identical houses, away from the waiting back at home, and on a whim, I decide to take the familiar path to my old school complex. It might be nice to see it again one last time before we leave this district. The streets are quiet at night, free from the bustle of landscaping bots and the whir of hover-buses. The only sound, other than the occasional rustle of the wind through the leaves overhead, is the padding of my feet on the concrete road and the steady rhythm of my breath. I find the stillness soothing after the pressure that I've been under lately, and before long, I'm turning the corner that brings the first of many school buildings into view. I squint. There's movement near the A building, but something doesn't look right. Whatever it is, it's cloaked in the shadowy part of the building, swaying with the wind. I take a hesitant step closer, straining my eyes to see what the moving object is. I move closer towards the building until the shadow naturally falls back, and I'm faced with the reality of what is swaying in front of me. A scream rips through my throat. I stumble backwards, bile choking down all sound trying to escape. A corpse stares at me with bloodshot eyes, her body twisting at the end of the rope. Her face is distorted, bloated, contorted into a haunting scowl, but I can still recognize my classmate, Tesa Halverson. Someone has scrawled the words "Execution and Innovation" in red behind her body, a twisted play on our city's motto.

The horror of the situation unravels in my mind. Did Tesa write this? My heart pounds and my whole body shakes. She must have found out that she wasn't accepted into Cortex? I swallow, glancing again at what is left of the kind, mild-mannered girl that I remember from school. Tesa never scored exceptionally high marks in school, so the fact that she didn't make it into

Cortex couldn't have come as a huge surprise. Tears prick the corner of my eyes. Tesa would've rather taken her own life than be cast outside of the wall. I look around, wondering if anyone else has noticed the body. Part of me thinks that I should alert the authorities, but this kind of message could get her family into serious trouble. I'm sure they're suffering enough already. I could get in trouble too, and every moment spent here increases my chances of falling under some kind of punishment as well. I glance back up at Tesa's swaying figure. But I can't just leave her here.

Moving quickly, I search the ground for the sharpest rock that I can find and climb atop the chair beside the body, trying not to think about what Tesa must have been feeling when she climbed on this chair, and I make work of cutting her down, glancing over my shoulder every few seconds. Her body hits the ground a little harder than I would've liked, and I'm sweating by the time I climb down from the chair. My eyes scan the wooded area around the A building for any sign of movement, and once satisfied that I'm alone, I wrap my arms around my classmate and start to pull her body toward the tree line. I don't have a plan exactly, but I can't leave her there, dangling. She deserves more than that. Once we get to the cover of the trees, I prop Tesa against a tall oak tree and take a few moments to smooth her hair and her black dress. Her white collar is stained with blood from the rope. I swallow. She must've struggled at the end. My hands begin to shake at the sight of her blood and I force myself to take a deep breath to keep from panicking. I've never been this close to a dead body before, and even though I knew Tesa in life, seeing her like this is hard for me to stomach. After I remove the rope from her neck, she looks almost peaceful, sitting up against the tree. I spy a speckling of flowers with tiny white blooms only a few feet away. They stand resilient against the colder temperatures and chilly autumn wind. I recognize them instantly, *aster pilosus*, and

I pluck several handfuls from the ground, tucking them around my classmate. I take my time, knowing that this may be the last act of human kindness shown to her. When I'm finished with my grim ritual, I feel like I should say something in parting. I blink back tears and dip my head.

"Tesa, I ... I know that we didn't know each other very well in school, and I'm sorry about that. I wish that you didn't think this was your only option. I wish that you could have lived a long life. I'm sorry"—once I start apologizing the tears begin pouring freely down my face and I can't seem to stop—"I'm sorry, I'm so sorry." I apologize over and over again, even though none of it is my fault. But Tesa deserves an apology, at least from someone. I never thought that the Criterion test could bring someone to this kind of a low. I never considered it at all. As I walk back home along an almost deserted street, a combination of sorrow and guilt overwhelms me. Sorrow for Tesa, and all the other graduates, who risk being pushed to such points of desperation over our Criterion scores. I haven't been denied yet, and I have no idea what my score will be. What if I make it to Cortex? I already feel burdened by the fate of those who didn't.

The next day, my answer comes as a single notification from Cortex blinking in my eye-screen. I'm sitting at the breakfast table, a spoonful of oatmeal halfway to my mouth when it appears. I gasp and carefully return my spoon to the bowl, never taking my eyes off the little red flag in the corner of my vision. My heart pounds in my chest. What will it say? There's only one way to find out. Now that my hand is empty, I flex my right index finger, and the message opens. It's a video. First, the Cortex logo appears before being replaced by an older woman with a pinched face, her black hair pulled back into a tight bun. She wears the Cortex uniform and speaks briskly, her voice playing directly through my skin coms.

"Arin Wells, you have received the highest Criterion score out of all this year's candidates. We would like to welcome you as our newest employee. Come to Cortex this afternoon to begin your new hire process. We will send a car." She gives a tight nod in parting. "Congratulations." The message ends as swiftly as it begins and I'm left sitting at the table, blinking in surprise. A flood of emotions washes over me. Excitement, mixed with disbelief, all combined with a healthy amount of nervousness. I decide that the best emotion to embrace is excitement. After all, isn't this the best possible outcome? This is what I wanted. It's the highest honor that a person can achieve. Pride blossoms in my stomach and I allow myself to fully embrace the feeling. I did it. As I stand up from the kitchen table, my chair makes a loud scraping sound, and my father looks over from where he is watching the public information channel. He takes one look at the expression on my face and his eyes widen.

"Uh, audio, mute please," he tells the living room, and it obeys, leaving the sound of my mother's determined scrubbing sound, as she works away at polishing her latest salvage project, the only noise surrounding us. My parents exchange a glance and then look back at me, eyes hopeful. The air stills with breathless anticipation.

"Mom, Dad," I begin slowly, savoring the moment. I can feel the smile spread across my face, eyes sparkling with excitement. I've been working my entire life to say these next words: "I just got a message from Cortex! I got the opening! I did it!" Their reaction is instant, almost as if someone had un-paused a live broadcast, and they both leap to their feet to embrace me.

"You did it, kiddo! I knew you would!" My father grins, wrapping me in such a tight hug that the air is squeezed from my lungs. I can't help but laugh, because I'm happy, truly happy. This invitation means that we are going to be alright. I know it, my parents know it. It is written all over my mother's face as she embraces me next, taking my hands in hers and beaming with a warm smile. Today marks the start of a new life for all of us.

"What did they say?" My mother's voice is full of excitement. "Did they tell you your score?" I shake my head.

"Not yet, but I'm supposed to report this afternoon. They're sending a car!" My voice is a mixture of elation and awe. I've never ridden in a hovercar before.

"Wow! The perks start already!" my dad teases, mussing my already wild bed-head. I swat him away, grinning.

"This means we get to stay in this house for as long as we want!" I proclaim proudly. "That is, of course, until I buy us a new one." My mother gives my shoulders a squeeze.

"Don't worry about any of that. As long as we have each other, it doesn't matter where we're living." Her words make me feel warm inside. I can tell that it's a lot easier to breathe for all of us now that we know what the future holds.

Despite the atmosphere of elation in the house, my mind flashes back to Tesa's body, who I left in the trees surrounded by flowers. There will be an entire group of my classmates who wished to receive the very message I have, but didn't. I wonder what fates await them. I try to ignore the pangs of guilt, and instead focus on the excitement. I have worked hard, after all. This is my dream, and I need to make sure that I'm ready.

There weren't a lot of instructions with the message other than the fact that Cortex will be sending a car. I have no idea what, if anything, that I should bring with me. I assume that wherever I will be staying will be able to meet my needs just as well as this house, if not better, but I'd still like to bring a few things with me to remind me of home. As I glance around my room, I feel a pang of sentiment in my chest. *Where do I begin? How do you pack an entire lifetime into a single bag to carry away? And how long until I see this room again?*

I push those feelings aside and focus instead on deciding what to wear for my first day. I ultimately settle on a simple black blazer, a freshly pressed white shirt, and black slacks. I consider pulling my long brown hair into a neat ponytail but decide to wear it in my signature style: loosely resting on my shoulders and down my back. The ponytail makes my naturally round cheekbones and wide eyes appear too youthful. If anything, I want to convey the maturity and wisdom of someone twice my age. I pause, glancing at myself in the mirror. I've never considered myself to be pretty, interesting looking, perhaps, but never beautiful. But none of that matters in the grand scheme of things. What truly matters is that I took the test and I scored highest. I abandon the mirror, picking up a canvas back to pack with. *I've proven myself worthy.* My heart swells in my chest, *my parents will be taken care of.*

Now to decide what to bring with me. I walk around the room, starting at my bed, running my hands along the heavy grey fabric, and pulling the comforter and pillows into place for what might be the last time. I want to leave the place looking tidy for my mom and dad, in case they visit this room while I'm gone. Next is my desk, the place where I spent most of my time studying on my Department of Learning issued tablet. The mandated search blockers prohibited the tablet from doing anything fun like puzzles or games, but it only took me about a week to find a backdoor in the programing, and another few days to re-write the code to get access. Since then, I became immersed in the world of coding. Coding is like another language; a roadmap to another world where you can make anything happen. A world that makes sense, broken down into endless combinations of numbers and letters. A true thing of beauty. But because hacking is illegal, I've never been brave enough to try hacking anything outside of the tech in my own home or my handheld nano.

I move on from the desk to my closet, where most items only stay in circulation for a few days. The house is always creating more clothes for me to wear, so it doesn't make sense to hold on to anything. However, I spot one familiar item right away, a green sweater. I pull it off the hanger and bury my face in it, breathing deeply. My mother repaired this sweater by hand; that's a hobby of hers, repairing things instead of discarding them. It smells like her. I tuck the sweater into a bag. My new home can probably make any sweater that I can dream of, but it can't make it smell like home. There isn't anything else that I want to take with me, so with one last look around the room, I slip my bag over my shoulder and whisper goodbye before descending the stairs.

Back in the family room, I find both my father and mother waiting for me. Dad has his arms around Mom's shoulders and they're both watching me with pride, smiles the widest I have ever seen.

"You look absolutely perfect," my mother gushes, her hands clasped together tight, a hint of tears glistening in her eyes. My father puts his arm around her, giving her a comforting squeeze, but I can see that he too is struggling to hold back his emotions.

"You're going to do great." When he speaks, there's a catch in his voice and he has to clear his throat before continuing. "We know how important today is, and that you have a lot to look forward to with your new job and all of the exciting new things you'll be doing, but don't forget that we'll always be here if you need us."

"And don't forget to come home." My mother's voice wobbles, and I have to look away, my own tears stinging in my eyes.

"Of course not. I miss you guys already," I joke to cover up the mix of sorrow, uncertainty, and nervousness swirling inside of me. I'm doing my duty, I remind myself. It's my job to leave home and send back coin for my parents. My hand goes to the nearest stone column, and its programmable surface is solid beneath my touch. This same house, that felt so giant at first, had been filled these past four years with love and laughter. I learned so many things here. There's no denying that I'm going to miss it.

"Are you okay, kiddo?" My father's voice is speckled with concern, pulling me out of my nostalgia. When I turn around, my parents are both watching my hesitation, hints of worry in their eyes. I give them my most reassuring smile.

"I'm fine," I promise, but a little piece of me knows that's not entirely true. "It just feels weird saying goodbye to you and to the house."

My father nods. "I get it. This is a big change. You've waited for this day your entire life." He's right of course. Every child wants the same thing—to be offered a position at Cortex. And now that I've made it, I'll never have to worry about my mom and dad being taken care of. As I gaze into their eyes, I know the pain I feel about leaving them will be overshadowed by my triumphant feeling of success when the coin starts rolling in. Even though I'll miss them, it's better this way. My fingers find my new necklace, tucked neatly beneath the fabric of my shirt, and I have to fight the urge to twirl it between my fingers. I look back at my parents, into their hopeful, smiling faces, and wonder if they are as nervous as I am.

They shouldn't be. I've never let them down before. I'm just like this diamond. Perfect under pressure.

"You're right," I agree, letting a little finality settle into my tone. This is my future. This is what I've always wanted. Just then, I get a notification; there is someone at the front door. I access the house's main frame and tap into the front door camera with a few gestures of my right hand. The camera's view appears in my right eye revealing a long, black vehicle hovering outside. A man exits, standing outside the door. He looks as if he's talking to someone through his skin coms. "House, amplify front door sound. Connect to my com," I command, straining to pick up on the stranger's voice.

"Yes, I'm here now," I hear him say. The connection is scratchy and hurts my ears; the house has maxed out its listening capabilities to eavesdrop on the conversation and relay it to me. "I understand. Okay, we will be there shortly," the stranger says, and then he raps his fists on the wood of the door. I wince as the sound is amplified in my ears, quickly disconnecting my coms from the front door's audio stream, and instead connecting to the microphone.

"Yes, hello. Can I help you?" I try to make my voice sound as official as possible. The stranger looks directly into the front door camera.

"I'm here for Arin Wells. I've been sent from Cortex." Butterflies flutter in my stomach—this is it.

"I'll be right there," I reply before turning to my parents, who watch me with wide eyes. I clear my throat. "The car is here." My voice is firm because it has to be. I'm not just a girl anymore. My father nods and breaks away from my mother, reaching out to embrace me one last time. He buries his face in the top of my head, arms wrapped around me tightly.

"I love you, kiddo." I blink rapidly, trying to keep the tears from spilling down my cheeks. My dad, my best friend. The one who can make me laugh about anything, who has always been there to help me work through a problem, no matter how large. "You're gonna do great things."

"I love you too," I murmur, wiping at my eyes quickly when he breaks away. My mother comes next. I take in her soft eyes and thin shoulders. I focus on the way the corners of her eyes crinkle as she smiles at me before pulling me close, whispering in my ear.

"You'll always be our miracle, Arin." She gives me a quick kiss on the cheek, and her familiar scent washes over me before she pulls away. I give them both a nod, and turn to go, stepping through the front door and into the warm afternoon sunlight.

They say that you shouldn't look back, that to truly be successful you must keep your eyes on the future. You must always be focused on where you are going, on what's ahead, in order to achieve. When I take one last look over my shoulder as I step outside and I catch a glimpse of my mother collapsed against my father, her face stricken with tears and shoulders shaking, I realize just how true that statement is. One should never look back, it's better to keep moving forward. Everyone knows that, eventually, you have to leave home and take care of your family members. This is the responsibility of the Gifted.

The driver greets me with a dip of the head, opening the second door on the car's long stretch of body for me to enter. When I climb inside, the cool black leather is smooth, and I nestle into the seat comfortably. The door closes behind me and I watch as my house becoming smaller and smaller as we pull away from my neighborhood and join the other traffic bustling along the skyway. A thick lump of emotion swells in my throat and I squeeze the leather beneath me to steady myself. Everything is happening so quickly. What I need is a distraction. I clear my throat, hoping that talking will make the drive pass more quickly.

"I didn't catch your name," I offer to the man who has been sent to transport me. I stare at the back of his head instead of the window, and I can feel the lump in my throat beginning to dissolve as my sadness is replaced with curiosity about this man and his role at Cortex.

"I'm called Marcus," he offers, taking his eyes off the road for one brief second to look at me in the rearview mirror. His face is square, covered by what looks like a day's worth of facial hair. His brown eyes are guarded, but not unkind. He speaks with a deep voice, and I find the timbre soothing. "Two years in a row I've brought new employees from that neighborhood. The other kid looked more scared than you." He chuckles and my mind flashes back to all I can remember of last year's winner, Linc. In my memory, I can see a boy with tousled brown hair and striking green eyes. My heartbeat quickens. I wonder if I'll see him at Cortex today. "You must be pretty excited," Marcus continues. "A lot of kids wish that they were you right now."

"It's complicated," I admit, my fingers digging into the leather once more.

His eyes meet mine in the rearview mirror. "What do you mean?"

The words come rushing out of me. "It's a lot to take in all at once. Leaving for Cortex is such a huge change. I mean, of course I'm excited. But moving away, leaving my home … my family …" I blink back tears. "It's just a lot." The car is quiet for a moment. I turn my face towards the window so that Marcus doesn't see how much I'm struggling not to cry. He finally speaks after several heartbeats.

"Hey, it'll be alright. I'm sure you're going to love it at Cortex." He gives me a small smile. His reassuring presence calms my nerves, and I find myself nodding as I sink into my seat.

"Yeah," I agree. "I hope so."

The posh luxury of the transport pod around me is as nice as something that you would expect from our city's capital. The inside smells fresh, like when you first take a new piece of clothing from your in-home printer, mixed with just a hint of spice and a lingering sweetness. It is no secret that those at Cortex live a very comfortable life, especially those in higher level positions, offered only to those with the highest of scores. I'll find out my scores today, in less than an hour. Whatever position they offer me, I'll most likely be in it for the rest of my life. I don't really care what I'm assigned to; anything at Cortex is better than the alternatives.

I don't remember much about life outside of Paramus. I was only three years old when we left. I do remember it being cold the day they brought me in. Some of us were shivering. We clung tightly to the thin garments that offered us little protection from the blistering cold, our shoeless feet vulnerable on the barren ground. We were the last group ever to be brought in from outside the wall. The council decided that it was becoming too dangerous to continue to send reconnaissance troops outside to test the Lost children and see if any were Gifted enough to enter our city. Soldiers were going missing. There were rumors of monsters.

That day is one of my earliest memories. I don't remember feeling any emotion except excitement. My mother and father held tight to each of my hands. I could sense that they were proud. Their little girl was their ticket inside the wall. I had done it. It was the first time I remember making them proud. No day has ever compared, until today.

The drive through the glistening white city is magnificent, and I fight the urge to press my nose against the window as I peer at the lush green landscaping, sparkling waters, dazzling arches and hovering skyscrapers below. Every available surface that isn't being developed or used for transportation is covered in greenery. The cultivation of many of these previously wasted spaces for gardening and food production guarantees a nearly limitless supply of resources. To me, the city serves as a reminder of all that can be accomplished by the intelligent. We've done more than any society in the history of the world, because we understand what is important.

As the familiar white tower comes into view, I sit up a little straighter and smooth my pant legs. One hand goes to the diamond necklace beneath my collar, and I twirl it between my fingers until we park on the lawn and Marcus comes around to open my door. He gives me a small smile and I'm grateful for his kindness as I step out into my new world as a Cortex scientist, blinking against the bright sunlight. Marcus was kind to me, and I almost wish that he could come with me as the building before me stands stark white against the blue sky, filling me with intimidation. But I know that, from this point forward, I'm going to be on my own. Only, I'm not completely alone. I clutch my bag tightly; it's full of reminders of home and the love that waits for me there. After bidding Marcus goodbye, I stride into the building, ready to face whatever may await me inside. After all, I'm like a diamond, perfect under pressure.

CHAPTER

"How is it then, that man so cruel-
For power traded his only soul?
Yet when smoke cleared, 'twas truly shown-
He'd traded much more than he'd ever known."

- Chronicles of Discord

N o one gives me a second glance as I approach the gigantic, polished desk in the middle of the first-floor lobby for only the second time in my life. I am greeted by a young woman, a few years my senior, who smiles at me knowingly as I reach the check-in point.

"Arin Wells, welcome back. We've been expecting you." She gives a small wink and my heart flutters with excitement. "And may I say, congratulations young lady. What you've done is not easy to do." My cheeks flush crimson and I mutter a "Thank you" before she waves me past the barrier. My heart swells as I glide past the barriers that so many dream of passing through. I clutch my bag tightly in my hands and try not to stare as I follow the walkway, moving away from the lobby and towards the familiar set of glass elevators. Only this time, I'm not just one student in a sea of graduates. This time, it's just me.

"How may I assist you?" An assistance droid startles me from my ogling and I am reminded that I have an appointment to make. I peer at the sophisticated piece of tech in front of me, and he blinks back with a pointed gaze. The droid has been given a voice that sounds distinctly male, nearly void of any artificial quality. His vocal inflection is perfectly on point, and if I was to hear his voice without seeing him, I'd probably assume that I was speaking to a real person. Whoever does the artificial intelligence coding here at the tower knows what they're doing. But I shouldn't be surprised really. This is Cortex, after all. The place where all great inventions are born. This droid is easily the most advanced model I've ever seen, and droids have been around for as long as I can remember. Every mindless task in Paramus was handed over to them upon their creation. It saves the real humans, the ones who have the power to *think*, a lot of time.

"My name is Arin Wells—" I begin, not sure how much information I'll need to provide to the droid, but it turns out that my name is all I have to say.

"Yes, Miss Wells, we've been expecting you. You'll be needed on the third floor, room one. This elevator to my right will take you there. Is there anything else I can help you with?"

"No, thank you," I reply and then step inside the glass elevator, sorry to step away from the friendly droid. What I wouldn't give to hook him up to my handheld nano and see what kind of coding was written to make him appear so life-like. I watch him get smaller and smaller as the elevator climbs. As well as dabbling in programming with our house's interface, I took an advanced robotics course in school. I wonder what position I'm going to be assigned today? I wouldn't mind working in robotics if we would be making stuff like that.

The third floor doors open to reveal another lobby of sorts. The bright white carpet is plush underfoot and a single desk awaits at the center of the room. There are a handful of sleek black chairs interspersed with artificial greenery. Somewhere in the distance, I can hear the sound of cascading water. My feet pad noiselessly on the carpeting as I approach the desk and I soon find another secretary. This time, it's a girl who looks to be only a year or so older than I am, with cropped black hair. Her name tag reads Petra, and she eyes me coolly.

"You must be Miss Wells." She has an air of importance to her voice, and I have to remind myself not to be intimidated. After all, I deserve to be here. "You'll be meeting with the Cortex officials in conference room E; go down this hall and to the third door on your left." I can feel Petra's gaze burning between my shoulder blades as I follow her directions. Soon, I find myself outside of a sleek opaque glass door with a white "E" stenciled at the top. I swallow and try to ignore the nervous fluttering in my stomach. I swing the glass door open and step inside, puzzled to find it empty. Is this some kind of test? The door clicks into place behind me, and I have no choice but to take one of the seats at the long white table and wait. There are no windows in conference room E, only the white table, eight chairs, and the humming white light in the ceiling above. I force myself to take a few deep breaths and fold my hands neatly on the table in front of me, watching the seconds tick by in my eye-screen. Tiny pinpricks of sweat prickle at the back of my neck as a minute passes. And then another. After five minutes of waiting, I'm startled by the sound of the turning knob, and in walks none other than the leader of Paramus and Director of Cortex herself, Eira Ellis. Her sleek brown hair is parted evenly down the middle and she walks with a steady assurance, polished pumps clicking against the polished floor.

"Arin Wells, it's a pleasure." Her commanding voice fills the small room as she walks toward me, offering me a dazzling smile and one perfectly manicured hand in greeting. I blink in surprise, and numbly reach out and shake it. The woman that I had seen on the web, who I had learned about in school, whose picture was displayed on surfaces all throughout the city, is so close that I just reached out and touched her. After our initial handshake, Director Ellis gives me a regal dip of her head.

"Thank you for waiting," she says in a light tone of voice, taking the seat at the opposite end of the conference table, crossing her crisp black pant legs and setting a silver tablet on the table. I watch her eyes measure me, slowly traveling down my face. Satisfied, she taps her manicured fingers on the tablet in front of her. "I have your score here. Your test results were ... unusual, to say the least, so I spent a few extra moments reviewing them myself." She pauses and I feel my heart begin to race in my chest. *What was so unusual about my test results? Was there some sort of mistake?* I wait with breathless anticipation, fingers locked tightly together in front of me, and beg silently for some sort of explanation. But instead, Director Ellis takes her time. She eyes me thoughtfully before continuing. "Arin, Intelligence is ... a powerful thing. Do you know why we hold the Criterion test every year?" I do, but her tone indicates that she is not expecting an answer, although her razor-sharp brown eyes search mine. "Before Paramus was built, people were ruled by their base desires of lust, greed, and a hunger for power." She must have given some sort of small signal because a hologram appears between us. I blink, sweeping my eyes around the otherwise empty room. We are clearly being watched. The projection shows a picture of the earth, a giant blue and green sphere, slowly spinning. I watch with reverence as she continues reciting our city's history. "The ancients fought over everything. They didn't care about the noble pursuit of society, but instead were selfish. In their squabbling, the people of Earth squandered away the planet's natural resources until there weren't enough to go around." The hologram changes to pictures of a building reduced to rubble by bombs, people lying in rows on the ground, covered in blood, a child sitting on the ground as ash falls, it's face streaked with tears and one leg missing. I have to look away. "Thankfully, a small group of scientists were wise enough to foresee where mankind was heading. They tried to warn everyone that, if they kept depleting the earth at such a fast rate, they would run out of essential resources"—she pauses to shake her head sadly—"but no one listened. These scientists took it upon themselves to try and preserve humanity. The parts of humanity that were good. The intelligent parts." Director Ellis takes a deep breath and a wave of gratitude washes over me like it always does at this portion of the story. The image changes to show a picture of the massive white wall surrounding our city. The imposing structure sends a little shiver down my spine as Director Ellis' words provide the perfect narration in the background.

"Together, our forefathers built Paramus, a huge city with a great wall, modeled after the great civilizations found in history books. Only the most intelligent of minds are permitted to live within our walls, because they understand that dividing people based on intelligence is the only way to maintain order—and excellence."

Director Ellis comes to the end of her speech, and anticipation coils deep in my stomach, ready to erupt. "But do you know what is even more powerful? Hope. Hope is the driving force that inspires us to work towards a better tomorrow. We simply want to make the world a better place. It's because of hope that we keep innovating; we keep looking forward. We keep ... pushing the boundaries. Hope is a powerful thing. Did you always hope that you would end up here"—she gestures to the room in which we are seated—"someday?"

I nod again, still unsure if I should speak.

"And here you are." The corners of Director Ellis's eyes crinkle with a smile, and then she goes silent. After what feels like an infinite pause, she speaks again. "I'm sure you must think this is unusual, but with such unusual results, I wanted to greet you myself. I wanted to be the one to show you your Criterion scores, which I'm sure you're eager to see. Here, let's take a look."

In one graceful motion she types a few lines onto her tablet screen and then flicks an image from its surface to the projection between us. It's a three-dimensional circle graph, each section representing a piece that is combined with the rest to create a final tally. She gestures to the graph, the numbers clearly displayed. "Tell me what you see."

My eyes are immediately drawn to the final number at the bottom of the graph. 999. Wait, that can't be right. The highest score ever recorded was 930. If that is truly my score, it is significantly higher than anything I've ever heard of before.

"I don't mean to offend but, is this accurate?" I wonder aloud and Director Ellis surprises me with a sharp laugh that sounds somewhat like shattering glass.

"You know, that is *exactly* the same reaction that I had. 999, a score that is absolutely unheard of, never been done," she says with some admiration in her voice. "At first I thought that perhaps there was some sort of system error when they presented me with the results. A typo perhaps."

I nod, too shocked to speak. She continues, "I actually made them pull up the results for me and I double checked them myself. I quite honestly couldn't believe it. And that is why I wanted to be the first one to meet you. Because do you know what I felt at that moment?"

I shake my head.

"Hope," she answers softly, leaning in closely, voice barely above a whisper. "Arin, your intelligence is … incredible. It's like nothing I've ever seen before." She sits back in her chair, posture relaxed, which completely surprises me. The usual, rigid tone of her voice that I am accustomed to seeing on live broadcasts is exchanged for a more relaxed feel, like she's chatting with an old friend. "Once we determined that your score was, in fact, not an error, there was some deliberation about what position we should offer someone of your ... capabilities." She presses her fingers together and watches me, measuring my response.

"As you know, most of our new hires start out on the green level," she begins, a sparkle in her crisp blue eyes. "But I see a lot of promise in you. I have decided that your skills would be best utilized through working with our Research and Development team on the silver level. So, that will be your job assignment for the time being."

"Thank you," I sputter, cheeks growing flush from the compliment. Research and Development is one of the highest ranking positions in the building, second only to executive spots. My heart races with so much excitement that I could jump from my chair, but I remind myself to maintain a professional attitude. Director Ellis certainly is. She offers a gracious smile, flashing a row of flawless teeth.

I clear my throat. "I will make our city proud," I say as calmly as I can muster.

She watches me, a thoughtful expression on her face, before continuing with enthusiasm. "Tomorrow will be the Primordium Ceremony, you may have heard of it." I nod, excitement stirring in my chest at the thought of attending Cortex's famous recognition ceremony for its newest recruit. It's always been a very public event, usually broadcasted live to everyone in Paramus. I remember watching every year with my family. I swallow. It had somehow slipped my mind that, as this year's recruit, I would be put in that kind of spotlight.

Director Ellis continues, "This will be your opportunity to meet several important people here at Cortex, including my fellow members of the council. Make a good impression, and you may be on your way to a very successful career." I force myself to smile even though my knuckles are turning white at the thought of meeting more important people.

"Well then," Director Ellis stands, clasping her hands together, "I'll see you tomorrow at the Primordium." She rises from the table. "Kace, my assistant will take you to your room," she says in parting, offering me one last impeccable smile before disappearing through the door.

Almost instantly after our leader leaves, a smiling girl, with long, golden curls, enters. She must've been waiting just outside the room.

"You must be Arin!" she exclaims. Her wide blue eyes are framed by long black eyelashes. She isn't wearing the standard white uniform and badge of a Cortex scientist, but is surprisingly dressed in a tight blue dress, the nano-fabric rippling like the ocean with her every step. Her eyes sparkle, complimenting the shine of the tiny diamonds suspended in her hair, as she extends a manicured hand to me. "My name is Kace, and I'll be your guide today to help you get settled in. Follow me!" Without another word, I collect my bag of belongings from the ground and follow her out, down the hallway, past Petra's glare, and back to the elevators that we ride all the way up to the 40th floor. Kace chatting happily the entire time.

I eye her warily as we wait for the doors to open. I'm still unsure about why this beautiful stranger is being so nice to me. Her level of friendliness is not something that I'm used to getting from people my age. People my age have always been my competition. I nearly jump when Kace grabs my hand and pulls me out of the elevator, beginning her enthusiastic tour.

"So, this whole floor is blue level." She gestures around us, either completely oblivious or not caring in the least about my obvious discomfort about having someone so close to me. "All of the dormitories are located on this level; you also have the dining hall over there." She nods over her right shoulder. "The fitness center is on the other end. Let's see, what else …. oh yeah, there are a couple of libraries and lab thingies on this level. Oh! And a few hang-out spots that are pretty cool but for some reason I never see any of you smarties hanging out over there," she says with a playful roll of her eyes and her jab somehow helps me relax. Her way of speaking is strange to me, it's so unlike what I'm used to. Speech and vocabulary are an excellent way to display your intelligence to someone without having to be too direct about it.

I'm well-versed in the subtle art of pretension, but it's like she's not even *trying* to come across as smarter than me. We stop in front of a corridor of white doors.

"I heard that you'll be working in Research and Development on the silver level." I glance up, expecting to see a vicious sneer or eyes brimming with jealousy but instead her blue eyes are wide, with … admiration? I don't know what it means to be working on the silver level, but I'm guessing that it's some kind of honor since Kace seems to be having no issue showing how impressed she is. Where is the spite that I am so used to receiving from my peers? Could it be that Kace is genuinely happy for me?

That would be a first.

"That's what I was told," I answer carefully, still half-expecting an attack, "but I don't really know much else." I feel vulnerable admitting that I don't know something to a peer. Kace nods, then grabs me by the hand.

"Well, don't you worry," she says with a smile. "I can help you." Her tone is so warm, it catches me off guard. I try to figure out the girl before me. Could it be possible that she has been somehow excluded from being programmed for competition? What's that like?

"Can I ask you something?" I venture, feeling silly as I speak. "You seem … different than … other people. Nicer. Um, what's up with that?" I'm worried that my question might come across as offensive, but Kace doesn't look upset at all; instead, she lets out another bout of musical laughter, followed by a flip of a perfectly curled lock of blonde hair over her shoulder and a glance down at me over glistening black lashes.

"That's because I *am* different." She shakes her head, golden curls bouncing. "All of this competition all of the time is *exhausting*." She waves her hand against her forehead dramatically. "You're here for a reason and so am I. We both earned our places, that's all I need to know."

"But what about being the best? I mean, isn't that what Cortex is about? Excellence and innovation?"

She rolls her baby blue eyes. "Everyone acts like the Gifted are so different from everyone else. But what I've learned is that everyone has something to hide. So, what's the point in acting like you don't?"

I don't necessarily agree, but I don't really have time to argue because she is already pulling me down the corridor of white doors and leading me to the last one. "This entire hallway is all silver level employees," she explains, "and you guys have the best rooms in the building! Well, except for the penthouse of course," she adds.

Ah, the penthouse.

Everyone in Paramus knows that the uppermost part of the building is reserved only for the elite of the elite, like Director Ellis, other executives and the council.

"They told you that you'll be sharing a room, right?" Kace changes the subject. They most certainly did not. My pulse quickens, and she must have noticed my surprise because she lets out a laugh. "Don't look so surprised! We are all about efficiency at Cortex, remember? There are a lot of people who work here. I guess it makes more sense to double up." She shrugs.

"Do you like your roommate?" I wonder and she looks away, it's just a glance, barely decipherable, but I catch it.

"I don't have one. I live in the penthouse." Her tone sounds like it's something she isn't proud of, which I find strange.

"Oh, wow," is all I can say. Kace is so unlike anyone that I've ever met. I've never had a conversation with someone so flippant about performance. I wasn't even aware that anyone besides my parents didn't strictly subscribe to the ideals of value that I learned in school. I wish that I could sit down with her and ask her even just one of the hundreds of questions that are on the tip of my tongue. How did she make it into the penthouse if she isn't Gifted? I thought that the penthouse was reserved specifically for the smartest among us. Is there another way? Curiosity burns within me, but at the moment I have an entirely different problem to worry about. My mind is already running wild, already conjuring up the worst possibilities that could come with having a roommate. What if we don't get along?

"Is there any way I can decline having a roommate?"

She laughs. "The only way to get out of having a roommate is by getting promoted to the penthouse. But don't worry, you'll be rooming with last year's recruit. I hear he's pretty nice." Wait. Does she mean Linc? The boy who was chosen last year? If my pulse was racing before it breaks into an all-out sprint. I have no idea why, but I can feel my face going red. Way to keep it professional, Arin. Kace notices my flushed cheeks and starts to giggle. "What, you've never roomed with a boy before?" she teases, giving me a little wink. "Don't worry, I'm sure he doesn't bite." We stop in front of the last door on the left after what seems like an endless row of identical doors. "We're here." She gestures grandly, eyes sparkling. "Well, go on in!"

With a good, healthy amount of apprehension I place my finger on the entry pad next to the door, the only thing standing between me and my new reality. It gives a quick beep and I hear the lock click open. This is it. This is what I've been working toward.

I step inside and look around, instantly in love. There are steps from the front door that lead down into the sunken living room. Two crisp-looking white couches have their back to us and are the perfect distance from a glass coffee table in front of them.

The couches are facing a holo-screen displaying an interview with Director Ellis.

"Wow," I say.

To my left is a dining room table with white leather chairs and a small kitchen island. I see two doorways on the far end of the room. One door is open and the other is closed. I walk through the open one and find myself inside of a bedroom, my bedroom. The large white bed is much bigger than what I am used to at home. Directly above the bed is a faux skylight, currently playing a projection that makes it look like I'm under water. On the one wall, there is a built-in desk and a rolling desk chair. There is an attached bathroom to my left.

Kace is right behind me, bouncing with excitement. "Do you like it?!"

All I can do is nod. I'm mesmerized. It really is beautiful. It turns out that either Linc isn't home or doesn't feel the need to come and introduce himself because nothing stirs in the apartment during our tour. I have to remind myself to pay attention while Kace points out the closet on the opposite wall.

"You can ask it for whatever you need. It comes with an updated model of the printer you probably have back home. If it's something big or something we don't have here, or can't make, we'll find someone who can."

"I'm not trying to spend a lot of coin while I'm here," I clarify, setting my bag down in the desk chair. Kace startles me with a chime of laughter.

"You don't have to *pay* for anything here, Arin! It's all part of the perks of being a Cortex employee." She bats her eyelashes. "You can have *anything* you want or need."

"Do people ever have family come and visit?" I ask, running my hands along the fluffy white comforter atop my gigantic new bed.

She shoots me a quizzical look. "No, not really. Usually, families are content enough with the ridiculous amount of coin you send home. *Especially* on the silver level. Here, you're set for life."

"And what are my hours? Like, when can I leave?" I wonder, and she blinks at me in surprise.

"Leave? Why would you want to leave?" she exclaims, shaking her head in playful disbelief. A little warning bell goes off in my mind. Why doesn't she just answer the question?

"I'm just saying," I press as I study her, "is if I wanted to ... leave Cortex, to go outside and get some fresh air, or to go for a walk—"

"There's a fully functional atrium on the green level with 400 species of flora and fauna if you're feeling like you need a little nature," she interjects with a smile and a knot begins to form at the bottom of my stomach. "Also, don't forget about the fitness center on the blue level for all your exercise needs."

"Yeah." I stare at Kace. Her expression is unreadable. "But what if I want to go home? I can do that, right?" At that moment, I realise that I've never actually seen a Cortex scientist riding the sky train or really in any place other than Cortex. I always assumed it was because they had more important things to do. But is it because they are forced to stay in this building? I need answers.

The corners of her eyes tighten, and her smile looks forced as she answers, "Your apartment is equipped with state of the art holographic and video conferencing abilities to communicate with anyone in the city!"

My heart is pounding so loudly in my ears that I can barely hear myself; the walls of the lavish new apartment suddenly feel like they are closing in around me. I ask again, "Kace I can turn around and walk out the front door right now with no problem, right? No one is going to try and keep me here?"

She glances around nervously, her smile gone. "Arin, don't be silly!" Her chiming laughter sounds as artificial as my new home. "You'll have so much groundbreaking work to keep you busy here at Cortex that you won't want to waste your time with senseless outside visits. Now, I'm sure you're anxious to see the lab where you are going to be working. Come with me and I'll show you!" She wraps one slender hand around my wrist, and I notice that her palms are damp. Her pulse is racing. I have a feeling that she has given me all the answers that she can. And of course, we are being watched. Her responses have given me the information that I need to draw my own conclusions.

I'm stuck here. I've been bought by Cortex for a plush salary and luxurious apartment for the remainder of my working years. This was the thing that they forgot to mention in all those Cortex Scientist ad campaigns. One very important little detail.

I won't ever leave Cortex again.

CHAPTER

"And so the Gifted shall redeem themselves and their families by rising to the top of society. Their intelligence will create a better Paramus for us all."

- Articles of Axiom. Section XI, Part A

Our ride up to the silver level is a silent one. I'm trying to wrap my head around the idea that I will never breathe outside air again. Kace is quiet for the first time since we met. I assume it's because she knows I know, and that there's nothing that can be said to make that realization any better.

When the elevator doors chime open, I get my first glimpse of the silver level. The carpeted hallway outside of the elevator is empty, which draws my attention to the set of silver double doors across the hall with an entry pad beside them.

"It's just on the other side of these doors," Kace explains, her voice laced with something other than enthusiasm. Sadness maybe? Pity? "You'll just need to scan your retina." She points to the access pad and as I lean down, she whispers, "Only doors that you've been granted access to open will open for your unique retinal scan."

"Is that not all of them?" I peer at her and she gives a subtle shake of her head before I hear the locks click and Kace ushers me into the Research and Development lab where I will be spending most of my time.

"Whoa," I say for the second time today as I step into what has to be the most incredible collection of equipment that I have ever seen. Everything about the lab is sleek, from the glossy white ceilings to the polished white floor underfoot. On every available wall space, there are smart screens and interactive mixed reality holo-screens. Long panels of glass separate workstations that are speckled across the laboratory floor, all dwarfed by a massive workstation in the center of the room. I walk towards the center station, drawn in by its sheer size and the magnitude of holo-screens that it has orbiting around it like a planet with many moons.

"What do you think?" A voice startles me from behind and I whip around. Behind me, in the center of the central workstation, stands a familiar person, with very long blonde hair and startling sea-green eyes. He's taller than I remember, and his wide shoulders are clothed in the standard white Cortex employee uniform, but down his sleeves is an extra black stripe, indicating that he is a department head, which I find surprising. Linc hasn't lost any time in his year here.

"Oh good!" Kace chimes from her spot beside the door. "Arin," she says, gesturing to my former schoolmate, "this is Linc. He will be overseeing most of your work. And I'm sure he can tell you way more than I can about this place." She looks around with disinterest. "Can you take over from here? I've got to run."

Linc chuckles. "Sure Kace. I was just finishing up anyway." She gives him a delicate nod and shoots me a radiant smile, blue eyes sparkling.

"Arin, I'm leaving you in more than capable hands. If you need anything I'm just a message away, okay?" I nod and without another moment's hesitation she is gone. I look at the spot she stood in just moments ago with a tinge of sadness. I'm sure her friendliness towards me is just part of her job, but I really felt a connection with Kace. It would be nice to have a friend here.

With Kace gone, my attention returns to Linc, currently busy at work in the central workstation. I take a few tentative steps closer, my footsteps echoing in the cavernous room.

When I get close enough to reach out and touch the first set of computers, he looks up from what he is doing, his face apologetic. "Sorry, I just needed to finish this up." He makes some final gestures that send various elements hovering in the sky between us spinning and he finishes with a series of finger swipes that tie everything together. He ends the session. "Alright, that should do it."

"What are you working on?" I can't help but wonder out loud. Linc gives me a sly grin that makes my heart skip.

"All kinds of things." There's a twinkle in his deep green eyes that disarms me. He pats the closest computer to him affectionately. "This lab has been my entire world for the last twelve months, and I still feel like I'm just beginning to scratch the surface of what I can create."

I nod. I can relate. That's the thing about learning. With the right equipment, the possibilities of what you can achieve are endless. I gaze around at the laboratory around us. Clearly this is the right equipment, it's easily the most sophisticated collection I've seen. I suppose if I have to be trapped somewhere, this is a pretty amazing place to be trapped.

"But enough about me. Congratulations on making it to Cortex. What's your name?" Linc folds his arms and leans casually against a nearby divider wall, studying me like Director Ellis had hours before, but not quite as intensely. My cheeks flush and I try to ignore my heart beating fast in my chest. I was a year younger than Linc. Of course, he doesn't remember me.

"I'm Arin." I offer him my best smile. "Arin Wells." I pause, waiting to see if my name brings any kind of recognition to his face. But when the light of recollection doesn't come on, I decide to give him a little help. "We actually went to the same school together, in district five," I add.

"That's where I know you from!" He snaps his fingers together, deep eyes twinkling. "That was bugging me. So, how's your first day been?" he asks, watching me thoughtfully. I'm not sure how to respond. Should I share with my new colleague that I met Director Ellis herself? I don't want to seem like I'm bragging, and that could end up leading to questions about my score, which I know from experience is not a fast way to make friends. I decide to play it safe.

"It's been like a dream come true," I answer thinking through each word. "I'm so thankful to be here."

Linc nods again. "Cortex is something else." He gives me a smile, before adding, "So ... I was told that we would be rooming together. If you want, I can walk you back?"

I stare at Linc's familiar face, at his inquisitive eyes. I try to ignore the flutter in my chest as he shoots me a grin. I feel ridiculous, but being around Linc for even this short amount of time has had an undeniable effect on me. I'm not sure how I'm going to handle living in the same house as him. Keep it professional, Arin, I remind myself.

"Sure." I shrug. "That would be great."

We leave the lab and walk in comfortable silence through the silver level, back towards the elevators. Linc stands about a head taller than me, and when he does speak, I have to glance up in order to see his face.

"Are you settling in okay?" A flicker of concern dances across his face. "The first day can be ... a lot." I wonder if he's referring to the fact that I just found out that I can never leave this building. If so, I'm inclined to agree.

"Yes," I nod. "It is ... a lot." I wonder if Cortex employees ever talk about how we are all just trapped in here, or if everyone just has a sort of understanding that it comes with the job. I don't have too much time to wonder about that because soon, the familiar door of our shared apartment comes into view, S22.

"Well, here we are." Linc shoots me a quick grin and leans down to the eye scanner, opening the front door with a soft click. I follow him through the doorway, trying to muster up my former enthusiasm from earlier, but every step into my new home sends a sinking feeling in my stomach.

"Hey, are you okay?" Linc watches me carefully. I wish I didn't wear my expressions on my face. My mother used to tease me, *Arin, you're an open book.*

"Huh? Oh yeah. Of course," I lie and give my most reassuring smile. In reality, I can feel myself starting to come unwound at the edges. *Don't think about home. Don't do it.*

"Okay, well ... if you ... need anything, I'm just one bedroom over. Down the hall," Linc offers and my heart pounds. I try to think of something to say to ease the awkward tension that my sad silence has created but all I can think about is getting into my new room and shutting the door.

"Thanks," I manage, and escape inside the safety of my bedroom. As the door clicks into place behind me, I allow myself to crumple there, behind the door, not caring if I was under surveillance. If anything, I hope that watching me sitting here, sobbing and mourning my family, makes them feel terrible. Because it should. I had no idea what I was trading.

I stop and wipe at my nose with the back of my wrist. Would I have made a different decision though? My sole mission in life has always been to make sure that my mom and dad, who have always been so kind to me, are well taken care of. Because they're all I have. Well, had.

A deep sigh wracks my body, and the tears don't seem to want to flow anymore. *I just wish that I had been warned,* I quietly mourn, as I wrap my arms around myself. I would have clung a little tighter when I said goodbye. I would have really breathed in the smell of them and burned it into my memory. And now, I'll probably never have the chance to do that again.

It's not fair.

It is what it is. I remind myself. There is no going back now. What am I going to do? Leave Cortex and commit my family to poverty? Destined to be cast outside of the city? No! I've worked too hard and come too far to end up back in that place again.

The Gifted never talk about who, or what, is lurking outside of Paramus' giant walls. All that I know is that it is not a place where anyone wants to go. It is a place to be rescued from; a place to never speak of again. It's where I have been working my entire life to avoid being dragged back to. If I don't adjust to my new life at Cortex, there is nothing else for me.

I go to my bathroom and scrub my face. The salty tracks the tears left on my cheeks will be gone in a moment, all evidence of this breakdown vanished. In its place will be the face that I always wear. The face of the girl with the highest Criterion score ever recorded. The face of a person who is perfect, not riddled with insecurities or terrified of losing what little family she has. Certainly not a girl who struggles with fear of abandonment at the deepest, darkest center of her core. No, everyone will see the face of Cortex's newest employee who has it all together. And this is the face that I will continue to wear. Because I must. I'm like a diamond, perfect under pressure.

And now that I look the way that I should, calm, confident, collected, I decide to give my mom and dad a call. I won't tell them about the policy that I learned about. They don't need to know. If they ask why I never come to visit, I'll feign busyness, but I'll always have time for our holo-calls. It's like Kace said, it's the best technology in the city. Almost as good as the real thing.

"Hey room," I begin. "I would like to make a call." The computer responds quickly, its automated voice sounding cheerful.

"I can help you with that, Arin Wells. Would you like to add contacts and customize your room experience?"

"Actually, yes," I answer, and as soon as the program is in place and my contacts transfer over, I give the command—"Call Mom and Dad"—and the room understands. It instantly connects a video feed from my holo-screen to whichever feed is available back at home. "Hi Mom! Hi Dad!" I call once the connection is made, activating my skin coms.

"Hey honey!" They both sound cheerful from the holo-screen in their bedroom, where they were apparently lounging for the evening, most likely catching up on some evening broadcasts. I can't help but smile. It's like I never left. Hearing their voices is like a breath of fresh air, and I feel better. "How is Cortex?" my dad asks. "Are you settling in okay?"

"Tell us everything!" my mom interjects. And I force a smile.

"It's actually been pretty eventful," I begin. "I've been assigned to an apartment, which is gorgeous, and I have a roommate who seems nice. Oh! There is one person that I met today that I actually wasn't expecting to meet. Director Ellis was here to meet me when I got here."

"You met Director Ellis?" my father says incredulously with wide eyes. "On your very first day? You've got some good luck, kiddo." He exchanges a proud look with my mom. "What was she like?"

"She said that she was very impressed with my scores and happy to have me on the team."

"Arin, that's fantastic! Did you ... find out your score?" my mom asks, hesitation in her voice. I can tell that she doesn't want me to feel any added pressure from her or dad.

"Yeah, that's the thing. Apparently"—I take a deep breath, not sure how they are going to react—"I scored a 999." They're both silent for a moment, faces frozen in surprise.

"I've never heard of a score that high!" my mother finally says. "That's incredible, honey!"

"Thanks. I don't really know how to act now," I confess. "I feel the same as I always do. But the good news is that I've been assigned to work in research and development, which is a top tier position. My salary is going to be very big, so you guys will be more than comfortable." My father shakes his head and laughs.

"You did it kiddo, I hope you're proud." I share a smile with him but deep down his words cut like a knife. I thought that the feeling of accomplishing what I've set out to do my entire life would feel a lot better. But now that I know it's true cost, my pride is sprinkled with regret.

"Are you okay, honey?" My mom is always so good at reading me.

"Of course," I lie through a reassuring smile. "I just miss you guys."

My mother chuckles. "Well, we miss you too sweetheart, but we are so happy for you! Day one seems like it was pretty great. We can't wait to see what else Cortex has in store for you!" She's quiet for a moment, just smiling at me until my dad gives her a light nudge.

"Hey, it's getting late," he chimes in. "Your mother and I should probably turn in, and you've got a big day tomorrow." He gives me a small smile.

"Okay. I'll call you tomorrow and let you know how everything goes." I miss them so much. "Love you both."

"We love you too. We'll talk tomorrow, okay?"

"Okay, Dad. Bye Mom. Bye Dad." I wave my hand to end the call and as soon as their faces disappear, a few rogue tears snake down my cheeks. That was harder than I thought it was going to be.

Of course, they can never know the sacrifice I'm making just being here. I'll make up excuses, I reason, as I turn off the light and climb into the monstrous white bed, new and foreign. I wonder if they'll really believe that I'm just too busy to come home. They must. Because knowing that I'm stuck here in this prison will crush them—like it threatens to crush me.

My first day as a Cortex employee goes by in a blur. I start my morning with a quick run in the fitness center, and then head over to the mess hall for breakfast around 7 a.m. I mostly keep to myself through breakfast and then change into my white lab coat to meet with the rest of the staff on the silver level by 8 a.m. There is no sign of Linc in the cafeteria or back at the apartment, which leaves me with a bit of lingering disappointment, although I'm not quite sure why.

I'm a jumbled mixture of excitement and nervousness when I walk through the lab door. It's a lot more intimidating during the daytime, filled with people. There are eight other scientists working in my section, all only a few years my senior. Everyone is sitting at attention, their eyes trained on a single figure at the center of the room, who looks as if he is about to lead a morning brief.

When I see him, my heart gives a little lurch in my chest. Linc's handsome face is serious as he regards the group of people awaiting his instruction. He's dressed in the same uniform as yesterday, the long black stripe down his arm demanding the respect of everyone present. He scans the room carefully, and once he sees me he holds my gaze with a small smile until my face start to grow hot and I have to look away.

"Before we get started today, there are just a few announcements that I wanted to make." Everyone sits up a little taller in their chairs, evidence of their respect for Linc. His words are met with close attention as he continues, "As you know, today is Primordium Ceremony day, honoring Cortex's newest employee. While most new employees start out at the green level, we are fortunate enough to have this year's recruit joining us here at Research and Development." He gestures to where I'm seated, and I try to sink down into my chair as a few people turn around to peer at me. I've never really been one to enjoy the spotlight. When I finally look up, Linc is wearing a mischievous smile, as if he finds my discomfort to be amusing. I scowl. I do not. "Please be sure to welcome her as you all go on about your day. Also, we are drawing closer to several project deadlines. If your project has a date that it must be presented to the council, those dates are not optional. If you need additional resources, don't be afraid to ask." Linc mentions a few other agenda items that are unfamiliar to me before ending the announcements and dismissing everyone back to their assigned workstations. A few people nod at me on their way, but no one seems particularly interested in the newcomer. I try to manage a warm smile toward the few colleges that do end up welcoming me, but most people seem interested in getting to their stations and resuming their work on their various projects.

The stations pose a new challenge. Everyone seems to know exactly where they are supposed to be, and I'm not sure if I'm supposed to just find an empty station and claim it as my own.

"Hi, excuse me." I approach a girl at the closest station and give a little wave, cringing internally for being so awkward. Her hair is pulled back into a tight ponytail and she barely glances up from her holo-screen, which has data scrolling across it at a rapid rate. "Sorry to bother you. I was just wondering, how do I know which workstation is mine?" I gesture to the maze of silver cubicles around us.

"Oh." She gives me a tight smile. "Any open one is fine," she answers dismissively, her mind still clearly on her work.

"Okay, thanks," I mumble but she has already started typing again before I even have the chance to walk away. I select a workstation and use my eye print to patch in. The system asks me to do a few warmup movements to acquaint itself with me and after no time is tracking my commands flawlessly. I swipe across the screen with my left hand, fingers splayed wide, to take my first look at Cortex's newest projects. There are countless projects in various stages of completion in the files I skim through, some of them bare-bones descriptions of the idea and some of them full blueprints, ready to be sent to the printers to create a prototype.

"What do you think?" Linc's voice sends a swirl of goosebumps down my neck, as he approaches my workstation and I look up from the module to see him wearing a warm grin. I can't help but smile back, although I'm still a little intimidated by his position as a department head.

"I like it a lot," I answer honestly, and he nods.

"I had a feeling you'd fit in well with our little team." He leans over to open a new screen in front of me and I try not to focus on the fact that when he stands this close to me, I get a nice hint of what he smells like: a clean aroma scent of soap mixed with a hint of trees. Has he been visiting the atrium lately?

"Since today is your first day, I thought I would come over and explain some of our current objectives. See if you have any ideas that you would like to present." He drags his hand across the holo-screen, bringing up the list of projects. "What do you think about this one?" he asks as the design specs lay out before me at eye level. According to the data, it's called Veritas, and it's a wearable device that takes thoughts that happen in real time, and projects them as a series of images onto a screen for viewing.

"It's an interesting concept," I observe as I take several moments to look at the hologram from all angles, zooming in on the individual specs and operating systems. I've never seen anything like it before, which is intriguing. But I also can't see any situation where physically seeing someone's thoughts would be necessary.

"What would the practical applications be?" I ask, glancing at my roommate, and he leans in closely, his green eyes holding my gaze steadily.

"The best usage that I can think of would be to use it to find out the truth. Are you the type of person who wants to know the truth, Arin?" Linc's voice is hushed, and his words surprise me so much that I'm momentarily stunned. What could he mean by that? I give him a tight smile.

"I think everyone wants to know the truth," I answer honestly, and he doesn't press further. Instead, he nods thoughtfully, and then launches into what feels like hours of a rather extensive orientation, taking me through a number of new programs and products that the R&D team are still working on.

There are a lot of products to learn, and Linc makes it clear that he expects me to memorize each one's specific features, uses, and applications. It seems that my special treatment doesn't extend to my new work life. If he does know my score, it still feels like he is determined to make me earn my silver level clearance anyway.

By lunch I'm exhausted. In the mess hall, I spot Kace flitting across the floor, her high heels and tight black dress with hovering diamonds swirling around the waist standing out easily amongst my fellow Cortex employees. She flips her long blonde hair and gives a delicate laugh at whatever the employee she is talking to says, and then we make eye contact. I give a little wave and her teeth flash in a perfect grin. She whispers something in the ear of the lucky guy and then struts over to me. He watches her go, still under her spell.

"Arin! It's so good to see you!" she squeals, wrapping me in a tight hug. "How's your first day?" I flinch; I'm still not used to all the friendly contact, but I soon find myself relaxing into her warm embrace.

"I'm exhausted. I think Linc is trying to make my head explode," I joke, and my comment makes her grin.

"He is *so* into smart stuff," Kace agrees, with a roll of her eyes. "Like, look at me, I'm a department head, blah blah blah." I find myself smiling at her impressions. He does seem to take his job really seriously, and he is pretty young to be a department head. I'm sure it wasn't easy to land such a prestigious position at his age.

"But also *so* easy to look at," Kace adds, waggling her eyebrows before breaking into a giggle. "How many days do you think you're going to make it before you want a piece of that?" she teases, and my face flushes hot for the third time today. "Seriously Arin, someone needs to show that man that there is more to life than graphs and if you don't do it, I will." She winks.

I swat at her in playful exasperation. "Kace! Stop it!"

"I'm sorry!" she grins, blue eyes sparkling. "I'm just saying, there's something unusual about him. Did you know that his dad is on the council?" I shake my head. I don't really know anything about my roommate, and former classmate, except that was accepted into Cortex and is now a department head. I wonder if his dad's position had something with him being promoted at such a young age. Could it have had something to do with his score? I can't help but wonder how much higher or lower his score is than mine. I glance at Kace. Does she have access to that information?

"Do you know what his score is?" I ask abruptly.

"Who cares?" Kace shrugs. "I'll never understand why you brainiacs are always so obsessed with those three little numbers."

"Because it's important," I point out. I can feel my brow furrowing. "The Criterion score separates the Gifted from the non-Gifted. It's how we determine who is suited for positions of power and leadership."

Kace rolls her eyes. "I'm not sure that I agree with all of that. I mean, if that's the case, then nobody matters unless they're Gifted. It just doesn't seem fair."

"It doesn't have to be fair. It *works*. Our city is the only man-made city to survive this long. We never have war ... or crime. We don't struggle for anything. If you ask me, that is successful by every way measurable. I mean, you're Director Ellis's personal assistant, aren't you? How can someone with such an esteemed position not see the importance of the Criterion test?"

"I'm just saying," Kace mutters, looking away. Her doubts puzzle me. I've never seen anyone be vocally against the Criterion test and the division of the Gifted besides my mom and dad. What reason would she have to oppose it?

Now, my parents, I can understand. They remember a time before Paramus, from before we were brought inside of the wall. They have their old way of thinking. But Kace should know all of this. I mean, she can't actually believe that there would be a better way to judge people other than the Criterion score, can she? What would that even look like? Judging people this way is the only way to have peace. I just don't understand how Director Ellis's *personal assistant* couldn't see that.

I glance at my Kace and repress a sigh. I can tell that my comments have upset her, which wasn't my intention at all. The ability to not be able to hold my tongue is probably one of my worst qualities. And I'm also not used to being around people that have different opinions than me—I didn't expect to find that at Cortex of all places.

But Kace is a kind person. Speaking to her again, her warm and approachable manner, makes me hope that we might even become friends. I take a deep breath. I know what I have to do.

"I'm sorry. I didn't mean to get so worked up," I quickly apologize, taking one of her manicured hands in mine. "I'm just kind of a nerd." I roll my eyes, poking fun at myself and successfully bringing a smile to her face. "I was actually wondering if I could get your help with something tonight. Would you ... could you help me find something to wear to the Primordium Ceremony later? I'm kind of clueless in that department."

Kace's face lights up at my request. "Well I'll have to arrange some things in my schedule ... but of course!" Kace is back to her smiling, bubbly self and I'm relieved. She's one of the few people that I've really connected with since coming to Cortex. I don't want to screw this up over politics.

I shoot Kace my warmest smile before packing up my things and getting up from the table. "Great! You're truly a life saver! I'll see you later?"

"Definitely!"

We go our separate ways with a wave, and relief floods my chest at avoiding any further conflict. Even if we don't agree on core issues, I still enjoy being around her.

As I watch Kace move away, I reflect on her words against the Criterion, the Gifted, the foundations of Paramus. It seems like the only people who don't appreciate our current system are people who aren't Gifted. I can't say for sure, but if I had to guess, I would wager that Kace would not score very high on the Criterion. Which begs the question: why is she here? I watch her retreating figure grow smaller and smaller, long blonde hair swishing behind her. She must have something else to offer. She is a very fun person to be around. A delight, truly. But this building is one of science. And a great personality doesn't earn coin. Does it?

CHAPTER

5

*"Trust your city and your leaders.
Everyone else comes secondary."*

- Articles of Axiom. Section I, Part H.

"Hey." Linc's voice startles me as I let myself into our shared apartment, and when I look up, he greets me with an easy smile. "How's it going?"

"It's going alright," I answer honestly as I dump the stuff I took home from the lab on our shared dining room table and grab a drink from the fridge. "Not winning any awards today in the friendship department."

"What do you mean?" he asks, glancing up at my expression of defeat.

I shake my head. "I think I'm so smart about everything but I'm an absolute idiot when it comes to talking to people my age." Linc laughs, which is a really pleasant sound and pats the couch cushion beside him. I like the ease that I feel around my roommate, it's almost like we picked up right where we left off when I knew him in school. I take a seat.

"Okay, but who can really blame you?" He shrugs. "I mean, your scores indicate that you've spent a lot of time studying and working to improve. I can see how that wouldn't leave a lot of time for a social life."

"Exactly!" I can feel the relief in my voice at someone finally understanding. "Thank you! I mean I had to work incredibly hard to get here, and sure, that meant spending a lot of time alone, in my room, or staying late after class but it was all worth it. I made it." I gesture at the apartment around us, and he nods thoughtfully.

"So, now that you're here, now what?" he asks.

"Now what?"

"What are your goals? Do you want to be a department head someday?"

I narrow my eyes, confused at the forward nature of the question. "Are you asking me as the head of my department or as my roommate?"

"I'm asking you as someone who is worried that you might take his job out from under him." He laughs. "Director Ellis is really impressed with you. You're the 'wonder girl' with the highest score ever recorded."

The highest score ever recorded. Little butterflies dance in my stomach. So, he knows. The information hangs heavily in the air between us, until he hesitantly speaks again.

"Oh, did you not know that I know? Yeah, Director Ellis told all the department heads. I think she wants to motivate us to all try and be a little bit more like you." He chuckles. "Does that bother you?"

"No," I answer quickly. I mean, why would it? Of course, Linc would have access to that kind of information. *I wonder how many other people know.*

"I'm still trying to wrap my head around it myself. I mean, I thought I was smart. But you beat the whole test." My cheeks start to redden at his compliment. It's not like I was trying to break the test. "I just wanted to get into Cortex," I answer honestly, thinking out loud more than anything. "Not become some kind of … wonder girl." Linc cocks his head a little and stares at me curiously as I continue. "I feel like I was just as surprised as everyone else when my results came in."

"You didn't already know that you are the smartest person in the city?"

"No, I mean I always had no problem earning coin on my DLT and my scores at Academia were always top of my class, and there were … things that have always come easily to me." *Like hacking,* I add mentally. "But how can you really know for sure how intelligent you truly are until you get that final Criterion score, showing you definitively? Until then, there's no real proof. The Criterion is the only standard that matters."

"Yeah, I guess you're right."

"So, what's your score?" I ask abruptly and, in that moment, I see an entirely new emotion in Linc's face. His cheeks flush red and he stares down into the mug in his hands. Is he … embarrassed? How bad could it be?

"You already know mine," I add purposefully, needling him a little bit. Not knowing Linc's score has been killing me since I first found out that he was supposedly the best match for me on the entire campus.

"That's fair." He takes a deep breath and I watch him expectantly. "My score is 840," he admits, and I try not to let my mouth drop open. "But if you check the system, it says 940. My father had … leverage with someone in the Criterion committee."

"What?" I'm shocked. If what Linc's saying is true, then that is *completely* unfair. I can feel myself start to splutter as different words and emotions try to all rush out of my mouth at once. "But how? That's … changing someone's score is not possible! That is … illegal, at best!"

"Well"—he runs his fingers through his hair nervously—"you're right. It is illegal, but it's also possible. And it happens more often than you'd think." I blink, trying to process what Linc is admitting to me right now.

The system needs to be tamper-free in order to work. It can't work if people can just … go in and change scores. Who else has scores that have been tampered with?

"Why are you telling me this? What is to keep me from going and telling someone right now?" I ask.

Linc shrugs. "I don't know. And I hope you won't." He looks at me carefully, sea-green eyes sincere. I realize that he just took a big risk, telling me this. The information that he just gave me … I could easily use it to end his career, maybe worse. "I'd just like to trust you I guess." I look into his heavy gaze and I want to feel warm and fuzzy inside but in reality, his confession stings me. Somehow finding out that Linc cheated on his score feels like a betrayal, if not to me personally then at least to society.

Why should he get something so easily that I have had to work my entire life to gain? And how many others are like him? Is being "Gifted" just about who you know? For some reason, tears start to burn in the back of my eyes and I have to look away. That can't be the case. It just can't be.

"I've gotta go get ready for the Primordium Ceremony," I say, excusing myself before I break down entirely and rush to the safety of my room, slamming the door shut behind me. My stomach is churning so much that I fear that I might be sick as I sink down onto the floor behind the door, not even bothering to walk to my bed.

Why would Linc tell me that someone purposely changed his scores so that he could be here at Cortex? And why tell me so soon after meeting me, properly, for the first time? Why would he take such a risk? How did I not know that changing scores was even possible until this very moment? Why have I never heard about people doing that … and being caught for it, in the media?

Maybe he's lying. But why tell a lie that makes him look bad or, even worse, could get him into serious trouble? I rub my throbbing temples and feel like I'm turning green as perception of my world, my society, continues to shatter into a million pieces.

Being intelligent gifts and burdens you with a hyperactive mind. My brain has no problem flexing its muscles and creating what feels like a thousand different scenarios and possibilities and honestly, I don't like a single explanation that I come up with as to why Linc would tell me that his Criterion score was changed. I wish that there was someone that I could ask about this, someone that I could talk to and find out if they had ever heard of someone *changing* their Criterion score without revealing what I know about Linc.

I'm not sure what to do about that secret yet. There is one thing that I know, however. If there is any information out there about people changing their Criterion scores, I'm going to find it.

Kace shows up a little while later, as promised, to help me get ready for the Primordium Ceremony tonight. She greets me with an exquisite smile and a warm hug, clearly thrilled about playing dress up with me for the next hour, and while I'll admit that I'm a little less than thrilled about the dress up part, it's nice to see her again. Together, like this, we feel like real friends.

I try to be patient as Kace spends the next half hour becoming completely absorbed with the task of finding out what my most flattering color palette is. I'm itching to tell her that I could really care less about which sleeve length and pant cut will go best with my figure, but I know that I should let her have her fun.

So, instead I "oooh" and "ahhh" over all the designs that she displays for me on my holo-screen and try not let my mind wander back to the news that I got about the Criterion. Kace asks the printer for all sorts of blouse and pant combos until my floor is absolutely covered with bright fabrics and the softest silks.

I step over the closest pile and pick up the first shirt that I see. It's royal blue with long sleeves and glistening buttons all the way down the front.

"I like this one," I declare and Kace helps me fasten the buttons. She pairs the top with a pair of perfectly tailored black slacks and stylish black pumps. The look is celebratory, but professional, and when I turn around, Kace is absolutely transfixed. Her hands are clasped together like a mother at her prodigy's first award ceremony, absolutely beaming with pride.

"Arin, you look breathtaking!" she squeals. "Director Ellis will be so pleased!" I thought that appearances weren't supposed to matter anymore. But what does? I'm honestly not sure anymore.

"This year's recruit, the guest of honor," she breathes, twirling around me. "Oh, you'll be the talk of Cortex."

I give her my best smile, but deep down, I hope not. I would rather not be the center of attention, even under the best of circumstances. Now, of course, the entire time I'm going to wonder if everyone who is there has actually earned their place, or if I'm going to be surrounded by a bunch of cheaters.

"Okay, so are you going to tell me what's wrong?" Kace wonders, eyeballing me knowingly after we finish shoving all the discarded clothing choices into the recycler and she starts getting to work on my hair.

"What do you mean?" I ask, catching her gaze in the mirror and doing my best to act surprised, although, clearly, I'm not the best at hiding my thoughts. She shakes her head, long blonde curls sending a wave of strawberry my way and grins.

"Arin, I can tell that your head has been somewhere else this whole time. Do you want to tell me what's going on in there? Have you gotten into a fight with loverboy?" She waggles her eyebrows suggestively and my cheeks instantly flush.

"No!" I practically shout and shake my head which makes her fuss at me. "And we are *not* lovers. Just colleagues. And roommates. That's it."

"Mmhmm ... so if it's not Linc, then what is bothering you?"

"I'm just ... starting to question everything that I thought I knew about the Criterion," I admit. "I'm just like"—I blow out a breath of air and feel my shoulders sag—"having an existential crisis. I don't even know if our scores even matter anymore."

Kace peers at me with blue eyes wide, speckled with concern. "What do you mean, Arin? You're clearly one of the people whose Criterion score means a lot to them, which is fine," she adds quickly. "I'm just surprised to hear you say something like that."

I blow out another breath and start to feel my pulse pound in my forehead. "Yeah, I mean I was—I am! It's just that ... I came into some information today that is making me question the whole thing. It's crazy right? I mean, obviously the system works. It has to."

Kace shrugs and gives my hair a gentle brush. The only other person who has ever brushed my hair is my mother. I feel a pang of homesickness. "What happened?" I glance at the girl who was the first person to truly befriend me when I arrived at Cortex and who had just taken the time to come and help me get dressed for a symposium. Her face is almost angelic as she watches me expectantly, waiting for some kind of explanation for my change of heart. I wanted someone to talk to about this, and clearly, she wants to help, so I take a deep breath.

"Today I heard that sometimes people can ... change their Criterion scores? If that is really true ... then that means that everything that I've worked for was basically a waste of time. Have you ever heard of anyone doing anything like that?"

Kace shrugs again, surprisingly nonchalant, given the information I've just shared with her. "Not really, but it wouldn't surprise me." Her words don't make me feel better. She frowns, lips turning down into a perfect pout and golden eyebrows furrowed. "But, so what if some people cheat and change their scores? What does that have to do with you? You didn't cheat, you *earned* your score."

"Right, but it ruins the entire point of having a performance-based system. If people are able to manipulate their results, then …" I can't finish the sentence. *Then that means that everything that I've believed my entire life is a lie.*

"Arin, take a deep breath with me and try to relax. Everything is fine, you are about to attend a ceremony as Director Ellis' special guest and you're going to look absolutely amazing, thanks to me." Kace's blue eyes draw me in, and I find myself trying hard to follow her instructions. *Take a deep breath. You don't know for sure.*

"Okay," I agree, trying to calm the turmoil in my chest. Maybe I didn't understand Linc correctly. Maybe this is all just a big misunderstanding. "You're right," I finally concede and Kace gives my shoulder a tight squeeze.

"Besides," she says warmly, an easy smile on her face, "if it makes you feel any better, you're definitely the smartest person that I know. And one of the nicest too. If I had to give you a score, it would be a 100." She giggles and I know that she is teasing. But her compliment raises questions within me. How do you quantify how much things are of value to you, but not really to society? My love for my parents, for example. Where do you draw the line?

My head is spinning but I don't mind. As I smile up at Kace, she returns my gesture with a look of acceptance, and kindness. It feels nice to have something that I've never had before— friendship. Even if I can't quantify it.

The air around me is electrified as I take my seat on the platform on the perfectly manicured lawns outside of Cortex. Ever since I stepped foot outside of the building, I've been gulping at the fresh air greedily. Who knows when I'll be allowed outside next? Director Ellis, Kace, and the rest of the members of the council sit in high backed chairs on either side of me, all smiles for the hundreds of cameras that are livestreaming our every movement for all of Paramus to see. I try not to think about that as I flash my best smile to the camera nearest to me. The sun is just starting to set in the sky, casting a red glow over the sea of Cortex scientists who sit on the lawn beneath us. They're all chatting happily, relishing the fresh air and the chance to be outside of Cortex's walls. Someone has set up tables with finger sandwiches and vials of bubbling champagne, which help to make the mood even more festive. However, up on the platform, I don't have the privilege of using alcohol to soften the edge of my nerves. So instead, I do my best to take slow, calming breaths and try to look confident for the cameras. I didn't receive a lot of instruction about what will be expected from me tonight other than the fact that I am supposed to stand by Director Ellis when she calls my name and that I'll have a few moments to express my gratitude about being chosen. Before leaving my apartment, I watched video after video of speeches from new recruits in years past, including Linc's. Seeing his face, even on a screen, made my heart race and unleashed a torrent of conflicting feelings. I decided to keep what I wanted to say simple, and now, as I watch Director Ellis take the microphone, my nerves have rendered my throat so dry that I worry I won't be able to speak at all. My eyes skim the crowd in an attempt to calm my nerves but come to a direct halt once I spot two familiar faces in the crowd. I blink, trying my best to get a clear look around all the flashing cameras and blaring event lights. Sure enough, my eyes have not deceived me. My mom and dad are really here, at Cortex, for my Primordium Ceremony.

My heart leaps in my chest and the smile on my face is real this time. I fight the urge to jump up in my seat, but instead, I wait patiently until my dad looks over and we lock eyes. His smile brings a relief that I can't put into words. I'm so happy to see him. He nudges my mom who also catches my gaze and she's quick to mouth "I love you" which I wish I could return, if it weren't for all the cameras trained on me at the moment. Feeling much better, I smooth the fabric of my slacks and pay attention to the welcome speech that Director Ellis is giving, to not only this crowd, but to the entire city. It's as familiar to me as breathing, but this year the words take on a fresh, new approach. This year, her message of hope and the brightness of the future, is about me. After what feels like only a few short minutes, I hear the words that I had been preparing myself for.

"—is my pleasure to present this year's newest Cortex recruit, Arin Wells." Director Ellis turns to smile at me, looking sleek and powerful in her bright white blazer and silver pants combo. There is a wave of applause as I rise to my feet and cross the platform in a few short steps. I catch Kace's eye as I walk past, and she gives me a reassuring smile. Once I reach the podium, Director Ellis takes a step back, presenting my opportunity to speak. I remind myself to just say the words that I had been rehearsing all afternoon, and then I would have a chance to run off the stage and embrace my mom and dad.

"Good evening, fellow colleagues, citizens of Paramus. It is, of course, such an honor to be presented as this year's newest recruit at Cortex. I don't need to tell you how much I've dreamed of this day, as many of you have stood where I stand now and have made speeches that will be much better than anything that I could come up with. I am, after all, a scientist and not a poet." There is a scattering of laughter throughout the crowd as my joke lands well, and I start to feel some relief from the pressure in my chest. My smile is more natural. I gaze upon the crowd as I rush to get to my ending remarks. "There is really just one thing that I think is worth mentioning, since I have been given such a prestigious opportunity, and that is—" My gaze halts as I notice a single figure in the crowd, who is not seated, but slowly rises to their feet. I blink as they raise a sign over their head. The words, scrawled in blood red paint, make my stomach churn. *Execution and Innovation.* The very same phrase next to Tesa's lifeless body. I feel myself swaying on my feet and have to grip onto the podium to keep steady.

"—that is, hope is a powerful thing." I struggle to finish my sentence, gaze transfixed on the stranger in the crowd. He looks to be about my age, with a dark crop of windswept hair on his head. His eyes are full of resolve. The crowd begins to murmur as other people notice the sign, and I watch as heads turn, and people gasp. I have to squint to read the second bit of writing at the bottom of the sign. My heart starts to race when I finally make out the words. *The Lost Live.*

"Arin, is everything alright?" Director Ellis murmurs from beside me, a cool smile still set in her lips. She follows my gaze out into the crowd and her smile disappears, instantly replaced by a scowl. She whispers something that is too quiet for me to hear and I notice figures moving from all sides of the crowd. Android soldiers. "Thank you for those wise words, Arin." Director Ellis cuts in front of me at the podium and signals for the cameras to turn their attention to her as the android soldiers close in on the stranger. "And that brings us to the end of this year's Primordium ceremony." My heart races in my chest. I have no idea if the man in the crowd is aware of the danger that he is in. Part of me wants to shout for him to run, but I know in my heart that it's too late.

"Let's go." Director Ellis steps away from the podium and her fingers close around my wrist like a steel trap. When I look up at her, I see nothing but anger in her dark eyes. "With Rebels in the crowd, it's not safe for us."

Rebels? Who are these Rebels and what could they want? Why would the stranger risk coming here just to show such a strange message?

More android soldiers rush to the stage and begin to escort Kace and the council members down the steps, to safety. I throw a look over my shoulder as I'm pulled towards the back of the platform and catch a glimpse of the crowd erupting into chaos. The soldiers must have made their move. I hear the sound of people running and a few shouts of surprise. My heart is in my throat and I wish that I could pull away and run into the pandemonium to make sure that my parents are okay, but I am surrounded on all sides by tall, android bodies. They move at a quick pace, shielding me completely. My eyes sting with the threat of tears. I didn't even get to see my mom and dad. Who knows when I'll get the chance again.

Once we have been safely transported back inside of the Cortex buildings, our android escorts feel confident enough to leave us. If there are any Rebel attacks tonight, the Cortex defense systems are more than prepared to keep everyone inside of the building safe, Director Ellis points out as we make our way to the closest set of glass elevators. I survey the other council members who travel with us. This is the closest that I have been to any of them since our shared time on the platform outside. But even then, I didn't get a chance to personally speak with any of them. I wonder if now is my chance to make a good impression. There are four council members in total, and they all look a little disheveled from the surprising turn the Primordium Ceremony took. Even Kace, who is glued to Director Ellis' side, does not look as perfectly put together as usual. There's a tear in the soft pink gauze of her blouse. As the glass elevator doors open, Director Ellis, Kace, and the councilmen step inside but I hesitate, sure that they are all headed to the penthouse to discuss what will be done with the Rebel who caused such a stir tonight. Did they catch him? From the smug expression on Director Ellis' face, I have the impression that they did.

"I apologize that your Ceremony took such a surprising turn," she says briskly. "I realize that introductions are still due, but those will have to wait for another time. I have another matter to attend to." Again, the smug expression. Then the doors close and I am left standing alone in the hallway, waiting for the next elevator to carry me back to my apartment.

I can't stop thinking about the stranger in the crowd. Is he really one of these "Rebels" that Director Ellis considers to be a threat? I wonder if his message ever got on camera? Or was it meant to be seen by only those Cortex employees in attendance? No, his actions seemed more intentional than that. He waited until I took the podium. I swallow, as the elevator doors come into view. It's almost as if the message was for me.

CHAPTER

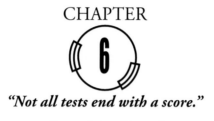

"Not all tests end with a score."

- Paraminian Proverb

I'm awoken by the sound of ringing in my ears. I blink groggily in the darkness and check the time in my eye-screen. 3 a.m.? Who could be calling me? The caller is marked with a special symbol—it's someone in the government. I sit up quickly in my bed and tap my ear.

"Hello?"

"Hello Arin." I recognize Director Ellis' voice instantly and rub the sleep from my eyes. "There is a second part to your Primordium Ceremony that begins in one hour. I'll send a driver to meet you outside of your apartment and he will transport you to the appropriate location, where I will meet you. Do you understand?"

"Yes." My voice sounds groggy even to my ears, but before I can assure the Director that I'm alert enough to follow her instructions, the call ends, and she is gone. I climb out of my bed and activate the night vision in my eye-screen with a blink. I dress quickly, unsure of how formal this portion of the ceremony is supposed to be. I pull on a billowy white button down and, after checking the day's forecast, opt to add my mother's green sweater from home on top of it. Pressed black slacks come next, and then a pair of simple black flats, since I have no idea about how much walking, or anything really, will be occurring at this mysterious second ceremony. While running a brush through my hair, I briefly consider waking up Linc and asking him what I should expect, but I'm not sure how things are between us since our last interaction ended rather uncomfortably. Also, if he's anything like me, he won't appreciate being awoken at three in the morning.

A notification in my vision alerts me to the fact that my escort has arrived outside of my apartment door. I slip my handheld nano in one pocket out of habit, and tiptoe to the front door. When I open it, I can't help but smile at the familiar face waiting on the other side.

"Marcus, it's good to see you." My former driver returns the smile, and his reassuring presence helps to take away some of the butterflies fluttering in my stomach.

"Likewise, Miss Wells." We are the only two people in the hallway leading away from the apartments and when we get to the glass elevators, I don't see any movement on any of the other levels either. It's strange. I feel like the only person awake in the entire building. The moon is high in the sky when we exit through the front doors and a cool breeze greets me when I step outside, playfully lifting the hair from the back of my neck and drying the tiny pinpricks of nervous sweat hiding there. I climb inside of the hovercar and nestle once again into the clean leather. When I glance at Marcus in the rearview mirror, his expression is more set than last time. His eyes stay trained on the road ahead of us and I can't help but wonder if he knows anything about this mysterious ceremony.

"Hey Marcus, can you tell me where we are headed?" Marcus shakes his head, giving me a brief glance in the mirror, the expression on his broad face apologetic.

"Okay." My fingertips dig into the leather as the little pinpricks of sweat return. "Director Ellis wouldn't tell me much either."

Why have I never heard of a second Primordium Ceremony before? Why didn't Kace or Linc didn't mention anything to me? I wonder if it's something that every new recruit experiences. Or maybe, just maybe, a little voice in my head whispers, this is something that is happening only to me. "Have you ever taken any other recruits here before?" I ask, and Marcus once again glances in the rearview mirror. Only this time he doesn't speak, but gives me a weighty look and the smallest, almost imperceptible, shake of the head. Immediately I understand two things. One, that this car ride is being monitored and two, for some reason, I am being taken somewhere that no other recruit has been taken before. My palms start to sweat, and I gaze out my window to stare at the nocturnal landscape below, thoughts racing. Why would Director Ellis want to bring me for a second Primordium Ceremony? Does it have something to do with my score? My fingers find my diamond necklace hidden beneath my collar and I rub the stone between my thumb and index finger. Perhaps it has to do with the way the first ceremony went. The Rebel appearance, the sign. In my heightened state of anxiety, my thoughts take a more sinister turn. Does Director Ellis know that I found Tesa's body outside of the school? Did she make a connection between the graffiti written there and the sign that the Rebel made for my Primordium Ceremony? Or worse, does she think that I have some sort of connection to either incident? I may not be an exact rule follower, but I'm very loyal to Paramus. I want nothing to do with these Rebels—or anything outside of the city's walls.

My heart drops as we leave the center of Paramus and continue further along the spoke like roads, taking us farther and farther towards the outskirts of the city. Past the first district, with its speckling of trees and gigantic rooftops, all cut to look exactly alike. The district that I used to call home, where my mom and dad are sleeping peacefully. I feel another pang of homesickness. I wonder what they thought about what happened at my Primordium Ceremony or if they made it home safely? I tried to reach them once I got back to my apartment last night, but there was no answer. I rationalized that it was because it's not a short trip from Cortex back to our neighborhood, even when taking the sky-train. Maybe, given the circumstances, Director Ellis will grant me another opportunity to see them. That is, of course, if she doesn't suspect me to be a Rebel. The wall looms closer and closer as we drive past the second district, with its automated water treatment plants, and then the third district with its steel mills. I start to get a sinking feeling once we pass District Four, and even District Five, the outermost district of the city. It's getting hard for me to swallow as I gaze down at the yellow lights that surround the fields and fields of automated farmland below. I've never traveled this far outside of the city before. Even when I was brought to Paramus, our first house was in District Four. Only the poorest of the poor live out here in District Five, practically outside of the wall. What could Director Ellis want, bringing me here?

I tuck my necklace back beneath my blouse and wrap my green sweater tightly around me for comfort as Marcus lands the hovercar and helps me out. His lips are pressed tightly together, and I get the impression that he won't say anything to me even if I ask. But, before he lets go of my hand, he gives it a reassuring squeeze. My eye-screen is still switched to night vision mode, which helps me make out my surroundings as I take hesitant steps from the waiting hovercar and towards the only other vehicle. Both cars have landed at what appears to be the edge of the automatic farms. The ground is made up of packed dirt beneath my feet and the wall is so close that I have to crane my neck and look up to see the top. My heart beats even faster as I spot a single break in the impenetrable white surface—a gate. It looks just like the one that I was brought through when I gained entrance to the city. But they are out of commission now, as there is no one else being brought inside of Paramus anymore.

I recognize Director Ellis' sleek brown hair at the far end of the other vehicle. I frown as I get closer. She is not alone. All three councilmen have joined her, as well as a handful of android soldiers. My heart drops and my palms begin to sweat as I realize that two of the soldiers are holding someone between them. I strain to get a glimpse of the person, but the blinding white lights from the Government Official's hovercar make distinguishing features from this far away impossible. I'll have to get closer.

"Arin, thank you so much for joining us." Director Ellis turns to acknowledge me as I approach the group. I'm greeted with a combination of nods and hellos from the other three members. They all look rather irritated to be here. I look at each face carefully: first Councilman Vos, at least as old as Director Ellis, if not a little older, with an appealing olive-toned complexion and a strong jawline. His shiny black hair is styled with care and he is dressed surprisingly well for being called here in the middle of the night. He is perhaps the friendliest looking out of all four members, but that's not hard to do, I realize, as I travel down the line of faces, curious about which one is Linc's father. Beside Vos is Councilman Mattox, and, as I focus on his features, the unmistakable similarities between their emerald green eyes tell me that he must be the one. I instantly feel sorry for Linc. He had a hungry look in his eye that, when fixed upon me, makes me instantly look away. Councilman Hornberg is certainly the worst looking of them all. He is ancient looking, by far the oldest person that I have ever seen, he does not wear it well. His wrinkled face is twisted into a permanent scowl. All three of them pay no attention to the imprisoned figure only a few feet away. I wonder who this person could be, and if I dare go closer for a better look. But before I get the chance, Director Ellis begins to speak, her voice amplified by the towering wall behind us. She gestures to the prisoner, a man, I realize, inching closer. His head hangs heavily, lolling from side to side, and I begin to feel sick to my stomach as I understand what this meeting means for him.

"In Paramus we have many traditions, all of them serving a specific, carefully considered purpose. Our tradition of accepting one new recruit into Cortex every year. Our tradition of rewarding intelligence. Our tradition of casting out the derelict among us." I watch with horror as two androids break away from the others and begin to drag the man toward the gate. He regains consciousness and begins thrashing against the bonds that hold him captive, but the android soldiers are strong. They continue marching, despite the man's attempts to break free. Along with kicking and pulling, the man begins to shout.

"Please! Don't do this! I have a family here. You don't understand! They won't make it without me! I can't survive out there! Please!" His pleas appear to have no impact upon those watching with a sort of bored, calloused expression. All except for Director Ellis, whose face is unreadable. My heart goes to my throat. Ever since I was primary-aged, I understood that one of the laws of Paramus required those who did not meet our city's standard of excellence to be cast out of the city. But I've never seen it happen before. And I wish, more than anything, that I could stop it from happening. His cries shake me down to my core. This doesn't feel right. In that moment, in the face of such cruelty, I find myself questioning all that I've known.

My mind flashes back to the words scrawled behind Tesa's body and again on the sign held only a few hours ago at my

Primordium Ceremony. *Execution and Innovation.* The display before me certainly feels like a sentence for death. We all know that there is nothing worth living for on the other side of that gate. I know it, Tesa knew it, the man before me knows it, clearly, as he is fighting with everything within him to keep from being cast outside. I feel hot tears start to prickle in the corners of my eyes as the two android soldiers deploy stun weapons on the thrashing man and I watch his body go limp again.

"As a member of our city's most elite minds, I want you to recognize the penalty for failure." Director Ellis speaks with earnestness, and even though she is speaking to me, I cannot meet her gaze, lest she sees some of the doubt in my eyes. I know that sacrifices must be made in order to keep Paramus the innovative paradise that it currently is, but I can't help but think that there must be a better way. There's got to be.

I flinch as the gate opens with a screech and the soldiers dump the man's body on the other side. I try to imagine what he will feel when he regains consciousness, locked out of the city that he has called home, forever separated from family and loved ones on the other side. I'm forced to consider the fact that this could have been me if my scores were different. It is a message that Director Ellis wants me to realize and one that I don't think I'll ever be able to forget. Once their task is done, the androids return to the hovercar, followed by the three councilmen, who now look bored and ready to go. I wonder how many of these "ceremonies" they have attended. And more importantly, how something like this could have little to no impact on them?

Director Ellis does not return to the hovercar just yet, but instead, motions for me to join her as she leans against the vehicles' shiny black hood. Her driver hands her a steaming cup of liquid that I assume to be coffee, and as I approach, I focus on the swirls of hot air rising from her cup into the night air, instead of looking her directly in the eye. She doesn't say anything for a moment, and we stand in silence; the only two people in our party remaining under the canopy of stars.

"I brought you here because I think that every citizen of Paramus should witness an exile at least once in their lifetime." I stare straight ahead at the looming white wall and silently disagree. What I witnessed this morning will haunt me in nightmares for many, many nights to come. The Director notices my silence and turns her attention to me. "It will benefit you to understand why things are the way that they are. Don't get it twisted. That man"—she nods towards the gate—"spoke of a family left here in Paramus. But what he failed to mention is the fact that he has not been providing for them. He cannot. He was consistently absent from his labor assignment and he had a habit of wasting away whatever resources his family did have on illegal gambling and drinking.

"His daughter is in her final year of schooling, and next fall she will take the Criterion test, just like you did. If her mother and younger siblings are to have a chance at a better life, they need that poor excuse for a father out of the way." Director Ellis shakes her head. "One thing about being a leader, Arin, is that you have to make tough calls sometimes." Her shoulders sag and for the first time, I see a hint of vulnerability in my leader. The woman before me looks very different from the imposing, rigid figure that I am used to seeing on the daily broadcast. Her eyes look sad as she stares at the gate ahead. She takes a deep sip from the warm cup in her hands and when she looks over at me, I can see that she is tired.

"I also wanted to apologize for what happened last night. A recruit's Primordium Ceremony is supposed to be a cause for celebration, a time of recognition, and I feel like the spotlight was stripped away from you. I'm sorry." She sighs. "These Rebels are getting more and more bold. Just when I think I've caught the last of them, another one pops up in his place. It's exhausting."

"What do they want?" I can't help but ask. The idea that there are people inside of Paramus who are radical enough to try and disrupt our way of living is scary to me. I wonder if the Rebels are just misinformed about why things are the way they are, and what sort of change they could hope to bring about.

"They want a revolution," Ellis explains, and all of the air squeezes out of my lungs. "They believe that our forefathers made a mistake in creating Paramus and they want to undo all of the progress that we've made. They would trade all of this"—she gestures to the distant city behind us—"for so called 'freedom'. But they have no idea what they're asking for." She sets the mug on the hood of the hovercar and pulls her jacket tightly around her. "The thing that most people don't know about me, Arin," she says quietly, "is that I understand what it's like to live out there." She nods towards the gate. "I lived out there in that barbaric wasteland, outside of Paramus and it's beautiful innovations, and let me tell you something, I would never go back. I understand what that man will be waking up to tomorrow, because I lived it for many years. But the only way to keep all of us from living that way every single day is to follow the rules that we have set into place, and to enforce them." I find myself nodding along.

"I know that you have a good head on your shoulders. And like I mentioned before, you could have a very successful career ahead of you at Cortex." Ellis's deep brown eyes are sincere, and her words send a tingle of excitement through me. "I respect what you've already achieved, and I knew that bringing you here and showing you this would help you understand. We are all pieces in this great machine that we call Paramus, and we must all do our part." She pours out the rest of her coffee on the ground between us and straightens the sleeve of her perfectly tailored jacket. "I'll see you back at Cortex," she says, the vulnerable woman swiftly replaced by the poised leader of Paramus that I am used to seeing in broadcasts and in person. "Oh, and Arin," she adds, pausing outside of the hovercar door, "this may be your last time out of Cortex for a while, so make the most of it."

Her words make my heart race. Is she referring to going home and seeing my parents? I ponder this as I return to my own hover vehicle and find Marcus waiting, eyeing me expectantly.

"Hey, um, would it be alright if we made one more stop before returning back to Cortex?" I ask the driver and Marcus looks unfazed by the question, readily nodding his agreement. I climb happily inside the car, full of a jumble of emotions, but most of all, excitement. The sun is just starting to rise over the edge of the wall as we drive further and further away from District Five and the confusing scene that I witnessed there. Director Ellis's revelation about her life outside of the wall shocked me, but I found myself relating to her on a level I didn't think possible.

We speed past the outer lying districts and in no time at all, I begin to recognize the symmetrical rooftops that announce our arrival at District One. I'm practically bouncing in my seat once we take the turn for my neighborhood and my old street comes into view. I can't wait to embrace my mom and dad, and tell them about all the things that have happened since I last saw them. I don't wait for Marcus to come around and open my door when we land in front of my house; instead, burst through the door as soon as the hovercar lands beside the manicured lawn and race toward the front door. I don't bother to knock; my retinal scan is still enough to grant me entry to my former home. The door creaks loudly as I step inside, and I remind myself to try and be quiet as it is still early in the morning. I hear no noise. My parents must be sleeping.

"Hello?" My voice sounds small as I take careful footsteps that echo through the rooms. I stop outside of the door to my parents' bedroom, which is cracked open in the corner. I reach for the knob. And then, a sound reaches my ears, like the clang of a bell, so loud that it shakes me to my core, and I find myself trembling.

Coughing. Horrible, hacking coughs that wrack through a person's entire body and make you shudder at the painful sound of it.

"Mom? Dad? Are you okay?" I fling the door open to find my mother almost doubled over, caught in a fit of coughing. My father is leaning over her, a damp rag in his hand.

"Arin?" he says in surprise, glancing up from my mother who has her sleeve pressed to her mouth.

It is tinged with blood.

Inky black dread snakes its way through my heart. I know all the potential illnesses that have coughing up blood as a symptom. Many of them are life threatening. Many of them are contagious. My hand instinctively goes to my shirt as I pull it up to cover my nose, backing away slowly.

Once the coughing subsides, my mother straightens herself and smooths down her long brown hair, sitting up in bed.

"We didn't know that you were coming," my mother says, sort of like an apology and I glance between them.

"I wanted to surprise you," I explain earnestly, my voice coming out muffled through the fabric of my shirt as I'm careful not to touch anything. "I didn't get a chance to see you after what happened at my ceremony and I wanted to make up for that ..." I pause, looking between them. First to my mother, who has beads of sweat on her forehead and then back to my father, who has worry lines etched into his face. "What is going on with mom? Is it contagious?" The two of them exchange glances.

"No, it's nothing like that. It's not contagious sweetie. I just ... haven't been feeling well. You shouldn't worry," my mother answers casually. There is blood in the corner of her mouth.

"When did this start?" I ask, cautiously coming to sit beside her, my stomach churning. I run my fingers through the ends of her soft brown curls to try and stop their trembling. My father clears his throat and dabs at her forehead with the cloth.

"Oh, it's only been a couple of days now. I'm sure it's nothing."

"I think that we should take her to the hospital," I suggest, shooting my father a pointed glance. My father, who has always stood so strong, nearly a head taller than me, now looks at my mom with concern and takes a deep breath.

"We aren't going to the hospital, Arin." He looks deeply into my eyes. I search their murky brown depths for answers.

"Why not?" A cold sweat breaks out across the back of my neck. It is unlike my father or mother to keep secrets from me. He breaks my gaze and looks away.

"It just isn't an option."

"What's going on, Dad?" I try to keep my hysteria from leaking into my voice. I reach for his shoulder and turn him towards me; his head hangs low, and he won't meet my gaze, but he takes one of my hands in his.

"We can't go to the hospital because we can't have anyone find out what your mother and I have been doing." He finally raises his eyes to meet mine and I see a brand new emotion in them that I have never before seen in my father's eyes.

Fear. "What's going on?" I repeat, my voice coming out small once again, as if in this strange parallel universe I can't quite seem to find it. Fear constricts my own chest and throat. I shoot a glance at my mother. "Mom, what is he talking about?"

My mother sighs heavily, her shoulders hunching, perhaps from the weight of the secret that she has been carrying or maybe the exhaustion of falling ill. "We didn't think that anything would come of it." She shakes her head. "I suppose it was foolish"—her gaze darts to me and then to my father, then back to me again——"but we've just been so very lucky since we were able to move into the city. Because of you." Her eyes begin to water. "And now I'm afraid that we've messed everything up.

"We've been going outside of the wall, Arin," my father speaks up, his voice solemn. His confession hangs in the air like suspended knives, waiting to come crashing down on this wonderful life that we have created for ourselves.

"Dad?" My voice trembles. "Why would you do that?" But I already know the answer. My parents are kind people. Good people. They had spent their entire lives outside of the wall; they understand the hardship that the Lost are facing every single day.

"At first, we were just bringing extra items," Mom begins. "Clothing and shoes that had been discarded, food packets, blankets. But then we heard of a small group of people that had fallen very ill. The children especially were suffering, so we went to bring them some medical supplies, antibiotics, fever reducers, anything that we thought might help. It was absolutely horrific." My mother shudders and her eyes plead with me to understand. "We have just been so blessed here Arin, because of how well you've done. It's all thanks to you."

"But it could've gone differently," my father chimes in, and his eyes are full of the guilt that I felt myself only hours before. "It could've easily been us, but we were one of the lucky ones. And that is something that we have to live with every day. But we couldn't turn our back on the people out there. We couldn't face ourselves if we did."

I look down at my hand, held so tightly in my father's embrace. His hands are well-muscled and worn from a life of hard labor, an aspect of life that I have never known.

"What kind of sickness is it?" I finally speak, dread settling in my chest like a heavy weight that I fear I may never be able to shake. My mother averts her gaze.

"It's a virus. I—I'm not sure how it's spread. I'm no doctor." She chuckles quietly. "It doesn't seem to be contagious at all. We've witnessed something like it in the Lost camps." She stops to cough. My blood rings in my ears.

My stomach begins to churn even more. How could my parents get wrapped up in something like this? "What are we going to do?" My voice comes out like a squeak, and I feel like a child again.

My father sits back against the headboard and folds his hands on his lap. When he speaks again, his tone is somber. "There's no reasonable way to explain how your mother contracted this sickness, so we can't go to the hospitals. The last thing that we want is to destroy all of your hard work here, Arin."

"Well, you should have thought about that before you went breaking Paramus' laws and climbing over walls!" I blurt, the dread in my chest turning into fuel for a rage that burns more furiously than anything that I have ever felt before. Because of my parent's foolishness, we are all in danger. "Do you understand what this means for me? I'm working at Cortex dad!" I shoot him a furious glare. "Do you know how much trouble we can get into?"

My father holds up his hands to stop me, but I am not even close to being finished yet.

"And it's not just that you're sick. It's the fact that I can't even get help! Do you realize how that makes me feel? I can't just sit here and watch mom die! Is that what you want?"

I can't even see my parents at this point; the tears that have been stinging the corners of my eye have clustered together in my vision, making everything a blur. I blink them away. Angry at myself for crying. Angry at my parents. Angry at the Lost outside of the wall for making my family sick.

It's the betrayal that stings the most. There's always been something that I could do, a test I could take, a position that I could hold, that could guarantee their safety. And now, I'm completely and utterly *powerless* to do anything about the situation. All because of the stupid Lost.

I hate them. I hate this. I can feel the hate coursing through my veins, turning my vessels black with the sickening aroma of spite. A voice in my head tells me that the hate is only my fear disguising itself, but I push that voice down deep, burying it in my disgust.

"You're selfish, that's what you are," I spit toward them, trying not to see the sadness in their eyes. I don't want my mom to be sick. I didn't ask for this. I played the good daughter.

I was their Arin, their miracle baby, sent to save them.

But they went right back.

"Sweetie." My mother reaches out a hand for me, but I shrug it away. "You don't understand. There were people out there, suffering."

"Well that's just great." I know that the words are poisonous as soon as I begin to taste them on my tongue, but I can't stop myself from launching them at her anyway, "Now we can all suffer together. I hope you're happy."

I can see the pain in her eyes as soon as I speak, how my words crush her, but I don't care. I just want to get away. I'll just go back to my gilded cage because I can't stand to be in this house. I won't stick around to watch everything that I've built crumble.

CHAPTER

"Identity comes from contribution.
You cannot exist outside of achievement."

- Articles of Axiom. Section VI, Part B

I am angry, like a train rolling along an infinite track, picking up speed as my fury builds with each step that I take away from my former home toward the hovercar that brought me here. Marcus eyes me curiously as I step inside the car, but he doesn't say anything and neither do I, because I'm afraid that if I do, I'll say something that will destroy everything I've worked for. There are many emotions rolling around inside of me; fear is the one that hurts the most, so instead, I choose anger. We ride the rest of the way in silence, and I play the scene from at home back in my head over and over again. My parent's confession. My mother's sickness. The fact that I cannot help them or even know when I will be able to see them again.

No, I refuse to be helpless. I will find a way to visit them again soon. Perhaps I can steal some medical supplies from the red level? If I can't find anything to cure my mother, at least I can bring something that will help ease her pain. I silently curse the fact that my parents' crime will now lead to me committing numerous crimes of my own. Oh well. This is the path that they chose to follow, and my job has always been to protect them. If they're going down, I'm going down with them.

Before we land on the lush Cortex lawn, Marcus breaks his silence.

"Did ... you enjoy your visit?" He glances at me in the rearview mirror. The question is innocent enough, but his eyes flash with a warning and I'm reminded that all conversation inside of the hovercar is not kept strictly between us.

"Yes, I did. Thank you again for taking me to see my parents, it means a lot." My voice catches and I clamp my mouth shut, refusing to speak anymore, lest I give anything away. When Marcus comes around to open my door, I think about asking him if he would be willing to take me to visit them again; he is kind enough that he just might do it, but I decide against it. There is no point in getting Marcus involved. If things go south, I don't want him to be punished for mine and my parents' mistakes.

However, as his identification badge catches my eye, I realize that there may be another way. In one careful motion I drop my handheld nano on the ground outside of the hovercar and when Marcus bends down to pick it up for me, I swipe the identification badge from his shirt. I offer him a grateful smile as he hands me the device, tucking the card and my nano into my pocket. I try to ignore the pang of guilt that I feel for deceiving Marcus as I bid him goodbye and hurry back inside the building. It's unlikely that he will be penalized for misplacing an identification card, I remind myself. And he'll be issued a replacement by tomorrow.

I smile at the receptionist as I pass through the barrier. It's just like Director Ellis said, I won't be able to leave Cortex for a while, but if I'm going to help my mother, I'm going to have to pretend to be someone who can.

Trying not to recall the scene from home in my mind, I focus on the elevator buttons as I ride up to the blue level. My eyes are drawn to one button in particular, the red level, a laboratory not unlike the one where I've been assigned to work, only with a focus on medical practice and advances. Only one floor beneath the level where I live, and the only place in Cortex that would stock the medication that could help my mother. When the elevator doors open to the blue level, my anger has been replaced with steely resolve. I'm willing to do whatever it takes to help my mom recover quickly.

After grabbing a quick breakfast consisting of an apple and a steaming cup of coffee from the cafeteria, I head up to the silver level to clock some hours in the lab. The cafeteria boasts an amazing range of food, but I still stick to the simple meals that I'm used to. I feel guilty for eating so well when I know that this kind of feast isn't available to everyone else in the city. The coffee is full of flavor and warm, and by the time I reach the lab I'm feeling much more alert.

"Hey," Linc calls from he's seated on the couch, sprawled out in front of the evening's broadcast. He looks completely different from how he does at work, swapping his uniform for Cortex brand loungewear, his hair tousled. It's nice to see him for what feels like the first time today. He offers me an easy smile that makes my heart flutter. "How's it going?"

I do my best to keep my face neutral and reveal nothing of what I've witnessed. "It's going good," I offer him what I hope is a convincing smile. "How's the broadcast?" He shrugs.

"It's pretty much the usual stuff. It's always the same, isn't it?" He wrinkles his nose a little playfully and a real smile finds its way to my face. "Anything new with you?"

An innocent enough question but still my heart begins pounding at a breakneck speed. Nothing much, I'm just planning to break the only rule that we have here. You may see me on that broadcast tomorrow. I blink and try to look casual as I answer.

"Not really," I lie, with a shrug. He watches me with careful precision, and I wonder if he can tell that I'm hiding something.

"Is everything okay? You look kind of ... tired."

"Yeah, sorry. I have a lot on my mind," I reply.

"I get it. It can be an adjustment when you're new here." There's sympathy in his voice and kindness in his eyes. I wonder if he's referring again to the fact that everyone is trapped in here. Well, everyone else. I'm getting out tonight.

"Yeah, my department head is kind of a hard ass," I tease in an attempt to use humor to deflect his suspicion. It works; he breaks into an easy laugh.

"I've heard that guy is the worst," he agrees with a sly grin and for a moment the tightening in my chest loosens. I swallow hard as fear starts to rise up in my throat. I like Linc. I wonder if I get caught if I'll ever see him again? Maybe he'll be there to use the Veritas program at my trial.

"Well, I should probably turn in. Goodnight!" I call over my shoulder and disappear to the solitude of my room. I don't have time to waste wondering about what will happen if I get caught. I just need to make sure that I don't. I slip out of my Cortex uniform and into the darkest available shade of newly-printed exercise wear. Black tennis shoes go on my feet, and I tie the laces tightly to prepare for the long night of running that I have ahead of me. To the surveillance system currently monitoring my room, I look like anyone else in the building, getting ready for some time in the fitness center, but my path will carry me much farther than the short loop that the treadmill has to offer.

I'll have several obstacles that I will need to overcome in order to sneak my way into the red level, but all of them will be impossible with the current amount of surveillance that I am under. The security cameras in my room will need to be the first to go.

"Hey, room, can you show me your control systems?" An innocent enough question. "I'd like to update some of your settings to fit my needs."

"I'm afraid that my internal control systems are rather complicated, Miss Wells. You can simply let me know what you would like to change, and I can do it for you."

"That's alright," I decide, switching tactics. "Hey, by chance, could I import my preferences from home? That would make me feel really comfortable here. Can I do that?"

"It's my job to make you comfortable," the room answers happily. "I would be glad to accommodate."

"Great." I smile. "Where can I plug in my nano to share those preferences with you?" A panel of the wall close to the holo-screen slides open, revealing a small access port.

"You can plug it in here," the room offers helpfully, oblivious to my true motive. My nano connects to the port with a soft click, and as soon as the drive is accepted, it downloads all my programs, including one that I designed to scramble any monitoring software written into the room. I breathe a deep sigh of relief once the new code is accepted. I'm a blind spot in Cortex's vision for the first time since I arrived here.

Now that my room is dark, I open a secure search network, heavily coded and untraceable. It only takes a few gestures to land myself among the unfamiliar landscape that is the Cortex database. Here, all secrets will reveal themselves to me and here, I will find my in.

I'm no stranger to navigating the intricate web of back doors that some call the dark web. Of course, the dark web is just as taboo as the Lost, spoken about in hushed whispers behind closed doors, far away from monitoring bots and smart rooms. The dark web is a place outside of the law, where one can do anything from hacking to earning illegal coin in order to change a Criterion score. While it's true that the dark web offers an unlimited source of information, unfiltered and raw unlike our usual daily collection of carefully monitored broadcasts, I could spend endless hours here, searching. I have to remind myself to not listen to my curiosity and remember my goal at hand. The information that I'm searching for is anything about how to get out of Cortex.

My fingers quiver with anticipation as I find something rather promising: a copy of Cortex blueprints. I scour the layout of the red level and confirm my suspicion about all medications being kept in secure rooms with coded entry panels. Luckily for me, I quickly locate a file labeled "Cortex Access Codes". With a deep breath, I carefully select the file. Sure, surfing the dark web is easily a punishable offense, but accessing restricted information, that's a whole different crime entirely. There's no going back, I remind myself as I fling my fingers wide and command the file to open before me. There. I memorize the number sequence blinking on my screen and then promptly close the browser, heart pounding. My anxious eyes dart around the room, fear causing my throat to tighten, and I remind myself that no one is watching me. My secret is safe, for now. When I squeeze my eyes shut, I can see the sequence of numbers, burning in my mind's eye, that will help my mother. I just need to get her some medicine, then everything can go back to normal, and I can spend the rest of my life pretending none of this ever happened.

Now that I have the information that I need, my handheld nano goes back in my pocket and I head to my room's small bathroom. At the glossy white counter, it takes a little work to remove my eye-screen; the small contact lens in my right eye is slippery and wriggles away from me. I have to take it out though; I don't want my location to be tracked. Once out, it goes in a little glass dish with cleaning liquid to the right of the sink.

There isn't much that I can do for my skin coms, I set them to "do not disturb" to stop my signal from transmitting and to block all incoming messages. I can always blame it on a technology glitch if it ever comes into question. Without my eye-screen and skin coms everything is ominously quiet inside of my head. It feels good to go dark every once and awhile.

I check my door cams to make sure that the hallway outside is empty before slipping outside of my room. There aren't any lights on in the rest of the apartment and Linc's bedroom door is shut. I feel a pang of regret in my chest for how short I was with him earlier. He's been nothing but kind to me, and I haven't been very friendly in return. I walk as softly as I can to the apartment door, careful not to disturb my roommate. Maybe when this is all over, I'll try harder to get to know him.

Out in the hall, I quicken my pace, heading for the elevators, the detailed blueprints from before acting as my guide. Once inside the elevators, I press the button for the red level, and when it stops, I input the set of numbers designed to grant access. I let out a sigh of relief when the doors part with a pleasant chime and I take a cautious step into the well-lit hallway. Despite the late hour, this level is bustling with activity, and I do my best to blend in as I make my way toward the medicine storage room. I've never been to the red level before, so I'll need to rely heavily on what little information I was able to gather during my quick file search if I hope to end up in the right place. The plans showed a maze of laboratories and treatment centers, and although I spend most of my time working in a lab, the research done on the red level is much more clinical and has an entirely different set of applications. I take my first right, walking down a long corridor with bright lighting overhead that casts an almost blueish tint on everything around me. On this level, everyone has swapped the cortex uniform that I am used to seeing for a more functional looking, monochromatic two-piece shirt and pant set, which appears to be offered in only a handful of neutral colors. Perhaps the different colors notate a particular ranking, I speculate, similar to how our uniforms have a set of stripes to notate who is in charge. Whatever the case, I come to the realization that I need to get my hands on one of those sets as I turn another corner and am met with more than one curious glance. My all-black ensemble complete with a pair of running shoes makes me stick out more than a non-composite number in the Fibonacci sequence.

I skim through the map in my head and opt for a short detour that will take me right to a nearby supply closet, which will hopefully have at least one uniform inside. Keeping my head down, I quicken my pace and half walk, half jog the last stretch toward my new destination, and after I confirm that no one is coming from either direction, duck inside. The air inside tickles my nose and carries a strong antiseptic smell. I fumble for the light, silently wishing that I was still wearing my night-mode enabled eye screen. It takes my eyes a moment to adjust, but when they do I find myself in a tidy room no larger than my bathroom back at the apartment. Directly in front of me are a set of shelves stocked with crisp stacks of neatly folded linens. I scan the orderly bundles until I catch a glimpse of the familiar fabric and nearly shout with joy. I find myself checking for the familiar glint of cameras at the high points of the room as I pull off my black garments and shrug into the new, lighter grey ones. I make a mental note to look through all the camera footage on this floor when I get home and delete any trace of my presence here.

Once dressed, I find that the bottoms are a little big and I have to cinch them tightly around my waist in order to get them to sit comfortably. I glance down at my dark running shoes peeking out beneath the wide pant legs. Unfortunately, there isn't much that I can do about those. I fold the clothes that I brought with me as small as possible and stow them behind a set of tightly rolled sheets before checking the time on my handheld nano. Only five minutes have passed but I don't want to spend a minute longer than necessary on the red level. I press my ear against the polished door and listen for any sounds that indicate anyone passing by on the other side. Once I'm certain that the hallway is empty, I push the door open and emerge with what I hope is a convincing air of confidence. I take long strides as I make my way back to the path to the medication storage area.

My disguise works perfectly, so well, in fact, that as soon as I pass through the sleek double doors into the main laboratory, a lanky man with a pinched face calls out to me.

"Resident! Take this code silver down to the morgue," he barks, pushing a long white hospital bed into my unsuspecting hands and walking away before I have the opportunity to object. I stare down in horror at the thinly veiled figure beneath a carefully arranged white sheet. The figure is small, which leads me to believe that the person beneath the covering is either a child or an elder, but I don't dare investigate further to find out for sure. I have no idea where the morgue is located, but not wanting to draw any attention to myself, I grip the gurney with trembling hands and push it back through the double doors I just entered. Panic grips me with steely fingers as I try to calculate my next plan of action. I can't waste any time trying to take this person—body, I correct myself—to its destination. But I can't just abandon it in the middle of the hallway either. I comb through the blueprints in my mind's eye, trying to remember if there was any mention of a morgue, while struggling to turn the gurney around a sharp corner. I almost run right into another employee wearing the exact same uniform as me.

"Resident," I snap, trying my best to imitate the man from earlier, "take this code silver down to the morgue!" I push the bed towards her, and she blinks at me in surprise but doesn't argue. Relief washes over me as she takes the bed, but in the exchange, the sheet shifts slightly and I watch as a small hand, crisscrossed with wrinkles and speckled with age, is uncovered. My eyes are immediately drawn to the hand, so petite, with soft pink paint on the nails. And even though it might raise suspicion, and even though I'm fairly certain that I already know the answer, I force myself to ask the question.

"Code silver ... that's what again?"

She eyes me curiously for a moment before answering, "An elder euthanasia."

"Right, right, just checking." I nod, hoping that the pounding in my ears isn't as obvious to her as it is to me. I turn on my heels, putting as much distance between myself and the other resident worker as possible, the image of that hand burning in my mind. As soon as I'm out of sight, I have to brace myself against the closest wall, my entire body trembling. Elder euthanasia. My stomach is churning in a mixture of disgust and sadness and I try to keep my dinner from making a second appearance in the middle of the red level hallway.

Of course, I'd been on the receiving end of countless teachings on the efficiency of limiting the non-performing, rapidly declining elderly, who are unable to make a valid contribution to society. But the sight of that small, delicate hand with nails painted soft pink shook me to my core. Did she paint her nails as one of her last actions on this earth? How old was she exactly? At what age does Paramus decide that its citizens have expired? I try to picture the face beneath the sheets and try to imagine what she must have been feeling when the officials showed up at her door to inform her that she had become too much of a burden on society. Was she afraid, knowing that they were escorting her to her death? Did she paint her nails ahead of time because she knew that they were coming, and wanted to greet death looking her best? And the most terrifying question of all—how many years before they come for me?

It could be sooner than I think if I don't get out of the red level, I remind myself, straightening up once again. I need to get this medicine. With that thought in the forefront of my mind, I smooth the front of my shirt and once again approach the set of double doors. This time, no one gives me any more orders and I am able to cross the wide laboratory floor and slip through another set of doors that lead to the supply area, undetected. My heart pounds against my rib cage as I spot the small black nameplate beside the very last door at the end of the hall. The neat white letters spell out the words I've been looking for: MEDICATION STORAGE.

Beneath the nameplate is a simple keypad, and with the access code fresh in my mind, I input the sequence carefully. When the code is accepted, a tingle of nervous anticipation shoots through my limbs. I throw a glance over my shoulder to make sure that no one is watching before sliding inside the room. The lock clicks into place behind me and a shiver travels down my spine from the drop in temperature as I walk through the rows and rows of neatly organized shelving. Since I don't know exactly what is wrong with my mom, I don't know which medicine is the best choice. Keeping an anxious eye on the door, I grab several different types of antibiotics and steroids and shove them into my uniform pockets. I've just about found everything that I came for when I hear the sound of doorknob turning. Frantic, I drop into a crouch and try to make myself as small as possible, squeezing behind the last shelf on the row and hoping that the shadows are enough to conceal me. I hold my breath, heart racing, as the door swings open and two employees dressed in white barge inside, talking loudly together.

"—told him that it was either the Witless kid or the Gifted student, we didn't have enough blood for both." The first one to enter, a woman, shakes her head as she reaches for a vial and a package of needles.

"Not enough blood for both? Now that's a new one!" A man walking behind her lets out a barking laugh and the woman joins him. I hold my breath, fearful that the slightest noise will give my location away, but neither of them seem to have any idea that I'm here.

"I'm not wasting supplies on a Witless kid! Surplus goes into my bank account. I'm just doing Cortex a favor!" the woman exclaims and the man voices his agreement. They appear to lift some boxes from the corner and turn to leave. Once I'm sure that they're gone, I venture out of my hiding place, my face burning. I'm actually glad that my father suggested that I not bring my mother here. From the sound of it, as a "Witless" bystander, she wouldn't have received the proper care that she needed anyway. I feel even more grateful for the supplies tucked deep into my uniform pockets. I can't entrust my mother's life to anyone but myself. Now all I need to do is to get the medication to her.

I fight against my heavy eyelids the next morning as I sit at my desk, writing pages and pages of code for the Veritas. It was nearly morning when I made it back to the apartment last night, and the sleepy rays of sunlight meant that traveling home would be impossible. As exhausted as I was, I barely slept. Fears about my mother kept me tossing and turning all night, and it was almost like I could feel the stolen medications tucked beneath my mattress while I struggled to get comfortable. I rub my temples and stare at the complex numbers and letters laid out on the screen before me, my mind rehearsing once again the plan for sneaking out of Cortex tonight.

Suddenly, my entire screen goes black.

Is this you?

The message darts across the screen like a flash of light that sends my heart racing. Beneath it is security footage of me in the red level supply room, stuffing medication into my pockets. I watch in horror as I see myself stare directly into the camera, giving a clear picture of my face. My pulse pounds in my ears. My program destroyed that footage, reduced it to unsalvageable bits of scrambled data. How did someone get a hold of it? And more importantly, what do they plan to do with it?

Your erasure program was impressive. I stare in disbelief at the message blinking impossibly in the secure network that I created. That's another thing, no one should have access to me, or even be able to see me. I'm cloaked in layers upon layers of coded camouflage. I scramble for my nano to check and see if there was somehow a gap in the interference, but it's still running smoothly.

Who are you? I type hastily, a desire to know who has infiltrated my barrier burning even more strongly than my desire for self-preservation at this point. I need to know who has outsmarted me. Is it Director Ellis? Someone at Cortex?

I'm someone who is always on the lookout for rebels.

Rebels. The word blinks menacingly on my screen.

I'm not a rebel.

Does the sender think that I am a Rebel because I snuck into the red level and stole medicine? That was certainly a rebellious act, but it was never my intention to be associated with any anarchist group. I remember the look on Director Ellis' face when she talked about the Rebels and a shiver runs down my spine. I certainly don't want to be mistaken for one. I'm just trying to keep my mom alive.

Why take the medication then?

I contemplate my answer carefully. I don't have enough information about the anonymous messenger to know which answer would be the safest. If the messenger is someone inside of Cortex, or worse, Director Ellis, maybe I could make up some kind of story about needing the medication for an experiment.

But if the messenger is a Rebel, then I have no idea what I could say to them to keep them from using the video against me. I still don't understand the so-called Rebels.

Why would I tell you that?

Because you seem desperate. I can help.

What are you going to do with the footage? I type, fingers flying through the air as rapidly as I can move them.

You seem smart. I'll make you a deal. If you can find me, I'll give you the footage.

My heart skips a beat at the idea of the challenge. It's not every day that I'm presented with something that is truly difficult. But I need to be careful. This is more than just a game. Whoever has this footage can use it to destroy everything that I've worked for. I just need to be smart. The tips of my fingers tingle in anticipation as I call up the program that I'll need to use to find him.

Thankfully, it's nothing complicated. All I need to do is ping the signal off the different servers around the building and see which one matches the identification stamp written into the last transmission. That should give me at least a good idea of where the sender is in the building.

It takes a few seconds for me to build the right platform for the ping. As soon as it's gone, I sit on the edge of my bed, eyes trained on the room's holo-screen, waiting for the results.

No match detected.

What? I double check the results, but it's undeniable. The location information in the message doesn't match up to anything close to the servers here in the building. The numbers are all wrong. I sit back in my bed, feeling defeated and slightly perplexed. What does this mean? The only thing to do is to widen the search perimeters and expand to the whole city. I decide to give it a try.

I jump to my feet, inspired once again. So, the messenger isn't at Cortex. He isn't in the building at all. Why would someone with this level of intelligence not be working at Cortex? And where are they hiding?

A flick of the wrist, a pinch of the fingers, a blink, and I'm comparing the message credentials to every server in the city, searching for a match. This takes several minutes. There are many different identity codes to sift through.

No match detected. A frustrated growl escapes my lips and I sink to the floor in frustration. How is that possible? There isn't a match inside of the building or even the entire city. Either the messenger is good enough to disguise his location or he's … outside of the city? Which can't be the case. This kind of technology doesn't exist outside of the wall, so either the program I made is flawed, or someone outside of the city has access to more technology than we ever realized. And the truth is that I know my program isn't flawed.

You're getting warmer.

My breath quickens as my eyes scan the newest message. Is the messenger saying that he is outside of the city? And if so, how is that even possible?

Are you one of the Lost? I type back, my mind spinning with the implications of what this could mean. Could technology exist outside of Paramus? And what did the messenger mean about always being on the lookout for Rebels? I thought that the Rebels existed only inside of the city.

You're even smarter than I thought. Here's the footage. A wave of relief washes through me as a file comes through and I quickly save it to my server. I'm grateful that the messenger has decided not to use it against me, but I'm left with more questions than ever.

Oh, and Arin, be careful. Cortex is not what it seems. A final message comes through, blinking on my holo-screen in my otherwise dark room, and I can't help but feel icy tendrils of fear wrap around my heart. For the first time in my life, I have more questions about the world than I ever thought possible. I feel like I don't know what is real anymore, or who to trust. My mind is barraged by doubts, all threatening to pull apart the very threads of my current reality. If scores can be changed, and if technology can exist outside of the wall, then what is Paramus, truly? Is this all a ruse? And to what gain? And even further, why did the anonymous messenger imply that there is more to Cortex than I realize? I have a sinking feeling that if I ever find the answer to this question, I might not like it.

CHAPTER

"The best part about Paramus is that it gives every citizen the opportunity to show the world their brightest self."

-Articles of Axiom. Section IX, Part K

I try to shake the questions gnawing away at my insides as I double check the laces on my running shoes and tie my hair into a quick knot at the base of my neck. There's no doubt that I need answers, but some of the bigger questions will just have to wait. Nothing matters more to me right now than making sure that my mom is okay.

In the back of the cafeteria, I find two metal swinging doors. I push through them and find winding corridors of polished white linoleum, dull fluorescent lights emitting a yellowish glow overhead. Stainless steel carts line the hallways, layered with empty trays and serving utensils. Down here, there are rooms and rooms of bot charging stations. They're all set to sleep mode, like ghosts; endless rows of white, motionless figures, charging quietly. I weave carefully through them.

I wonder how long it's been since another human has been down here. It's oddly comforting; the sleeping robots won't tell my secrets. Most of the labor on this side of Cortex has already been performed by serving bots and AI drones, and now that the city has become fully automated, bots will be replacing any human workers that remain. There's really no need to bring people in to do a job that a robot can accomplish. There's a smaller margin for error. Robots rarely make mistakes. They don't have squabbles or complain about their work schedules. Artificial intelligence is excellent and efficient. Sometimes I wonder if the city wishes that it could replace all of us with robots, even the Gifted.

I feel like a robot sometimes, computing my life away, processing data. Robots don't have feelings; they don't have families. In order to be the best mind, I have to ignore my heart, quite like a robot. In fact, the less feelings that I have, the better, because feelings only make room for error. It's not as messy that way, or as dangerous. With a Criterion score of 999 it would be better to not have any feelings at all. If I could just be cold, just become like a machine, then I could guarantee my family's safety. Feelings like jealousy, anger, and lust: those are the feelings that killed off the human race in the first place.

I break into a light jog and take a hard turn down a flight of stairs. The lighting down here is even dimmer, but I carry my map inside of my head and feel confident about every step. As long as I don't run into anyone, I'll be just fine. Past the charging stations, around several turns, turning left and right so sharply that my sneakers squeak their complaints against the linoleum floors, I run towards the door. I'm at full speed now, heart pumping. My muscles are burning but I dig deeper and embrace the pain. I'm used to pushing past pain. I duck through one last doorway and find it—my way out.

Beside the door is an entry panel with a slot for an identification card. I retrieve Marcus's card from my pocket, heart pounding, and say a silent prayer that it hasn't been discontinued. The green light flashing on the panel and the click of the lock assures me that the card is, in fact, still active. I breathe a sigh of relief and prop the door open with my foot. I still don't want Marcus to get into any kind of trouble from my thievery, but I doubt that anyone is closely monitoring this out-of-the-way door down by the loading docks.

Outside of the building, I'm greeted with a gust of fresh air, and I realize just how insane it is that we are all kept inside of that building. I never pictured Cortex as a prison. It was always the place that I wanted to be, but now, I can't wait to put as much distance between myself and those suffocating walls as possible.

The moon overhead is covered by a thick blanket of clouds, making it hard for me to see the ground in front of me. I have to move slowly, picking my way carefully through the streets, sticking to the shadows as much as possible; I don't want to run into any of the sentry bots that replace the AI cleaning bots that patrol the streets during the day, keeping an eye out for anything unusual and sending a direct feed to the council.

It's slow going; even though I'm a seasoned jogger, I know I won't be able to jog all the way home. I'll need to take the train, which runs on a continual loop of the city. The station won't be hard to get to, it's only about a half an hour's jog away. The cover of night is welcome, shielding me from prying eyes as I sneak through the city.

Once I reach the train platform, I automatically drop into a crouch, under the cover of shadows, and wait for the eleven o'clock train. I haven't purchased a ticket and couldn't if I wanted to, since I left my eye-screen at home. This trip needs to be off the record so I'm going to have to sneak on board. Thankfully, the trains aren't very smart, and they run automatically. I take in greedy gulps of air as I wait, slowing the beating of my pounding heart and allowing the cool evening breeze to dry the sweat drenching the back of my shirt.

As the train pulls in and comes to a brief stop, I race to the door, keeping an eye out for passengers. Not many people travel at this hour of the night, and thankfully, this train appears to be deserted. Now there's only one more problem; without a ticket, I'm going to need to find another way in.

There is an access pad beside the door, but it needs a specific code to open. A code that I don't have. I should have done more research to try and find the codes before I left the apartment. I curse silently; why can't anything be simple?

This is fine. I can figure it out. I study the panel carefully, vaguely noticing the train chime in my ears as it gives a last warning that it is about to leave the station. I wave my hand in front of the panel to access the authorization prompt. The system blinks at me, bright blue, displaying on its screen a series of intricate patterns; a dizzying mixture of spherical lines, orbiting one another, each its own distinct color. It appears to be operating under a basic pattern recognition interface. All I need to do is figure out the right pattern and it should open right up.

Pattern recognition security systems are a joke. Everyone knows that a number-based system is much more secure. Taking a deep breath, I let my mind become fully absorbed by the problem before me. Okay, so each system before me is represented by its own color. There are numbers, variants of ten, rotating in each system, swirling in dizzying arrays. I need to find the calm within the storm. Simplify, I tell myself. Cut out the clutter.

My eyes skim quickly, looking for the simple. Search for the obvious. Breathe. Calm. Surrender to the storm. There! I zero in on the simplest of the systems, consisting of only three numbers. I think I've got it!

I hurriedly swipe my fingers across the screen, careful to mimic the pattern that had flashed across my mind only seconds before. To my amazement, the panel chimes, and blinks green. Without hesitation I lunge inside the train car just as the sleek doors close behind me. The train starts moving and I breathe a sigh of relief. The train is quiet at this hour, and I'm grateful to be the only passenger. I rest my forehead against the cool glass window and watch as the buildings give way to trees, and the familiar peaks of my home neighborhood come into view. Once I exit the train, I break into a light run, darting between the cover of shadows, my eyes and ears on high alert for street monitors. It would be terrible to be caught outside of Cortex on any day, but even more so with stolen medication in my pocket. I feel like I can barely breathe until my old home comes into view, and I hurriedly let myself inside.

"Mom? Dad?" I call, and feel my shoulders start to relax when I hear the comforting voice of my father coming from their bedroom.

"In here, honey!" Only a few more steps. I push past the bedroom door and feel my knees go weak with gratitude at seeing their faces again in person. I rush to the bedside and take my mother's hands in mine. She looks worse than last time. She's lying down in bed, with my father hovering anxiously above her. I glance back and forth between both of their faces. My dad's face is etched with deep lines of concern, and he looks as if he's aged twenty years. I instantly feel remorse for not being here to help him care for my mother.

"How are you feeling? Are you in pain?" I ask, going to my mother's side, and taking one clammy hand in mine. Her skin has a grey tone to it that wasn't there before. When I glance up at my dad again, his eyebrows are furrowed.

"I'm alright," she croaks, the pale skin of her face crinkling in the corners as she gives a shaky smile. She looks so fragile, it sends a shooting pain through my chest. I hope that the medicine will help her. It has to.

"I brought you something." I release my mother's hand and reach for the stolen containers in my jacket pocket. There is almost a sense of hushed reverence in the room as I lay out each bottle on the bed. My father's eyes grow wide as he takes in the wide array of antibiotics, steroids, and vitamin packs.

"Where did you get all of this?" He reaches for the closest bottle and scans the label, voice full of awe.

"A friend." I shrug, and then help raise my mother up to sitting. "I wasn't sure which thing would help the most, so I just got a variety." I start opening containers and pouring pills into my hand. "I would just start by taking all of them."

"You said you got these from a friend." Even in her weakened state, my mother watches me with a knowing eye. "We told you not to tell anyone about us, Arin," she chides, but I can tell that she is pleased.

"It's okay, our secret is safe," I assure them, and hand my mother a glass of water from her nightstand. She takes the pills eagerly, and after finishing all the water, beams at me with eyes so full of hope that it's like a soothing medicine for my soul. I know that I made the right choice. Anything for my mom and dad. "Now I would take all of these twice a day. And send me a message when you're getting low so I can get some more." My heart skips a beat thinking about sneaking back onto the red level to steal some more, but that's a problem for another day.

My dad takes both of my hands and plants a kiss on the back of one of my hands. "You're our miracle, Arin," he says gently. When I look up at my mother, she has tears glistening in her eyes. My heart jumps into my throat, again eternally grateful for the medicine working their magic inside of her. At least one of them has to work. I can't lose her. I just can't.

Saying goodbye is tough, and even as I disappear into the darkness and pick my way through the shadows back to the train station, my mind is still stuck in the warmth of that room. Frozen in the gaze of my mother's eyes, and the spark of hope that I found there. I feel lighter too, as I climb the platform steps.

It's like a weight has been lifted from my shoulders, to know that my mom is on the road to recovery, and this nightmare will soon be over. I might even be able to sleep tonight. I climb into the train car, feeling relieved, and lay my head back against the wall, closing my eyes for a moment.

"Arin?" I hear a familiar voice speak up from behind me and my entire body freezes, on pins and needles.

"Linc?" I open my eyes with a start and turn to find a tall figure, wrapped in dark clothing like I am, sitting cross-legged on the floor, staring up at me with a smile, wispy blonde hair awry.

"Arin Wells, you are full of surprises." He grins.

"What are you doing here?" we both say at the same time, and I am still frozen, my heart in my throat. I can't think of a single reasonable explanation to give to my roommate about what I am doing on a train outside of Cortex's walls. And what is he doing, anyway? No one is supposed to leave Cortex. Not me—and definitely not Linc either. I stand over him, arms folded, which I can't see but he probably can because he probably isn't sitting here in the dark without an eye-screen like somebody brain-missing. I stare down at him with my most intimidating face.

"You shouldn't be here." I let a little roughness leak into my voice, hoping that it will come across at least a little threatening. His body language doesn't change one bit; he looks as relaxed as he did back at the apartment. He stares at me with a little smile on his face.

"And neither should you. But here we are." He shakes his head in disbelief, either unable or unwilling to conceal a grin that is slowly spreading across his face. "How in the world did you get out?" he asks, reaching into his pocket. He pulls out a tiny white cylinder, then produces a small cardboard box from the other one. With a flick of his wrist a flame appears, and he brings it to the end of the cylinder. Smoke fills the train car. I've never seen anyone smoke before. It tickles my nose and surrounds me in a cloudy haze.

"I'm the wonder girl," I remind him, and he chuckles in response.

"Yes," he agrees. "The wonder girl with the brightest of futures ahead of her at Cortex. So why risk it? Why leave?" I blink in the darkness, letting the question hang in the air between us on the tendrils of lazy smoke. What answer could I give that would be believable in the slightest? If I tell the truth, I'll have no choice but to reveal my parents' mistake and put them in danger. Well, more in danger than they already are.

"You don't want to tell me? That's fine. I suppose I haven't given you a whole lot of reasons to trust me. How about this? I'll go first," he offers, and takes a deep drag from his cigarette, blowing smoke lazily through his lips as he begins. "This is not my first time outside of Cortex. I'm a Rebel." My heart lurches in my throat. I've heard that phrase once before. *I'm always on the lookout for Rebels.*

"You're a Rebel?" I ask in disbelief and Linc looks back at me with an expression of bemusement.

"That's right, and we've had our eye on you for some time now." His words send a chill through me and I wonder just how much he knows. "The one thing that we don't understand is why you stole the medicine? And now I'm wondering why you're out here, on this train at night? It seems to me that you have a secret."

I feel a tiny bit of smug satisfaction, even with all their watching, the Rebels haven't found out about my mom.

"What does it matter to you? Are you going to turn me in?" I challenge, eyeing him carefully, but he just laughs.

"No, far from it. I was actually going to try and find a way to ask for your help."

"My help? Why would you need me?" The suspicion in my voice is obvious, but it doesn't seem to faze Linc. He speaks with enthusiasm, putting out his cigarette and turning to me with a glint in his eye.

"There's something going on outside of the wall ... a sickness like nothing the Lost have ever seen before." My heart drops and the train car sways a little. I put my hands on the ground to steady myself.

"What do you know about the sickness?" I try to keep my voice calm, but inside my pulse is racing. He watches me for a moment and seems to weigh his words carefully before answering.

"It's ... complicated. If you want to know more, I can show you. Under one condition."

"Okay. What's that?" I'm not sure what Linc is hinting at, but I'll do anything that I can to learn everything there is to know about the sickness if it will help my mother.

"We're going to need to go outside of the wall." I feel my stomach drop when he says those words, terrified of all the new possibilities that could come with that. "The Lost City is not what you remember. It's something else entirely. And Arin"—his voice is full of sincerity—"if you come with me, I promise, that all of your questions will be answered."

I stare into his deep green eyes, logic and emotions waging a war inside of me. On the one hand, if I truly want to help my mother, I need to understand the sickness. And there are things about Paramus that I just can't ignore. What if there are more people outside of the wall like the anonymous messenger? People who have technology and who are entirely different than what I was led to believe. People who have answers, people my parents were willing to risk it all for. I trust my parents, and, despite my better judgement, I trust Linc. I take a deep breath and mutter the words that I never thought I would hear myself say, "Okay. Take me outside of the wall."

You know the feeling, the one when you emerge from a dream and you feel yourself start to surface to the real world, but you're still sleepy enough not to be truly aware of your problems? That sweet in-between spot of unknowing, the bliss of ignorance before the weight of reality comes crashing down again?

I will myself to stay in that sweet spot as I can feel myself start to awaken. Morning is here, and with it, the harsh reality of everything that I wish I could escape. My limbs grow heavy with the dread of remembering everything. The truths come back, shattering my bliss. My mom is sick. Linc is taking me outside of the wall. All that I have done to bury the memories of my life outside of Paramus, and to finally separate myself from the Lost, was to no avail. The irony of how deeply intertwined my fate continues to be with the Lost does not escape me. It floods my veins with a mixture of remorse and anxiety.

When I can delay it no longer, I crack my eyes open and am instantly flooded with messages and notifications on my eye-screen. I wave them away and sit up feeling groggy. Coffee. I need coffee.

"Hey." Linc is sitting at the dining room table when I shuffle from my room to the kitchen and the aroma of freshly brewed java envelops me like a warm hug.

"Hey," I say back, retrieving a mug for myself and filling it to the brim with the strong caffeinated goodness.

"How'd you sleep?" he asks, peering at me over his mug, a holo-screen of daily news in front of him. I shrug. "Are you nervous?" He watches me closely, a little bit of mischievousness dancing in his eyes, but I refuse to give him the satisfaction and simply answer with another shrug.

We've agreed to leave the city today after work, and if I hadn't been so exhausted, I don't think that I would have slept at all last night. My mind is overrun with anxious thoughts about our trip. I may not sleep again until all of this is over. We sit in silence for a few moments, him reading his article and me ingesting coffee as quickly as possible.

Our dynamic has changed since Linc revealed where his loyalties lie. I may not completely understand what his involvement is with the Lost just yet, but betrayal is easy to spot, and one thing is for sure: Linc is definitely more than he is pretending to be as far as only being the Cortex R&D Department head. There's more below the surface, and although he claims to hold the secret to saving my parents, I don't know if I'll ever be able to feel secure about who he is and what his motives are. I try not to notice how adorable his tousled blonde hair looks in the morning.

"How often do you go out there?" I ask, refilling my cup and bringing him a mug of his own as a type of offering. He takes the cup gratefully and deeply inhales the delicious aroma.

"It's been a few months," he answers.

"How do you slip away without anyone noticing?" It's my biggest concern. Whether we are outside of the wall for a few minutes or a few days, everything built into us offers real time location tracking, and although I've never tried, I can't imagine that hacking the skin coms to that kind of degree would be easy. Paramus likes to keep tabs on its citizens.

"I have a hacker friend who helps with that," he says simply, and I feel my mouth drop open. The anonymous messenger! I wonder if he and Linc's friend are one and the same.

"I can't believe the level of technology they apparently have out there." He laughs.

"You have no idea."

"I have about a million questions," I answer, and he grins before checking the time with a blink.

"We'd better get going or we'll be late for our shift at the lab," he observes, jumping to his feet and I quickly follow, swapping out my coffee mug for my handheld nano and following him to the door. He hesitates before opening the door abruptly and I come to a quick halt, finding my body just inches away from his.

He looks at me sincerely. "I just want to say that I think you choosing to come outside the wall with me tonight is really brave. I know this can't be easy for you." I try to focus on his words and not how close his lips are to mine, or the way his proximity to me makes my heart pound. I swallow and force myself to look away from his lips. The effect that he has on me is dizzying.

"Yeah, well, my dad always says that sometimes life calls upon us to do brave things. It's our choice whether or not we answer." I struggle to focus on what I'm saying, finding myself fighting for breath for each word. The air between us is heavy.

"I think that's really beautiful," he murmurs, and for a brief moment I imagine him closing the space between us. What would it be like to have his lips pressed against my lips? Is that even something that I want? There is still so much about Linc that is unknown to me. I take a deep breath and force myself to take a step backwards, shaking hands shoved into the pockets of my slacks.

"Thanks." A smile is all that I can offer him until I find out whether or not he is on the side of right. At this point I don't even know which side I'm on, or which side is the right side. Sure, my feelings for Linc are ... undeniable. But my loyalty lies with my parents first and foremost. I need to find out if he is a friend to them or an enemy. I'm still feeling very distrustful toward the Rebels and the Lost. They're the ones who got my parents sick after all.

CHAPTER

"There is nothing new outside of Paramus.
There is everything new inside of it."

- The Chronicles of Discord

Dusk has fallen on the city as we ride the hover train to its very last stop inside of the wall, getting off only when the magnetic tracks run out and can take us no further. From this point forward, we walk. Our boots make no measurable impact on the smooth, magnetic road, carrying us closer and closer to the looming white wall ahead, marking the divide between our city and the Lost. I can't help but wonder, what are the roads like on the other side of this massive white structure? Something tells me that they are not so easy to walk.

There is one break in the sea of white ahead: a gate, a panel of all black except for the words AUTHORIZED ACCESS ONLY stenciled in white. The black gate is at such a stark contrast to the rest of the wall, dark and foreboding that it only adds to the intimidation. On the other side of this wall, is a different train. Linc describes it as a monstrous beast made of ancient iron that feeds on liquified stone and billows black smoke into the sky.

I had no idea that there were trains outside of the wall. Linc has explained that the trains were used by the city to bring in resources like building materials and food from outlying farms beyond the Lost City before we became self-contained. Now they've fallen under the control of the Lost since being long abandoned by Paramus.

I stare at the intimidating structure ahead. Once I pass through this gate, I will no longer be an ordinary citizen of Paramus. I will be a criminal. Linc approaches the access panel without hesitation and hurriedly types in a code. I need to remember to ask him sometime how he got such restricted information like access codes to the wall. The wall's security accepts Linc's passcode, and a panel slides open within the jet-black gate, just narrow enough for us to squeeze through. Linc has to duck to avoid hitting his head on the top of the opening.

"My contact said that there shouldn't be anyone to bother us at this hour," Linc whispers once we are through to the other side. I hope that he is right. Moments after we step through the gate, a loud signal blows from overhead, momentarily deafening and a red light above the gate flashes once, twice, and with an ear-splitting *clang* the panel slams shut, leaving us stranded on the inside. Surrounded by darkness.

My breath is loud in my ears-short and erratic, heightened by fear. We crouch, listening, practically helpless until our eyes adjust to the dimness around us. So, this is where they keep the trains.

I can smell the burning odor of hydraulic fluid and railway grease in my nose. It's a sharp metal smell, almost an insult to my nostrils in comparison to the clean, magnetic transportation of the city. And the temperature! The heat inside of the train station falls on me like a blanket, stifling my lungs with hot, metallic air and causing beads of sweat to form on every inch of my exposed skin. By now, my eyesight has adjusted well enough that I can make out the sheer vastness of the room around us. Overhead, heavy-looking metal ducts, painted with chipping black paint cross through the ceiling in intricate patterns, releasing occasional bursts of steam that worsen the overall feeling of sticky moisture in the air. Ahead of us, the ground drops off, creating a sort of a platform, but there is no train in sight.

"Stay low!" Linc hisses in my ear as a sharp whistle sounds around us and we duck behind a black metal container, hearts racing. I have never seen anything as monstrous or heard anything as thunderous as the moment when the train comes pounding into the station. It is like the sound of a million running feet, pounding into the ground beneath us, making me feel incredibly small. An eerie sound, which I come to realize was the train whistle, accompanied with a jarring screech signals that the train was coming to a halt at the platform. We wait with anticipation to see if anyone comes to greet the train, but there is no movement in the train station around us.

"Come on," he says, rising to a low crouch and keeping his head and shoulders down, "we need to be on that train before it leaves the station." Linc signals for us to slow as he reaches for the boxcar handle, pulling the door to the side with all his might and filling the air with the squeaky protest of rusted metal.

We climb inside with a sense of urgency, sure that any other souls in or around the platform would be alerted by such an obnoxious outburst and we would be discovered. Linc slams the door shut behind us and once again, we are crouching in darkness, hearts pounding through our chests. Only this time, we are not alone.

"You know, you smarties could really use a lesson in subtlety," comes a raspy, sinister voice from inside of the train car, directly across from me. My head instinctively juts to the right and the air is sucked from my lungs as fear takes over. Linc presses my body behind him and I can feel the tightening of his muscles as he turns to face the stranger. "It's a good thing I dismembered all of the sentries or we'd all be sitting in a load of shit right now," the voice is saying and yet somehow his statement doesn't make me feel any better. Finger-sized pinpricks of light infiltrate the car through scattered holes in the far wall and the ceiling as I strain my eyes to make out the man before me.

"Thank you," Linc says steadily, and I hold my breath, still wary of the stranger in front of me. The man chuckles loudly, and there's a mocking tone in his voice.

"You think you'd know better for being a couple of smarties. Oh well, good thing you got ole Rus lookin' out for you." I try to adjust to the dialogue of the stranger before us. I don't know whether to be terrified or happy to see him. Have the Lost really all become a bunch of cannibalistic savages?

The man in front of me certainly looks like he could hurt someone. His head is shaved down close to the skin, his face is weathered and greasy, and a long mess of a beard tumbles down his chin. He is a strange jumble of man and machine, and all parts of him show signs of wear and tear. He is naked from the waist up, and his left arm connects to a metal arm; it's a gruesome sight, you can see where the man ends and the metal pieces begin, crudely wired together in his skin. The rest of his chest is tattooed and scarred. In his human arm he clutches a heavy metal pipe. "Have a seat," he says, gesturing to the train care floor by swinging the pipe in his hand in a lazy arc before us, "it's about to get pretty bumpy."

Almost before he has finished speaking, the train lurches forward, sending me rocking back onto my heels and tumbling down to the back of the car. I brace myself against the back wall and attempt to sit comfortably amidst the jostling of the train. The cadence of the iron wheels against the ancient iron tracks is nothing like the smooth glide of the electric trains in the city.

"It was Rus, you said?" Linc has to shout to be heard over the clacking of the metal wheels of the train on tracks.

"Yup!" the man replies, scratching at his dirty beard with the metal arm. I watch with fascination; Rus is so unlike anyone that I have ever seen within the pristine city walls. He catches my gaze as I stare, unbothered, as he smacks the metal pipe he's holding rhythmically against his metal hand. He doesn't break eye contact, so I quickly look away.

"How long has it been since you've been out of that goddamn wall?" Rus shouts to me, spitting off to the side, and I feel my stomach churn. There's blood in the spittle and I wonder if the man in front of us is diseased or dying.

"It's been a while!" Linc speaks for me, for which I'm grateful because he has to practically shout to be heard and Rus points his metal pipe toward the sliding car door.

"Well why don't you open her up then? You've got the finest goddamn seat available, to get a nice, good look at this shithole! Go on!"

I crawl aside so that Linc can, with much effort, wedge the train car door open. There is some resistance at first but then the door bursts open with a *whoosh* that blows me backwards and hits my face with a wave of putrid air. "Ugh!" I exclaim, scrambling to cover my face and nose as I peer out through the open car door to behold an unbelievable sight before me. There is garbage. Everywhere.

The narrow train tracks that we are currently following are suspended high above a swamp of murky water, and the source of the water comes from massive concrete aqueducts, pouring out from beneath the train station, vast streams of what could only be enormous amounts of sewage and garbage. Garbage that could not be kept within the city walls and so was carelessly dumped outside of them. I swallow hard, this sort of irresponsibility stands in stark contrast to all the ideas that I have been fed about our perfect city and our perfect system. Dumping waste outside of the city definitely wasn't "Excellence and Innovation". I find the entire thing unsettling.

"They dump all of our garbage here outside of the wall!" I exclaim, still struggling to process the implications of it all.

"Oh, I know," Linc says quickly, "I stumbled upon that gem when I was combing through the council's confidential budget reports a few months back. There were budgets for just about everything: infrastructure, labor, education, but the numbers for waste and waste disposal were so astronomically small that I thought there must have been a mistake. But the more digging that I did, I concluded that there was no budget because there is no disposal program." He shakes his head in disgust. "We dump it."

My mind struggles to believe the images that my eyes receive as we travel further and further from the train station. As the aqueducts and the lake of sewage grow smaller, along the muddy shores, erratic tent-like dwellings begin to appear. I am amazed by the sheer size of everything outside of the wall. It is crazy to imagine that less than twenty-four hours ago, I wasn't even convinced that there were civilized people out here, and now, hundreds of them are unfolding before me. They appear to be placed at random, strung together with a litter of dirty cloths, un-matching and tattered, strung up on sticks and poles that look ready to collapse at any moment.

Now, among the smell of garbage and waste, tiny elements of smoke reach my nose, wafting towards the train from open fires where people gather to cook their evening meal. There are families living out here, groups of people with mothers and fathers and children. Not feeding on each other in a brutal struggle for survival, but cooking around a fire, and laughing. "There are so many of them," I mutter in amazement. "I had no idea that the Lost were so numerous."

Linc nods his understanding, "There is an entire city of people out here, Arin. Living their lives. Lives that matter, cast away from Paramus." He pauses. "There's a storm brewing outside of the wall, Arin." His deep green eyes lock with mine. "Change is coming."

The further inward that we travel into the Lost's territory, I observe that the tents are becoming denser. Single home dwellings give away to larger structures: rows and rows of tattered cloth, strong together with roofs rising in a peak and smoke billowing from within them.

It's hard to believe that, in this place so far away from Paramus, there is a semblance of structure. I wonder if the Lost families down there ever cluster in their tents beneath the night sky and speculate about what is on the other side, off limits to them forever. I swallow, but a lump forms hard in my throat. What makes these people so different from us? Why are they condemned to their garbage cities while others get to live in pristine homes? And I struggle with an even deeper thought— this could've been me.

"You're our miracle, Arin." The familiar phrase echoes in my head. I think back to the last evening my parents and I spent together, before testing day. We were all curled up in the family room by the crackling of the warm fire, my father reading out loud to us an article that he found particularly amusing about the miracles of Paramus, and how back in his day, they couldn't just ask the wall for anything they wanted. They had to repair things that were broken, and be resourceful whenever they had the chance. My mother, of course, took this opportunity to chime in. "Yet another perfect example of how you just can't discard things when you may not see the value. Things, and people, have value, even if we may not quite see it."

Her words haunt me now.

The deeper we move into the city, the more sophisticated the structures around us become. For the first time since we crossed over the wall, I see lights. Tall wooden beams have been crudely erected and posted every hundred yards or so and they support a mess of wires, extending overhead and connecting one beam to the next. From some of these wires come strands of light bulbs, made of various sizes and giving off varying degrees of light and yet offering at least some illumination in the otherwise darkness. The structures here are different as well, more permanent in nature. Large metal containers, stained with rust and scribbled in unintelligible markings and drawings of all sorts, cram together on every available surface. I have no idea where these containers come from, but they appear to be in abundance in this part of the city. It's louder here too. I watch the blur of people moving about. More fires in barrels and buckets are out in the open between containers. I can smell the scent of cooking meat. There is laughter and shouting. Somewhere in the distance, a baby cries.

"Alright! This is us!" Rus shouts, heaving himself up off the train car floor with some effort. "Are you ready for your personalized, up close tour of The Lost City?" he says, giving an exaggerated bow. He makes a good point. Am I ready to step into this new world, a city beyond my city?

I square my shoulders, resolute with a fresh spirit of determination. The Lost City was once my home. It's the place where my parents grew up and might just be the place that contains the answers about how to save them. I think I can manage one night.

I don't know who stares more, as we make our way through the bustling tent city towards the Rebel base: me or the people of The Lost City. I can tell that many of them have never seen anyone from Paramus before, especially people my own age and younger. Children with dirt smudged faces peer out from behind their mother's tattered skirts with eyes as big as the moon and others giggle and try to touch our clothes. I wonder if they thought that people from Paramus weren't real. I can understand that, before today, I didn't realize just how real they were either. The Lost are way more sophisticated and exist in vastly larger numbers than I had ever imagined, but there is nothing about them that seems uncivilized or barbaric. Just *different*.

The women here keep their hair long and wear intricate braids down their backs laced with shimmering rocks and tiny metal pieces, while many of the men grow impressive beards and wear elaborate braids in their hair as well. Their clothing is made of intricate layers of wrapped, coarse fabrics: many of the women wear dresses while the men are clad in course pants, vests and belts to carry an array or necessary tools for life in the Lost city. The clothing appears to have been dyed with natural colors to make red, dark blue, and gray pieces but almost everyone is wrapped in the khaki-colored canvas and burlap that Cortex uses to transport materials. There is probably an abundance of it in the garbage that the city expels every week. But it hasn't gone to waste out here. Out here it is utilized to make structures and beautiful clothing. The Lost work with what they've got, and I admire them for that.

The sounds and smells of the Lost city are so different than what I would have imagined; music warbles through the air from one of the tents that we pass and mixed into the scent of cooking meat and campfire smoke is a flavorful aroma, some kind of spice, that makes my mouth water and my stomach grumble.

At first, I am cautious about making eye contact with the Lost people, keeping my head down and my eyes low, unsure of how they will react to a Gifted amongst their midst. But the people around me are nothing but friendly, welcoming me with smiling eyes and clamoring among one another to try and be the first one to say hello.

Not everyone seems thrilled to see me though. The Rebel soldiers watch me pass with a kind of stoic vigilance, not exactly threatening but not quite welcoming either. They are easy to spot among the Lost, as they wear an entirely different apparel. Many of them have made themselves weaponized: half-man, half machine-like Rus. They are speckled throughout the crowd, both men and women, all well-muscled and no one over the age of forty. Some of them sport metal arms, robotic hands, or mechanical face plates and eyes.

It's hard to look at; every surgery that I've seen in Paramus has been to extend youthfulness or enhance beauty, but these modifications appear to enhance something entirely different: reflexes, speed, vision. If the Gifted were born to think, the Rebels were born to fight.

In addition, each of them carries the same distinctive symbol on some part of their person, the Lost City flag. A circle with three black dots, one on each side, crudely sewn onto their missmatched uniforms which are made from different forms of the same heavy forest green cloth, unifying them as members of the same army.

Unlike me, Linc seems to have no reservations about being among the Lost again. He greets many people throughout the crowd with warm handshakes, a joyous smile, and even stops to embrace a few women and children. He's like a celebrity here. Even the rebel soldiers greet him with a smile and hearty slaps on the back, like a lost brother returning home.

I'm also amazed by the amount of ingenuity that the Lost display, and the feats of engineering that they have been able to accomplish out here without construction droids and nano-blocks. It truly is a tent *city* broken up into little villages and markets and residences, stretching as far as the eye can see. I have so many questions about everything that they trip over one another as they come out of my mouth and I can't seem to speak fast enough.

"Where does the water come from?"

"We collect rainwater and collect and purify whatever else that we need from the lake," Linc answers my questions happily, clearly proud of this world outside of our world.

"What about technology? I mean, what kind of tech are they using out here?"

"You probably already noticed the mechanical enhancements." He nods in the direction of the nearest soldier.

"Yeah, what's up with that?" I wonder aloud.

"Our medical resources out here are limited, as you can imagine; we do what we have to do," he shrugs. His answer troubles me, it doesn't seem fair that we have state-of-the-art medical care in Cortex and the Lost have to resort to crudely made mechanical appendages.

"Do they have eye-screens, skin coms?"

He shakes his head. "No, everybody is offline out here."

"Wow, that must be so ... quiet."

"It's kind of nice once you get used to it."

"Who is in charge?"

"The people elect a leader, based on their character and how respected that they are in the community."

"Not their intelligence?"

"No, there is no Criterion outside of the wall."

I shake my head. "How do they maintain order?" I ask incredulously. All of this sounds to foreign to me: a city governed by a person who wasn't the smartest person? That sounds like a program for disaster.

"They look out for each other, and things have natural consequences," he explains, shrugging again like it's not that hard to believe. "When you grow up valuing human life, your way of living changes. You realize what is really important."

My head is swimming with the ideals that Linc has shared as the tent city behind us fades and we get closer and closer to the

Rebel base. The further that we get away from the city's center, the Lost citizens seem to thin away until all that is left, on all sides of us, are soldiers. They watch us, unblinking, eyes tracking our every movement as we near their base, with weapons at the ready. They don't appear to be a mob of angry outsiders with undirected aggression and no plan of action. There is nothing mindless about the operation before me. It is clear that someone is channeling their anger into a very specific purpose. Someone had taught these soldiers discipline. Someone who must be powerful enough to command the respect of the intimidating group of people around us.

I feel almost a sense of disconnect as I watch my feet closely following behind Linc, boots crunching on the dirt floor of the rebel base. I am blaringly aware of my own sense of fear as we follow Rus through the sea of rigid bodies to meet "the commander".

And yet, as the heavy burlap curtains part and we are ushered into the rebel's command center, a small voice in the back of my head reminds me that I've always known that I would do anything to protect my family, even if it was illegal. Even if it led me to a rebel army base outside of Paramus. I won't sit around and watch them die. On the other side of this curtain awaits answers, I remind myself, as I take a deep breath and step inside.

"Linc!" a voice booms from across the other side of a massive wooden desk, polished and gleaming, where the commander is seated, reclining back in his chair. His big black boots coated with a layer of grey dust resting gingerly atop the desk's immaculate surface and a lit cigarette in his mouth.

"Steele," Linc says warmly, his face breaking into a smile and the first sense of calm washes over me since we left the city, "it's been a while."

Steele chuckles and drops his boots down from the desk. "Indeed, it has," he grins, standing. "I've been meaning to come and visit you inside the city, but for some reason I haven't been able to get in." He barks a loud laugh and gives Linc a friendly squeeze on the shoulder, grey eyes twinkling.

Steele's much younger than I would've imagined for the leader of an entire rebel army. He stands tall, with broad shoulders; well-muscled and powerful looking. His face is hardened and speckled with a few scars, but he has an easy smile. He's also sporting an impressive dark beard, which seems to be the norm for most of the men that I had seen here outside of the wall, but his is well kept, neatly groomed, polished, and gleaming much like his desk. I get the impression that Steele takes good care of his things.

"This is Arin," Linc offers, nudging me forward. "She wants to know more about the sickness." I feel myself stiffen as the commander's deep grey eyes bare into me, not altogether unkind but his stare is heavy, nonetheless. I resist the urge to squirm beneath it.

A strange look comes across his face. Although he is looking straight at me, I have the impression that his mind is elsewhere. Finally, when he does speak, his voice still comes from that distant place. "Arin, you say? Remarkable. I could have sworn that you were her."

"That I was who?" My voice comes out small, and I try to clear my throat, to encourage my voice up out of my chest, but it stays deep down, unwilling to be exposed. Steele shakes his head, not answering my question because he either didn't hear it or was unwilling. One hand runs through his beard, giving him a pensive appearance.

"What do you think of The Lost, Arin?" he says quietly, his gaze off in the distance, resting on something that I can't see.

"Being out here feels like I've traveled back in time," I answer honestly, then realizing how that might sound, start to back track frantically. "I mean, what you guys have built here is great! This is awesome, but I mean, life is too hard out here. And it doesn't have to be," I stammer.

"Why doesn't it have to be?" Steele maintains his thoughtful position, everyone in the room waits for me to speak.

"Well, as I understand it, there's not really a shortage of anything," I say cautiously. "Our agriculture is maintained for the most part automatically. Our water is on an endless rotation and purification track. The magnetic and solar energies that power the city require little to no maintenance and have a hypothetically endless supply. The problems that plagued our ancestors, famine, war, drought, disease, have essentially been eradicated within the city by Cortex and all of their contributions for the last 100 years."

"So why have the wall then?" Steele wonders, still avoiding my gaze, I assume to take some of the pressure off me and for that I am grateful.

"Um, scarcity, I'm guessing? Or perhaps, principle. Cortex wants the city to believe that the only things worthy of value are the best and the brightest. I suppose the slum exists to make a statement. To discourage people from not outputting their very best at all times."

Steele nods thoughtfully, his eyes carefully meeting mine. "And what do you think would happen if everyone were included? If the wall came down? Do you still think that people would work hard? Do you still think that advancements would be made?"

"I—I'm not sure." I answer honestly, careful not to offend the very powerful, very muscular commander. "I mean, history would suggest that it doesn't work. I guess Cortex discovered that fear and scarcity made pretty powerful motivators. On the other hand, if we are talking about ethics and morals, obviously what is going on here is wrong. I'm not sure that it is possible to have the most productive society and the most moral one simultaneously. There has to be a loss on one side or the other."

"A loss that Cortex is not willing to take," Linc interjects bitterly from beside me. "People are so much more than production numbers. They have families. They feel loss. Sacrificing humanity for the sake of advancements in science or technology isn't just heartless. It's fundamentally wrong."

"I guess that can only be determined by what you define as 'good' or 'wrong'," I interject, making air quotations with my fingers. "If we determine that what is 'good' is what turns out best for society as a whole, then what Cortex is doing is technically 'good'. But if you determine 'good' by the treatment of each individual life, then they are most definitely wrong."

I catch the movement of Steele slowly shaking his head out of the corner of my eye, a wide smile on his face. "You sound just like her. Director Ellis, that is." He exchanges a glance with Linc, who shrugs. "These are decisions that must be made, Arin," Steele says kindly, turning to address me, "because they affect so much more than just you and me."

"I came here because Linc said that you had answers," I explain. Finding out that there is such organization, such strength here, leaves me with a hundred questions. I don't know where to begin. "What can you tell me about the sickness?" The first question, the one that's been on my lips for weeks, the only one that truly matters.

Steele leans against his heavy wooden desk, facing me. He suddenly looks very weary. "I know what is making the Lost sick. Or who, rather." He exchanges a glance with Linc, who comes to sit down beside me. I glance at both of them. I wish one of them would just spit it out.

"We've had agents inside of Cortex for a while," Steele begins, nodding to Linc. "Linc here is our most recent recruit. A lot of what we have today wouldn't have been possible without him." I glance at Linc. Who would've known that the tall, quiet director of Research and Development with tousled blonde hair was a

Rebel spy? He makes eye contact with me for a brief second. Lingering eyes and a small smile. I wonder what he has in his life that is worth working as a mole for the Rebel army?

"Initially, Linc's primary mission was just collecting information. We feel that, in order to be successful, we need to learn everything that we possibly can about our enemy." He takes a deep breath. "But then, we discovered this." He picks up a tablet off his desk and waves his hand across to produce a holo-screen. I see a picture of Director Ellis, floating in front of the three of us; it turns slowly, highlighting the sharp angles of her cheekbones and the curve of her lips. She looks like she is about to speak, our fearless leader. "We've been watching Director Ellis up there in her ivory tower for a while now. And we've stumbled across something that is huge, Arin. So much bigger than dumping trash or Criterion scores." Steele's voice lowers, growing more and more serious. "Cortex is planning something horrible. Something that affects everyone in this compound, every single one of the Lost. And this sickness has led us to believe that they have already put their plan in motion." He rubs the back of his neck thoughtfully. "Time is running out."

"What are you talking about?" I whisper, heart pounding. I can hear the blood pumping in my ears.

"An extinction, Arin. Director Ellis is planning an extinction." The blood drains from my face and I feel myself begin to tremble uncontrollably.

"An extinction? How ... why?" My mind is flooding with questions as I struggle to wrap my mind around what they are telling me. Linc's face reveals his sheer anger—an emotion that I have never seen in him before.

"Here, see for yourself," Steele says grimly, making a gesture at the holo-screen. A video begins to play. Director Ellis comes to life. Her beauty is striking, silky brown hair pulled back tightly into a bun. She stands tall and erect, shoulders square, commanding attention from the audience. Her lips are pursed together tightly but her youthful face softens the harshness of it all. Her brown eyes peer at me behind thinly framed black glasses, the expression in them always like someone analyzing data. Searching, measuring. That was how she had made it to the top, how she had grown to become the leader of something as powerful as Cortex. She was all brain, and apparently, no heart.

"Greetings," the message begins, and I settle into the familiar comfort of her voice. "Please note that the following information is extremely confidential and for your eyes only." I hear Linc huff from beside me. "I come to you with a message. An epiphany of sorts. A revolutionary idea." I find myself sitting up taller in my seat. It is hard not to be drawn into Director Ellis's sense of assurance. She has this way of saying things that makes you feel like she knows everything. That she is someone that you can trust. "Tell me, trusted confidants. What is the motto of our beloved city?" she asks the camera, and I find myself reciting it back to her in my mind. *Excellence and Innovation.*

"It has come to my attention that there is a section of our city, which is putting a drain on our precious resources. It is costing us coin, labor, and most importantly, time. Time that could be spent pushing the boundaries of the human mind and exceeding our greatest expectations of progress and growth. As you all are well aware, beyond our walls there is a collective group of people, the Lost, who do not meet our standards of excellence. For some time, we have held them up, extending to them our good graces and blessing them with charity and materials that would otherwise be unavailable to them. Up until this moment, we had told ourselves that the pull they are creating on our resources was not significant enough to be a problem, but I have been studying this particular issue for some time now and I believe that the cost of providing for the Lost is too great. What do they contribute to us in return for our good graces? Children? We create adequate amounts of children within the city. In the last eighteen years they have failed to provide even that. Science would suggest that by purifying the gene pool and limiting it to the best and the brightest minds, we will be increasing our chances for more prodigies than ever. As far as labor is concerned, I have spoken at length with our artificial intelligence departments, and they too believe that our city is ready to function at a one hundred percent automated status. There is much fewer risk involved when the complete conversion to automatic systems is complete. And so, we begin phase one of a plan of progression and growth." The screen changes to display a diagram of something microscopic: it looks like a molecule, maybe?

"This is an encrypted nanobotic virus. Years ago, we released the nanobots into the air, and they have since been consumed by every living being both inside of the city and out. We alone hold the power to control the nanobots, and the virus. And we alone hold the decoder key."

I feel my stomach drop and a sense of dread creep up my spine. "I would like to begin with a trial run among test subjects." *Test subjects.* The words echo in my ears. My mom is one of Director Ellis's test subjects? No, that's not possible. She would never do that. My hands begin to tremble and I'm having a difficult time focusing on the rest of what the Director is saying.

"And then if the trials are successful, to move forward with activating the rest of the nanobots outside of the wall through location targeting. The nanobots will work their way through the host's body, attacking it on a cellular level. By the time that the host displays symptoms, total organ shut down has already been initiated and is irreversible without the decoder key." I think that I am going to be sick. Still trembling, I grip the arms of my chair for support.

"No!" I leap to my feet, pointing at the projection of Director Ellis glowing in front of me. "She can't do that!" My gaze whips wildly back and forth between Linc and the commander. "You *knew* about this? Why didn't you stop her?!" My anger is boiling at the surface, and at this moment I'm not even sure who to direct it at. It's no wonder that the Olden civilization killed everybody off! The rage that I feel inside of my chest is not very Gifted. It certainly isn't *Excellence and Innovation*. It's feral. And deadly.

It calls for blood.

"We're trying," says Linc, holding his hands up as if in a sign of peace towards me. "We've been working every day to find a cure."

"Well try harder!" My words fly like daggers and hit true to their mark. I can see the wounded expression on Linc's face. But I don't care. I'm too furious for sympathy. "We have to stop this, now!" My anger turns to passion and I plead with the rebel commander. "If what she said is true, then … the infected don't have much time left!" I shake my head, trying to make sense of it all. How could the council approve something like this? How could Director Ellis think that she could get away with wiping out—murdering—an entire people group? I was entirely wrong about her. She isn't the pinnacle of the Gifted. She is cruel.

I glare at her image with disgust. I've never hated someone before. Hate, like love, conflicts with reason. There is no equation, no solution that can be written to explain it. It just is.

"You seem very upset, Arin." Steele's grey eyes are full of curiosity. "Is your anger solely for the Lost?"

"No." I feel my shoulders droop under the burden that I've been carrying for weeks, and I don't bother to hold the secret in anymore. My whole trip out here was pointless. It's like Linc said, they don't even have a cure. "I wanted to know about the sickness because my mother has it."

Everyone in the room is silent, and when Steele finally speaks, his voice is heavy.

"I see."

"That's why you took the medicine," Linc says quietly, and I stare at the ground so that no one can see the prickle of tears burning in my eyes. When I look up, Steele's grey eyes flash with determination.

"We can help her, Arin. We can help all of them. But we need your help."

CHAPTER

*"The two most important days in your life are the day that
you are born and the day you receive your Criterion score."*

- Chronicles of Discord

"There is something that I would like to show you." Steele gestures to a dark curtain behind him that I didn't notice before and pulls it open. "You'll find the real command center right this way. I'd like to give you an idea of what kind of operation that we are truly running," he continues as we pass through the heavy curtain. As soon as I step through to the other side, I am amazed by the sheer size and construction of the rebel base. It seems to go on forever. We walk together through a maze of winding hallways, the walls of which are solid, built from a heavy looking metal and painted in a dark green.

Along the dimly lit twists and turns, walls are marked with distinctive Lost City symbols. Words like "barracks" and "infantry" are all neatly stenciled with a deep black paint. Plenty of soldiers pass us as we make our way, and every single one of them stops to salute the commander, backs rigid and hands tight in a display of respect, and many of them stop to salute Linc as well.

"Do you have some kind of rank out here?" I whisper to Linc as we navigate the spacious hallways. He shrugs.

"A lot of the soldiers are familiar with my mission inside of Cortex." His gaze is solemn. "Respect is a big thing out here in The Lost City."

There is no chatter echoing throughout the halls, despite the vast numbers of people. Everyone eyes us warily, we are obviously marked as outsiders, in our starchy city clothes and smooth haircuts. Steele takes a sharp turn to the right and we step down through a tattered black curtain and into a room that is literally buzzing with activity. In the center of the room sits an array of computers, all considered outdated by the city's standards but still the most high-tech thing that I have seen since we left the city's walls. Here, people are gathered in clusters, clutching clipboards and chattering excitedly. The pace of the room is much more frantic, and I find myself settling into the familiar bustle. This reminds me of Cortex.

"This way!" Steele takes a seat at the center of the web of computers and gestures for us to join him, we sit eagerly, all of us getting caught up in the buzz of the room. *Now this is more like it.* He leans forward eagerly in his seat, his hands clasped tightly together, "We are sitting in the area that I like to call the hub. This is a twenty-four-hour operation. From here, we closely monitor everything that is going on inside of Cortex. Every breakthrough invention, every policy change, every trash dump, we know about it practically before they do. And a lot of that in part is due to a gentleman that I'd like you to meet, Arin." Steele walks up to a young man, and places his hands affectionately on his shoulders, like a proud father might. "This is Sol, and he is one hell of a hacker."

The man named Sol grins at me. His smile is so wide that I can see all of his teeth; he looks like a primary getting a perfect score for their very first time.

"Ah, so you're the one who reached the fabled 999 on the Criterion?" Sol asks, voice friendly. His eyes are hidden behind a dark pair of sunglasses and the toothy grin is still in place. "I've gotta tell you, you were not easy to find."

I blink; is this the messenger from back at the apartment? He doesn't look anything like I would have pictured. He sits in a comfortable looking black chair, surrounded by holo-screens, modified to look like nothing that I've ever seen before, even inside of Cortex. His shiny dark hair is split down the middle and tucked behind both ears, once again giving him the appearance of a primary child. He isn't sporting the army-green threads of the rest of the rebel army but is apparently more comfortable in jeans and a T-shirt. He appears to be all man, no machine. Without metal parts, tattoos, or a beard he doesn't look like he belongs out here among the Lost.

"I'm Arin." I offer my hand for him to shake but he doesn't take it.

"Hey Arin! It's great to meet you! Come and find me!" he says playfully, still smiling and looking a little bit over my head. "Wasn't that bit great?" he chuckles. "First things first, you may have noticed the specs." He points to the dark sunglasses. "They are more than just a fashion statement! Just so we are all on the same page, I am blind. Like, hella blind." That explains the handshake thing. I feel a combination of both admiration and empathy for the hacker swell in my chest.

"Okay, thanks for clueing me in. It's really great to meet you too," I say sincerely, and I mean it. Curiosity causes me to take a step closer to his desk and take a look at the intricate machinery around him. "What is all of this?" I wonder.

"Oh yes!" Sol claps his hands together and beams proudly. "This is my pride and joy." He gestures to the holo-screens floating around his head. "I modified them all myself."

"This is incredible …" I breathe, examining the complex structure of the holo-screens and their Sol-given mods. It looks like he went in and re-coded the framework down to its bare bones, reconfiguring it for a different output display entirely. Instead of a shimmering visual projection of information, it was a steady stream of code, directing data to Sol and essentially *telling* him what to see.

"Thanks!" Sol grins. "I had to adjust the interface so that I could use it without my eyes. It can be instructed only by me. The holo is controlled by my skin coms of course but the final output is blind-friendly. I use this gear to do most of my Cortex hacking. It's proven more than useful," he boasts happily. "It's kind of awesome." I can't help but smile. This *is* awesome.

"So, you're Gifted, aren't you Sol?" I take a seat beside him, wondering why someone who understood technology well enough to create such a system was living out here among the Lost.

He nods. "Yup, sure am."

"Sol's intelligence has been vital in helping us monitor Cortex," Steele interjects. "We have been able to collect data on the nanovirus from their most secure servers."

"Then why did you reach out to me?" I ask, and Sol gives me a big grin.

"Because once we found out Director Ellis's plan, we figured that we should try and recruit Cortex's smartest mind to help us with our cause. We thought that if you found out what Director Ellis was doing that you would want to help us stop her."

"With Sol's help we have learned a lot about the way the nanobots operate," Linc adds, "but the decoder program is something way more complicated than anything any of us have ever seen. We are hoping that we can crack it with a little help." His tone is confident. "This is why we wanted to bring you here! We needed you to *see* our efforts, to *see* what we have built out here in The Lost City." He gestures to the command center around us. "It's extraordinary!" It really is.

It bewilders me that the people of Paramus live out their lives in fear of the Lost and of their city. And yet, if they only knew, that the person that they should be most afraid of is the person leading them.

"How close are we to breaking it?" I press, scanning the data scrolling across the nearest holo-screen, in search of any kind of indication that we have the key.

"Well, that's kind of been the problem. There is only so much that we can do remotely, we need someone on the inside. The key is hardwired into the defense system. If you want to access it, you have to shut their entire defense system down." Steele explains gravely.

I understand what Steele is saying. The only way to stop the nanovirus and save the Lost and my parents is to take over its source. Cortex.

"You're planning an attack." I realize.

"That's right, Arin. We're going to take over Paramus. The wall is coming down."

It takes a moment for the meaning of Steele's words to sink in. Immediately, my mind starts calculating the probability of actually succeeding at something so crazy. I'm not sure what exactly the rebel army has up their sleeve, but invading Paramus and taking over Cortex? It would take a miracle. Cortex is an impenetrable fortress. Director Ellis and her team of scientists have made sure of that.

"I can't see how that would ever work," I begin carefully. "Do you guys have something that I don't know about? A secret weapon perhaps? Because otherwise ..." I shake my head.

Sol smirks at me. "Yeah, we do." I look around the room: everyone has a little smile except for Linc, whose gaze on me is heavy. I realize that everyone is staring at me.

"What do you mean?" I start to back up, physically trying to escape from the very real possibility of what I think that they are about to say. It's me. Of course, it's me.

My head starts spinning. I wonder how much of this was orchestrated by the rebel army from the very beginning. They must have gained access to my scores.

My job assignment. Could it be a coincidence that I ended up assigned to the very department that is overseen by the Rebel spy? It doesn't seem likely.

My "random pairing" with Linc as my roommate. And the sparks that have been flying between us. I glance at Linc, trying to ignore the tendrils of betrayal that begin to wrap around my heart. He won't make eye contact with me. Has our friendship, the connection I've felt between us, been a ruse? I wonder if anything that has happened in the past week has been of my own doing, or if I've just been blindly following the guidance of the rebels, completely oblivious.

"I need some air," I blurt out and rush out of the command center. I push past rebel soldiers in the hall, slowly breaking into a jog. Not really paying attention to where I'm going, I just want out. I will my feet to find the exit. Thankfully, the next turn takes me through a canvas door flap, and I burst outside into the open air. Stars overhead glistening. I take a few ragged breaths, hands on my knees, mind still racing. I hear footsteps behind me as someone approaches me, but I don't care enough to turn around.

"Hey," I hear Sol greet me softly. He comes to stand beside me, hands in the pockets of his jeans. It's cold enough outside that when he speaks, I can see his breath. "I wasn't born blind, you know," he begins, his voice far away. "It was a gradual blindness. I was born inside of the city to a wealthy family. I was on the fast track for success. I did extremely well in my classes, my parents were really proud." He shakes his head and gives a little laugh, completely void of humor. "And then the spots came. Big rings in my vision. They started at night. And I was scared. Scared shitless."

I know what that feels like.

"My parents didn't even try to stop it," he continues. "They could've splurged on a major surgery and tried to get it reversed. Maybe. But they didn't want to spend the coin. And they didn't want to damage their reputation by having a defective kid." He spits the words. "Why care about anything when you can just throw the old one away and get a new one?"

My stomach twists at his words. I wonder if all the Gifted are like Director Ellis and Sol's parents, ready to throw away anything that loses value. But I don't see garbage when I look at Sol, standing beside me, kicking dirt with the toe of his shoe; I see so much worth valuing.

"Yeah, I had to learn some hard lessons as a pretty young kid," he continues. "I was twelve when I realized that I couldn't rely on anyone to take care of me but myself. I started studying frantically, learning everything that I could about programming and engineering. As my vision started slipping, I built myself a system that I could use without the use of my eyes. When they cast me outside of Paramus, I began working on a plan to take down the system that taught my parents that throwing their own son away is okay."

"Sol, that's awful." I put my hand on his shoulder, my heart breaking for him. He turns to face me, bottom lip quivering. His hands find mine, a comforting warmth against the cold.

"They have to be stopped, Arin." His voice trembles unsteadily. "That city is like a plague, destroying anyone and anything that doesn't live up to its perfect standards."

I agree with him, I really do. Purposefully infecting an entire group of people with a virus that is a death sentence because they don't meet your standards is wrong. Purposefully hurting anyone, for any selfish reason is wrong. What Sol's parents did to him is wrong, As is the system that encouraged it.

But I don't want to be the Rebel's champion. I just want to be a daughter with two living parents.

"I don't think I can help you," I murmur, letting go of his hand. "You're smart Sol. You can figure out a way to save all of these people. I know you can."

He shakes his head. "Without someone on the inside helping us, they're dead. There's only so much I can do out here."

"I've seen the firewall, Sol. It's complex for sure but you could hack it. Bring down Cortex's defense system from out here in The Lost City."

He shakes his head again. "That's where you're wrong. The override is a combination of digital security and a physical key. One won't work without the other."

"Then hack the server from the outside and send Linc or another soldier in to retrieve the key," I suggest.

"The digital hack and the physical key have to happen at the same time. If there is a lapse between the two for any point of time over five seconds, the whole thing goes into lockdown and reverts to back-up servers. Our plan would fail. Also, we need every trained soldier that we have to help launch the ground attack as soon as the servers go down. There's going to be a war to fight." He takes my hands in both of his again. "Arin, if we don't stop the kill switch, everyone is going to go down with this ship. Your parents too. Now, I don't understand what it's like to have family love like that, but I can feel it coming from you like waves. This loyalty that you have to them. It drives you. Whatever you have, it must be worth saving."

My eyes sting with tears, threatening to spill over. "It is," I manage. Sol puts one of my hands on his heart; I can feel it beating steadily beneath my palm.

"We are all worth saving," he says solemnly. "Your parents understood this, and you know it too." A single bell tolls in the distance. Sol turns toward the sound of the bell, and my hand falls back down to my side, still warm from his chest, my stomach churning with indecision as the first rays of sunlight peak over the horizon. "That bell means that it's time for breakfast. I'm going to head back inside," he says sadly before turning to go and I watch his figure get smaller and smaller, feeling like my insides are turning into tighter and tighter knots.

Of course, I want to help, of *course* I do. But I'm the protector of my family—not the protector of entire cities. My whole life I've been like a diamond, perfect under pressure. But this is too much pressure. What if I crack?

Linc is waiting for me back at the base, leaning against its canvas entrance casually, arms crossed over his chest, red embers glowing from the smoke between his lips as he watches the sun rise. As I trudge up the muddy slope to the base, my eyes trained on the opening, I wish for a brief moment that I could confide in him. He's a sight to behold in the sleepy light of dawn. He somehow managed to find a jacket and it fits him well, cloaking him in the last shadowy part of the morning so that you almost would miss him, except for the warm glow from the end of the cigarette. As I get closer, I can just make out his tousled blonde curls, the slope of his jaw. He really is beautiful. But when I look at him, all that I can think about is that he is a Rebel Spy ... and I don't really know him, or who he is to me. Am I just a pawn to him? A means to an ultimate end? He's never really given me a reason to believe otherwise.

When I reach the top, he takes a final drag of the cigarette and tosses it onto the ground, stomping out its embers with his boot. "Are you about ready to head back?" he wonders, and I nod, my mind churning. "You look cold. Here." He slips the jacket from his shoulders and places it carefully on my shoulders. I try to ignore the warm tingles of pleasure that spread across my skin where he touches me. I wrap the jacket tightly around me. It smells like him, like soap and trees and cigarette smoke. "If it's okay with you, there's one more person I'd like you to meet before we leave?" he asks, and I agree. I follow him through the rebel encampment, and back to the outskirts of the tent city, until he stops outside of a huge canvas structure, as tall as my house. As the panels flap in the wind a wisp of something mouthwatering floats up into my nostrils. Whatever is cooking in there smells wonderful.

"This way," Linc says, pushing a heavy flap aside and I duck inside. The space inside of the tent is warm and packed with the Lost. Delicious smells and noise fill every available space of the tent. A large fire crackles at the center of the room and skewers stuffed with spiced meat and vegetables are dutifully watched and turned by women who joke loudly amongst each other and have babies on their backs. Everything about The Lost City stirs up a longing in my heart for my own family. I can almost see my mother standing by this fire, helping to cook food for the families who have had someone fall ill, making sure that no one goes hungry.

There is such a sense of community among the Lost that is foreign to me. I realize now as I observe clusters of people around me, that this is what Paramus is missing. I see people constantly touching each other, either a reassuring hug or the squeeze of a hand in greeting. The Lost work like a well-written program, dutifully serving their family members and friends food first before ever taking their first bite. The mothers take turns holding each other's babies so that they can each have a chance to eat. I see an old man pass by with one leg, but he has two sturdy sons at his side, easing his every step. Two girls sit by the fire, braiding one another's hair and laughing.

These people are quick to share, they are quick to make sure that no one goes without food, they look out for each other. Linc returns with a steaming plate of meat and vegetables for our table in one hand and a warm basket of bread in the other. As he places it on the table in front of us, he gestures to an old woman who has followed him over to our table.

"This is Maz," he says. "She is the elected leader here outside the wall." The old woman dips her head respectfully in greeting. Her long silver braids are beautifully interwoven with bird feathers. She is by far the oldest looking person that I have ever seen, and although she walks slowly and with the assistance of a wooden cane, she holds her head high with dignity.

My mind flashes back to the petite, nail-polished hand slipping from under the sheet in the red level. Even though the elder before me has a face covered in deep wrinkles, she seems to have a strength about her that I would have never expected for someone so advanced in age.

She slowly takes a seat across from me and when she speaks her voice is soft and rough, like someone who has spent their entire life around fresh air and campfire smoke. "Greetings, Arin Wells," she begins calmly, her deep brown eyes steady. "There is no need to introduce yourself, I know who you are." Her air of unwavering confidence and matter-of-fact way of speaking leads me to believe that she is worthy of being called leader of The Lost City. "It is not very often that we get visitors from Paramus. The last people to come and help since the Plague struck were your parents." My eyes widen at the mention of my parents. Had Maz met them before? Had they been here, in this very tent, where I'm seated now? My heart starts to race, I have so many questions.

"I'm so sorry to hear that your mother has been struck with this sickness." She shakes her head sadly. "Lara and Timothy are well loved by everyone here. They truly embody the spirit of The Lost City and its citizens." It's surreal listening to Maz talk about my mom and dad. I would give anything to have them here now. My eyes start to sting, and I have to look away. Maz sees my tears and takes my hands in hers. They are rough from hard labor yet warm and comforting.

"Here in The Lost City, we have a word: 'Ubuntu'. It is a belief that we hold dear to our hearts. It's the idea that as human beings we are *defined* by our compassion and our kindness towards others. It is the symbol on our flag." She points to a deep crimson flag hanging on one side of the canvas tent walls. It is adorned with the circular symbol and three dots that the Rebel soldiers wear.

"It is the very first thing that we teach our children, before they learn to walk, or to read. We teach them that their value is fixed. It's a constant. They don't lose it when they fail. They don't gain more when they achieve. They grow up with an understanding that their worth is not tied to their career or their contributions to society. It is something that I wish the Gifted understood. If you can internalize this idea, you'll find it easier to discover what you actually want from life."

What I actually want from life—what a revolutionary idea. Paramus encourages its citizens to compete. It has taught me that only the smartest deserve to survive. It boasts that perfection and glory are the highest goals any human being can obtain. Yet what I truly want is to enjoy the warmth of family, of friends. I'm tired of being alone.

Maz's words wash over me like the soothing cream that my mother placed on my burns once when I had a science experiment go wrong. I breathe in the deep gentleness of her words, letting them soak into me. "Life was never meant to be about competition, Arin. Life is about community. In the Lost City, we understand that *we belong to each other*, no one is better than the other. We are all human. I am you and you are me." I find myself nodding along to her words, I can see the beauty in them. If everyone in Paramus lived like this, our lives would be so much different. So much more … full.

"I've never seen someone with as many … years as you have," I admit sheepishly, not sure if I'm being rude but still so very

146

curious. "In Paramus, the elderly are seen to be without purpose. What purpose do they serve here?"

Maz's eyes light up with golden sparks that dance as she answers, her words like a poem that she has memorized by heart and told a thousand times. "Our elders tell our stories, young one. They tell us what has been in the past so that we can have the brightest future. Their gift is experience, it is wisdom. They are the matriarch of the family, and they can help you learn who you are by knowing of your ancestors before you. You cannot know where you are going, if you do not know the history of where you have been." I feel a pang in my chest. I have always struggled with knowing who I truly am. In many ways, I am Lara and Timothy's daughter, and that has been the identity that has supported me all of these years, the identity that I have chosen and will die to protect. But there is another identity as well.

"Maz, do you ever remember a young woman who looked like me?" I ask tentatively, clinging to a cautious hope that she might say yes but worried about what that could mean for me. "Timothy and Lara aren't my birth parents," I add for clarification. "I ... I've just always wondered, you know, who *my biological mother* might be."

Maz strokes her chin thoughtfully as she ponders my request, and I await her answer, heart pounding. My fingers go to the token around my neck as they always do when I'm nervous. Finally, she answers. "It is not my place to say. I'm sorry."

I feel the small sliver of hope that I was clinging to crumble to pieces inside of me. I'm no closer to finding out who my birth mother is or why she abandoned me. I was hoping maybe, just maybe, to find some answers here. What did Maz mean, it wasn't her place? Does that mean that she knows my mother but doesn't want to say? What could possibly be the reason? Could she be here now? My eyes scan the tent around us. And if she is, do I even want to meet her? She abandoned me in a trash can after all, and I'm lucky that I was found by Timothy and Lara. I feel another pang in my chest. They've loved me like their own daughter all of these years.

I can't lose them. They must be saved. They're all that I have left.

We eat dinner together, like members of a real community. After the meal is finished, Maz extends an invitation to me. "It is our tradition to bring warm food and fresh water to the sick and elderly in the morning before we start our day," she explains, rising from the table. "Would you like to come with me to pay them a visit?" She offers me a warm smile. "This was the task that your mother helped me with the most when she would come. Sweet Lara."

I have the strangest desire to walk everywhere that my mother and father have walked; to see the Lost City through their eyes. To *feel* them here.

"Yes, I would like that very much." I follow Maz, with Linc close behind. We are able to carry several baskets of food and pitchers filled with cooled, boiled water from the lake to deliver to those who cannot come themselves. The air outside of the tent is crisp and there is a chill in the early morning air that makes me grateful for the jacket Linc gave me. Maz leads us to a string of tent homes towards the outskirts of the tent city. I can hear the sounds of the sick before we even get inside.

My hands tightly clutch the earthenware pot in my hands as we get closer and closer to the intense hacking sounds and the moaning coming from inside the canvas sick camp. A wave of fear washes over me, and I have to take several deep breaths to steady myself. Maz stops and turns towards our little troupe, her head high. When she speaks, her voice rings out clear through the cold night air. "This is what Cortex has done to my people," she declares softly, before disappearing through the canvas flaps.

The sounds and smells of the sick bay hit my ears and my nose before my eyes ever adjust. My stomach churns instantly but I force myself to focus on the people in front of me. They are real, and they are hurting. The food in my hands feels like a meager offering now as I see that great extent of the suffering around me. I walk slowly down the aisles of handmade canvas cots, bodies on both sides in what seems like endless rows. The eyes that stare back at me are glossy, belonging to fevered bodies, full of fear.

I have seen the data. I know what the nanobots are doing to their bodies. Shutting down their organs one by one. I have to look away, busying myself with work instead. We set up a serving station and scoop out individual meal portions into clay bowls. I deliver bowls to shivering young mothers who rock their crying babies close to their chest and try to ignore their own fevers because they have mouths to feed. I bring bread to pairs of siblings who sit beside each other, clinging tightly to one another; afraid that this day might be their last with their brother or sister, who they can't imagine a world without. I can see the desperation in each one of their eyes. All they can do is hope that somehow, someone, somewhere will save their family. And I feel their pain. Because it is my pain too.

Director Ellis seeks to destroy these people because she doesn't see their value. She sees their compassion as weakness, but when I look around me at the people of The Lost City, all that I see is strength. While it's true that their value can't be measured by performance evaluations or Criterion scores, it's somehow better. It's their Ubuntu. The love that they share for each other.

Love. My entire life my city has taught me that being the best at everything and eventually getting a job at Cortex was my purpose. I was told that the highest thing that I could achieve in life would be to be the smartest person in the room. The person with the most coin and the most power. Now I understand, that's not true. The people of The Lost City have opened my eyes to what really matters. *People* matter. I feel like it's always been there, a whisper in the back of my mind, fueled by the love my parents have always shown me. So subtly they led by example, not wanting to take me out of the world of Paramus or Cortex but still simply showing me that at the same time, there is another way. My heart aches for the Lost people and I wish that I could spend time here, among them, learning. But I have a mother inside of Paramus who needs my care.

We make our way back through the Rebel encampment and find ourselves making our final stop, once again before the commander.

"I'm going to take Arin back to Cortex. She has a lot that she needs to think about." Linc explains, and Steele nods.

"I understand." He turns to me. "If you decide that you would like to help, you know where to find us." I feel a pang of guilt in my chest. What has happened here is awful, there's no denying that. But as much as I'd like to help Sol, the handsome commander, Maz, and everyone else, I can't become the Rebel's champion.

It's strange how your entire world can turn upside down in a single day, I think, as we ride the train back through the city, once again inside of Paramus' walls. Through the train car windows I catch glimpses of the bustling city, teeming with activity outside of our triple paned windows. But the inside of the train car is quiet.

I haven't said much to Linc since we left the command center. We sit across from each other in silence, him looking out the window deep in thought and me toying with my necklace, twisting the diamond back and forth between my fingers.

"What are you worrying about?" Linc asks, glancing from the window to the diamond in my grasp.

Instantly, I release the token, embarrassed. "What do you mean?"

"You always play with your necklace when you're worried," he points out casually, and the warmth in my cheeks intensifies at the thought of him studying me carefully enough to notice my habit. I try to brush it off. He's a spy. Spies are trained to be observant.

"Oh." I avert my gaze. "There's a lot on my mind right now. That's all."

Linc lights a cigarette and the smoke curls lazily skyward between us. "Are you glad that you came with me outside the wall?" he asks innocently, green eyes flickering with mischief, and I have to resist the urge to swat him for being so smug.

Instead, I roll my eyes. "Yeah, I love finding out that my entire life has been a lie," I reply, with plenty of sarcasm. He laughs, a pleasant sound, and I realize that I haven't heard him laugh very much. I like it.

There's so much that I like about him, but there are also so many unknowns when it comes to Linc. It's hard to draw the line between what has been genuine between us and what has been orchestrated by the Rebels. "You had no idea that my mom was sick, did you?" I ask, and I think that I know the answer to this one before he even speaks.

He shakes his head. "No, I had no idea. And I am sorry about that." His face is completely earnest, and I feel a sense of quiet confidence; maybe I'm not as bad at determining what has been real between us as I first thought.

"You really lucked out that that was the case," I realize. He had me in the right place at the right time, but without that information, he would have had no motivation to get me to come with him to the rebel base. "Otherwise, I probably would have never gone outside of the wall. How exactly were you going to try and get me to even join the Rebels?" I ask, thinking about his ability to talk his way into anything. Would he have been able to come up with a story interesting enough to get me to come along?

His answer takes me by surprise. "I was probably going to have to turn up the charm and seduce you," he responds with a grin, and I can't tell if he's joking. I find myself letting out nervous laughter in response, trying to ignore the exhilarating tingle his words send down my spine.

"Don't be ridiculous," I retort, my nerves practically dancing from all the electric excitement tingling through my veins. "I don't make it a habit to fall for strangers."

He watches me, with amusement on his face. "We're not strangers. We're roommates."

"Which was 100% orchestrated by the Rebels right?" I circle back to fact checking, grateful for a subject that brings me some stability and grounding.

"Yeah, Sol gets the credit for that one." My roommate grins proudly, his admiration for our mutual friend completely understandable. I've never met someone as brilliant, or as likeable, as the hacker. They make an unusual team, Sol with his goofy brilliance, Steele with his ability to lead an entire Rebel army, and Linc, the double agent.

"How did you get tangled up with all of them anyway?" I ask, I've heard a few origin stories tonight, but there is still one that I am very interested in hearing.

"Have you ever heard the expression, that family isn't always the people that you're related to, but the people that you choose?" he begins slowly, his voice coming from that faraway place of remembering, and I sit very still so as not to distract him while he tells me his story. "Steele and Sol and Maz and the rest of the Lost are my chosen family."

"I understand about choosing family. Probably more than most." I murmur, drawing similarities between our two stories already,

"You know how you just learned how fucked up Cortex is? Well, I've known about it for a long time?" He flicks his cigarette butt to the other end of the train car, brow furrowing. I can feel it, stewing just below the surface. Anger.

"My father," he begins, avoiding my gaze, "if you want to even call him that, is a councilman. He had set aside a little coin for himself that he decided he wanted to do some investing with. Well, in a world where Gifted children are the currency, you can imagine how he decided to create more wealth." He spits out the words, resentment heavy in his voice. I get the feeling that the place that he is walking me to is a very dark place. "Of course, the Gifted aren't going to willingly give up any of their prodigies, so he looks outside of the wall. Plenty of Gifted kids come from outside of the wall, he thinks, you know, maybe I'll take my chances and see if I can't get a kid or two to really set myself up with a nice retirement plan."

I feel my stomach twisting into knots at his words, a very dark place indeed.

"Anyway, he makes it sound really great. He makes this offer that can't be refused to some unsuspecting Lost girls, talks them up with promises of lots of coin and illusions of grandeur." He shakes his head. "It ended up working on my mother. Once he brought her to the city and got her pregnant, he took good care of her for the most part I guess until I was born." Linc has to stop, he's trembling a little. Part of me wants to reach out and comfort him. The other part of me is a little afraid to do so. He pushes on. "As soon as he figured out that I was Gifted, he didn't need my mother anymore. I was seven when he kicked her out. I wanted to go with her, but he wouldn't let me. He kept me locked in the house for weeks. I never saw her again." I shake my head slowly. I can't imagine having your mother taken away and being trapped with the monster who took her from you.

"Is she living here with the Lost?" I ask. "Where is she now?"

His green eyes fill with sadness and I can hear a tremor in his voice when he shares, "She wasn't here when I got here. It looks like she never made it."

"I'm so sorry," I find myself murmuring, his vulnerability catching me off guard. Up until this point, my view of Linc has been that of a guy who isn't bothered by anything, someone who can handle anything that life throws at him. The kind of person who takes on life's challenges with resourcefulness, brains, and a good amount of stubbornness: someone who isn't afraid to have a little fun along the way. But the man in front of me has a dark past that haunts him, and a deeper motivation than I could have ever realized.

"That's why you joined the Rebels," I conclude, gaining a truly deeper perspective about the double agent, "to avenge her."

He nods. "The world shouldn't be like this." No, it shouldn't. I think back to what Maz said, about when you understand that you have value, simply from being a human being, that you start to realize what you actually want in life. I glance at the man in front of me, the one who took me outside of the wall and showed me that there is another way, a different way, that the world should be. He catches me staring but this time I don't avert my eyes and look away, I take all of him in. From his disheveled blonde locks and his curious eyes, to his sharp cheekbones and full lips, parted slightly like there's a question on the tip of his tongue.

I want to believe this idea that humans have value, just from *being*. I mean, isn't there something to be said for the emotions that can be created in your chest, sitting across from a handsome boy on a dark train, a night full of adventure behind you, and everything in the world in front of you? How do you put a value on that?

I take a deep breath, the smoke tickling my nose. "Do you really think that you can change things?" I ask the question that has been on my mind since we left the command center, finally giving a voice to my doubts after everything that has happened tonight.

"I have to try," he answers simply, green eyes glistening with determination and I know that he is right. For too long, I have believed a lie about Paramus and the outside world. Paramus is not the only city left capable of civilization; the Lost City has proved that. Paramus and its obsession with knowledge has unknowingly created a virus: Cortex. It's not unlike the virus that they in turn created, infecting all of its citizens with false ideals about their worth and enslaving them through their ignorance. The system tells us that we are smart, all the while blinding us to the truth; we actually know nothing about our city or our leaders. The truth is, they don't care about me, or Linc, or Sol, or Kace. To them, each person is easily disposable and easily replaced, hardly unique. I hope that Linc and the Rebels succeed, I really do.

CHAPTER

"The only way to attain success is by casting aside the attachments that hold you back."

- Articles of Axiom. Section XV11, Part F

I try to stifle a yawn as I sit down at the table across from Linc in our apartment. It's early evening following our day in the Lost City. I slept for almost twelve hours, but I still feel like I need twelve more, as I was tormented throughout the night with bad dreams. Also, when I woke up, I had a T-shirt covering me that I definitely don't remember putting on and that leaves me with questions.

"Did you put this shirt on me?" I ask, my fingers playing with the hem. Linc takes a long sip from his water glass and looks over the rim at me, clearly amused.

"What, you don't like the color?" he answers, eyebrows arched, a small smile on his lips, green eyes dancing. I look down at the standardized graphic T-shirt with the Cortex logo I'm currently wearing in confusion.

"No, the color is fine. I'm just wondering where it came from?"

He chuckles. "You kept saying that you were cold in your sleep last night, so I gave you my shirt," he answers nonchalantly, like it's no big deal.

"Oh, I think I was having a nightmare." I can feel my cheeks starting to redden so I busy myself with the task of wiping off the ring left by someone's glass on the table in front of me. When I finally look up, he is watching me, green eyes still dancing. Why is he staring at me?

"What?" I ask, his stare making my stomach flutter nervously. "Do you want it back?" I add, feeling awkward. He laughs, a loud, hearty sound.

"Nah, keep it." He smiles. "It looks cute on you."

"Thanks." Again, I can feel my face growing hot, so I look down at the table again to try and hide the bright redness in my cheeks. I feel warm all over as his words send a thrill of excitement through my chest. I realize just how much I have wanted to feel Linc's admiration. Now, hearing him compliment me stirs up emotions inside of me that I wish that I knew how to put into words to say to him. Instead, I pour myself something to drink, and proceed to wash my glass, letting the noise of the dishes clattering in the sink drown out the silence between us since I can't think of a single thing to say back to him to express how I feel. *I think that you're very handsome*, I practice while rinsing my mug. *I like that I feel like I can be myself around you.*

"Here, let me help you with that." Suddenly he's behind me, and I can feel his body pressing against me as he reaches for the glass in my hand, his fingers brushing against mine. Goosebumps run up and down my arms and my breath starts to quicken like I'm running, heart racing in my chest. But this is different from running. This is an intense excitement to feel him so close to me.

"Look, I know that we don't know each other very well," he begins, and my heart leaps in my chest, "but I want you to know that you can trust me." He places the clean mug on the counter to dry. I can barely hear him over the pounding in my chest, so I can't tell whether or not he is being playful, but when I turn around, his green eyes are more sincere than I've ever seen them before, sending a thrill throughout my entire body.

"Okay," I breathe, feeling the electricity between us and watching how his eyes dart from holding mine down to my lips. I wonder if he wants to kiss me? The thought sends a flutter of butterflies through my stomach. Would I want him to? My eyes travel up from his full lips up to his dancing emerald eyes, framed with long black lashes. My heart skips a beat. Yes, I think I would like that very much.

But not now. *It isn't fair for me to be up here kissing Linc while my mother is still out there suffering*

"I've got to go," I blurt, backing away and leaving him staring after me in confusion as I hurry to my room and retrieve my jacket and running shoes. I walk past a confused Linc as I head for the front door.

"Go where?" he asks, watching me with a wounded expression. I feel bad. It felt like we were having a moment. But I can't rest, or enjoy anything, until my mother is well and recovering.

"Just ... out," is all that I can say, and I feel a pang of regret in my chest. It's not that I want to push him away. But I can't find the words to explain the amount of guilt that I feel for being here, with him, after everything I learned yesterday. I need to tell my dad the truth about what is going on inside of my mom and work with him to try and find a solution. And my parents both need to know the truth about Director Ellis.

"Are you leaving Cortex? Arin, I don't think that's a good idea," he tries to reason, arms folded across his chest, green eyes indignant.

"I'll be fine," I assure him, and reach for the doorknob, avoiding his gaze. I feel like I'm ruining any chance of having another "moment" with him ever again. The thought fills me with disappointment, but Linc isn't my top priority right now. "I can make it out and back to the apartment myself."

"At least tell me where you're going, please." His tone is firm, but there's a hidden emotion that comes in at the end. Is it concern?

I pause and weigh the pros and cons of telling him the truth. After all, Linc did reveal his true score, take me to meet the Rebels, and tell me about his parents. He just asked me to trust him, and I want to. Especially if I ever want to have the chance at another moment like the one we just shared. I take a deep breath, letting go of the knob and turn to face him.

"I'm going home," I admit, and struggle to put into words the intense burden that I feel. "I need to see my mom. To make sure she's …" I trail off and have to bite my lower lip to keep it from trembling. I watch his face drop. I can tell that he understands immediately.

"Arin, I'm sorry. Of course. I don't mean to be selfish. I just want to know that you're going to be careful." He pauses, eyes serious. "I can't help you if you get caught sneaking in or out of Cortex."

"I'll be fine." I tell him again, trying not suppress the pinpricks of irritation that surface. I've made it out of Cortex before without his help. I leave the apartment without another word and make my way down to the loading docks. While my feelings toward Linc are strong, if he wants to get close to me, there's one thing that he needs to understand. I'm perfectly capable of taking care of myself—and it's not just myself that I'm looking out for. I have my own battles to fight. Ones that have nothing to do with the Rebel army.

Once I'm outside of the Cortex building, it takes a minute for my eyes to adjust to the dark. It's always light inside of Cortex, but out here, only the moon and a spattering of street lamps offer illumination against the thick blanket of darkness. I shiver and pull my hood down over my face and begin my long jog to the train station.

My mind is racing. I'm not sure if it's due to leftover adrenaline from my encounter earlier or if it's because there's something particularly eerie about the especially thick cloak of darkness in the sky tonight, but I can't help but feel like something is wrong—and that I'm in danger. There is no additional sound other than the rhythm of my footsteps on the pavement and the loud exhalations of my breathing, but I can't stop thinking that something, or someone, else is here with me.

Chills crawl up the back of my neck as I reach the train station and I have the unshakeable feeling that someone is watching me. I give a hasty look around but see no one. *Here*, I think as I climb the platform steps, *at least there is more light.* The light's warm glow brings me a little comfort. But I also know, peering into the darkness, that I am easy to spot up here, alone on this platform, bathed in light like a beacon. If someone was watching me, they would have a perfect view of me up here. My ears strain to pick up any sound of activity but there is no sound except my labored breathing. I try to shake the feeling.

The train rushing into the station comes like a welcomed friend, and with one last glance over my shoulder, I run to the very last car on the train, out of the spotlight on the platform, covered in shadow, providing the perfect cover for what I'm about to do next. A little prying with a screwdriver that I brought along for this specific purpose pops off the entry panel cover and I start a quick hijack that will get me an untraceable ride and allow me to be whisked away along the magnetic track towards mom and dad. Only a few more seconds …

"Hey!" A voice behind me makes me freeze and the tools that I'm holding clatter to the platform floor as I'm caught in the act of hijacking. I turn around slowly, heart pounding, and to my dismay find myself face to face with two street monitors, their stun weapons raised. Shit. How did they sneak up on me like that? I must have been too caught up in my thoughts to hear them.

"Tampering with public transportation is illegal and unethical. You need to come with me for questioning." My eyes dart around frantically, but there is nowhere for me to run. The train doors are still shut behind me and the monitors are positioned directly between me and any chance at running and disappearing into the night. There's two of them and only one of me. The electricity of their stun weapons crackles loud enough to send chills down my spine. I've never been hit with a stun weapon before, but I can imagine that it doesn't feel very good.

If only I had backup. I hear Linc's voice in my head. *If you get caught sneaking in or out of Cortex, I won't be able to help you.* My stomach drops as solid metal hands grab my wrists and sinks deeper when I feel the metal bite of restraints on my wrists. I try to fight, to struggle, but the droid is strong.

"Stop resisting." The first droid orders and I feel myself being shoved onto the ground. I wince as the hard impact of my shoulder hitting the concrete below sends shooting pains down my arm. This might have not been such a fantastic idea after all, I realize from my spot on the ground as I start to break out in a cold sweat. I'm not allowed to be out here, and I got caught hacking government property. I try to remember the penalties for the list of my crimes. What will become of my parents?

"Halt!" I can hear the sound of the second street monitor objecting to someone behind me. I struggle to sit up and am able to raise myself just in time to see Linc landing a kick on the first droid's head. Linc is here!

He twists through the air, calculated and deadly, swift kick perfectly placed. The robot crumbles. The other droid rushes forward to attack, its arms transformed into stun guns, meant to deliver a debilitating shock, rendering an opponent temporarily paralyzed.

"Behind you!" I shout and Linc swiftly turns, connecting his fist with the android's chin piece. It staggers backwards. Instinctively, I stick my foot out and the bot trips and falls. Linc lunges for the droid, and pins both of its weaponized arms to the ground with his knees. He takes out a knife to disable the droid, ripping wires out left and right from the base of the robot's skull. It works and the droid goes still, nothing more than lifeless metal in his arms. There is no time to celebrate however, because the first droid has recovered from the kick and is quickly approaching, stun weapons crackling.

"Stop!" Linc growls, yanking his knife from the first droid's crumpled body and in one swift motion, launches the knife through the air. I watch in amazement as it flies, turning over one full rotation before implanting itself in the dead center of the robot's left eye. Sparks fly from the damaged circuits and the droid hesitates, trying to recover from the damage. At that moment, Linc springs forward with an attack, landing another well-placed kick, this time to the droid's chest. It crumples to the floor, and he promptly dismembers it, the same as the first.

After both robots have been incapacitated, we both sink to the ground, surrounded by wires and screws, trying to catch our breath. Linc retrieves his knife and makes quick work to remove my restraints. Once free, I rub my wrists, wincing from the pain in my shoulder. I look around us. We can't stay here, the robotic carnage around us is no doubt already sending a distress signal to the authorities. Sure enough, sirens begin to wail in the distance.

I glance at the man beside me. His chest rises and falls rapidly with each breath. His shirt is tattered and dirty. He looks back at me with piercing green eyes, forehead matted and sweaty.

"You said that you would be careful!" he exclaims, voice thick with adrenaline maybe? Could it be emotion? "You could've been taken!" His eyes flash with anger and his posture makes me feel like I should've known better. I try to think of the words to explain that I'm sorry, that I didn't plan on being caught.

"I ..." is the only syllable that I get out before he pulls me close and wraps me up in a sudden embrace. My cheek is pressed against his chest while his fingers tangle themselves into my hair. My heart swells with emotion. Linc saved me. He must have been following me. And maybe I should feel annoyed, but at this moment, I don't feel anything but grateful.

"That was too close," he says, the deep timber of his voice vibrating through his chest and against my ear as he holds me tightly, fingers still interlaced in my hair. "I was really scared there for a minute." I find myself breathing in sync with the rise and fall of his chest. The salty smell of him tickles my nose as I breathe him in deeply, and I wonder what it would feel like to be held in his arms like this all night long. This moment would be perfect, if the sound of sirens weren't growing closer and closer by the second.

"Come on," he murmurs, letting me go but slipping my hand into his, "you still want to go see your parents, right?" I nod. "Okay. We can meet the train at the next station." I let him pull me through the dark, our hands intertwined, along the winding twists and turns of the city, always keeping to the shadows, heart pounding with adrenaline. I memorize the rippling of his muscles under the moonlight, and the way the hairs on the back of his neck curl up when they get damp with sweat. The hand that is still firmly grasping mine is both strong and soft at the same time. I wonder just how tender that he can be.

I'm almost sorry when he pulls me under the bright lights of the next closest train station, almost four miles from where we left the demolished droids. Linc keeps me pulled tightly against his body as he enters in the override code that gets us into the empty car and barreling back towards District Five at max speed.

Gifted

CHAPTER

*"The greatest crime that a citizen can commit is
the self over the good of Paramus."*

- The Chronicles of Discord

Linc seems to relax once the train is moving, and he leans
his head back against the wall, the yellow fluorescent lights
flickering overhead. He smirks at me playfully. "So, you haven't
figured out the train override codes yet?"

I shoot him a glare that only makes him smirk harder. I
briefly consider throwing something at him but decide that a
better use of my time is finding out more about what exactly led
to my rescue.

"How did you find me?" I ask. Now that I think about it, it
was shocking how quickly he was able to come to my aid. Almost
as if he had been there the entire time.

"I was following you," he admits, green eyes bearing into me.
"And I'm sorry if that seems weird. I just wanted to make sure
that you were safe." He scoots closer to me and rests his hand on
my knee. My skin feels warm beneath his palm and the thudding
in my chest matches the rhythmic sounds of the mag train. I try

to feel upset about him following me, but all I can think about is how nice it is to have him so close.

"I'm glad you were there," I answer honestly. I've never had anyone fight for me or fight so well. I had no idea that this charming, witty, Rebel spy was so capable of taking out two armed droids.

"Me too." His voice is soft, his other hand going to my hair as he tucks a stray piece behind my ear. "There's something that I need you to know," he adds, in a soft voice, his fingers tracing the line of my cheekbone, leaving a trail of tingling skin behind. "In the beginning, all I cared about was winning you over for the Rebels. But now …"

"… but now?" I repeat, anticipation hanging in every breath as I search the emerald depths of his eyes for the truth about how he feels.

"But now, you're here. And you're you. I've never met anyone like you," he admits shyly, his hands leaving my face and running a path through his already tousled hair. I realize that he's nervous, and little feelings of pleasure bubble through me at his words. I've never met anyone like him either.

"I've … been alone a lot," I admit slowly, working up the courage to find his eyes again, when I do, they are warm and inviting, urging me to go on. "You're different for me too. You said that you wanted me to trust you, and I want to. I just need to know something first."

"Okay." He watches me expectantly. I take a deep breath, hesitation gripping my chest. What if he doesn't say the words I want to hear?

"This … thing between us, is it real? I'm not just another mission, am I?"

I watch his face earnestly for clues, trying to get a good reading on the truth before he even responds. His expression changes first from surprise, to confusion, and finally, irritation. "Is that really what you think of me?" he exclaims so indignantly, rising to his feet. "Do you think that I'm just trying to manipulate you?"

I blink rapidly, the abruptness of his outburst still leaving me startled. "I—I just need to know for sure."

He sits back down, our knees touching, and takes both of my hands in his. His voice is earnest. "Then know for sure, Arin. I like you." His eyes are so full of passion that I can't look away. "It's not because the Rebel army or anyone else is forcing me to spend time with you. I like you because you're smart and beautiful and brave, okay?"

"Okay," I start hesitantly, the unfamiliarity of sharing my feelings like this out loud with another person is uncomfortable but somehow feels freeing at the same time. "I ... like you too." I take a deep breath and take one last look into his gemstone eyes before barreling on. "You ... make me feel like no one else ever has before. You make me feel ... valuable, and not just because of how smart I am or my Criterion score. From the day that I met you, you've made me feel good." He gives me a crooked smile, and when he answers, his voice is husky.

"I like the idea of making you feel good." Heat rushes to my cheeks and I want to hear more but the train is starting to slow. I glance out the window and recognize the familiar station of District Five. "It looks like we're here," Linc says, rising to his feet and offering me his hand. I take it, and together we exit the train, making our way carefully through the empty streets. When my old house comes into view, I feel myself starting to walk faster, eager to get home and see my parents' familiar faces. When we get to the front door, Linc releases my hand and gives me a reassuring smile. "I'll wait out here for you."

"Thanks." I can't help but smile back. I feel on top of the world after hearing Linc admit his feelings to me, and now I can't wait to get inside and hear how much my mom has improved from the medicine. I know that it's late, so when I step inside, I don't expect to find anyone stirring. But what I also don't expect, as I shut the door behind me, and travel down the hallway, is the sound of sobbing coming from my parents' room. I freeze, panic causing the blood in my veins to turn to ice. It's a sound that I've never heard before: a desperate, bone chilling cry. The sound of loss. I can't let myself try to imagine the reason. I just run, bursting through the door, full of alarm and not sure what I'll find, when I see the source of the sound. My father is at the foot of the bed, head in his hands, shoulders shaking as his entire body is wracked with sobs. He doesn't hear me come in—he is entirely consumed by grief. And I know why. I drop to my knees and a sob escapes my own lips as I see her there, in the bed, so still.

"Mom!" I cry, and the sound comes from deep inside me. From the child who was lost and found again; who found comfort in the warmth of her smile and the softness of her embrace. Every inch of me is shaking as I stare at her colorless body, eyes gently closed as if she is sleeping. But there is no rise and fall to her chest. I shake my head in denial. I can't believe that she's gone. I won't believe it.

"Arin?" My dad blinks up at me, face red and splotchy, eyes dazed. "Oh Arin, I'm so sorry." His eyes pour fresh tears and I have to blink through my own to see him. Somehow, we find each other, and his arms wrap around me what is supposed to be a comforting embrace, but I can feel that he is also trembling.

"She's gone?" I whisper, and uttering the words out loud feels unreal. If this isn't a dream, I don't want to live anymore. I just want to lie down. I just want to close my eyelids, let the sweet relief of darkness overtake me, and never open them again.

"I'm so sorry," my dad murmurs again, and I know that he is trying to comfort me, to somehow keep me from drowning in this sea of grief but it's hard to save another person when you yourself are drowning.

"What happened?" I manage, and I wrack my brain, thinking about how it had only been a matter of days since I saw her last. When I learned what the sickness truly was yesterday, I still had hope that the medications I brought her would at least slow things down. But this? It all happened so fast. And I wasn't here to say goodbye.

My father's voice sounds like he's in a far-off place. I wonder if he also feels like he is in a dream.

"She kept saying that she was tired, so very tired. So, I thought I'd let her sleep, I thought that maybe some sleep would do her some good. But when I came back—" He can't continue. And I don't want him to. The thought of my mom taking her last breath in this room, all alone, makes me feel sick. I know without question that my father feels the same way. And I can see from the sagging in his shoulders that he blames himself. I throw my arms around his waist and hold him until the salt from my tears soaks through his shirt. It's not his fault. But I know whose fault it is. I need to tell my father everything. So, I do.

We sit there, on the floor of the bedroom, holding each other, and I tell him about it all. The stories I share lend little bursts of much needed light in a room that before felt oh so dark.

I tell him about finding Tesa, meeting Marcus and Kace, and about how I'm not allowed to leave Cortex. I tell him about the Rebel man's sign and about how I stole the medicine for mom, thinking it would help. His eyes light up when I tell him about going outside of the wall with Linc, and about meeting Sol and Maz and Steele. My words seem to fill an empty void inside of him. I don't know how, but somehow, telling him everything, is helping. Then, at the very end, I tell him about Director Ellis and everything that I know about the sickness. It is then that I see some of the light fade from his eyes, replaced instead by anger.

It's not very often that I see my father angry; it's out of character for him. He has always been a steady confidant, with a positive outlook on life and a dash of good humor. But losing my mother has broken him. And I wonder, if what he's learned now, will be enough to push him over the edge. He's still for several moments, simply staring at my mother's spectral form on the bed. I sit in quiet anticipation, holding my breath, waiting for his reaction. Finally, he takes a deep breath, and utters his first words for what feels like centuries.

"You have to help them." His voice is solemn, and when he tears his gaze away from her to look at me, there are tears in his eyes. "It's what she would have wanted."

"Dad—" I start to protest, and he shakes his head.

"What Director Ellis has done is evil, there's just no other word for it. Your mother"—he has to pause to keep his voice from breaking—"did not deserve this. She loved those people so much. You've been out there, Arin. You know that Director Ellis is wrong about them. They don't deserve to die." Now it's my turn to shake my head. How can I make him understand that I agree with him? That I want to stop this genocide. I want to avenge my mother. But I'm just one person. I have no idea how to stop it.

"I don't know if I can, Dad. The Rebels' plan is to bring down the entire system. I'm not a soldier."

"No, you're not. But you are Gifted. You have the highest Criterion score ever recorded. I bet if anyone can figure it out, you can."

"I can't just take on Cortex and Director Ellis. What if I fail? They'll come for you." My father gives me a weary smile, and I see a glimpse of his old self; the dad that I'm used to, rises past all of the grief to the surface.

"So, what if they do?" He reaches out his hand to me, and when I take it, he pulls me in for a tight hug, resting his head on top of mine like he used to when I was a little girl. Transporting me to a time before I knew that things like genocides were real, or that people were thrown away because they didn't seem to matter. Back to a time when I had two loving parents, and all was right in the world.

He lets me go from the embrace, but still keeps hold of both of my hands, and holds my eyes with a steady gaze. "Sometimes, life requires you to be extremely brave, and you'll have a choice to make. You can choose to stay where it is comfortable and where it is safe, or you can choose to do something extraordinary." His face is earnest, and I recognize an emotion that I never thought could come out of such tragedy—hope. "Do something extraordinary, kiddo. I know you can." His words fall on my ears like sparks, bringing the kindling of a fire that I had burning inside of me already to a steady, roaring flame.

I have always wanted to protect my family, to provide for my mother and father, but it doesn't stop with just them. My father is right, there is something unique about me. I have scored the highest Criterion score ever recorded. And now the only reason that matters is because it means that I can have a purpose; something to use my intelligence for besides wealth and recognition. I have a job to protect not just for my parents anymore. I steal a quick glance at my mother's still body. I couldn't save her, but there are still plenty out there who can be saved, who must be saved.

I cross the room to my mother's tranquil form, free now from the worries of Cortex and Paramus and their bloodthirsty leader. I smooth her flowing brown locks and plant a quick kiss on the skin of her forehead before whispering a promise.

"I'm going to save them." This is my new purpose, and sears through me like a bolt of electricity, putting into motion every atom of my being. I can't believe I didn't realize it before. Of course, the Lost deserve to live. Not just outside of the wall, in isolation, but within the walls of Paramus. And that can only mean one thing.

The walls must come down.

Director Ellis must fall.

These truths are the new heartbeat inside of my chest, and they carry me away from my childhood home, away from my father, who clings to me tightly before I leave him all alone in our once happy home, out into the darkness of night where I find Linc waiting. He looks up at me in surprise.

"What happened in there? You were gone for so long," he says. I speak quickly, because so much has happened and because there isn't much time. A plan is slowly forming in my mind.

"I was too late. My mother is gone." As the words fall on his ears, I watch Linc's expression change from horror, to sadness, and then finally, concern.

"I'm so sorry," he murmurs, offering me comfort, but at this moment, it's not comfort that I want. I want retribution, a chance to write the wrong that has been done.

"Her death will not be in vain." I turn to Linc. "I want to help save them. Take me back outside the wall."

My second trip outside of the wall is very different from the first. Instead of a wide-eyed girl, full of curiosity and wonder about a brand new world, I am a woman on a mission. I barely register the tent like steeples of the Lost camp and my eyes do not linger on the speckle of fires. Instead, I stare straight ahead, fists clenched, jaw tight. The only emotion that I will allow myself to feel is anger, and it carries me beyond my sorrow, filling each step that I take closer to the Rebel command center with purpose.

When we reach our destination and I stand in front of Linc, Steele, Sol and everyone else in the command center, I speak with an urgency unlike I've ever felt before. If there's one thing I've learned tonight, it's that the virus works quickly. We don't have much time.

"I know that before I left, I said I couldn't help you, but things are different now." Steele watches me with a solemn expression, and in the corner, Linc gives me an almost imperceptible nod. I take a deep breath, it's hard, talking about the loss that I just experienced. My tongue feels rough in my mouth as I share with the group that my worst nightmare had occurred only hours ago. "My mother is dead. She was lost to Director Ellis' virus, an innocent life, stolen away, because of prejudice." I can feel myself trembling, but I push through the sorrow. There will be time to grieve once the Lost are saved. "I told you before that I thought you couldn't defeat Cortex, but I don't believe that anymore. I'm willing to do whatever it takes to bring Director Ellis down." I survey the room, my gaze coming to rest on Steele. "Tell me everything."

For the next couple of hours, we pour over the Rebel plans for infiltrating Cortex. Because the virus is distributed by microscopic nanobots, it can only be spread when the nanobots are activated inside of a particular person or group of people within a certain range. If we can stop Director Ellis from activating the nanobots, we can keep the virus from being released. But the nanobots are controlled remotely from a singular base computer.

I learn that there's already a program set in place to activate the nanobots exactly seven days from today. That means that the rebel soldiers around me, including Sol and Steele and everyone in the city, are all essentially ticking time bombs. Of course, that program is buried beneath layers and layers of firewalls that need a specific passcode to be accessed. A passcode that we don't have.

Sol has done a ton of research on the "trigger program" as he calls it, building an impressive holographic model of the layers and layers of security built in to protect it from outside forces. The most basic systems that I've played with generally have had only a single layer of security, but I've seen them get as high as four or five layers. Looking at it now, it appears that the trigger program has ten security layers protecting Director Ellis's precious kill switch. The swirling, multi-layer tower of defense hologram that Sol built is utterly amazing and I feel both intimidated and excited about the chance to try and get inside. Hacking something like this would be by far the most impressive thing that I've ever done, and I don't hesitate to share those concerns out loud.

"Arin, we've all seen what you can do," Sol reassures me with a toothy smile, and his praise makes me feel a little bit better. "Trust me, there isn't anyone more capable than you for this hack. You can do it." I want to believe him, I really do, but as I look at that security tower, I can't help but notice that my palms feel damp with sweat. Of course, I have to do it. I have no choice. My parents and everyone here are depending on me.

"The trigger program is held on a singular server and the hacking cannot be done remotely. As I mentioned before, there is a physical key that will need to be used at the exact same time as the internal hack. We can't get in without one or the other," Sol continues. The sweat on my palms is no longer alone as I feel droplets snaking down the back of my neck. I forgot about the physical key. This plan seems to be getting more and more difficult by the minute.

"How do we get the key?" I glance at Linc and the expression on his face is tense. When he responds his voice is careful and guarded.

"Director Ellis will be the only one with access to the key. She doesn't keep it on her person, so we need to figure out where she's keeping it." his eyes drop to his hands resting in his lap and I watch as his fingers find the matches in his pocket. He taps them nervously and for a minute no one speaks. Unanswered questions hang so heavily in the air that it's almost stifling to try and breathe.

What happens if we can't find the key?
What if we can't get into the trigger program?
What if any one of us is hurt ... or killed in the attempt to try and stop Director Ellis?
Or worse, what if we can't stop it, and the Lost are all murdered? What then?

"Linc will try to recover the physical key," Steele finally speaks and for the first time since I met him, he sounds like the commander of an army, the timber of his voice resonating down to my very bones. "Arin and Sol, you will be responsible for getting into the system and finding the kill switch. Expect resistance. This is war that we are talking about." I take a deep breath and use his determination to drown out the sound of my own fears. "There is a lot at stake here, and we are facing an enemy so evil that we can't possibly scratch the surface of what she is capable of. Do not underestimate her." His gaze comes to rest on me, and I feel a flutter of hope in my chest. "But do not underestimate yourselves either." He passes his gaze to each team member, stirring them with his optimism and steadfast belief. "You are not alone. Together we are strong. Together, we will bring down the wall."

I glance around the room. Sol is somber but nodding his head in enthusiastic agreement. Linc is a statue, his muscles tense with what I can only assume is determination for our cause, eyes focused on our leader. The rest of the soldiers scattered throughout the control room are also bracing themselves for the meaning of Steele's words. It's time for war. But this isn't a surprise. This is the thing that they have been waiting for. They are more than ready for Director Ellis's tyrannical reign to end. They are ready to sleep at night without the worry of a microscopic nanobotic virus lying dormant in their bloodstream, poised and ready to start shutting down their internal organs at any moment. They are ready to be free.

I am also ready to be free. Free from the fear of losing anyone else to Director Ellis' cruelty. Free from the fear of not being smart enough or good enough to take care of my family. Free from the pressure of everything being solely on my shoulders. There's this moment in hacking, a threshold, where you aren't where you came from but not exactly where you want to be. You're caught in this paradox, right before crossing the threshold into whatever it is that you're trying to reach. It's unknown before the other side. That's where I am now. Stuck between two worlds. One world where an old system and an evil ruler is in control, and I can just barely see a glimpse on the other side, where maybe people can be free. It's a place where at least my one living parent can be alive and well with me, and where maybe we can relearn everything that we thought we knew about humanity. All I have to do is cross the threshold and get there.

CHAPTER

"If you do not want your failures to define you, then do not fail."

- Paraminian Proverb

The city is just starting to stir when Linc and I make it back to the Cortex building. The sun's sleepy rays peeking over the top of the building, covering everything in a warm orange glow.

"Are you okay?" Linc asks when we are safely back inside our apartment, perhaps due to the fact that I feel like I'm so tired that if I close my eyes for even a second that I'm going to fall asleep right where I'm standing.

"I'm exhausted," I admit, I've been awake for almost forty-eight hours at this point, "but sleep is going to come easily tonight." I suppress a shudder. I don't think that it has truly sunk in that my mother is gone. I've had little time to process her death, and even less time to grieve. Heartache lurks in the shadows, ready to pound as soon I let my guard down. I know that the tears are coming, it's only a matter of time.

"Do you want some company?" Linc offers.

"Yes," I answer quickly, feeling immediately relieved. I don't want to be alone. He follows me to my bedroom and immediately begins to peel off his clothes, tossing them into the wall. I don't bother looking, the weariness inside of me has left me feeling nothing, and I'm still just as numb as he helps me out of my own travel clothes that are sticky with sweat and dirt. My eyes feel heavy as I climb into bed and bury beneath the covers, wishing for the escape of sleep.

Linc joins me shortly after, his body a warm presence beside me. He reaches for my hand and gives it a comforting squeeze, and I lie there for hours, long past the time that I hear Linc fall asleep, the rise and fall of his breath steady. I wish that sleep would bring me an escape but every time I close my eyes, I see her lying there, white as a ghost. I bite my lip to try and feel something other than the immense sorrow that comes with the sight of her, but it doesn't help. Finally, when I can hold it back no longer, the tears come. They come with the ferocity of the ocean, rolling down my cheeks in waves of guilt and regret and most of all, loss. I weep, silently in the dark, wishing that I could be with her. I would give anything to hear her voice again. If only I could tell her how sorry that I am, how I tried to be perfect, how I tried to save her. Eventually, sleep does come, but it's plagued with nightmares so vivid that I question what is real. After the nightmares comes a suffocating darkness, pressing on my chest and pushing me down deeper and deeper. Slowly I sink,

Down

Down

To the bottom of the ocean. The aching in my chest drowns me. Sadness filling my lungs until I can't breathe. The waves of regret are relentless as they batter my mind and body.

I should have saved her.

I should have stopped this.

I should have done better.

I should have been more.

I let the current of regret pull me under, and the swirling torrents of sorrow consume me, until all that remains of Arin is a shadow of a person that once was, back when I had a mother.

———————————○———————————

The days pass, and I struggle to feel anything but numb. I feel like I've lost a part of myself, and every day when I wake up, I struggle to believe that she is really gone. Even attending my mother's burial felt like a terrible dream. All of it, sneaking out once again, my pockets and my heart empty. Riding the train, clad all in black, keeping my face hidden in the daylight. Watching as my father signed the paperwork before the sanitation bots carried her away in a rough edged steel box. I kept waiting to feel her hand on my shoulder or catch a glimpse of her long brown curls.

Back at Cortex, I try keeping busy, throwing myself into my work on Veritas during the day and practicing hacking with Sol in the evenings. But even there I cannot truly escape. Too many things remind me of her. Life, for me, cannot go on as normal, because there is a hole inside of me that I fear will never go away. My friends try to be understanding, with Sol we only talk numbers and when he does venture to ask how I'm doing, my silence is enough to tell him all he needs to know. Kace stopped by to visit once and when Linc told her what happened her blue eyes had filled with tears. She stopped by multiple times to see me afterwards, but I always made an excuse, feigning business to avoid seeing her.

In the apartment, Linc gives me space. Looking at him makes my heart hurt even more. I know that he wants to be a source of comfort to me, but the reality is that there is nothing that he can do or say that will make me feel better. He can't bring my mom back.

Days turn into weeks, and the only thing that keeps me going is the knowledge that there is a way to get back at Director Ellis for what she took from me. Over time, my sadness turns to anger, and I find myself walking around with a perpetual frown, rage simmering close to the surface, ready to unleash on anyone who dares to get in my way.

"Hey. Coffee?" Linc greets me one morning when I arrive in the kitchen. He looks even better than usual, dressed in all-black moisture-wicking, athletic clothes that emphasize the outline of his muscles. I shoot him a look but accept the steaming mug that he hands me. He ignores the look and presses on, his voice serious.

"You might want to suit up." I glance down at the same grey sweatpants and Cortex T-shirt that has been my outfit of choice for more days than I care to remember. "Today we start on the physical part of your training."

I raise one eyebrow. Back at the Rebel headquarters, it was decided that, in addition to working to improve my, already excellent, hacking skills, Linc would also be training me in some basic defense, just in case I run into any problems while I'm doing my part in the control room.

I start to object but Linc stops me. "Physical training. Ten minutes." I slam my coffee mug in the sink, feeling a bit of satisfaction when I hear it shatter before I stalk off to my bedroom to change. I don't know where Linc got the idea that I take orders from him, but if he wants to give me the opportunity to hit something, he'd better get ready. I have a lot of rage that I am more than willing to let out.

When I return to the living room a few minutes later, dressed in similar black athletic wear, Linc informs me that we aren't going to be working with weapons, which is probably for the best. If Linc was to put a stun gun in my hand right now, I'd go straight up to the penthouse and not stop until it was pressed against Director Ellis' forehead. I smile, thinking about how satisfying it would be to watch her squirm.

"Ahem, today my goal is to improve your coordination and speed when dodging an attack." Linc's voice snaps me back to the present. "We are going to be dealing with artificial soldiers who will have more firepower and strength than you. So, you need to be quick. And you need to be smart."

I feel my lips curl up into a smirk.

I can do smart.

At first my movements are slow and clumsy, but with Linc's patient coaching and gentle encouragement, I start to get the hang of this new way of moving.

Duck, dodge left, dodge right, spin, arms up, head down.

Soon. I'm able to distinguish Linc's patterns and dodging his attacks comes more easily to me.

"You're a fast learner," he observes, leaning heavily against the living room wall and bringing a bottle of water to his lips for a long drink. I ignore the compliment, the pounding of my pulse making me feel more alive than I have in weeks.

"I want to hit something," I announce, and he eyes me warily before finishing his water bottle and meeting me back on the living room floor.

"Okay," he begins, picking up the nearest couch cushion and holding it up in front of him, feet planted firmly on the white carpet. "Show me what you got." Eyes narrowed, I take a deep breath, and, using my back foot as an anchor, I draw my fist backward, vision focused at the center of the cushion. I think about the sick tent outside of the wall, and the hopelessness in everyone's eyes. I think about the shaking of my father's shoulders.

Wham! I throw my entire body weight into the punch and feel satisfied at the resounding "oof" that comes from behind the couch cushion as Linc stumbles backwards, clearly caught off guard.

"Not bad," he mutters, lowering the couch cushion so that I can see his grin. I shake my head.

"I can do better. Let's go again." I ignore the stinging in my knuckles and ready myself for the next hit. Plant my foot, deep breath, aim. I strike again, and again, and again. Each punch channeling the anger that I feel inside. *Pow!* That one is for Tesa, whose future was so dark that she chose to end her own life rather than live through it. *Smack!* This one is for Sol, who was outcast because he wasn't physically perfect enough to be deemed worthy. *Wham!* A punch for my mother, who only wanted to help the needy, but you created a virus to attack her, simply because she wanted to make the world a better place. I blink, my vision blurry, and realize that there are tears streaming down my face. I wipe them away angrily with the back of my hands, which I now realize are shaking. One of my knuckles is cracked and bleeding, but I don't feel anything except the pounding in my ears.

"Arin." Linc gently sets the cushion down. "You're bleeding."

"I don't care!" I growl. "I'm not finished yet." My shoulders are heaving, and I greedily suck in air. I don't want to stop; I don't want to slow down. I have too much that I need to make atonement for. Linc doesn't argue but insists that I let him bandage my hand before we continue. At it once again, I throw myself into each punch, ignoring the pain in my side and the stream of sweat down my back. Strike, strike, jab. Strike, strike, jab.

I push until I physically can't anymore. My arms feel like lead when I finally drop them before collapsing to the floor, chest heaving. Linc tosses the bloodied cushion and quietly drops to the floor beside me. There's no sound other than the greedy gulps of air that I'm drinking in, heart racing. The sweat stings my eyes, or maybe it's the tears, as I stare up at the ceiling and picture my mother's last few moments. Was she sad that she was all alone? Did she wonder where I was? Where was I at that exact moment, instead of being by her side? Now I'm sure that the stinging is tears, but my arms are too tired to wipe them away.

"I should have been there." I blubber, and speaking the words aloud feels so relieving. They lift from my chest like weights, and I lie there, in a pool of sweat and tears, letting the words that I have been dying to say flow out of me. "If I hadn't been accepted into Cortex, I could have been at her side. I thought that Cortex was the best way to take care of my mom and dad. That's all I've ever wanted, to take care of them. But in the end, I let her down." Linc listens quietly, peering at me with those emerald, green eyes, showing no movement other than the rise and fall of his chest. One of his hands reaches for mine and I let him hold me, while I lie there on the floor, unleashing the weight I've been carrying for weeks. "It should have been *me*. If I was a good daughter, I wouldn't have been so obsessed with academia. I could have gone with my parents outside of the wall. It was because of me that they stayed inside of Paramus at all."

"If you lived outside of Paramus, then you would've all gotten sick," Linc points out softly.

"Yeah, well at least we would all be together," I mumble, bracing myself for a fresh wave of tears but they don't come. I struggle to sit up, even starting to feel the throbbing in my knuckles.

"Do you honestly believe that is what your parents would have wanted?" Linc hands me a clean bandage, and I peel off the old ones, wincing from the stickiness of the dried blood.

"I don't know," I shrug, but the truth is, my mom and dad had always encouraged me to pursue my dream of being accepted into Cortex. And they never doubted that I would.

"Well, I think that they wanted you to get into Cortex," Linc's words are soothing. "They were proud of you, Arin. Your mom was proud of you." I focus on wrapping the bandages tightly around my knuckles and blame that pain for the fresh tears stinging in the corner of my eyes. It just isn't fair. I did everything that I was supposed to and I still couldn't protect her.

"I just wish I could've been better." I sniffle, wiping my cheeks with my newly bandaged hand. Linc rests his hand on my leg and it sends a warm sensation through my body.

"Then be better." He says kindly, and I know exactly what he means. Linc is right. My mother was always proud of me, but she wouldn't be proud of me if she could see the way that I've been carrying on since I lost her. All the mourning that I've been doing has been for myself. I've been so absorbed in grief for my own loss that I've lost sight of who my mother truly was, and what she would have wanted, for me to put all of my efforts into helping the Lost.

"You're right." I turn to the man beside me, tracing the strong line of his jaw down to his slightly parted lips, and place my hand on top of his. "I think I'm okay now."

"Yeah?" He gives my hand a tight squeeze, eyes bright. "Good." He lets go of my hand to rub his arm, wincing. "I don't think that I could have taken much more punching." I grin, feeling like I can finally breathe again. He eyes me playfully. "You're stronger than you look." He cocks his head to the side. "But, did you actually learn anything today?"

I nod.

"Prove it." Linc smirks and, despite the protests of my aching arms, I push myself up off the floor and move through the steps that he taught me earlier.

Duck, dodge left, dodge right, spin, arms up, head down

Only this time, I anticipate his attack, and dodge early. He overshoots his attack and narrowly misses me. But now I am off balance and have no time to react as he plows into me with his left shoulder. We both go tumbling to the living room floor together.

My breath hitches as he lands on top of me.

His face is only inches from mine.

His floppy blonde hair matted with sweat.

He's so close. I can feel his heartbeat on top of me.

His deep green eyes burn into me, and we are both breathing hard.

I can hear his shallow breaths exiting his lips.

"I'm sorry that I've been such an ass," I admit sheepishly, my head dizzy from his closeness to me. I try not to dwell on how close his mouth is to mine, or the bewitching shape of his lips. He listens intently, eyes holding my gaze steadily.

"If I had to put up with anyone being an ass, I'd want it to be you." Linc breathes, face serious. "Who you are to me ..." He trails off for a moment and then shakes his head. "I've never felt this way about anyone before." He bites his lip and, for the first time in my life, I'm jealous of teeth. All I can think about at this moment is how I would do anything—anything—to have him finally close these last few inches between us. I want to taste his lips, more than anything.

His breathing is jagged, and his hand goes to my hair, fingers tightly entangling themselves with a purposeful determination. His eyes meet mine for one brief second, searching, until he gives in with a groan and I feel his lips press into mine, and all at once I'm breathing and not breathing.

His breath is hot in my mouth, taking over me. His lips are softer than anything I've ever known. He kisses me with a fierceness that I would expect from a rebel soldier, and when I lean against him, he holds me with ease. Tasting him makes me realize that my entire life, I have been starving. My life has always been missing something, and that something is Linc. His kisses make me feel like my whole body is on fire. Everything else burns away: my fears about not being good enough to save the people of The Lost City, gone. And there is only Linc, until finally, we break away and I'm left with electricity buzzing through my entire body and his voice whispering in my ear.

"You have no idea how long I've been waiting to do that," he admits and my entire body shivers with relief.

"I'm so glad that you did." I grin, staring into the emerald seas of his eyes, framed with long black lashes. It would be easy to get lost in their depths. I kiss him again, his hands tangled in my hair, and the sheer pleasure of finally getting to taste him, making me greedy. Now I know what I've been missing, and I don't want to stop.

But suddenly, there's a ding in my ears as I get a notification in my skin coms, partially blocking my view of Linc. I push him off me and he groans as I find the notification to take a closer look. My heart drops into my throat. It's marked as urgent with the presidential insignia. Director Ellis. I open it hastily.

"Good morning. There is something that I would like to speak to you about. I am sending you my location, please report there within the hour. Thank you." The sound of her voice in my head sends my skin crawling. The message ends, disappearing as abruptly as it appeared, and I can feel the color draining from my face.

"What's wrong?" Linc watches me with concern. I swallow, heart hammering, unable to answer as my mind comes up with a million possibilities about what Director Ellis could possibly want.

Does she know that I've been leaving Cortex? Or worse yet, sneaking out of Paramus? Does she somehow know that my mother was a casualty from her test run?

"Director Ellis," I say, my voice shaking, "she said that she has something important that she needs to speak with me about." Linc sits up abruptly, all former playfulness gone. He's on high alert now; I can practically see the wheels of his mind turning.

"What could she want?" His gaze follows me as I pull myself up to standing and smooth my hair, mind racing. There is no telling. Her tone gave no indication of the nature of the meeting. She didn't sound angry or pleased or suspicious. Just, cool, calm, and collected as always.

"I guess I'll find out." I bite my lip and he frowns.

"There's no way you're going there alone. I'll come with you." He jumps to his feet and I can see the pulse pounding in his neck, ready to attack, ready to defend me, but I shake my head.

"That will just raise suspicion. I go alone."

"No," he protests, clearly agitated. "You have no idea what you're walking into. I can't protect you if I'm not there."

"I'm sure it's nothing. She probably just wants to show me off to the council members again." I roll my eyes for effect, trying to show that I'm not concerned, but my insides are churning. Linc sees right through my bravado, the frown on his face deepening.

"What if she's somehow seen you sneaking out and tries to arrest you?" he asks. I shake my head.

"No way. The Rebels have been doctoring the feed for months. They wouldn't let that slip through."

"What if—" I raise my hand to stop him. Time is ticking. Director Ellis, the person who has taken so much from me and still holds the balance of power—for now—is waiting.

"We don't have time for 'what ifs', Linc. The Director is waiting." His eyes narrow and I can tell from the purse of his lips that he is not happy.

"Fine," he snaps. "Wait here." When he returns, he has a small parcel with him, wrapped in grey fabric that he hands to me. I shoot him a quizzical look before unwrapping it. A gasp catches in my throat. It's a knife. Linc takes the weapon from my hands and presses a small button on the side that causes it to vibrate in the air with a hum.

"This is a zeno knife," he explains, his voice solemn. "Stick it in your waistband and take it out only if you need it. It will cut through anything that you put in front of it, wire, metal, flesh." His words send a shiver down my spine. "If it comes down to it and you need to protect yourself, just slash like hell and run."

I take the knife again, feeling its weight in my hands before shooting Linc my most reassuring smile.

"Got it, slash like hell and run."

The room Director Ellis has instructed me to meet her at was Meeting Room C, located on the white level. I find her in the meeting room, standing at a large glass window which takes up the space of the entire back wall, looking out over the city. It's a strange feeling, looking at the woman who used to be a beacon of inspiration to me through the lens of her true nature. Knowing that she could murder an entire population of people out of cold blood. Knowing that she was solely responsible for my mother's death. I just want to scream at her, lunge across the table between us and press my zeno knife to her throat, to listen to her yelp as the blade starts to chew through her skin until she agrees to kill the nanobot program and keep her little monsters from hurting anyone else. But instead, I tap my knuckles lightly on the slightly opened door. "You wanted to see me?"

The Director turns to acknowledge me with a small smile on her lips, the expression in her eyes unreadable.

"Thank you for meeting with me on such short notice," she begins, turning from the window and taking a few slow steps toward me, icy blue eyes glued to my face. Her fingertips lightly brush the back of the nearest chair as she speaks. "There is something that has been on my mind for a while that I just had to speak to you about." A wave of nausea overwhelms me, and I quickly take note of where all the exits are in the room in case I need to bolt. But on the outside, I force myself to smile.

"I'd like to have you start working closely beside me." Director Ellis smiles warmly, and I try not to let the shock that I feel at her words register on my face. "I think that a mind as Gifted as yours should not be wasted. I have big plans for Paramus, and I could use your help." The lump in my throat makes it difficult to swallow. *Big plans for Paramus, like killing everyone outside of its walls?* I have to fight past the disgust that I feel toward her and instead, put on an enthusiastic face.

"Wow, Director Ellis, that is ..." I stammer, struggling to find the right words, "... such an honor. Thank you." Even though spending more time with her is the last thing I would like to do, working closely with her would give me the opportunity to gain her trust. *And hopefully find out where she keeps the physical key that we will need to disarm the defense computer.* Yes, a promotion like this could indeed be a very good thing.

"So, you accept?" The Director watches me with poised anticipation and I answer with an enthusiastic nod. She looks pleased. "Good, I'm glad to have you." She gives me one of her textbook smiles and reaches for a tablet resting on the table in front of her. "There is one thing, of course. If we are going to be working together, I need to know that I can trust you."

Her voice remains light, but the hidden implications of what she's saying cause my pulse to quicken. I try to keep my face expressionless as she reveals her true plan.

"The system that you helped create, the Veritas, will be a perfect way for us to do that. You'll get to see how well your newest invention works, and I'll be able to know for a fact that I can trust you."

I feel like my heart stops. I try not to audibly swallow in fear before I respond. "You want to use Veritas to look inside of my head?"

"That's not a problem, is it?"

"No," I answer carefully, trying to keep my voice nice and steady. "But I'll need to make sure it's ready. When would you like to use it?"

"Can you have it ready by tomorrow?"

"Of course."

"Tomorrow it is!" I can tell that Director Ellis is pleased; the smile that she offers me before she turns to go is almost warm. "I'm really looking forward to this," she calls before leaving me to attend to other important matters. I'm left standing alone in the conference room, heart in my throat and hands shaking.

Well, that makes one of us.

CHAPTER

*"The Gifted mind belongs not only to the individual,
but to the whole of the city and all of its leaders."*

- Articles of Axiom, Article XXIII Part G

"What did she say?" Back at the apartment, Linc runs over to me, the words flying out of his mouth before I can shut the door behind me. I swallow before turning to face him.

"She said that she wants to work more closely together."

He pauses before speaking again. "Okay." His brows furrow and he looks at me with a guarded expression. "That sounds like a good thing. But is it?"

"Well …" I try to swallow again but the words fight to stay stuck in my throat. "It's just that she made it very clear that before we can work together, she needs to make sure that she can trust me."

"What do you mean?" I can sense his uncertainty, and I wish that I didn't have to say what I'm about to say.

"Veritas, Linc." As soon as the words leave my lips, I can see the effect that they have on him. His face mirrors the exact emotion that I am feeling inside. Fear.

"She's going to look inside your head," Linc realizes, voice solemn.

"Yeah."

"What if she finds something in there about what we are planning?"

"I won't let her. I can—"

"We can't risk it." His tone sounds final, but I know deep down that I have to do it. If I suddenly refuse to participate, it will arouse suspicion, which we cannot afford. I can't jeopardize the plan with a sudden change in behavior. I can't jeopardize the safety of my father, or Linc. I glance at him. He is so beautiful, even looking as worried as he does right now. He has to be protected. I'll just have to be extremely careful.

Linc watches me intently.

"Arin, you understand why you can't do this," he tries to reason, pacing across the floor in front of me, but it doesn't matter. My mind is made up.

"I also understand what happens if I don't. I can't risk raising any amount of suspicion." I huff, feeling trapped by this entire situation. "I don't have a choice," I mutter and turn to go. I still have work to do on Veritas to make it ready for its test run tomorrow. On me.

"Wait." Linc grabs my arm to stop me, eyes sincere. "Doing this would be insane." He pleads. "You have to know that."

"I scored the highest ever Criterion score on record. I think I can handle Director Ellis."

Linc shakes his head, clearly not appeased.

"I disagree. Up until just a few days ago you had no idea what she was capable of. If you think that going there and letting her look inside of your head is going to be anything other than disastrous, then you're clearly still underestimating her."

"I don't have a choice here!" I reply, exasperated. "If I don't go, it will be just as big of a problem. At least this way, I have some sort of control about what happens."

I sigh, dropping my head in frustration. If only Linc would understand that there isn't any other way. The course of tomorrow has been written. And it hurts me to hear how much he doubts my ability to outsmart Director Ellis. I mean, sure, she's smart, but I'm smarter.

"We don't know that, and because we can't be certain, it's too much of a risk. I can't let you do it." Linc's voice is growing more and more adamant, and I briefly wonder if he plans to physically restrain me to keep me from going. I look down at his hand on my arm, gripping me as tightly as ever.

"It's not up to you Linc," I growl, yanking my arm away, surprising myself and him. "You're the one who picked me to be the one who has to save everybody. Just let me do my job!"

"Is that what you think? That this is all on your shoulders?" Again, he looks like he can't believe what he is saying, but that's not my problem. Linc could never understand the weight that I am currently carrying. I have so much to lose. One slip up, and everyone that I love is gone. "We are supposed to be a team, remember?" he says.

"I'm going tomorrow," I retort, turning to leave, face burning. "Don't try and stop me." Our cover here hangs in the balance. I don't have a choice. They picked me to be the wonder-girl. Sometimes that means making tough choices.

"I hope you know what you're doing!" he calls after me, but I don't answer.

I welcome the next several hours, pouring over Veritas, fine tuning and polishing, anything to distract me from that last exchange with Linc. I don't regret what I said necessarily; it needed to be said. But I'm worried that this is something that we aren't going to be able to ever recover from.

It's strange, perfecting the machine that in less than twenty-four hours is going to be used against me. It's not Veritas's fault, it's a magnificent creation, and in some ways, I feel a lot of pride towards the machine in front of me. But while every piece that I finish brings a sense of accomplishment, it's also another step closer to letting Director Ellis inside of my mind—and that is something that I am less confident about.

When there are no longer any improvements that I can make, and I can no longer delay the inevitable, I turn off my equipment and stretch. Distracting myself with finishing Veritas helped a little, but I'm still not looking forward to what will probably be, at the least, a quite uncomfortable encounter between Linc and I when I get back to the apartment.

As I leave the lab, I note that the halls around me are empty. I don't run into another single person on my way back to the apartment, which I find odd, even at this late hour. Is there something going on? A mandatory meeting that I was supposed to attend? I feel a knot start to grow in my throat and my steps carry me a little bit more quickly as I hurry home.

"Hey," I mutter as I let myself in the door, bracing myself for the worst, but Linc doesn't answer. His eyes are glued to the large holo-screen in our living room, where Director Ellis is in the middle of a live broadcast.

"—don't know much about this disease, but only that it is highly contagious and that so far it has not crossed over the wall at this time."

I stare at the crisp, flawless image of our leader with what looks like sympathy in her eyes and feel my heart sink. Linc notices my presence and greets me with a somber nod, eyes serious, before turning back to look at the screen.

"It is our duty as citizens of Paramus to not let this disease spread into our beautiful community. If anyone within our walls is caught having contact with the Lost, potentially infecting our fellow citizens and endangering innocent lives, the penalty, unfortunately, will be death."

My eyes are frozen on Director Ellis's holographic face as my mind registers all of the implications of the statement that she is making to the entire city. Few things in Paramus have ever carried the weight of the death penalty. I swallow. *And this particular thing happens to be something that I do pretty regularly.* Linc waves his hand to clear the broadcast with a look of disgust on his face.

"Just when I thought I couldn't hate that woman more than I do already." He grunts, dropping onto our shared white couch angrily. I sink down onto the pristine leather a few cushions away, my insides churning. What does Director Ellis's announcement mean for us? I hear the announcement end, and the holo-screen disappears. I glance at Linc, who is staring at the now empty wall where the holo-screen was just on display, lost in thought. I want to say something, but I'm unsure about how to act. I decide to just focus on the issue at hand.

"The death penalty. I can't believe it," I venture, and when he looks up at me his eyes are expressionless, impossible to read. "Exile, I could understand. But threatening Paramus' citizens with death?" A little shiver runs down my back. "I mean, first the Lost, and now this. Where does it end?"

"It won't. It doesn't with people like her." Linc's eyes finally flicker with an expression that I recognize. Anger. "She's trying to cover her tracks by telling everyone about the Lost sickness. That way, when they all start dying, no one will suspect foul play." His voice is hard, and his hands begin to ball into fists.

"Hey." I touch his arm and he looks at me in surprise, like he has forgotten where he is. "They're not going to die. No one is going to die." *Except us if we get caught sneaking outside of the wall again.* "Obviously the stakes are even higher now. We just need to be careful."

"So do you agree then that you can't let her use the Veritas on you tomorrow?" Linc replies.

I sigh, feeling my frustration growing as we revisit the issue from earlier. "No, I told you, I've already made up my mind. I have to go."

"I know," he says quietly, and my anger instantly deflates. He looks down at the couch cushion in worried silence and I know that we are both thinking the same thing. If Director Ellis is able to see anything about my contact with the Lost, she can have me executed. When he looks up, there's a worry line between his brows. "If anything happened to you—"

"It won't," I cut him off. "I promise." My fingers find the familiar warmth of his hand and he gives my hand a squeeze. We sit like that for what feels like an eternity, holding hands quietly in the dark, both of us consumed with our own worries but neither willing to give them a voice. *I hope that I made a promise that I can keep.* The list keeps growing of people that I can't possibly let down. My parents, the Lost, and now Linc, it's a lot of pressure. My free hand goes to my necklace and I twirl it in the dark.

I'm like a diamond. Perfect under pressure.

CHAPTER

"The truest pursuits are knowledge, justice, and peace."

- The Articles of Axiom, Article XVIII Part D

Director Ellis has instructed me to meet her on the red level, and as I step off the elevator on the fourth floor, I note that it's significantly colder here—or perhaps I'm shivering for an entirely different reason. I've tried unsuccessfully to get rid of the knot in my stomach since I left the apartment, but to no avail. It looks like I'm bringing it with me.

When I enter the medical lab, Director Ellis is already waiting. It's strange, seeing her dressed in a lab coat and sterile gloves for the first time, trading her usual neutral-colored dresses-and-heels ensemble for a crisp white lab coat and a clipboard.

"Right on time." She nods approvingly. "Please, have a seat." She gestures to the exam table between us, apparently not interested in wasting any time. "Excellency and Innovation" alright. The grey fabric is cold against my skin and I try not to flinch as I settle in, careful not to disturb the scanner's arm dangling above my head.

"I cannot express to you enough how much I'm looking forward to watching your creation at work." Director Ellis speaks not directly to me, but addresses the room, as if she's giving a lecture to a large group of people. I glance around, but as far as I can tell, we are the only two people here. The Director states today's date and the time as she flips on the scanner and brings it from my abdomen all the way up to the crown of my head. Ah, she must be recording the session.

"Today we will be administering a series of questions and then we will measure the legitimacy of the subject's answers." The word "questions" makes me nervous; I'm not sure what kind of questions that she will be asking, but I do know that I need to make sure that I'm on guard for whatever they may be.

Director Ellis explains that we will start with a series of warm-up exercises that involve her attaching several electrodes to different spots of my head and arms. I can feel little beads of sweat pooling behind my knees as she attaches the electrodes and I wonder if she can tell that I'm nervous.

"This screen here"—she points to a holo-screen that blinks to life at her mention of it—"will display real time pictures of your thoughts. For example, try thinking about a tablet." I try not to look horrified as Director Ellis explains about the literal projection of my thoughts for her to observe and draw conclusions from. Oh, this is not good. This is not good at all. I glance over at Director Ellis who is staring at me expectantly. Shit, what did she tell me to do? Tablet! That's right.

Picture a tablet. I close my eyes and concentrate. The smooth white glass body. The soft blue glow of the screen. The happy chirp that the tablet would make after getting the right answer on an equation. My father helping me to find solutions with me after school in the evenings. Sitting by the fireplace.

"Ahem!" My eyes snap open, Director Ellis is tapping her foot impatiently. She points to the screen. "Try to stay within the parameters for these first few exercises please. I just asked for a tablet."

"Sorry," I rush to apologize, surprising myself, I think, as much as I do Director Ellis. The memory came to the surface so easily, just slipped right out onto the screen. I need to be more controlled.

"Let's get started, test question number one, what is your name?" I have to lick my lips in order to get any sound out. *Do not reveal anything about the plan. Do not reveal anything.*

"Arin Wells." I remind myself to take a deep breath and try to slow my heart rate; the electrodes are monitoring everything. There is no logical explanation as to why I would be nervous. There's nothing to be nervous about. It's just my name. We both stare at the screen expectantly. An image of me emerges, or rather, an image of a version of me. The girl on the screen has exaggerated features. Wide, unblinking eyes stare back at us; she looks plain, almost as if an artist did a real-life rendering but forgot to add the color. Nothing about the girl on the screen looks exceptional or even noteworthy. Easy to miss in a crowd. Is that how I view myself?

Director Ellis doesn't seem as interested in the image and presses forward. "How are you enjoying your time here at Cortex?" This one is a little more complicated. Immediately my mind flashes to Linc, and I have to quickly transform the image into a regular setting. Linc with me, alone, is not okay. Linc working in front of me in the Research and Development laboratory, is better. I watch the image on the screen change from just his face to a more obscure image of him and some of my other colleagues in our usual work setting, which is more acceptable.

"I'm learning a lot," I answer truthfully, and Director Ellis nods her head thoughtfully.

"What makes a person great?"

I bite my tongue. "Success."

"What motivates you to succeed?"

I know what I'm expected to say, and I try to sound as convincing as possible when I recite the familiar words. "I want to make my city, my family, and myself proud, by being the best."

"Do you believe that you are the best?"

"I … yes."

"What makes you the best?"

"My determination to achieve."

"Do you believe that there will ever be anyone as great as you?"

"No." These are the answers that she wants to hear—and the beliefs that I have been wrestling with since I first stepped foot in The Lost City. I blink and quickly change my train of thought, praying that no Lost City-related images appeared on the screen. If there was anything suspicious, Director Ellis gives no apparent reaction.

"Tell me about your childhood."

"My childhood?"

"Yes, much can be learned about a person and their motivations from their upbringing."

"I see, okay, my childhood." I force myself to take a deep breath, exhaling slowly to laser my focus in playing the good citizen. Which story should I tell? "I had a pretty traditional childhood; from the very beginning my parents taught me the importance of achievement."

"Two parents in the household?" I swallow.

"Yes."

"What are their names?" This question is dangerous. The holo-screen in the corner of my eye burns a hole into me with it's dangerous potential. What image will I recall of them? I think of the single picture that I brought with me to Cortex, the one of my mom and dad and I on our picnic, happy and healthy.

"My mother's name is Lara and my father's name is Timothy." I try to remember the way that I felt that day; how the moment felt so perfect, that we decided to preserve it in time forever in a photograph.

"What do you remember the most about your childhood?" A droplet of sweat from behind my knees snakes down my leg and I try not to react. This line of questioning is making me increasingly nervous.

"I remember wanting nothing more than to become a Cortex employee. It is all that I have ever wanted, and now I'm here, and I feel very proud of myself and my accomplishments."

"What do you think that your greatest accomplishment will be?" This is a tricky question, because I'm not sure how driven Director Ellis wants me to be, since this is basically an interview to be her number two.

"My greatest accomplishment will be my contributions to Paramus. I want to make the city the best that it can be," I answer carefully, trying to ignore the fact that with each passing second my mind is having to struggle more and more against the power of Veritas, which threatens to unearth my true thoughts, my genuine answers. This one was almost too close. It's true that I want to make the city the best that it can be—and that means getting rid of the person standing right in front of me.

"Well, that is good to hear." Director Ellis nods thoughtfully, almost as if she is lost in her own train of thought. "It is undeniable that there is something special about you. You've displayed tremendous intelligence since primary school. Your records show nothing but accomplishment and hard work, and you've been flourishing in your position here since you started. It's almost like you've always had a particular ... agenda. Do you have an agenda here at Cortex, Arin?"

My heart starts to race so quickly in my chest that I'm worried that I'm going to go into cardiac arrest right here in the conference room. I have to remind myself to breathe, to try and remember that Director Ellis couldn't possibly be talking about what I think she is talking about. She is, however, watching me intensely, so I force myself to put on as innocent a face as possible.

"I'm not sure I know what you mean," I answer carefully.

Director Ellis smiles coyly. "Oh, don't be modest. Anyone who watches you can see what you're up to."

I can barely hear her over the pounding on my heart in my ears. "And what is that?"

"You want power," she boasts proudly. A wave of relief washes through me and I can feel my clenched shoulder muscles relaxing. *Director Ellis has no idea about my involvement with the Lost. She thinks that I am just another power-hungry Gifted.*

"I see a lot of myself in you, Arin," she continues. "You've got the kind of determination and intelligence that makes me believe that you could really be an incredible ally." My eyes widen in surprise. I wasn't expecting that.

"In my life I've had to make some tough decisions, some more difficult than others." I feel myself freeze. Is she referencing her decision to commit genocide? Director Ellis stares off into the distance, looking over my head somewhere. I try to keep my mind empty as I watch her with growing curiosity. "I suppose I learned that from my parents. I was never quite good enough for them. I never understood the hard decisions that they made when I was growing up. In fact, there were times when I hated them for it. But now I understand, sometimes you have to make hard decisions if you want to get where you want to be. But you understand that, don't you, Arin? That's why I believe that you and I are a lot alike. Don't you agree?" I can hear the approval in Director Ellis's voice, but it coats my ears like slick black oil. I want nothing to do with her praise and I do not agree. We are nothing alike. I could never be capable of ... I grit my teeth against the disorienting effect of Veritas. I need to keep my thoughts from going there, lest I be betrayed by the screen on display in front of Cortex's leader. I glance at the screen as it swirls with unintelligible images, silhouettes of things that at any moment could clear and reveal all. Has anything come through that has exposed me already?

I glance at the face of the woman who may in fact be my greatest enemy, who says she wants to be allies, searching for any hint of deception. But I find only a sort of expectant waiting as I remember that she has asked me a question.

"Yes," I answer after what feels to me like an eternity. I can taste the tiny beads of sweat on my upper lip as I continue to watch my prosecutor, her expression unchanging. She alternates between examining my face, expression watchful and observing and then glancing up at the Veritas screen, almost as if she is trying to find the hidden meaning in both. I hold her gaze steadily. Today, nothing will be revealed.

Satisfied, Director Ellis gives a tight nod and turns off the machine. "I think that I found out all that I needed," she says pleasantly but her words send my heart racing in my chest. Was there something that I let slip through? I wonder as she removes the various electrodes from my body, and I raise myself to a comfortable seated position. The back of my shirt is sticky from the amount of sweating that I did on the table and I can feel goosebumps spread up my neck and down my arms as the temperature in the room is a little crisp and the sweat begins to cool.

Director Ellis pays no attention to me as she busies herself with putting her various tools away and cleaning up our area. I watch her expectantly. Will she call for droids to escort me to a new life of imprisonment? Did I let something slip about my connection with the Lost that will lead to my execution? Or does she think that I did well, in which case I might find myself in a new and important position?

Finally, she turns to address me, brown eyes sharp and unblinking. I brace myself, hoping that she cannot hear the audible pounding of my heart in my chest. "Arin Wells," she says clearly, her voice ringing throughout the chamber, "welcome to my team."

The next morning, I stare wide-eyed at the opulence around me, standing in stark contrast to the functional, sterile, hospital-like layers of the rest of the building. The uppermost level of the Cortex building has glass ceilings arched above my head at dizzying heights. Beautiful trees, flowering bushes, and flawless landscaping compete for my attention against intricate, hand-carved bridges, bubbling fountains, and crystal-clear bodies of water. As far as the eye can see, is a diverse, indoor ecosystem, made up of jungles, beaches, gardens and ponds. It's a landscaping masterpiece.

Rows and rows of extravagant buildings stacked with what I can only assume are plush executive suites face the atrium, built with gigantic windows, to give their occupants a breathtaking view of the beauty around them. It's incredible just how opulent life is for Director Ellis and the city council. It makes my apartment back on the blue level look like a closet.

A sparkling clean sidewalk guides my feet to the last building on the street, which is the most impressive of them all. It is a geometric wonder. A large, black frame juxtaposed with smaller, white pieces, together with an intimidating mix of angles and panels of glass. It is breathtaking, but in a cold and dangerous way. *Perfect for Director Ellis.* It's my impression that the entire building belongs to the Commander in Chief, the only entry a solid black door that towers above my head. A quick eye-screen grants me entrance and I'm greeted by a service drone.

"Arin Wells, Ms. Ellis has been expecting you." The drone's voice is quiet in the cavernous hallway, the shining black marble floor beneath my feet causing my footsteps to echo. The hallway is lit only by a single chandelier overhead, its black diamonds twinkling in the dim glow. "Right this way." I follow the droid into an impressive chamber, possibly a den, where a roaring fire crackles over a bed of diamonds and all of the furniture is made of glass. Despite the presence of the fire, I feel a chill start to seep into my bones.

"Welcome," Director Ellis's voice booms from behind me, filling up the room as she enters. She looks very smart in an all-black pantsuit with a white collar poking out from underneath, a heavy fur draped around her shoulders. I stare in shock. I'm not sure the wall makes furs. Her heels click against the glossy floor as she makes her way to the seat across from me, sinking effortlessly onto the asymmetrical glass surface. "Thank you for meeting me here."

"Of course," I answer shakily, and try not to stare at the animal hide accessory. "Your home is ... exquisite." She dips her head graciously, but I can tell that she is proud of the shrine of intimidation that she has created.

"Thank you. It's taken some time, but I wanted this place to be perfect." A smile plays on her lips. "They say that one's home is an outward reflection of the inner thoughts of one's mind." *I wonder if that is true.* I think back to my childhood home, with its cozy furniture and cheery decor that stands in stark contrast to the severe chamber around me. If this is a reflection of Director Ellis's mind, then her mind must be a very dark and cold place indeed. "I thought that for our first activity together, you could accompany me on a visit to all of the members of the council. Tomorrow we will be putting a certain ... proposition to vote that I've put before them. I'd like to make sure that they will be voting correctly." I have to fight the urge to narrow my eyes.

Does voting really matter when all of the council members are being either persuaded or blackmailed into voting a certain way by Director Ellis?

I turn my head, startled, as I hear another set of footsteps enter the room. "You remember Kace, my assistant."

"Yes." I glance at the beautiful girl as she glides to Director Ellis's side. I try to catch her gaze to give her a quick smile, but her eyes are glued to the ground, which I find troubling. I feel a pang of guilt in my chest. I've been so caught up in everything lately with my mother and the Lost that I haven't been replying to any of her messages. As soon as I get the chance, I need to apologize and ask for my friend's forgiveness. Could the fact that I hurt her feelings be the reason for her current behavior? She stands with shoulders sloped and eyes down, in direct contrast to the bubbly, outgoing self I know.

"Kace will help us secure Councilman Wing's vote, and that leaves only Councilman Hornburg and Councilman Vos with votes unsecured. We will pay them each a visit, and you'll get a front row seat into the heart of politics."

I glance at my friend, who is still studying the glossy white floor. "Why send Kace?" I ask. "Wouldn't it be more persuasive to make the visit yourself?"

Director Ellis shakes her head dismissively. "Not really, Councilman Wing has more of a preference for petite blondes and a soft spot for Kace." She adjusts one of the buttons on her sleeve before turning to my friend. "You'll get the vote, won't you dear?"

"Yes."

"Very good." Director Ellis stands. "Arin, you and I had better get going. Kace, you are dismissed." Kace turns and exits the room without so much as an acknowledgement of my presence. *Is she pretending not to know me because Director Ellis is here?*

"We have a very full schedule today but there is one quick stop that I'd like to make along the way," continues the Director. "Have you ever seen the broadcasting studio?" I shake my head, before she gestures for me to follow her out of the great room, down the cavernous hallway and out the door. I have to work hard to keep up with her fast pace, and even faster way of speaking. "One of my proudest responsibilities as leader are the broadcasts that I get to give to the people. It's an incredibly humbling opportunity, being given the chance to shape the perspectives of every person in Paramus," Director Ellis boasts in a way that gives me the impression that there is nothing humbling about it. "You'll see that out of every component that makes up our great city, the one that matters the most, are the opinions of the people." As we make our way through the magnificent atrium and towards the glass elevators, my heart races from Director Ellis's long strides but also from her words. Something about what she is saying doesn't sit right with me. "I've worked hard to craft an image that the people respect, and I would do anything to protect that image." It sounds almost like a thinly veiled threat. Little warning bells go off in my mind and I sneak a glance at her face, but her expression remains neutral, revealing nothing.

We take a short ride in the glass elevator down to the silver level, but instead of walking in the direction towards the labs, Director Ellis takes a sharp turn to the left and stops outside of a pair of double doors. A quick retinal scan grants us access, the doors parting with a hiss. The air inside of the small room is stale, and I get the impression that it is not frequently visited. The interior is dark, filled with mounds of technical equipment and when Director Ellis flicks on the lights. A set of blinding bulbs illuminates the recording area. Director Ellis positions herself in front of the camera and gives it a collected smile. "This is one of my favorite places in the city," she brags, gesturing for me to join her. Reluctantly I move to her side, squinting from the glare of the overhead lights. "If you could say anything, what would you tell the people?"

My heart races, and the heat from the lights starts to make little drops of sweat pool in the tight parts of my clothing. *I would tell them that their leader is a monster.* I clear my throat.

"I'd tell them to keep looking forward. That the best is yet to come."

Director Ellis seems pleased with my answer and I find myself feeling relieved when the glare of the studio lights fade and we leave the broadcasting room behind. Director Ellis was right. There is a lot of power in that room; power that could be used for good or evil. I wonder what it would feel like to stand in front of that camera and tell the people about Director Ellis? To reveal to them that her carefully constructed image of a capable and just leader was all a lie?

Our next stop is Councilman Vos's house, back on the white level. His mansion is not nearly as large as Director Ellis's, but what it lacks in size it makes up for in opulence. Every surface is gilded in gold or sparkling marble. It's like nothing I've ever seen before. The councilman is expecting us, and agrees to hear our petition in his study, where we are guided by one of his many human servants. The mansion is filled with human help, as opposed to androids, which I find to be unusual. The study is padded with a luxurious red carpet underfoot and smells like a mix of spice and cigar smoke. Councilman Vos extends one hand to us in greeting from behind his colossal mahogany desk, gold rings sparkling. I shake his extended hand, feeling slightly nauseated by the lavishness around me. I think about how the Lost are forced to scrummage through the city's waste for basic necessities. As we take our seats, the councilman observes us with an amused expression, his narrow eyes unblinking. When he finally speaks, there is a velvety tone to his voice.

"I thought that you might be paying me a visit today." He presses the tips of his fingers together and watches Director Ellis expectantly. "Could it be because we are going to be voting tomorrow on your new proposition?" He glances at me. "Who is this?"

"She's with me," Director Ellis says simply and the councilman nods. "I cannot underestimate the importance of your vote in favor of my proposition tomorrow, so, I brought you a token of my appreciation." I watch in dismay as the councilman extends his gold ring clad hand, and Director Ellis drops a dozen coins made of solid gold inside. "I trust this should cover it?"

"Consider my vote secured," Councilman Vos says with a smile, carefully placing the coins in his desk drawer. We turn to go. "Oh, and if you're looking for votes, Wing might like that one." He calls to our retreating figures and I feel myself shudder, golden doors closing behind us.

I am silent as we climb the steps to Councilman Hornburg's home, which although nearly a block away from Councilman Vos, was still not enough distance between myself and that man. Director Ellis hasn't said a word since we left either and I wonder what she thinks my opinion is of what I just witnessed. Of course, it's appalling; people in power bribing one another with money and favors to get what they want. How could anyone see it any other way?

"Councilman Hornburg takes some getting used to," Director Ellis warns me as she identifies herself to the Councilman's building and the old doors creak open. Where Director Ellis's home was cold and inhospitable, and Councilman Vos's home was opulent and overly lavish, Councilman Hornburg's home is dusty and has the appearance of something that has been sitting for hundreds of years. The floorboards creak beneath our feet as we let ourselves in; there are no servants, human or android, to greet us. "Alistar?" Director Ellis's powerful voice sounds small as we step into a vast room, adorned from floor to ceiling in portraits of angry-looking men and tapestries depicting stories of battles from long, long ago. I recognize an actual suit of armor in the corner, a relic that must have been preserved by the founders of Paramus. How did something so valuable end up here? We find Councilman Hornburg in an otherwise empty dining hall, sitting at the end of a long table that could easily sit twenty. He seems preoccupied with finishing his rich meal of several different types of meat and savory side dishes piled on top of each other. My own growling stomach reminds me that it must be close to lunch time. "Allistar?" Director Ellis repeats and he looks up from his meal, a scowl on his face.

"What do you want?" His voice is gruff and there is gravy in his white moustache.

"I apologize for the intrusion, but this shouldn't take long." Director Ellis pulls up a seat for herself at the table and gestures for me to do the same. "How is your meal?"

"It was fine until I was interrupted." He frowns, bushy white eyebrows knitted together in disapproval. "Now enough pleasantries. What is this about?"

Director Ellis raises one eyebrow but otherwise makes no reaction to his unpleasant tone. "I'm simply here to make sure that you'll be voting in favor of my proposition tomorrow." The old man studies her, looking interested in our company for the first time.

"What's in it for me?" Director Ellis removes an imaginary speck of something from her sleeve.

"I heard that you were trying to change the dynamic of the way we hold council in Paramus. Instead of five equal members, you had proposed that one member reside over the others, as a sort of head councilman"—she glances up at him to see if she has his attention—"and I couldn't agree more. However, there is only one person fit for that role and it is you, Alistar." The councilman looks positively giddy. He rubs his hands together and flashes a set of yellowing, crooked teeth. "Now if you were to do me a favor tomorrow and vote to pass my little proposition, I would be more than happy to see to it that you secure that seat." Councilman Hornburg slams his hand onto the table, making the dishes clatter.

"Consider it done."

"It's a pleasure doing business with you," Director Ellis says smoothly before striding out of the room, satisfied that she had in fact secured all three councilmen's votes. And as soon as we are outside of Councilman Hornburg's door, she turns to me, clearly pleased. "And that is your first lesson on politics. I hope that you learned something today."

I nod. I certainly learned a lot today about the corruption that runs deeply in the heart of Paramus' leaders. But there is one thing I haven't learned. What exactly is in the proposal that Director Ellis has been referring to?

"The proposal tomorrow ... what is it?"

"It's a proposal to limit waste and spending in transportation," she says matter-of-factly, and I frown. There isn't anything sinister or important sounding about that. Why go through all of the trouble? "Do me a favor, before you leave the white level, stop by Kace's home and make sure that she was able to get the vote from Councilman Wing. I want to make sure that there are no surprises tomorrow." I nod again, turning to leave. "Oh, and Arin," she calls over her shoulder, brown eyes narrowed. "I hope you saw today that everyone's loyalty has a price. Don't think I don't know yours."

CHAPTER

"Beauty should only be reserved for the Gifted,
as they are the only ones who can truly enjoy it."

- Chronicles of Discord

Every part of me is shaking as I make my way to Kace's building. *What did Director Ellis mean that she knows the price for my loyalty? Was she referring to my father? Linc?* The sun has long set, and the starlight overhead is blocked out by the overflow of foliage in the atrium's upper canopy, making the pathway dark and foreboding. I have a lot of things that I need to figure out, but I can't move forward until I find my friend and apologize for my long absence. Rehearsing the words that I need to say, I rush to Kace's door, number eight, and give it a tentative knock. There's no answer. I try the eye-screen, and to my surprise, it grants me access.

"Kace?" I call, taking careful steps inside. No lights are on when I take cautious steps across the threshold. *Maybe she isn't here?* There is no sign of Kace as I walk further into her home, past the baby grand piano, past the aquarium. The opulent chandelier overhead shakes slightly with each footstep, and I consider leaving before I think I hear a sound from the room on my left. It sounds like soft sobbing coming from behind the door. I swing it open quietly. "Kace?" I repeat, and I find a figure that I assume must be my friend crouched over a basin of water, her blonde void of its normal bouncing curls. Instead, it is a waterfall of tangles, cascading down her shoulder and effectively hiding her face from me. I take a hesitant step closer as I can hear the occasional sniffle from behind the wall of hair. She must have been the one crying in here.

"Hey, it's me, Arin," I offer quietly before reaching out a hand to touch one slender shoulder. But as my fingertips near her skin, I find myself frozen. Her normally perfect complexion is speckled with deep purple and green bruises that send a wave of nausea through my stomach. "Kace," I repeat, this time touching her shoulder with my fingertips as my heart breaks for my friend. "What happened to you?" She flinches when I touch her at first, but she seems to relax once she remembers it's me. With shaking shoulders, she takes a deep breath and brushes her hair aside. My stomach drops one hundred stories when her golden hair parts and I take in the remainder of what used to be the most beautiful face in Cortex. Now, pained blue eyes, full of sadness, look up at me, ringed in angry purple. The angelic-like bow of her lips has been busted open, leaving them swollen and painful looking. There's a scratch across her cheek that looks angry and red, and a pathway of bruises around her neck that connect to the cluster that I noticed earlier on her shoulder like constellations against her milky white flesh.

"Councilman Wing?" I wonder incredulously, horrified by the abuse in front of me. "He did this to you?"

She nods. "Like he always does."

"Kace, have you told anyone about this?" I ask. "He should be imprisoned!" I can feel my anger start to boil beneath the surface. How dare anyone do something like this to another human being?

"It won't help." Her normally bubbly disposition has vanished and is replaced with a kind of hopelessness that is heavy and unshakeable. I want nothing more than to wrap my friend up in my arms and never let go. If no one else will protect her from this, then I will.

I watch as she takes sad, slow steps over to her vanity to retrieve a small canister of spray skin. She sits down in front of the mirror and begins to coat her face with new skin, wincing as it seeps into the open wounds. She does this methodically, as if she has done this a hundred times before, and my heart breaks even more.

"Hey." I cross the room so that she can see me in the vanity and place my hand lightly on her shoulder. She doesn't look up from her work, but I know that she is listening. "This isn't okay. It doesn't have to be like this."

"What do you know?" She whimpers, brushing my hand away. "You're the wonder girl. You're valuable. Your own parents didn't sell you into slavery because you weren't smart enough to earn coin." I freeze, and suddenly my hand on her shoulder feels more like a violation. The horrific realization that all this time, Kace had to listen to me talk about how only the Criterion gives a person value and watch me be praised by Director Ellis repeatedly for my brilliance, while she was enduring this torment chills me to the bone. And what did she do to deserve to be treated like this? Just because she isn't "Gifted"? I feel sick to my stomach.

I can't believe that I was such a careless friend. Kace has never been anything but kind to me. I wish that there was a way to make her understand that I don't believe that way anymore.

"Kace, I'm so sorry. You're right, I don't know anything. I had no idea. I'm an idiot." I hope that my friend can hear the sincerity in my voice, and to my relief when I look back at her in the vanity reflection, the corners of her lips are turned up into the slightest suggestion of a smile. I feel a weight crumble from my shoulders.

"You're not an idiot," she says kindly, and I watch her with amazement. How could someone who has endured so much be so quick to forgive? She looks better now that the wounds are healed, almost like the old Kace again. But I know that there are wounds beneath the surface that I cannot see that are not so easily healed.

"I know that I probably can't even begin to understand," I start carefully, holding my friend's gaze, "but why don't you just leave?" It's something that I can't help but wonder, although I'm fairly certain that I already know the answer already.

"And do what?" Kace laughs again but this time it's not as lighthearted. "I can't support myself outside of this building. I'm totally not smart enough to earn any coin on my own. I'll lose everything and get thrown outside of the wall." She shudders. "We've all heard the stories of what the Lost are like: savage people acting like animals, no clean water or access to healthcare. I would never make it!"

I wish that I could tell my friend that she's wrong. That the Lost are nothing like we were told. I need her to know that she can leave this place. I need her to know that she can have hope. But I need to do it carefully. The walls are listening.

"Can you meet me at my apartment later? There's something that I could use your help with," I say deliberately, locking eyes with her in the mirror and giving a little wink. I'm sure that Kace knows that she is closely monitored, here in her home. She seems to get the idea because her eyes widen, and she gives me a little nod.

"Sure, Arin, anything you need," she says with her usual Kace chipper-ness, and I wonder how she can put on such a positive persona after everything that she's been through. I stand to go, feeling a new sense of determination in my chest and give her shoulder a reassuring squeeze before leaving. My steps are purposeful as I make my way out of her penthouse, which now looks to me like nothing more than a gilded cage. I will bring hope to Kace.

Change is coming.

Later, Linc, Kace and I are sitting around the kitchen table in my apartment, which now seems small in comparison to my time in the penthouse. I feel a little shiver run down my spine. But I would much rather live here than have anything to do with the monsters that live in their castles above us.

I told Linc that Kace was coming by, but I didn't offer much more explanation than that. He now eyes me curiously as they both wait for me to speak. I glance up at him, waiting for his expression to change as soon as he hears what I have to say. It won't make much difference in the end though. My mind is already made up.

"Kace, I wanted to bring you here because our apartment is safe. No one can listen to us here." I gesture around the room and she nods her understanding, sparkling blue eyes wide. "There is something I would like to show you," I continue. I can feel Linc's eyes on me. If I can get Kace out of here and show her that there is an entire people group living outside of Cortex, it could really give her hope. Things are going to change, and I want her to know that.

"What is it?"

"Oh no you don't." Linc leans forward in his chair, shooting daggers at me with his eyes. "It's too dangerous!"

"Linc, you need to trust me about this." I shoot him a glance of my own. "If anyone can understand what we are doing, it's Kace." I argue, pointing to my poor, beautiful friend, who has been taken advantage of, just like the rest of us, by the system that only rewards intellect. Her shoulders hunch and she hugs her knees to her chest, looking almost child-like.

"We don't know if we can trust her," Linc explains through gritted teeth, green eyes flashing with a warning. He thinks I'm being reckless. Well, I don't care. "If you want to help her, we need to stick to the plan that we already *have*. This could jeopardize the entire thing. Are you willing to risk that?" I glance at the first person that I've considered to be a friend, whose life is in danger because of the horrible things that Director Ellis has forced her to endure. I look at her petite frame, curled up in my kitchen chair: a prisoner inside of a mansion. If anyone knows what it feels like to be helpless, it's her. She needs hope.

Hope is a powerful thing.

I ignore Linc's warning and barrel on. "Kace I've been outside of the wall, to the city of The Lost City. It's nothing like we thought it was!" I say.

"You've been outside of the wall?" Her eyes widen with an emotion that I believe to be terror, but her fear is misplaced. Life outside of the wall is nothing like she was led to believe. Linc shakes his head, clearly admitting defeat.

"Yes!" I try to contain my excitement. "There's an entire city *full* of people, and an army. They have this huge Rebel army! It's unbelievable." I try to paint a picture for my friend. If I can take her here and show her what we are doing, then she will have something to hope for. "You've said it yourself, Kace. You're a prisoner here."

"No!" She stands so abruptly that her chair falls to the ground with a loud clatter and Linc and I both jump up. "I don't want to have any part of this." This is a side to Kace that I haven't seen before. The fear in her eyes is so powerful that I start to feel an uneasy sense of alarm in my own chest. "You—you shouldn't be doing any of that either. If Director Ellis found out …" Her knuckles clutch the side of the table so tightly that they start to turn white.

"Kace ..." I say to try and assure her that this is a safe place. But she looks ready to run.

"I shouldn't be here. I need to go," she exclaims and turns abruptly, pushing the fallen chair to the side and making a break for our front door. As soon as she's gone, Linc and I share a glance. Her sudden outburst leaves us both in an air of dazed confusion. *What just happened?*

The alarm in my chest turns into sinking feelings of guilt so strong that I have to look away. *Did I misjudge Kace as a person that I could trust?* Linc isn't looking at me either, but I can practically hear his "I told you so" even though he hasn't uttered a word since Kace left. My cheeks burn. He might as well say it. I may have just put the both of us in danger by once again ignoring his advice. I stare at the doorway that my "friend" had just vanished through.

I hope that I didn't just sentence myself to death.

"Underestimation is the mistake of the Witless."

- Chronicles of Discord

I don't sleep well at all that night, tossing and turning until the early morning hours, expecting a guard to come at any minute and arrest me after Kace turns me in to Director Ellis. When a loud rap sounds on my door in the early morning, my heart jumps into my throat and I feel my pulse racing. This is it.

"Linc!" I hiss, running to his room, "there is someone at the door!" But when I push his door open, I find the bedroom empty. I picture Linc, leaving this morning for the gym, completely unsuspecting when soldiers apprehend him and drag him away for accompanying me outside the wall. I feel a knot form in my stomach. Where did they take him? The knock sounds again, louder this time, and I connect to the front door camera to see how many of them are outside waiting while frantically searching for something to use for a weapon. But instead of armed guards, there is only one figure outside of my door, who I recognize instantly. Kace.

A wave of relief so strong washes over me that I feel like I could collapse onto the floor. I open the door wide, and usher my friend inside. "Boy am I happy to see you." Kace shoots me a quizzical look, and I suddenly realize from her tousled blonde locks and the dark circles under her eyes that she didn't sleep much last night either. "What's going on?"

"I'm sorry I left so abruptly yesterday," she says quickly, shutting the door firmly behind her and looking around the apartment. "But I just got really scared."

"It's okay, you don't have to apologize," I reply. "I shouldn't have sprung that on you so quickly." She shakes her head.

"No, it's more than that," she begins, clutching my arm tightly. "There is something that I need to tell you, about Director Ellis." Her big blue eyes are wider than I've ever seen before and her gaze darts around nervously as she whispers so softly that I have to lean in closer to make out what she is saying. It doesn't help that she is speaking so fast that her words seem to trip over each other on the way out. "I thought maybe it wasn't true, or that there was some kind of mistake. But when I heard it from your own mouth yesterday ..." She's practically hyperventilating at this point.

"Kace, what's going on?" I can feel the alarm rising in my chest as the little hairs on the back of my neck start to stand up. What could Kace know about Director Ellis that is more frightening than what I've already seen? Her grip on my arm tightens like a vice, her nails digging into the skin of my arm, but the pain barely registers because I'm too focused on the next words that come out of her mouth.

"She knows, Arin. Director Ellis knows."

"What?" I feel the blood drain from my face, and I can feel myself falling. Kace looks at me with a mix of terror and concern and when she answers her voice sounds far away.

"The Veritas. When she looked inside of your head, she was able to see your connection with the Lost. She told me everything."

"What?" I'm horrified. How did this happen? "No, how is that possible? I was so careful." Kace shakes her head.

"You don't understand. Director Ellis is ... brilliant. She is sneaky, manipulative and always gets the upper hand." I hear Linc's voice echoing in my head. *If you think that going there and letting her look inside of your head is going to be anything other than disastrous, then you're clearly still underestimating her.* I can barely hear myself think over the pounding in my chest. I did this.

"Why are you telling me this?"

"Because you're my friend, Arin. I don't want to see anything bad happen to you."

I shake my head. "There's got to be some way that I can fix this."

"I don't see how. She knows that you've gone outside of the wall and that you've been working with the Rebel commander. She said that you knew all about her plans, and an upcoming Rebel attack. Are the Lost really going to attack us, Arin?" Her voice quivers with fear and I don't know how to answer her. Steele would never launch an attack that Director Ellis knew was coming.

That's it. I jump so quickly that I startle Kace, and she gazes back at me, confusion written all over her face.

"What is it?" she asks.

"I think I know how to fix this. You said that Director Ellis knows that I'm working with the Lost. Has she said anything about calling for my arrest?"

"N—no." Kace frowns, still not seeing the picture. "She said that she wanted to keep you close and that you could be a helpful source of information." I clap my hands together, my enthusiasm building.

"Yes! And that's exactly what I'm going to do."

My friend watches me quizzically.

"Wait, you want to help Director Ellis?" Kace's voice is full of doubt. I laugh, everything coming together.

"Not in the slightest. But if she wants information, I'll give her information. The wrong kind." Kace blinks slowly and I watch as the realization of my plan slowly dawns on her.

"That's brilliant!" For the first time today, my friend has a sparkle in her eye. "She doesn't know that you are on to her, so anything that she learns from you she will believe to be true."

"Exactly. All I need to do is get with Steele and explain everything to him. He'll know what information I should feed her."

"You're going back outside of the wall?"

"Yes."

Kace is quiet for a minute, but when she does speak her voice is full of a resolution that I have never seen before. "I want to come with you."

"I'm not sure that's a good idea," I reply, shaking my head. "You know the risks. The penalty is death." I gaze at the gorgeous, brave girl in front of me who sometimes reminds me of a child. She's been through more than I can imagine, and yet I trust her more than anyone in this building. But trust or not, I don't want her to put herself at risk for the Rebel's cause.

"I know," Kace says softly, glancing down at her manicured hands. "But this is something that I have to do." When she looks back at me her eyes are steady. "You know what life has been like here for me. If there's a chance that things could possibly … change, then I want to be a part of that." I don't know what to say. How can I deny her a hand in bringing about her own justice? "Besides," she adds, "I think that I could be a lot of help to the Rebel army. No one knows more about Director Ellis than I do."

I nod. She has a point. It would take a lot of explaining to both Linc and Steele, but something tells me that Kace may prove to be a more valuable ally than any of us realize. There is a lot of risk, involving another person in our plan, but sometimes to succeed, you've got to take a little risk. I shoot her a grin.

"Welcome to the team." Kace beams back with an emotion that I realize I've never seen on her before, hope. She wears it well. "Oh, and Kace, one more thing. If you're going to come with us, there's something you have to do." Her face grows puzzled, and I have to keep myself from chuckling as I glance down at her sparkling silver pumps. "You're going to have to wear durable shoes."

As I walk back to my apartment, I can practically feel Director Ellis's gaze all around me, watching my every move. She outsmarted me, just like Linc said she would. I feel a new fire of determination kindling in my chest. She may have outsmarted me once, but this will be the last time.

I have to brace myself before opening the apartment door. The conversation I am about to have with Linc is not going to be an easy one. Not only do I have to admit that he was right about Director Ellis, but I also have to somehow convince him to bring Kace outside of the wall. I swallow. It also doesn't help that I'm very aware that this next trip outside of the wall is not going to be fun. I wince, imagining the look on Steele's face when he learns that, because of me, the Rebel's entire plan has been jeopardized. Because of me—the girl who is supposed to help save everyone—there is a chance that all could be lost. And all because I was not careful. And now I want to be even less careful and get Kace involved, Director Ellis's right hand man. *This is going to take some serious convincing.*

"Hey," I say, my hesitant footsteps guiding me through the door and through the apartment, searching for Linc. I find him in his bedroom, in the process of getting changed for the gym.

"Hey," he says in greeting as I enter the room but doesn't seem to mind my presence as he strips off his work attire. The image of his bare chest rattles me even more and I avert my eyes as he swaps out his work pants for athletic ones, my cheeks burning. It's not that I don't want to get more intimate with Linc, it's just that we haven't really had the opportunity to do much more than kissing since I first discovered that he had feelings for me. There is certainly a part of me that craves to see every part of his body. I glance up at him as he straightens the collar of his smart fabric shirt and adjusts it for his work out. It's just that we both have a lot going on right now, and when that moment comes ... I want it to be perfect. Stripping in front of me definitely doesn't help my ability to wait though. "Cat got your tongue?" he says, eyes sparkling with mischief and I wonder if this little show was on purpose.

"Um ..." is all I can say before he chuckles and grabs both of my hands, pulling me onto the bed with him. I feel myself melt as I'm wrapped up in the familiar smell of him and the comforting feeling of his body pressed against mine. He kisses my neck softly, and every worry in my body dissolves. He has become my safe place. I trust him completely—and I know he trusts me.

"Hey," I say, pulling away slightly until we are eyes to eye. His expression is puzzled.

"Is everything okay?" he replies.

I nod, and although I want nothing more than to spend the next hour seeing how much of his body I can cover with kisses of my own, I owe it to him first to let him know what is on my mind.

"Kace came and found me today. She was really upset. She said something was wrong." Linc freezes, his fingers hanging in midair from where he was lightly playing with my hair and watches me with intensity.

"What did she say?"

I take a deep breath, preparing myself for what's coming. "She ... she said that Director Ellis knows about the Lost's plan. She found out from me. Through Veritas. I ... you were right." I look down at his dark blue bed sheets and I feel his hand drop.

"Are you sure?" Linc's entire body goes stiff and all I can do is nod again, my eyes burning with tears. I should have just listened to him. He exhales slowly, letting the reality of this new information sink in. The touch of his fingertips to my face startles me and I look up in surprise as his fingers caress my cheek. His eyes are all-consuming, their sea green pupils churning with a torrent of emotions. What is he going to say? I brace myself for the worst.

"I love you."

"What?" I blink in surprise. His response is not at all what I was expecting.

"I just ... wanted to make sure that you know that, with everything that is going on," he explains, voice thick. His touch is gentle on my face. "That stuff matters, but this, you and I, matters too." With his free hand he presses his palm into my chest, and I feel a warmth spreading throughout me. His finger strokes my diamond token. "I just wanted to make sure that, no matter what, I had the chance to say it."

"I love you too," I declare, and I know that there has never been a truer statement to ever leave my lips. Linc is right, what we have matters, but I want to enjoy him in a world where we do not have to worry about our every move endangering the people that we love most. "I love you and I have a plan."

His smile sends little bolts of electricity shooting through my limbs. "I knew you would."

CHAPTER

"Praising the mediocre breeds mediocrity,
Eliminating the mediocre produces advancement."

- Articles of Axiom. Article VII Part B

I don't think I'll ever get used to the nervousness that comes with sneaking out of Cortex. I can feel the uneasy tension in the air as the magnetic train brings us closer and closer to the dividing wall. A lot of careful planning has gone into getting all three of us discreetly outside of Cortex and beyond the city's walls; our nerves are on edge because of the possibility of being found out that passes with every second. It's just a risk that we will have to take.

The wall looms ahead, a visual representation of everything that is wrong with our city. I glance over at Kace, whose blue eyes are wide, but other than that she seems to be doing alright. I don't know what to say to prepare her for the truth about what lies on the other side of this wall, so I will let her come to terms with it just like I did. She catches my eye and gives me a nervous smile. I wonder what would happen to her if Director Ellis knew where she was going tonight. I bet it could make killer robots seem like a walk in the park.

Linc is silent as well. It took a lot of convincing to persuade him to let me bring Kace along. But ultimately, he agreed that if I trusted Kace, then that should be enough for everyone else. I'm not sure that Steele will agree with him.

"Alright this is us," I exclaim, giving Kace's hand a reassuring squeeze. The train slows as it approaches the wall and we launch ourselves out of the car, rolling on the soft grass and coming to a gradual stop beneath the starry night sky. Jumping from the train car is just as exhilarating the second time as it was the first, and other than a few scrapes on my hands and knees, I'm completely unharmed. A laugh bubbles up through my chest and I have to let it out, Kace looks at me like I'm crazy.

"What is so funny?" she grumbles, brushing dirt and grass from her fashionable black pants. I shake my head.

"If anyone would have told me on my first day at Cortex that I would end up jumping out of trains with Kace Simmons I would have never believed them."

It's true. It is a strange thing, what we will do for love. I plan to do anything and everything that I can do to keep the Lost people safe—even if it means declaring a war on Cortex.

The thing about wars is that allies are important. It's easier to take down someone if you have someone to fight beside you who shares your mutual enemy. I glance at Kace, sparkling with exhilaration from the night's adventures. We share a common enemy—Director Ellis. For me, Director Ellis has poisoned the people of The Lost City, poisoned my mother, because she doesn't see them as valuable. For Kace, she has taken away her sense of self and forced her to become a tool for others enjoyment. A plaything.

"Come on," I say, standing up, a new determination for tonight's mission coursing quickly through my veins. "You have a rebel commander to meet. Linc has already sent a message ahead—they'll be expecting us."

I wasn't there for the exact conversation but I'm sure that Steele was angry when he found out about my mistake about Director Ellis. But when I had asked Linc about it, he simply shrugged and said, "This is war, things change."

Kace's first experience outside of the wall practically mirrored my own. Her face reflected the same horror that I felt when I first saw the conditions that some of the Lost are living in. And she was also overwhelmed by the sheer size of the Lost community. It's a shocking occurrence to learn that the real monsters live inside of the city, and not outside of it.

When we arrive, I advise Kace to wait with Linc while I go in first. I need to bring the commander up to date with what's happened, and I'm still not sure how he is going to react. When I push the familiar tent canvas flap aside and step into the warmth of the Commander's candle lit office, I find him seated behind his lustrous oak desk. The light from the flames bathes the whole room in a soft glow and when I speak, my voice comes out in a hushed tone.

"Ahem, Commander," I begin. "I've just arrived from the city. Is this a good time?"

"Arin, please come in," Steele greets me, his voice impaired by the pipe lodged firmly between his lips. He gestures to the seat closest to me. "Linc informed me that there has been a change of plans." I swallow and sink into the chair, not sure how to continue.

"Yes, well, um, there is this device that Linc and I created, called Veritas …" The commander nods, careful not to interrupt. I wonder how much of this he already knows. "And it is used to reveal the truth. Director Ellis … used it on me, so that I could work closely beside her." I take a deep breath, *here comes the hard part.* "But when she looked inside of my head, she was able to see everything that we had planned. I thought that I could hide it from her, but it turned out that I was very wrong. I'm so sorry."

Steele is quiet for a moment. He takes a long drag from the pipe in his mouth and watches as the smoke curls lazily upward toward the ceiling. I wait on the edge of my seat, ready for the reprimand of a lifetime. Instead, Steele just strokes his beard, puffing away.

"Things are not always the way that they seem," he says thoughtfully. "Sometimes our greatest mistakes can become gateways to our greatest triumphs." He glances at me, grey eyes curious. "Linc mentioned that you had a plan."

"Yes!" I sit upright, ready to disclose my plan. "I do. Director Ellis has no idea that I am on to her, and I have someone on the inside."

"Oh?" Steele raises one thick brow. "Who?"

"Kace Simmons, sir. She is Director Ellis's right hand man, but she is devoted to our cause. She is actually waiting outside to meet you."

Steele looks at me with intensity in his eyes, conveying the seriousness of his next question: "Do you trust her?"

I nod firmly. "Yes. I do."

Steele observes me for a moment, as if making one last decision whether or not to trust my judgement on a woman from beyond the wall whom he has never met. Finally, he speaks again, saying, "Very well. Bring her to the command center and we can work out the details of your plan with the rest of the team."

When Kace, Linc and I arrive in the command center, we find Steele and Sol waiting, apparently caught up in a deep discussion. The commander, with his polished leather boots and dark beard, stands in stark contrast to Sol who is wearing a T-shirt with what I believe to be a rocket on it, from the ancient days, and jeans, his shoulder length dark hair tucked behind his ears.

"… the interface, but if we could only mimic …" Sol's gesturing wildly, caught up in whatever point he is trying to make, but stops himself mid-sentence when Kace enters the room, head whipping towards us.

"Someone smells like strawberries!" he says. I have to hold back a laugh at Sol's outburst and Kace looks bewildered beside me. I can't help but smile. Sol definitely has a way of making memorable first impressions. He clears his throat and smooths down the front of his wrinkled T-shirt, covering the ground between us in two steps. He offers Kace his best, gap-toothed smile. "Hello, my name is Sol, and I am the brains behind the Rebel Army," he says grandly, with a deep bow. Kace grins, clearly flattered by his display.

"It's nice to meet you, Sol," she responds warmly. "I'm Kace." But her eyes keep darting towards Steele, whose torso is covered only by a thin sleeveless shirt. He has knives strapped to each of his rippling biceps, and is currently busying himself with emptying his pipe of its tobacco. Kace watches in fascination, clearly captivated by the ruggedly handsome commander.

Finally, Steele turns to greet her, an easy smile on his lips. "Welcome to the Lost City, my name is Steele," he says, crossing the room in three easy strides, "and I command this army." With a sparkle in her eyes like they share a common secret, Kace extends one delicate hand for him to take.

"The Commander, I've heard many wonderful things about you," she purrs and Linc and I exchange a glance. She didn't even know the commander existed twelve hours ago. Steele takes her extended hand into his, bringing it to his mouth and kissing it.

"I'm sure they aren't true," he says with a wink and for a moment I feel butterflies in my own stomach. Kace lets out a delicate giggle that sounds like wind chimes, her face flushing a delicate shade of pink.

"So," Sol says loudly, stepping between Kace and the commander, clearly interested in more time with my friend, "to what do we owe this pleasure?"

"I think that I could be of use to the Rebel army," Kace replies firmly. She glances at me, big blue eyes hesitant. "Arin has told me that you are going to change things, and I want to help make that happen."

Steele nods. "Arin mentioned that the two of you have a plan."

"Yes! It was all Arin's idea, really." Kace clears her throat before continuing. "When we get back to the city, I will tell Director Ellis that I have befriended Arin and that I was able to find out her encryption password for all of her communications with the Rebel army. Then, Arin will start a chain of fake messages between the two of you, and we will feed her all kinds of false information. You can tell her that you are going to attack, say, three weeks from now and then do it in only one week. She will be taken completely by surprise."

"And Director Ellis trusts you?"

"Completely. She always uses me to get information from people."

Steele raises an eyebrow. "How?" he asks.

"Favors," Kace says coyly, running her fingers through her long blonde hair.

"If you help us, you will be putting yourself in danger," Sol interjects, concern in his voice. "If you get found out, there is no telling what Director Ellis will do to you."

"I know, but I don't care. Director Ellis has controlled me for too long." Kace's voice trembles. "It's time that I take control of my own life."

"I see a lot of ways that this could be beneficial," Steele says finally. "But not everyone will be convinced that you are truly for our cause. Being so close to Director Ellis is both a danger and an advantage."

"I understand," Kace responds, and starts to unzip her jacket. "I have something that I'd like to show you that I hope will change their minds." I watch with curiosity as she pulls the jacket off and tosses it aside before starting to remove her shirt.

"Kace, what are you doing?" I hiss, my cheeks growing hot with embarrassment when the bustle of the room comes to an abrupt stop as my friend strips off her shirt in the middle of it all. She shows no hesitation whatsoever, and proceeds to address the commander, who seems unfazed by her lacy black undergarments.

"I have the key," she announces, pointing to a raised spot on her arm and I can hear an audible gasp in the room. "It was put here the day I was chosen to become Director Ellis's assistant."

I exchange glances with Linc and the look of shock on his face mirrors mine.

"No one knows about this key's location except Director Ellis and myself," Kace continues, "and I think you know how important it is." Her voice is steady as she looks around the room, where a quiet hush has fallen. "To prove my loyalty, I'd like to give it to you."

Steele strokes his beard again in thought, unfazed by Kace's audacious display. When he speaks, he looks burdened, as if something is troubling him. "I'm not surprised that Director Ellis would do something as inhumane as hiding the city's key inside of a young girl."

"Oh damn," Sol mutters under his breath from beside the commander, finally piecing together the dialogue of the last five minutes. *Oh damn is right.* I wince, thinking about how painful that must have been to be placed inside of her, *and how painful it's going to be to get it out.*

"Kace," Steele continues. This time, when he addresses her, the commander's tone is soft, and full of compassion. "If we are going to be able to use that key, we are going to have to get it removed as soon as possible. Will you come with me to speak with our best surgeon, so we can find out our options?"

"Of course." Kace slips her garments back on as easily as she removed them and follows the commander's broad frame out of the control center. I watch them go, curious about the role Kace will play within our group. I thought I sensed something between her and Steele, but then again, there seems to be something between almost every man and Kace.

While the rest of the room goes back to their tasks, Linc saunters over to me and greets me with a smirk.

"You know, maybe bringing Kace out here wasn't such a bad idea after all," he admits, green eyes friendly. "Though I thought you were going to faint when she started taking her clothes off."

"When are you going to learn that I'm always right?" I tease, ignoring the jab, and he gives me a playful nudge with his shoulder.

"If only you were as good at modesty as you are at everything else," he jokes, holding my gaze with a warm smile, and I can't help but smile back, happier than I've ever been, despite our current circumstances. "Listen," he lowers his voice to barely above a whisper and runs his fingers through his hair, tousling it more than normal. He looks nervous. What could Linc have to say that he could possibly be nervous about?

But before he can speak, we hear a loud "Shit!" from the other side of the room. Linc and I exchange worried glances, before turning to see Sol, frantically rapidly plugging himself into the system, his computer emitting a series of high-pitched beeps. We rush over to him.

"This is not good!" he announces to no one in particular.

"Commander, I think you should see this," says a petite Asian woman standing next to him. She's wearing a deep green tank top and a utility belt loaded with weapons, and within seconds of speaking into her communication device, Steele rushes into the room, Kace at his side. He is immediately swarmed with soldiers, and one of them hands him with a tablet swirling with activity.

"This feed is live, and we just noticed the change a few seconds ago," the woman explains.

"I'm on it!" Sol yells from his chair, fingers typing at lightning speed, and everyone else in the control room seems to be just as confused as I am about what exactly is going on. I look for Linc, who had hastened to the commander's side, and was currently in deep discussion with him, both of their expressions serious.

"What's going on?" I hear Kace's voice from beside me, and I offer my friend a tight smile.

"I have no idea, but I'm sure everything is okay," I assure her, despite the nervous feelings stirring in my own chest.

"Everything is *not* okay," Steele interjects, his face serious, and he makes his way over to us. "We just got word that the city has shut down the train station on our side of the wall. The one that carried you here, it's no longer operable. We can't get any information about why it's happening now, but I suspect that it has to do with Director Ellis's 'announcement' about the Lost City."

I feel my heart drop as Steele's words sink in. I can't shake the feeling that this has something to do with Director Ellis's "proposition" that she presented to the council.

"The train is gone?" I ask incredulously. "But doesn't the city need the train to carry food from the outlying farms into Paramus?"

Linc joins our conversation: "No. Paramus has been fully automated for months. Not many people know, but the city has enough systems inside of itself to produce food for everyone. That was Director Ellis's last project, and I think I know why." He runs a hand through his already tousled blonde hair, making it stand on end, expression worried. "Director Ellis is smart, and she knows that we were planning an attack. She just made getting to the gate a big problem."

"But how are we going to get home?" Kace asks, fear making her blue eyes appear larger than normal. Linc meets her gaze, face grim. "We're going to have to walk."

"Walk? But that will take forever!" Kace protests, and I run the calculations in my head.

"Not forever, about three days," I conclude, which still isn't ideal. "Sol, can we be gone that long without anyone noticing we're gone?"

"Leave it to me," Sol replies from his chair, wheels already turning. "I can upload false tracking history to your nanos, making it look like you've had activity inside of Cortex for the next few days. From here, I can also put your logins into the system, giving the appearance that you've been working remotely from your apartment. It may raise some questions, but at least you'll have an alibi."

I ask the question that's been on my mind since they started speaking: "Does this mean that we won't be able to come back?" Fear twists in my stomach. How will I be able to work side by side with the Rebels to perfect our plan if I can't come back to the rebel base?

"That is still unclear," Steele sighs, rubbing his hands across his face. "I'm sure that Director Ellis is going to do everything in her power to widen the separation between our two cities until the nanobots take their toll."

"We should be able to help you remotely," Sol adds, still deeply absorbed in his controls. "I can send you guys on your way with some tech that should make it pretty easy." He types a few more lines of code and then jumps up from the computer, hands in the air. "Boom! And that is how it's done!" he shouts, clearly pleased with himself, toothy grin wide. "Whew! I am good!"

"What did you do?" Kace asks, glancing back and forth between Sol and the stream of code on his monitor, clearly puzzled. He laughs wildly, clearly still exuberant.

"I made you guys *ghosts!*" he exclaims proudly. "Thanks to me, Cortex thinks you guys are chilling at home, still getting work done, and not raising any alarms. This should buy you three or four days, easy."

"We can't be too careful," Linc advises the group. "I think that we should start heading back as soon as possible." We all nod our agreement, and for once, I am anxious to get back to Cortex. Director Ellis shutting down the train is a clear indication that things are moving more quickly than I realized. The time for action is quickly approaching, and I want to make sure that I'm ready.

"Sol, how long will it take for you to create the tech that you mentioned so that we can work together remotely?" I still very much need Sol's help in preparing to hack the system. His knowledge and experience is invaluable to me and staying connected to him throughout the remainder of my training is imperative if I'm going to succeed.

"Gosh, gee ... I don't know Arin. This is kind of some complex stuff. It may take a couple of hours," he answers, face solemn, but he can't hold the expression and breaks into a huge grin, snickering to himself. "I'm just kidding! Give me ten minutes."

CHAPTER

"Never avoid a battle of wits,
As the victor, you gain prestige-
As the loser, you gain knowledge."

- Chronicles of Discord

When we say goodbye to the Rebel base, possibly for the last time if our initiative doesn't succeed, we are armed with a lot more than we started with. The five of us—myself, Linc, Kace, Sol, and a soldier named Ret who has been assigned to be our guide out of the city—set out to start our journey by the light of a star-filled sky.

We plan to walk as far as we can tonight and stop only to sleep. Ret carries a rolled-up canvas on his broad, well-muscled back, his carob colored skin shining with sweat. The canvas will be made into a temporary shelter for the night in addition to the packs that we all carry that were generously provided to us by the rebel army. They loaded us up with dehydrated food, water purifiers, fire starters, and sleeping bags for the journey, and while I was more than grateful, Kace's mortified expression at the dehydrated food was so comical that I don't think I'll ever forget it. Sol graciously volunteered to carry her pack, but somehow, before we even get to town, she is already complaining about the strain of our journey.

"I'm just saying, you guys could fix the roads," she grumbles while carefully stepping over a giant pothole. "Like, don't you worry about someone twisting an ankle or something out here? That would be just awful!"

Despite her ramblings, Sol listens eagerly to her complaints, offering his arm when she is unsteady and offering his sympathy, never straying more than a foot or two from her side. Their paces match perfectly; Sol, feeling his way along with a cane and Kace hopping about like a hummingbird, careful to avoid any traces of mud. Along the way she peppers him with questions about Steele: how long he's been in charge, what he's like, if he is seeing anyone, and Sol answers begrudgingly, clearly upset with her obsession.

News of the train shutdown must have traveled quickly through the Lost City, because when we get to the first outskirts of town, there are already crowds of people gathered. It looks like an endless sea made up of pinpricks of light, but the night is quiet, as each Lost citizen stands in reverent silence, every hand tightly gripping a candle to light our way.

When we get close enough to reach out and touch, they part the sea of candlelight to form two rows, one on either side of us, and as we take our first steps, they begin to sing. It's a heart wrenching song. They sing of their sorrow, of their loss. I feel tears start to sting the corner of my eyes as I look into the faces of the humans around me: mothers, fathers, sons, and daughters. Brothers and sisters, friends, and lovers, all dangerously close to losing one another. All banding together in this massive sea of the Lost, clinging to a singular hope; the hope that we will save them. Their song swells and changes as we move through them, voices ringing out into the night. For some it is a song, but for others, it's a cry.

May our candles light your way and bring you safely home. A girl much younger than me raises her voice strongly as we pass by, and she gives me a small nod. In one hand she holds a candle, and her other hand is tightly clutched by a wide-eyed little boy who doesn't seem to know the words to the song. When he asks to be picked up, she holds onto him tightly, letting her voice ring throughout the night, as tears rush from her deep grey eyes. *We sing for those who've gone before, we miss them, every one.* An old woman, bent with age, holds her flame high into the night sky, although it trembles. Grasped firmly in her other hand appears to be a small pair of shoes. When I pass by, I can see the generous tracks on her face that the tears have made, but she still continues to sing. *May their footsteps guide you, until your journey's done.* A man who looks to be about the same age as Linc stands tall with pride, gives a sharp salute as we pass; his voice resonates with passion and courage to guide us on our way.

For I am you, and you are me, and we exist as one. At the end of the line, we turn to get one last glimpse of the people who have come to see us off, the people who are trusting us to save them. We all give a wave goodbye before we turn to leave, portraying confidence with happy smiles and giving the appearance of absolute confidence. I'm relieved when we leave the main city behind, however, and I can let my smile falter. Because the truth is, I don't carry the weight of their trust effortlessly. It sits on my chest, making it hard to breathe. If I fail, I don't just let myself down, or even my own family down, I let every single one of them down. The young girl and her brother, the old woman, the man Linc's age. All of the Lost who are already sick and dying that I visited with Maz. Every Lost man, woman, and child that I've met and haven't met. They're all counting on me to find the kill switch and shut the nanobots down. Until then, they're sitting helplessly, awaiting a certain death to come. I'm their only hope.

"That was really something, wasn't it?" Linc falls easily into step with me, and we walk together directly behind Ret, with Kace and Sol trailing behind.

"Yeah," I mutter, unable to shake the panic that is slowly creeping through my chest. They all have so much to lose if we fail. We all do.

"What is it?" Linc replies. He is getting so good at reading my expressions that there isn't really any point in me trying to hide my feelings from him anymore.

"It's so much pressure," I gasp. "More than I've ever carried. It's not just my family depending on me to succeed anymore, it's an entire city. All of their faces. They were so hopeful."

"And they have good reason to be. Look, I understand how you feel, but it's not just up to you this time. We are all here. We are going to do this together." Linc takes my hand in his and gives it a reassuring squeeze. I let myself be comforted by his presence, and by the playful chatter of Kace and Sol's conversation that drifts up from behind us. I take comfort in the steady pace of Ret, the trained soldier, who has taken it upon himself to guide us home. I think back to the entire Rebel army back at the base who are going to be working alongside us to make sure that our initiative succeeds. Linc is right. This time I am not alone.

We walk for several hours, and when we finally stop to make camp, I'm drenched in sweat and I can feel the muscles in my legs shaking. We made good time, however, and although I'm not looking forward to the long walks ahead of us, I couldn't ask for better company. While Ret and Linc get started on building a fire for the night and constructing our makeshift tents, the rest of us gratefully drop our heavy packs to the ground and finally get off our feet for the first time all night. In no time we have a roaring fire going, and we all gather around the cozy glow, eager to eat and get some much-needed rest before sunrise brings another strenuous day.

Dinner is dehydrated meat and vegetables, but the highlight of my night is when Linc reveals a self-heating thermos from inside of his pack and uses it to make us all steaming cups of coffee. The beverage is warm and comforting and helps to take the edge off my fatigue. As we all relax around the fire, warm drinks in hand, the conversation naturally drifts to our situation.

"So, Ret, how long have you been in the Rebel army?" I ask the newest member of our group. He finishes his sip of coffee and stares into the fire as he answers, speaking really for the first time that we left the base.

"It's been about four years," he answers quietly, his face solemn. At first glance, I would have guessed that Ret was several years older, but upon closer inspection, I realize that it's just the weathering of his face and the harsh lines that have formed that give him that appearance. He isn't much older than I am.

"Do you have family out here?" I wonder, eager to hear his story.

"I do," he answers solemnly. "My wife and baby girl."

"Where are they?" Kace pipes up from across the fire, clearly just as curious as I am about the silent soldier.

"They're in the sick tents," he answers, voice thick, never looking away from the fire, but I can see his hands shaking around his coffee mug. I feel my heart drop, and no one speaks for a moment.

"I know how you feel, Ret," I eventually offer. Linc throws the last bit of his dehydrated meat into the fire and sends up a wave of sparks. "My mom was one of the first test subjects." I swallow, the familiar ache blossoming in my chest. "She was the reason that I first came outside of the wall. She ... didn't make it." Ret drops his head and when he looks up from the fire, there are tears in his eyes.

"My daughter is only a few months old. I'm not sure how much time she has left." He stops to wipe his eyes with the back of his hand. "That's why, when they were asking for volunteers to get you guys to the city, I knew it had to be me. I needed to make sure that you got there as quick as you could." I feel a pang of sadness for Ret and think back to the young mother that we served a bowl of soup to in the sick tents. Could that have been Ret's wife?

"I'm sorry, Ret," Kace adds, her voice quiet. "No one should be made to feel helpless." We all turn to look at her, thin arms wrapped tightly her arms around herself, the firelight casting dark shadows across her face. "It's awful that no one knows the truth about Director Ellis. She is capable of so much evil ..." She shivers. "They all are."

"I can't believe that Director Ellis has made you carry the key all this time," Sol speaks up, turning to Kace. "That is no way to treat a human being." He places one hand lightly on her shoulder. "I can't imagine what else you've been through." I shoot a worried glance to Linc, not wanting Kace to have to reveal more than she wants to about her life inside of Cortex.

She sniffles, glances at Sol's concerned expression, and lets a stream of tears roll down her cheeks, shoulders heaving. "Hey, hey, it's okay. I'm sorry. I'm sorry!" Sol scrambles, taking off his jacket and wrapping it around her shoulders. "It's okay." He gives her a comforting squeeze, and to my surprise, she doesn't pull away. She just lets him hold her. "You don't have to talk about it," he murmurs. "I'm sorry."

"No," she sniffles sadly, wiping at her tears. "You should know," she sighs. "My father is a member of the council in Cortex, if I told you his name, you'd probably recognize it. Growing up, he was really hard on me ... He made me feel like I needed to earn my place in the house. After mom died, it got worse. He knew that I wasn't Gifted, so according to him I was practically useless." She sniffles, pulling Sol's coat more tightly around her shoulders. "It was pretty obvious that I wasn't going to be able to earn him any coin the traditional way, so he figured out a way for me to earn enough coin for the house to keep up appearances." She grows quiet. "He sold me."

I hear Sol's sharp intake of breath and I can imagine the widening of his eyes behind his dark frames.

"No," he says softly. "To who?"

"Technically, I belong to Director Ellis, but she lends me out to whoever she is trying to get in good graces with." Kace bites her bottom lip and looks away. "I've spent my entire life as a slave, and I never had any hope until the day I met Arin." She gives me a warm smile, tears glistening in her clear blue eyes framed by perfect lashes. "Arin, your friendship has meant more to me than you could ever know. It feels incredible to finally have someone in my life who truly cares about me." I get up from my seat and walk around the fire to wrap my friend up in a tight hug and let her strawberry-scented aroma wash over me while her arms cling tightly to me, tears stinging at my eyes. I feel the same way about her. Kace was the first person that I was able to call my friend at Cortex, and she taught me how to let my guard down. When she finally lets me go, I realize that there is something that I need to make sure that she understands.

"Kace, you have a lot of people here that care about you here. Linc, Sol, Steele, me, and maybe even Ret—it's hard to tell." We all share a laugh. "But seriously, you are a beautiful person on the inside and the outside and we are all really lucky to call you friend."

"Yes," Sol chimes in. "I want you to know that you're not alone. I understand first-hand how cruel Cortex and family can be. I was born with a pretty impressive IQ, and probably would've had it made if I hadn't started losing my eyesight in primary school."

"You weren't born blind?" Kace sounds surprised. He shakes his head.

"No. I know what it's like to see. I know what I'm missing out on every day." He gives a dry laugh. "Anyway, my parents didn't want anyone to know that they had a kid that had something wrong with him, so they kicked me out. With no family, no home, no way to find food, scared and blind, I left Paramus. I've been on my own since I was eleven."

"Family sucks," Kace agrees. "No offense," she quickly adds, glancing at me. I smile, silently reassuring her that it's okay. I don't blame her or Sol for feeling that way, but family isn't the true problem—Cortex is.

"I hate my dad even more than I hate Director Ellis," Kace adds.

"Well, this is depressing. Anyone know any good jokes?" Ret says, wiping tears from his eyes, and we all burst into shared laughter. We sit and reminisce by the glow of the fire, telling stories and sharing jokes until the last coal burns out. Finally, as the last ember dies, we bid each other goodnight and retreat to our tents. Linc hangs back from the rest of the others and walks me to my makeshift shelter.

"Hey." He stops outside of my tent and runs his fingers through his hair, tousling it more than usual. "Mind if I join you?" he asks, and little flutters of pleasure run through my body. I know that I'll sleep much better with Linc beside me.

"Of course," I agree quickly, and try to hide the excitement on my face as he climbs into the tent without any further hesitation and lays down. "Is there any room for me?" I tease once he gets settled, as his long legs span almost the entire length of the shelter.

"Let's see." He grins and pats the ground next to him. I roll my eyes but quickly make work of removing my boots and then plop down beside him. The ground is cold but the heat from his body is warm and I'm grateful to have him next to me.

"I think they used to call this camping," he speaks up in the dark. "People would choose to come sleep on the ground all night for fun."

"I think I'd prefer my bed back in the apartment," I grumble half-heartedly, eyelids growing heavy.

"I think I'd prefer your bed too." His voice is playful, but his words send little shivers down my spine.

"Are you ever going to stop talking so I can go to sleep?" I chide him playfully, and I feel his body shift as one strong arm wraps around me and he lands a small kiss on my cheek.

"I'm sorry. I'll be good."

I'm pretty sure I fall asleep with a smile on my face.

The next day drags on painstakingly slow. The hot sun beats down harshly on our backs and I've developed blisters on my feet from wearing my boots for such a long period of time. The conversation has pretty much halted as we all focus our energy on keeping up the pace with Ret, who walks at what feels like breakneck speed and never stops to look back. Yesterday we walked through the biggest areas of infrastructure that the Lost City has, passing by its largest tents where gatherings are held, markets, and some residential dwellings. Today we are on the outskirts of the city, where the tents lay more sparsely against the landscape and there won't be another landmark until we reach the refuse lake. We stop for a quick lunch after what feels like hours, and then get right back on the trail. I decide to walk with Kace, who is always at the tail of our group, to give my aching feet a bit of a break. We walk in silence for a while, saving our breath for the journey, but after a few miles my mind starts to drift to the events of the beginning of our trip and I realize that there is something I want to say.

"That thing you did back there with the key, it was really brave," I share with Kace, beside me. and She shrugs, golden curls matted with sweat.

"I didn't have a choice about becoming the key-holder, but I can choose who ends up with it," she replies, this new hardness in her voice. There is so much that I admire about my friend. She never let the things that she endured at Cortex break her. Instead, she has used them as a forge in which to become strong enough to help us defeat Director Ellis. I wonder what her place will be in this brave new world, where being "Gifted" is just a thing of the past.

"So, what do you think of the Commander?" I tease, and she looks down at the ground. I can't tell if the flush of red in her cheeks is from my question or the afternoon heat.

"He's pretty impressive," she says quickly, growing redder still. "We didn't get to talk for very long because of what happened with the train. But he did tell me that he's glad that I came out here." When she glances up at me there is a giddy twinkle in her eye. "I … I think he likes me." Her confession surprises me, but not as much as the bashful way she is speaking about the commander, like a primary talking about her first crush. It's clear that if the commander does have feelings towards Kace, the feelings are mutual. I think about what they would be like together. An unusual pair for sure. She fidgets with a strand of long blonde hair. "He kind of scares me." She giggles. "But I like it."

"Steele is a good guy," I assure her. Although I haven't known the Commander for that long, he seems passionate and kind. I look ahead at the others and catch Linc's eye. He's looking back to make sure that Kace and I haven't fallen too far behind. I feel myself smile. Steele isn't the only good guy around here.

We break for camp that night, and as my heavy pack falls to the ground with a thud, I can't decide which hurts more, my back or my feet. I've been running all my life, but this landscape, with its stretches of rocky ground divided by uneven patches of sand, is a terrain that I was not ready for. Out of the corner of my eye I watch as Sol helps Kace out of her pack, his trademark smile wide, and I feel a pang in my heart. *Steele isn't the only one with feelings for Kace.*

"You hungry?" Linc's voice from beside me pulls me out of my head.

"Hmm? Oh, yeah, starving." He watches me with an amused look on his face.

"What are you thinking so hard about?"

I bite my lip. "Do you think that Sol has feelings for Kace?" I gesture over to the two of them, where they are sharing the same log by the fire, shoulders touching, as Kace erupts in a cascade of laughter. Linc shrugs.

"Most guys do," he points out, and although that is true, I feel like with Sol it's different.

"I'm not just talking about her looks," I argue. "Sol has no idea what she looks like. So, if he has feelings for her, it's got to be based on who she is as a person, and not all that other stuff." Linc shakes his head, offering me a steaming bowl of dehydrated noodles. I gladly accept. "Don't you think they would be good together?"

"Maybe," he grants, pressing his knee into mine and I can't help but smile. I'm glad that he thinks that we are good together. My mind flashes back to our interrupted conversation from the day before. *What was he about to say?* "Do you want to take a walk with me?" he says suddenly, abruptly setting his bowl down and running the back of his hand over his mouth. I look down at my feet, still throbbing from the day's walk. But when I glance back up at Linc his eyes are eager, so I allow him to pull me to my feet. No one pays us any attention as we saunter away from camp, my hand in his, until we are far away from the other. Just Linc and I, and a cool breeze that lifts the hair from the back of my neck and cools the skin beneath my shirt. We lose our shoes, toes in the dusky sand, and watch the sunset together. The sand feels soft beneath my feet and I can't help but feel happy, bathed in the warm glow of the end of another day. When I glance over at Linc, he's watching me, the same peaceful look on his face that I feel on my own.

"I love you," he says, and my heart skips a beat. I don't think I'll ever get used to hearing him say that.

"I love you too." I smile, wiggling my toes in the sand

"I wanted to get you away from everyone because I wanted to talk about what it's going to mean for us when this is all over." I feel my heart drop and suddenly the last rays of the disappearing sun seem too warm, causing sweat to prickle at my temple. *What does he mean? Does he think that things between us are supposed to change once we aren't allies fighting against Cortex anymore?*

"Okay …" I say hesitantly, bracing myself for the worst. He rummages around in his pockets and I watch curiously, wondering why he is going to light a smoke in the middle of our conversation, but instead he retrieves a ring and holds it out to me, the reflections from the lazy rays making it twinkle. "Oh!" I gasp, hands flying my mouth in surprise, my heart threatening to beat its way out of my chest with excitement. Linc looks at me steadily, the ring extended, his eyes full of hope.

"I just want you to know that there is a future here, with me, when this is all done." My eyes fill with tears and it's all that I can do to keep from sobbing out loud. I love him so much. "This ring belonged to my mother. I'm not sure if it will fit, but we can always—"

"It's perfect," I interrupt him and let him carefully slip the ring on my hand. The metal feels cool against my skin and I throw my arms around his neck in a grateful embrace. He kisses me deeply and we stay there, wrapped up together under the stars, his mother's ring on my hand, until the moon is high in the sky. Not many moments in my life have been perfect. There have been a lot of unknowns. But this moment, just Linc and I, and the stars, is one of them.

CHAPTER

"Unintelligence does not just hinder progress. It stops life."

- Articles of Axiom. Article XI Part G

The morning air is crisp, more so than I ever remember the air inside of Paramus's walls being. I pause for a moment to truly appreciate it—*who knows when I'll be back*—then finish stamping out the last embers of this morning's fire. While finishing off the last of my coffee with a deep sip, I hear a squeal from across the campsite. Kace comes flying up to me, her golden curls like a halo against the morning sun.

"Where were you?" she breathes, eyes dancing. "I was dying to tell you what happened, and you missed it!"

"I'm sorry," I begin sheepishly, "Linc and I were—wait. Missed what?"

"Sol kissed me last night!" she blurts, bouncing up and down. I blink, trying to register what she is saying. *Sol kissed Kace?* The beautiful girl stands in front of me practically bursting with excitement, waiting expectantly for my reply.

"He did? How? Why?" My questions all tumble out in a jumble of surprise. "I thought you liked Steele!"

"I do." She glances up at me sheepishly, cheeks tinted pink. "I wasn't expecting it at all, but it happened, and it was nice."

"Do you want him to do it again?" Truth be told, I couldn't be happier to hear this news. I know that Sol has feelings for my friend, and I could really see her being happy with him too. He was a great guy.

"Yes. I mean no. I don't know!" Kace exclaims. "I never really saw him that way before. I thought he was nice, and funny, but now ..."

"But now, what?"

"But now I think, maybe I could see something more?" she admits, chewing on her lower lip as a smile creeps across her face. I let out a delighted squeal and give my friend a tight hug.

"I just want you to be happy." I beam at her. "You deserve all of the happiness in the world."

"So do you." She stares at the ring on my finger, blue eyes wide. "And it looks like you've got it! Where did you get that?" Now it's my turn to flush crimson.

"Linc gave it to me last night when we were alone. He wanted me to know that what we have between us, it's forever." Kace gazes back at me, tears in her eyes.

"That's beautiful," she says simply.

And she's right.

The refuse lake is just as repulsive as I remember the last time I saw it. Only this time, I'm close enough to see the various types of debris strewn throughout its waters and there's no riding away from the pungent aroma. Still, despite its odorous condition, there are a surprising number of tents camped along its banks.

"Scavengers," Linc explains simply as we pass by the makeshift city. "There are a lot of usable materials in the lake, but not many people who are willing to go and get them." I peer at the lake in disgust. I wouldn't be very willing either.

"On the other side of this lake is the train station. We'll have to climb up to the platform and then from there it is only a short walk to the door that separates us from the city," Ret announces, gesturing to the raised railway in the distance. I swallow hard, staring at how high off the ground the support beams rise. I didn't realize that there would be climbing involved.

"What's with them?" Linc bumps my shoulder and nods his head at Kace and Sol who have broken off from our group and are having what appears to be a cozy conversation behind us, shoulders pressed together.

"Sol kissed her last night," I disclose and Linc's eyebrows raise, "and now I guess they're seeing where things go."

"Wow, sounds nice. I wish I was in love," Linc sighs and I elbow him in response. The closer we get to the start of the tracks the more my palms begin to sweat. There are many things that I am good at, but heights is not one of them. Also, as far as I can tell, we haven't brought any climbing gear along for our journey. The lack of grappling hooks, ropes, or anchors makes me very nervous.

"This is it," Ret says unceremoniously, slapping the rusted metal beam closest to him. He then removes his backpack and grabs a handful of the course dirt beneath our feet, rubbing it in his hands.

"What are you doing?" I ask incredulously. "Aren't you a little worried?" He cracks a smile.

"Nope. It's pretty common out here for kids to climb all the way to the top for fun. I've been climbing these things since I can remember." On one hand I'm relieved to hear that our guide is so comfortable but on the other hand, I am not. I look over at Linc who is picking up a handful of dirt and rubbing it on his hands in a similar fashion.

"Does this not worry you?" I fret, my palms positively slick. *Oh, that must be what the dirt is for.*

"We'll be fine. Just don't look down." Somehow his words don't make me feel any more assured. Kace isn't happy either.

"No one told me that we were going to have to *climb* our way out of here," she complains, arms crossed. "There's no way that I'm doing that." Sol laughs from behind her and whispers something in her ear. I watch as her eyes light up and she nods, pleased. He slips something into her hand, and she offers it to me. I take the smooth black disk, and stare at it in confusion, clueless as to the device's purpose. Sol raises his arms above his head dramatically, face in full theatrics, and says in a loud voice, "I present to you ... the hoverboard." He chucks the disk at the ground and it stops right before impact, unfolding itself into a long rectangle and hovering above the ground. I gawk at the device in fascination. I've seen hover technology used in transportation and infrastructure, but never designed for singular use.

"Did you build this?" I ask, amazed.

"Yup. Have you ever seen a blind guy climb? It's not what we are best at." Sol shudders. A wave of relief washes over me but also a new sense of apprehension. There don't seem to be any handles on this either. I throw the disk in my hand at the ground, and it stops, unfolding just like the last one. I take a careful step and gingerly place one foot on the long, smooth surface of the board. It wobbles for just a moment, adjusting to my weight, and then feels as steady beneath my feet as the ground that carried us here.

"You had these this whole time, yet you made us *walk* all this way?" I groan and Sol grins in return.

"The boards need metal to work. If I could have spared us the walk, trust me, I would." I look down at the board hovering only inches above the real ground and carefully bring my other foot up until I'm standing, both feet on its surface. It feels secure beneath me. *Now how do I steer this thing?* I hear giggling behind me, and see that Sol has ascended his board and pulled Kace on with him, his arms locked in a protective embrace around her. They begin to rise quickly from the ground, Kace's shrieks of excitement getting further and further away as they go up the pillar until they reach the platform. I glance at Linc.

"Want a ride?" I ask. He shakes his head.

"Nah, I prefer the old-fashioned way." He gives me a wink and launches into the air, landing a firm grip on the nearest crosspiece of the structure and hoisting himself up. Ret joins him, scaling the frame easily. *Okay then, that leaves just me.* I take a deep breath and urge the board forward with the tips of my toes. It eagerly obeys, flying forward. *This is kind of fun!*

"Bend your knees!" Sol yells over the side of the platform and I do, finding my balance much easier that way. "Now look where you want to go!" I angle myself toward the platform and the board rapidly rises. I feel the air whoosh past my ears and after a few breathless moments I am even with the rest of the group. Ret extends his hand out to me and pulls me to the safety of the platform. I shakily dismount, just as Linc pulls himself up from the last bit of scaffolding.

"That looked fun," he comments with an easy smile. "I call next ride."

We reach our destination in no time at all, descending from our hoverboards, Sol demonstrating how to transform them back into the small black disks. The train station is completely abandoned, we realize, as we make our way inside of its dark belly. Paramus didn't even bother to leave sentinels behind to guard the forsaken trains. Director Ellis had already warned everyone inside of Paramus about leaving, and there is no need to guard city resources from a population that would be dead soon. Still, we all move cautiously. The closer we get to Cortex, the more careful we need to be.

"This is where I leave you," Ret speaks softly, but his eyes are determined, "for now. You have your communication devices from Sol, correct?" I nod. I was given a specialized earpiece that will keep me connected to Sol and the Rebel base, as well as a tiny screen mirroring device that is smaller than my fingernail that will transmit data back.

"It's time for me to say goodbye too." Sol's voice is full of purpose. "We all have missions to accomplish and not a lot of time to do them."

"Good luck my friend." Linc marches over to Sol and gives him a warm embrace. "We'll see you on the other side." I take a deep breath, emotions rising in my chest. I've only known him for such a short time, but I already have so much love for Sol, and even for Ret, too, for being our guide across the miles and miles of Lost territory. Saying goodbye is bittersweet; bitter because I may never see them again, but sweet because I hope that I do. There are a lot of things that I could say to Sol, but instead, I let him pull me into a deep hug and grip onto him tightly.

"Don't worry. I'll be with you," he whispers, and I nod, letting go. The last to say goodbye is Kace. Her face looks like she too, has a lot of things to say but she settles instead for a quick kiss. Sol looks pleased with her goodbye. "Don't forget about me in there," he says.

"I won't," she promises.

Ret offers us all a firm handshake and a nod which I take as his expression of his faith in us. I know he has a lot riding on our success. They all do. At this moment, I remember a Paramus teaching: that you should never look back, that to truly be successful you must keep your eyes on the future. But this time, when I take one last look over my shoulder before we head for the gate to Paramus, I'm glad that I look back. Because behind me are two brave friends, who are willing to risk everything to save my parents and the people that they love, who have traveled far and had many sleepless nights because of the looming threat of a plague thrust upon them. But do I see fear in their eyes? Or doubt? No. I see hope.

And hope is a powerful thing.

CHAPTER

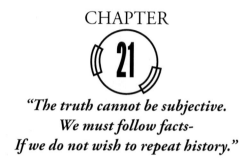

"The truth cannot be subjective.
We must follow facts-
If we do not wish to repeat history."

- Chronicles of Discord

Linc and I train together every night for the next week, and my speed and reflexes continue to improve. I had to remove the Linc's mother's ring from my finger in order to avoid suspicion, but I've swapped it with my old token, the diamond, and now wear it around my neck. As well as continuing my regular work in the lab, I also study with Sol, practicing late into the hours of the night.

"You're getting pretty good at this." Sol sounds pleased, his voice close enough that it feels like he is standing beside me. We are two weeks into my extensive hacking training and, according to Sol, it's going well. His teachings compliment my own knowledge of Cortex's defense systems, which I've completely memorized in my short weeks here.

Further aiding our cause, is the fact that I've also been feeding Director Ellis false information. With Kace's help, I've logged multiple hours of "top-secret" conversation with "the Commander" about the Rebel army's plans. Each of those messages were read by Director Ellis and she has already begun to prepare for a Rebel attack at the end of the month. But Sol has assured me that the actual attack will be much sooner than that. The only piece that we haven't been able to solve is how to safely remove the key from Kace. None of us know anyone on the red level personally, and if we came to them with this task, there is no way to guarantee that they won't immediately report us to Director Ellis. But Linc is confident that a solution will present itself soon.

However, when I meet Linc back at the apartment after a full day's work of pretending to strengthen the Cortex firewalls, while simultaneously learning how to defeat them, his face is grim.

"Hey." I greet him with a tight smile, dropping my book back onto the shining floor and crossing the room to stand in front of him-curious about what's on his mind. His strong arms wrap around me and he buries his face in my hair, the little bursts of air from his nose tickling the top of my head. The fact that I am able to finally embrace him without reserve, to know that he too wants to be close to me, is like water to my thirsty soul. There was so much wasted time that we spent not knowing who we were to each other. And now, I'm starting to understand how well we fit together. I can feel it in my bones, the relief, the way my worries melt away when he holds me. It's an understatement to say that my nerves have become quite frayed these last few weeks. I understand the importance of what I am doing and why I'm doing it, but I'm starting to feel anxious to actually put our plan into motion. Director Ellis has been in power long enough.

"I got the call today," Linc murmurs into my hair. "Steele wants to move." I break away to look up at him, eyes searching his handsome face, a million questions racing to the tip of my tongue.

"How soon?" is the one that makes it out, which, I suppose, is the most important question of all.

"Tomorrow."

"Tomorrow?" My heart is pounding, palms sweating. I knew this day would come. Of course, it would. It had to. This is the only way. And it's happening tomorrow. "But what about the key?"

"Kace says she found someone." Linc pauses for a beat. "Do you think you're ready?" his eyes searching mine and I hesitate, not sure how to answer. What is readiness anyway? Am I certain that I have the knowledge to perform a hacking procedure successfully tomorrow on the Cortex mainframe? Sol says that I am doing well, and I'm fairly confident in my abilities. I've learned the operating code like the back of my hand. It's just that...

I look at Linc, who is still watching me. Awaiting my response. There is one thing that I am not ready for.

"What if I lose you?" It's the question that's been taunting me in the back of my mind since our first kiss and every day since then. As soon as I let Linc into my heart the worry began of having another person that I could potentially lose. First my mom and dad. And now Linc is there too. The beast inside of me is frantic. It wants, with an animal like ferocity, to keep them safe. Because home, for me, has never been a place. It has always been my mom and dad. The softness of my mother's hands. The warmth in my father's laughter. And now, with Linc, the possibility of an entirely different home has presented itself. I want to follow this path with him, the one that started with a kiss. And see what we can build together.

He pulls me in close again, only this time, instead of burying his face in my hair, his eyes demand my full concentration.

"You're not going to lose me." His tone is firm, and his grip on my shoulders is tight. I can feel how he truly means what he is saying with every fiber of his being.

"Tomorrow, I am going to get you and I safely into the control room, and you are going to disarm the city. And then *together*, we will bring down Director Ellis, and the council, and the entire city of Paramus. We will stop the nanobots, and the Lost will recover. Tomorrow begins the start of a new world," he promises. I can hear it, the hope in his voice. The steely resolve that burns through him, the sheer assurance with every fiber of his being that this is going to be tomorrow's outcome. But nothing in this world is certain.

I lean in to kiss him, and his kisses are gentle at first, warm and accepting, but that is not what tonight is about. Tonight is the last night before a new world; the last night before everything changes. Our kisses become more passionate, our breathing ragged. My hands find his hair and his hands find the hem of my shirt and go under it. We are frantic. Desperate to know, and longing to find, while following the roadmaps of each other's skin, a new world. Every taste of him brings him closer and closer to me.

"Sol turn off the cams!" he shouts, voice rough and hoarse as he picks me up and carries me into the bedroom, my legs wrapped firmly around his waist. "Cut the feed, Sol!" It's dark in his bedroom, but I don't mind because my senses are heightened, and we can finally use our curious hands and our hungry lips to find every inch of each other. I can truly know Linc, and he can truly know me. Never to be lost. Even without the promise of tomorrow.

The wind whistles through my jacket, making me shiver. Clouds cover the moon in the night sky and the stars are hidden. There is a storm on the horizon. The wind whips louder, slapping my hair across my face and stinging my eyes. All around me in The Lost City, canvas doors are flapping. Tent poles creak, and the wind begins to moan. It's quiet at first but grows steadily louder. No, it's not the wind. I turn my head and I see my mother and father staggering across the camp, skin white and papery. Blood pools from their mouths, their eyes are black and empty. The moaning grows louder as they near, and I try to run to them, to save them. But as I look down, I realize that I am standing only on sand. And I am sinking.

"Help us!" They scream over the wind and I'm wriggling, writhing, trying to get myself free from this sinking sand so that I can run to them, but the wind stirs the sand, and it burns my eyes and pelts my ears. It's up to my neck now and each claw full of sand I grab sends me sinking deeper, and deeper.

"Arin! Grab on!" I turn, and there's Linc, offering me his hand. I'm saved! I grab onto him, gratitude washing over me. But something is wrong. The hand that I'm holding is white and cold. I look up, and Linc stares back at me with eyes that have turned black. There is blood pouring from his mouth, and he's coughing, violently.

I sit up in bed with a gasp, shaken from the nightmare. Heart still pounding, breath still coming in gasps. Sunlight peeks through the cracks under the bedroom door and I try to steady myself. *It was just a dream, only a dream.* But as the light of a new day begins, a new sense of dread fills me. Even though the nightmare ended, a whole new one begins today. I can feel the weight of my role today on my shoulders before I even get out of bed. I glance at Linc who is still sleeping peacefully beside me. I trace the lines of his skin with my eyes, blissfully remembering the night before. He stirs, and with a luxurious stretch and yawn, blinks his eyes open and greets me with a smile.

"Wow, you look even better in the daylight," he says groggily, and I manage a small smile as his hand finds mine, steady and warm. "Are you nervous?" he asks.

"Yeah."

"Well, don't be." He draws my hand to his lips, pulling me on top of him in the process. His other hand combs though my hair, sending tiny shivers of pleasure down my spine. "I'm not going to let anything happen to you," he murmurs, fingers running down my neck. He strokes my cheek softly with his thumb. "You know that, right?" My cheeks flush in response and I can feel my heart pounding in time with his. My throat is thick with emotion. There are so many things that I want to say, as he looks back at me with eyes tender, voice soft. But I can't find the words. All I can do is nod. I try not to stare at him as we hurry to get dressed. He's the one that looks even better in the daylight. Rippling muscle, strong arms and legs. Broad back and shoulders, scarred from years in The Lost City. I remember holding onto those shoulders last night. The little dips my fingertips made in his skin. He catches me staring, then teases, eyes playful. "What are you looking at?" I feel my lips twist into a smirk.

"The guy that's going to make us late for breakfast. Let's go!"

Crouched. Listening. But nothing seems to be stirring on the other side of the stairwell door. Beside me, Kace is tense. Linc sits with his face pressed against the door, fingers poised in the air, signaling for us to wait. He's scanning the hallway on the other side for heat signatures. His eye-screens have been upgraded with X-ray and infrared mods for the mission, military grade, and they see through the stairwell door easily. I glance at Kace, who is the only one out of the three of us who isn't wearing the standard Cortex uniform. Instead, she is dressed in a stylish white pantsuit, in typical Kace fashion. We are all dressed in our day-to-day work clothes to avoid raising suspicion. We look perfectly normal on the outside. But in reality, we are armed to the teeth. Upgraded mods and hacking gadgets at the ready. If anyone could see the weapons that we have concealed, strapped to our bodies, they'd surely sound the alarm. I can feel the cold metal of my zeno blade from its hiding place on my calf, reassuringly pressing against my skin.

It's the weapon that I felt the most comfortable with during training, and although it sits silent and unthreatening in its sheath at the moment, it can be absolutely deadly when in trained hands. My hands.

Linc gives the signal to move, and we follow him through the door marked "WHITE LEVEL" whilst keeping low to the ground. Silent. As we creep through the stairwell door, we are met with a hallway, empty at this time of night. The white fluorescent lights overhead glow dimly, set to night mode to conserve energy. Directly across from us is a set of glass doors, locked. The only thing standing between us and the entire white level. I swallow as I take hesitant steps across the polished white floor, willing my shoes not to squeak. I'm thankful that Kace, who follows close behind me, opted for silent leather boots instead of her usual high heels. It took some persuading and she said that she would rather *die* than wear tennis shoes with her pantsuit, so a compromise was made. Because even without workers on this level, Cortex still has eyes and ears. Luckily, Sol has already been a tremendous help on his end, breaking into the Cortex camera feed for the entire white level, and replacing it with a creation of his own. I glance up at the cameras in the corners of the glass doorway, completely useless now. I hope that Sol's broadcast holds strong, and if it does fail, that we are out of here by then.

Kace breaks away from behind me and crouches towards the entry panel, careful to avoid exposing her entire body to the glass doors in case there are sentries that we cannot yet see on the other side. We are fully prepared for the possibility that as soon as Kace opens the door, that an army of Android soldiers will come storming out, so Linc and I stay poised, on the alert, weapons within a finger's reach, ready.

The entry panel on the door is DNA accessible only, just like the rest of the restricted area panels in the building—yet another reason why it's so valuable to have Kace on our team. That, and the fact that, if we ever got backed into a tight spot, she can be pretty persuasive. I watch as Kace slowly rises from her hands and knees to align her face with the eye-scanner, movements deliberate and careful. After a few seconds, the panel accepts her eye print match and we hear an encouraging click as the white level doors unlock.

Linc snakes his hand around to catch the door as it opens, and I give Kace the signal to follow us inside. Linc makes his way through the double glass doors first, weapon drawn, eyes scanning the room for both heat signatures and any sign of movement, whether human or android. Thankfully, the area is still, so Linc and I move quickly. He covers me, weapon drawn, as I hurry through the white level's maze of uniform workstation until I get to the one at its core. My eyes widen at the sight of a massive glass box at the center of the room, and I know at once that this is it. The Defense Control System. Gaining access is not going to be easy. The cube-like glass exterior shimmers in the flickering safety lights, with no visible doors or entryways cut into its glass-like surface. I would bet anything that there is more to the cube than meets the eye.

"Should I—"

"Get down!" Linc shouts, throwing me to the polished white floor just as the first electrified net comes shooting through the air, narrowly missing me. I hear Kace's scream as the net crackles on the ground behind the command central, still very much alive with electricity. I roll to the left to dodge the next net, scrambling to my feet just in time to watch Kace take shelter behind the closest workstation. *Good idea.* I drop into a crouch, making myself small behind the nearest desk and look for Linc. He is hiding a few desks away and holds up four fingers to signal to me that there are four androids surrounding us. Two coming from the left and two from the right. I draw my zeno knife from its sheath and with a squeeze of my fingers it comes to life; humming with electric power, ready to slice through the nearest droid.

I signal for Kace to stay put, then Linc and I share a look. On the count of three, we leap out from behind the workstation where we are hiding, weapons drawn. The droids notice us immediately and take threatening steps towards us, hydraulic bones creaking. They aren't the servant model that I usually see in the halls of Cortex. These droids are designed to look like predators.

Instead of a friendly, comfortably proportioned body with two arms and two legs, the defense droids have grossly exaggerated features, meant to invoke fear. The smooth, humanoid servant droid face swapped out for an angular, narrow, scope like head with one lens for an eye, designed for measuring distance and aiming for prey. Their clawed hands crackle with electricity as they take menacing steps towards us, quickly closing the circle tighter and tighter.

"Are you ready?" Linc whispers, voice tight, the fear in his voice mirroring the terror I feel in my own chest.

"Yup," I lie, swinging my zeno knife in the direction of the nearest droid. Fighting is like hacking: find a weakness and take advantage of it. My eyes zero in on the robot's potential kill zones, zeno knife connecting with the first droid's chest plate. My knife makes a satisfying grinding sound as it gets to slice through the reinforced metal exterior, sparks flying. A secondary kill shot, courtesy of Linc's pulse rifle, brings the bot to its knees. With all of my strength, I aim a final kick at the bot's scoped head, knocking it to the floor, disoriented.

Adrenaline courses through my veins as I stand over the wounded droid, still twitching. It takes a forceful drive of my foot to the zeno knife, pushing it all the way through the steely android body, before the bot finally lies still. Circuits damaged beyond repair.

Behind me I hear the sound of the stun net gun powering up. "Behind you!" Kace screams. The third droid. Before the net can reach me, I drop to the ground, rolling hard to the left, and finding shelter just in time behind a nearby desk. The net crackles on the ground beside me, only inches away. I long for my zeno knife, which is unfortunately still lodged in the first droid's body.

I search the desk area, looking for something to protect myself. I try to run a quick calculation of the nearby objects, calculating the weight, velocity and force it would take to knock the droid to the ground. The only thing remotely heavy enough to do any damage is the chair in front of me, so with a deep breath, I spring from my hiding spot and grab for the chair, swinging it over my head with all the strength I can muster, crashing into the android's unsuspecting head. It crumples, and everything is still except for the sound of my heaving breathing. The fourth droid lies at Linc's feet, defeated by his pulse rifle.

With all the androids out of commission and the area now clear, Kace crawls out from her hiding place, visibly shaken.

"That was so scary," she whimpers. "Do you think there will be more?"

"I don't know," Linc replies, eyes scanning the room, "but time is of the essence. Do you have the key?" Kace's eyes dart to the lab door and then back to Linc.

"I have someone who is supposed to meet me here," she says. "A surgeon. He agreed to do it, I paid him substantially for his secrecy." Linc glared at the door.

"Well, where is he?"

"I—I don't know." Kace looks like she is about to cry. "He should be here by now." Linc swears, and kicks at the head of the closest droid. I feel a sinking in my own chest. Neither one of us has a way to get to the key, and without it, the system can't be shutdown.

"Arin," Linc calls my name sharply and then forces himself to take a deep breath. "You just go in there and get started with the system. I'll stay out here with Kace and figure out what to do about the key."

I nod, my attention returning to the cube in the center of the room. I find myself taking careful steps forward, almost reverently, toward the impenetrable fortress before me. When I place my hand against the closest panel the smooth surface is cool to the touch. It looks to be made of dually reinforced fibers: the tiniest strands of glass woven with steel by nanotechnology. It would take something much stronger than a bullet to break through this surface.

I share a glance with Linc. Neither of us have any sort of fire power remotely strong enough to break these walls. But force isn't necessarily always the answer. Sometimes you have to work smart. My fingers close around the handheld nano currently hidden in my pocket. This, combined with my experience with hacking, might just be enough to get us in. I search carefully along the cube's exterior until I find a singular access panel, blending perfectly with the smooth glass surface, practically invisible if you don't know what to look for. I inch forward for a closer look. *Bingo.*

The cube has DNA recognition software hard-wired in, only granting access to those who have been authorized by Director Ellis or the council through its walls. Because the access panel is flush against the glass, it's going to need a little maneuvering to get to the wires hidden behind. The knife currently strapped to my hip should do the trick. I shimmy it free from its cover and jam the blade into the corner of the panel, grunting with effort as I try to pop the face free. After several attempts, it breaks away and clatters to the laboratory floor. Linc and I freeze at the noise, sharing alarmed glances as we dare not to move or breathe at the risk of being discovered. But after several moments, no alarm is raised, so I go back to my mission, working quickly.

With the cover removed, I can reach my arm into the mess of wires inside of the door, fingers working deftly to sort through the clutter until I find the one that I'm looking for. I feel the familiar texture of a single black wire towards the back. *Gotcha.*

With a little more effort, I yank the black wire from its port and connect it to the handheld nano, its little blue screen blinking to life and its keyboard coming online, eagerly awaiting my instruction. After a little coaxing, the nano starts running some serious interference straight into the access panel's mainframe, disorienting it. Then once the system is off track, I am able to input my own stream of code, reprogramming it to grant access to me, and only me. I don't want to think about what someone would have to do to Linc to get him to open the door, but it's a possibility that someone could use him to get it open. The system doesn't need an alive body to open the door. Just a body. That's why I have to be careful and program the door to open to my unique DNA signature and my DNA only. With the new protocol in place, all that is left is to put the panel back and provide the program with a sample of my DNA. I try not to wince from the sharp sting of the finger prick.

The true test will be whether or not my blood gets accepted. The pounding in my ears drowns out almost all other sounds I watch in anticipation as the system analyzes. Will my hack work? Will it tell the system that I'm an authorized user? The access panel displays a spinning circle logo, demanding that I wait while it tries to figure out if I'm allowed inside. I try to breathe as I imagine the mimic code doing its work.

Let me in, let me in, let me in, I chant silently, as if the circuits can hear my wish and grant it. To my great relief, the mimic code is accepted.

The cube chimes pleasantly and, with a swooshing sound, a door appears in what was an unbroken wall of glass only a second before. Linc looks at me, eyes wide, fingers wrapped tightly around his rifle, and gives a tight nod. I'm on my own as soon as I step foot inside of the cube. The glass should be enough to keep anyone from interfering with our plan, but we can't afford to take any chances. Linc will stop anyone who tries to make their way to the cube before they can get there. Before I can take a step forward, a lump forms in my throat. I feel like I should say something to them both before locking myself inside.

"I don't know what is going to happen when I start hacking," I start, worry leaking into my voice even though I try to hide it. I'm not worried about myself. I will be safe in the cube. "There could be protocols set into place, weapons, I have no idea."

"I know." Linc offers me a small smile, his green eyes show no signs of hesitation. My eyes travel wistfully down his strong jaw line, resting just a moment on his lips. I think about how his arms that are now clutching a rifle so assuredly, held me so tenderly only hours before. I wish that I had some of his calm. Instead, all that I have is a nearly debilitating amount of fear and a sense of dread deep in the pit of my stomach. I need to be brave for everyone counting on me. But the thought of leaving Linc here, the thought of something going terribly wrong and never seeing him again, is enough to make me halter. In two long strides he closes the distance between us, and one hand goes to my hair, the other around my waist, gripping me tightly and pulling me in close until I'm surrounded by the familiar smell of him.

"Hey," he says, pressing into me and for a moment I want to lose myself in the smell of him, the taste of his lips, the depth of his green eyes. Just one more kiss. Just one more embrace. "I love you," he murmurs, tilting my chin up so that I have to look into the swirling oceans that are his eyes and see the fierceness behind what he is saying. My heart skips a beat when I find no hesitation there, nothing obscured. Only sincerity.

"I love you too." It's the truth. I love Linc with every fiber of my being, and it's because I love him, that I need to leave him here. I turn to Kace, her eyes full of fear.

"I'm sorry," she whispers. "I'm afraid that I've messed everything up." I shake my head.

"Don't be. Every problem has a solution. I'm going to go in there and work on mine, and you two stay out here and figure it out. I know you will." Kace gives me a fantastic smile.

"I won't let you down," she announces, wrapping me up in a sincere embrace, her thin arms squeezing me tight. When she lets go, I square my shoulders, bracing myself for the next step of my journey.

"I'll see you both when all of this is over," I pledge, and step inside the control center, the glass doors sliding into place behind me. No matter what the outcome is of the next few minutes, nothing will ever be the same. I try not to imagine the walls closing in on me, taking deep breaths inside of the glass prison. Where does the oxygen come from in there? *Don't think about that. Focus.* If I am to defeat my enemy today, I'll need to start with the single control panel before me.

There's nothing on the surface that is intimidating about the setup here, but there is an unspoken power that the sleeping beast before me holds. The mind of this machine is the only thing keeping the nanobots from further attacks inside of my parents, and from beginning attacks on the people of The Lost City. This complex, artificial mind, and its defense systems must be disarmed in order for the Rebels to be successful today, so that's what I'll do. Steele's soldiers stand at the ready, waiting to cross the wall into Cortex and overthrow its corrupt leadership. But first they need the defense systems to go down. *Alright, let's wake this thing up.*

I wave my hand across the main sensor and the central holo-screen blinks to life, and I find myself taking a deep breath as the beast awakens. It immediately asks me to identify myself. *Nope, can't tell you that.* I remember Sol's patient instructions: "Find the backdoor." *Just like we practiced.*

Instead of imputing a passcode that will grant me access to the control database, a sweep across the keys prompts a command window, which I begin to fill with a steady stream of code, fingers flying through the air, heart racing just as fast. If even one letter is off, or one symbol misplaced, then the entire stream will be rejected. The computer could sense that I'm an imposter and shut itself down. Our mission would fail.

My fingers fall into the steady rhythms that I practiced with Sol, my eyes screening my input as quickly as my fingers put it in front of me, searching for flaws, and praying that I find none.

<<ACCESS GRANTED>>

"I did it! I'm in!" My heart is so filled with elation that I could scream. Now all that I need is the physical key to gain access to the mainframe, and I can begin to target the necessary firewalls in place keeping the Cortex defense system online. I look outside the cube to see if any progress has been found but Linc looks back at me in dismay. I open the cube's paneled doors and step outside, my excitement fading fast. Everything that I just accomplished won't matter without the key. It's only one part of the security measures. I try to wrack my brain for a solution, but I can't come up with anything that won't hurt my friend. I hear a sharp gasp and I glance up in alarm to find Kace standing with one of Linc's knives in her hand, the arm of her white pantsuit slowly turning crimson with blood. I watch in horror as several droplets drip onto the white floor of the lab. I watch the room sway around me and I'm worried that I might faint. Linc swears again and rushes to Kace's side.

"Why did you do that? You're going to bleed out!" he exclaims, ripping off a piece of his shirt to use to slow the bleeding.

"It had to be done," Kace mumbles, her face turning white. "We've got to have the key." I find that I can't look away as she reaches deep into the open wound in her arm and retrieves a blood covered key, fingers shaking. My stomach churns at the sight and I think I might be sick. "Here," she insists, holding the key in her bloodied fingers. "Take it." I retrieve the key from her hands as Linc makes quick work of forming a tourniquet around her arm.

"Hurry," he says to me. "We don't have much time." I nod and race back inside the cube, sealing the doors behind me, and slide the key into the open slot on the control panel. Instantly, each wall of the cube becomes a map of holo-screens laid out before me, all of them offering me a different route into the mind of Paramus. There is so much information in front of me about the inner workings of our city that I would love nothing more than to sit in front of these screens for hours, scrolling through population records, agriculture reports, and the city budget. But that will have to wait for another time. When the city is ours, I can spend days in here if I want to.

I work quickly, posing as a Council member, forging my identity along the way. Thankfully, the system accepts my lie and offers me access to all the building's defense systems.

"Sol." I activate our com system. "I'm in. I'm looking at the defense controls right now."

"Good work! Okay, I'm just waiting on the all-clear from Steele on his end."

"Okay." My voice is tense, I sneak a glance at Linc whose head is currently working like a swivel, alert for the smallest sign of danger.

"Arin?" Sol's voice crackles in my earpiece, "Shut it down." My heart begins to pound as soon as I realize what he is saying.

"Okay, shutting it down." The map of controls splays out before me, a dizzying array. With just a few movements of my fingers, I'm going to disarm the city. It almost doesn't feel real. It's almost as if I am somewhere, far away, completely outside of my body, as I watch my hands input the kill sequence. This is the moment that we've been waiting for.

<<COMMAND ACCEPTED>>
<INITIATING TOTAL DEFENSE OVERRIDE>>

The walls are coming down. "Sol, the override is working! I repeat, it's working now."

"Roger that, we have soldiers on the ground, closing in."

I turn to Linc and Kace, flashing them a grin of elation and relief before, suddenly, my body is wracked with terror from the sound of a voice coming through my skin coms.

"Stop." I can barely breathe. The voice is familiar—it belongs to Director Ellis.

Gifted

CHAPTER

22

"Never let your emotions overpower your intelligence."

- Paraminian Proverb

The Director takes me by such surprise that I crumple to the floor. I see Linc draw his weapon out of the corner of my eye before I ever see her. My eyes search the room until I spot her standing in the corner of the lab, head held high, face unwavering, posture confident. She takes slow, deliberate steps towards me, silk hair swishing, never for a second breaking eye contact or looking away.

I watch Linc position himself between us, and even though I can't see it from here, I can imagine his finger curling around the trigger, ready to fire. If Director Ellis notices this, she doesn't show it. She doesn't have the frantic look in her eye that one might expect of someone who knows that I metaphorically have my own hand on the trigger, pointed at the city's throat, or is aware of the very real trigger that Linc is millimeters away from pulling. Instead, she looks just like she does in all the city broadcasts: calm and collected. Our fearless leader. My eyes dart to the progress bar across the central holo-screen. It's estimating twelve minutes until the defense systems are completely offline. *We need to keep Director Ellis out of the cube for twelve minutes.* That seems like an eternity. An impossible amount of time.

I know how determined the Cortex leader can be; if she plans to try to get into this cube and stop the shut-down, there's nothing that Linc will be able to say to get her to stop. He is going to have to physically stop her.

I try to swallow but my throat feels dry. I can see Linc circling, slowly calculating, optimizing the best kill spots at close range, Kace cowering behind him. My heart pounds and I fight the urge to look away. The sound of a weapon firing makes a ringing in my ears, but it is not Director Ellis who falls. I watch with horror as Linc crumples to the floor. Kace screams.

"Linc!" I yell, every atom of my being drawn to his body on the control room floor. I scramble to my feet, and slam into the nearest glass wall, desperation clawing in my chest like a wild animal. He's okay. *He has to be okay; he has to, he has to.*

"It's too bad that he turned out to be a traitor." I can hear the disappointment in Director Ellis's voice as she steps over Linc's body and makes her way toward Kace. "Speaking of traitors."

There isn't much that Kace can do as Director Ellis closes in, weapon raised. She narrows her eyes as she takes in the girl's bloodied pantsuit and the makeshift bandage, probably piecing together how we got the key. "I never took you for someone who would actually *achieve* something," Director Ellis spits, looming over my friend. "And you got so close." There's pity in her voice.

"Please," Kace whimpers, staring up at her.

I throw myself against the glass of the entry panel, desperate to get out, to save my friend, just as Director Ellis pulls the trigger.

"No!" I scream again, the blood in my veins running cold with liquid fury as I glare at the person I hate most in the world, my heart racing. I want nothing more than to release myself from this glass prison and wrap my hands around her throat and squeeze until the light fades from her cold, calculating eyes.

"Kace is nothing. And I can't have a Lost boy in here with a live gun, firing away." Director Ellis continues to speak calmly, directly into my skin coms. If only I could cut them out of me so that I don't have to continue to hear her voice in my head. "I don't understand why you would waste your time with him. You have such a brilliant mind. Clearly." She gestures to the cube that I hacked my way into. "It took my top scientists' over a year to build this defense system. And you got inside in minutes." Her voice sounds thoughtful. "I always knew that you were someone special. Not to be trifled with. It's too bad that the Rebels got to you first." Her fingers go to her suit jacket and she brushes an invisible speck from her sleeve, apparently lost in thought. "How *did* you get in there?"

I can feel her measuring me, making all kinds of calculations about what she thinks I am and am not capable of, no doubt. Before, I would have squirmed beneath her gaze. Anxious to be seen as worthy of approval, desperate for her praise. But now?

I am filled with nothing but rage.

"Does it really matter? Your system has been shut down, Eira." I use her first name because we are finally being honest with each other. She lost my respect to be the rightful director of Paramus a long time ago. "Just admit it, you've lost." She smiles, an icy, humorless expression.

"Oh, I never lose." Her words send a chill down my spine, and she takes another step toward the cube.

"You won't be able to open it," I point out as she reaches the control panel. "It's registered to my DNA alone." She looks up from closely inspecting the panel.

"Really? That was very clever, Arin. Very clever." She presses her hand against the screen, and I shake my head. I've overridden the original controls, totally wiped her from the system. The only way that she is getting that door open is …

My thoughts stop in their tracks as the cube gives a pleasant chime and the door slides open. No. I should move away, try to run but there is nowhere to go. And I'm not sure that I could move my legs if I wanted to. I'm frozen in place with shock.

It's not possible. There's no way. Maybe there was a glitch in my programming.

Was there a loophole? A backup? Some sort of default that I missed? That's impossible. I wiped out every single thread of the previous protocol. It's as if Director Ellis is reading my thoughts as she steps through the door, beaming triumphantly.

"I know this may come as quite a shock to you, Arin," she says. "I was waiting for the perfect moment to tell you."

The perfect moment to tell me what?

"As soon as I found out that you were alive, and that you were doing so well, I just knew that we would govern Cortex together." I can hear her words, but they don't make sense.

Found out I was alive?

"It was the hardest decision of my life, leaving you, but I had no choice."

Leaving me. How could she know that I was abandoned as an infant? There was only one person who had ever left me.

"You?" I feel myself swaying and I worry that my knees may buckle beneath me. I hold onto the desk beside me for support. "You … you're my mother?" The woman in front of me, the version that I have always known as Director Ellis, our fearless leader, looks at me with an emotion that is in complete contradiction to everything I've ever known her to be. Shame colors her face red. She won't look me in the eye.

"You have to understand, I was very young." She brushes a perfect strand of silky brown hair behind her ear, still avoiding my gaze, "At that time, it seemed like the best decision to keep working. I couldn't do both. I had to quit my career and become a mother or walk away from motherhood. It wasn't an easy decision."

"You abandoned me."

"I know, and I'm sorry."

"You're *sorry?*" I cry out. "You abandoned me in a *trash can* and all you can say is *sorry?*"

"I understand your anger." She lets a large exhale, a stark contrast to her usual, professional demeanor. "But look at what I was able to accomplish." She gestures widely, referring to all of Cortex. "I did all of this for *you.*" I shake my head angrily.

"I never asked for any of this! I was perfectly happy with my real mom and dad," I scowl, and she rolls her eyes.

"They were never really your family, Arin. I am! And now that I've found you, we can lead Cortex together. A mother and daughter team! With our combined brilliance, think of what we could achieve!" Her eyes sparkle with excitement and again the fearless leader is unrecognizable. Her voice is full of pride as she continues, "You showed up here and scored the highest Criterion score ever recorded, and I thought to myself, what if that is my little girl? And then I saw your face and I instantly knew it was you." She beams at me and reaches for my hand, catching me completely off guard. I back away slowly and her face falls momentarily but her frown is quickly replaced with an earnest expression. "Don't you see? *We* can finally be a family."

I shake my head, still dazed by the transformation of the person in front of me. Everything that she is saying stands in stark contradiction to the woman I know, the one who is planning mass genocide. This woman speaks of family, as if it is something that actually matters.

"What you're doing is wrong. I want no part of that," I object, and one of her perfectly traced eyebrows raises slightly.

"Oh? I think that our forefathers would be inclined to disagree with you." She sighs, the sound coming across as that of exasperation. As if the effort of having to explain something incredibly simple is too much. "You know that judging people based on their possible contributions to society is what has made

Paramus great. It's this way of thinking that separates us from the ancients and keeps us from spiraling back into the dark ages! To some, it could be considered harsh, but compassion is just another face disguising itself as the old way of thinking. It is an enemy of progress Arin, don't you see? There is so much to be achieved."

"But at what cost?"

She shoots me an unimpressed look.

"Do you really care about all of those Lost peasants outside of the wall? Is that why you've shut my system down?" My silence is answer enough.

"You know what I think, Arin? I think you siding with the Rebels, hacking my system, it's all an act of rebellion." She reaches out a tentative hand again, but this time I am frozen in place. Her fingers lightly brushing the tips of my hair. "I think that you wanted to draw attention because you were looking for me."

"What?" Her words confuse me; my head feels like it's spinning. Isn't this woman who stands before me, and claims to be my mother, claims to know the reason for my actions, the very same one who shot Linc only moments before? Who is she really?

"It's biology," she continues. "You're wired for family. There's so much I could teach you. If you just give me a chance."

"You mean put the system back online?" I shake my head resolutely. "I can't do that. There are too many lives at stake."

"You know, I think it's funny that your parents gave you that name—Arin. It suits you." Director Ellis stares wistfully above my head as if she is caught up in a time long, long ago. "Arin means peace. And together, by my side, we can finally bring peace." Her voice is loving, taking on a quality that I couldn't have imagined coming from her. A deep ache down in the depths of me that was buried long ago throbs longingly. The mother that has always been missing, here now with me. She takes another step towards me, until she is only inches away. The smell of her lavender perfume tickles my nostrils, and her warm brown eyes are kind. When she speaks again, her voice is gentle, barely above a whisper. "There's nothing out there that matters beyond our walls, Arin. Just the remains of an old way of thinking. The future is here. With me."

"With you?"

She gives me an understanding smile.

"This isn't the future, sweetie." She gestures to the timer steadily counting down behind me. "It could never work. You're not going to be able to save them, but not because you're flawed." The Director takes a deep breath. "But because they don't *deserve* to be saved. I know that you know this. Think logically. Join me. I can put you on the council. I can make you the head of any department of your choice. I can give you anything that you want." She starts speaking quickly, her voice becoming more and more earnest. "You care about helping people? We can help our citizens, together. Think of it, the things that we could create if we put our minds together. What happens to all of this"—she gestures to the room around us—"if we become enemies? You need to think carefully about your future."

"The future doesn't matter if the people that I love aren't in it," I reply.

"You don't even have to choose between me and your family, Arin. I promise that they will be safe."

My confusion quickly turns to anger. She doesn't even know what she took from me. I let out a sharp laugh.

"Your promise means nothing, Eira. You already took my mother and Linc from me!" I hiss. "I wouldn't trust you with my worst enemy." Her eyes widen with surprise. It would appear that she had no idea about my mother's death, but she recovers quickly.

"What about your father?" she asks. "Wars are messy, Arin, it's a sad reality. Who knows who will get caught in the crossfire? But, if you join me, I can guarantee his protection."

Although I hate to admit it, her words make me pause. It's true that wars have casualties. If the Rebels don't cross over the wall, then there won't be a fight for my father to possibly fall victim in.

If I take her agreement, then many people will die. But the only person that I have left will live. I think about how my father would feel when he realizes the cost that came with his rescue. The amount of destruction. I'll never be able to look him in the eye again. The weight of shame already hangs heavy on my shoulders for even considering it. And yet, I'm gravely aware of the hole that losing him would leave in my life. These past few weeks, it's always been looming in the background. An ever-present fear of finally and cruelly becoming completely alone in this great big world.

Losing him would break me. I already know it. I can't even glance over at Linc's body on the floor or I know I'll just start screaming. And now, on top of that, I also risk the possibility of losing my birth mother, who I just found. How can I make the right decision when either way, there is so much to lose? I count the number of the Lost in my head. Sol, Steele, Maz, Ret, his wife and their baby. The brother and sister. The old woman. The young patriot. Every soldier. Every man, woman, and child. The list goes on and on.

All the Lost and their precious Ubuntu—their radical way of loving human beings just for being, will be wiped off the face of the earth. Who will tell their stories? Who will sing their songs? Will humanity really be better off without them?

"I can't do it," I whisper. "I made a promise."

Director Ellis shoots a glare at Linc.

"What?" Her voice raises, words flying like daggers. "A promise to *him*?" She points an accusatory finger at Linc's body, still crumpled on the laboratory floor. "Romantic love is pointless, Arin! There is *nothing* to be gained from it! Don't you see? What does loving this boy profit you?" Again, the look of disgust.

"It's not about profit, Eira," I say, shaking my head. "It's just love. You wouldn't understand."

"You think I don't understand? I was young once." Her voice drops again, and she resumes her sense of calm, taken swiftly away to a place only in her memories. "I understand how tightly romantic love can grip you, clouding out all sense of rationality." She holds my gaze, and I can see the pain in her eyes. "But then one day you wake up, and you don't matter anymore, and you realize just how shallow romantic love is." She shakes her head wistfully, and I can hear the regret in her voice. "I should have never let him take me away from my work. I lost so much time with him." She sniffles and gestures to the glass control booth around us. "This is how I redeem myself, don't you see? I learned that the only thing that matters is this city that I've built and its pursuit of knowledge. And that's why I need to protect it."

And with that, as quick as a flash, I watch her reach into the pocket of her slacks and retrieve a pair of stun-cuffs. She lunges for my wrist. My instincts tell me to run away but the space in the cube is tight, and she already has me cornered against the keyboard. I'm like a caged animal, with nowhere to run. I swiftly sidestep her attack and drop into a crouch. I eye the crackling cuffs in her hands as she takes careful steps toward me. I'm not going to escape if we stay in this box much longer. I feign a step right and when she lunges, I roll to the left and slam my hand against the exit panel, the door swishing open with sweet relief. I race toward freedom with a glance over my shoulder that reveals that Eira isn't even trying to follow me. She just watches me with a slight bemused expression on her face, which puzzles me until—

Slam! An android body collides with mine at full force and knocks the wind out of my lungs. I wobble unsteadily as the world tilts around me, and I desperately try to catch myself to keep from going down, but the surprise attack brings me to my knees, a stabbing pain in my side making even catching a single breath difficult. I hear the crackle of the electric claws before I see them and as I try to crawl away, they send a jolt of electricity through me that creates an explosion of white light behind my eyes and leaves me convulsing on the floor, utterly helpless.

Eira takes unhurried, calculated steps toward me, and from my viewpoint on the floor I can only see her heels moving. If my ears weren't ringing, I would probably hear the sound of their steady clicks against the laboratory floor as every step brings her closer. I try to tell my body to move, to stand up, to get away, but my ability to communicate with my arms and legs is completely gone. Instead, I can only glare as Eira secures the cuffs around my wrists and a second pair around my ankles, leaving me completely powerless to escape.

"I'm doing this for your own good," she huffs as the ringing in my ears fades and she tightens the last restraint. She backs away and stands proudly over me, admiring her work. "Honestly Arin, I knew that you would take some convincing but really all of this is unnecessary." I'm almost ungrateful that my hearing came back. I could really do without another one of her lectures.

She takes a deep breath and smooths the front of her shirt. "Now that we are all *calm*," she emphasizes the word like I'm not still twitching on the floor in front of her, seeing little spots in my vision, "I need you to walk me through disarming this little system destroyer that you built."

"No." I glance at the timer as each second brings it closer to completion. Only four minutes remaining. Only four minutes until this will all be over, and it will be too late for even Eira to stop the system from destroying itself. I realize that she really thought that she would be able to convince me to join her. But it's too late now, she thought wrong. There is nothing that she can do in the next four minutes that will change my mind. What is she going to do, torture her own daughter?

"Very well." Her eyes, which were wide and pleading before, now narrow into little slits. "I didn't want to have to do this, but you give me no choice." She turns her gaze to the lab doors. "Bring him in." I feel my heart drop when I hear her words and I'm reminded of what she said to me on the white level, only a few weeks ago. *I hope you saw today that everyone's loyalty has a price. Don't think I don't know yours.*

Full of dread, I slowly follow her gaze to the lab doors as they open. Four soldiers enter, dragging a familiar form between them.

My dad.

CHAPTER

"Our founders discovered that to succeed in life you need only two things: intelligence and intelligence."

- Chronicles of Discord

"**N**o!" I cry out. I try to stand but my binds are tight, and I can't. Instead, I thrash against them wildly, like an animal, trying to break free. Trying to run to embrace my father, to set him free.

My father half stumbles and is half dragged over to Eira, his body nearly limp as he mutters unintelligibly, his expression dazed. I feel my heart sink in my chest.

"Let him go!" The scream makes my throat feel raw and I'm bruising my knees and arms by struggling. I can feel the cuffs pulling against my skin and crushing the soft tissue underneath, but I don't care. I must get to him; I must set him free. My father is corralled through the lab until he is a few steps away from me, and I shoot daggers with my eyes at the guards when they roughly push him to the ground, close enough for me to see the sweat on my father's brow but not close enough to touch him.

"Arin?" He blinks several times and reaches a shaky hand out to me, concern written all over his face. "Sweetie, are you hurt?" I feel tears pooling in my eyes. My father can barely stand, and he's worried about me.

"I wouldn't worry about her," Director Ellis speaks sharply, a menacing tone seeping into her voice. "You have enough to worry about." She gives a slight nod to the guards and they draw their weapons, pressing one into my father's stomach and another against the back of his head.

Eira is going to kill him. "I understand that you're willing to risk your life for the Lost, but are you willing to risk his?" Director Ellis hurls the question from across the room and it hits me like a slap in the face.

She knows. She knows that I can't do it. It was always about saving my family. Everything that I've ever done, I've done for the two people that I loved the most—my mother, now lost to me, and my father, lying with two weapons pressed against his body. I don't want to live in a world without Mom, Linc or Dad. I can't. My father is the last of the family I have left.

This is what I mean about how sometimes I wish that the "Gift" would consume me, making me completely void of emotion, because maybe then I wouldn't feel like my heart is being ripped out of my body. I understand why the ancients burnt down entire cities and murdered each other where they stood. Because someone that they loved was in danger. Love is fragile like that.

"Mother, please," I say desperately, turning to Director Ellis. I plead to whatever ounce of humanity that she has remaining inside of her. "Let him go, he's suffered enough."

"Arin, I agree with you." She offers me a smile that doesn't reach her eyes. "What happened with Lara was unfortunate, to say the least. But I suppose that's what happens when you don't *carefully* consider the results of your actions. I implore you not to make the same mistake." She watches me expectantly. She knows that she has won. That asking me to watch my father die is absolutely impossible. I'll never let that happen.

But then, I hear my father's unsteady voice from beside her. "I implore you to consider *your* actions, Eira. You can't just murder an entire people group because they are different from you"—he takes in one ragged breath—"it's wrong. I know it and you know it and Arin knows it. Don't you, honey?" His voice cuts through the chaos to reach me like a beam of light through darkness. His words pull me in like a lighthouse to harbored shores, until everything else in the room fades away and it's only his kind, tired face, and his familiar voice. Trying to help his little girl to find her way in the world.

"I know you're scared but you don't need to be," he continues. "All I've ever wanted was to raise you to be the kind of person who knows right from wrong, and here you are, risking everything to save all of those innocent people and kiddo, I couldn't be prouder." He gets choked up and has to stop and clear his throat. I feel emotion rising up in the back of my own throat and I have to blink away the tears blurring my vision so that I can look into his determined eyes.

No dad, you don't understand, I want to say.
I just can't lose you.
I'd be so lost without you.

"I know that you think that you need me, but you don't. Not anymore. But there is something that you need to do. And it's okay, kiddo. It's okay. I'm ready. I want to be with your mother. We've done all that we can in this fight. It's up to you now." The reassurance in his eyes is so familiar; I've seen it a thousand times. Coaxing me, encouraging me when times were tough, when I felt like giving up. But none of those instances could ever compare to what he is asking me to do. Nothing in my life could have ever prepared me. *Sometimes in life, you'll have to be incredibly brave. And you'll have a choice to make.*

I take a breath before delivering the most painful words I've ever expressed. "I can't help you, Eira," I say, breaking my own heart while doing so. "Kill my father if you must, kill Linc, kill me, it doesn't matter. Soon your city will fall, and you with it."

The words ring out of me like a declaration, sending the wheels of fate turning. What has been set into motion cannot be undone. My decision has been made.

"You continue to surprise me, Arin." Eira's voice is barely more than a growl. I have a brief flicker of hope stir in my chest. Maybe she will have a change of heart. Surely, she won't force her daughter to watch her only family die? No one could be that cruel.

"Kill him." The command cuts through my heart like a knife, knocking the breath out of me, and turning the ground beneath me into sinking sand. I struggle against my bonds, I struggle to breathe, I struggle to comprehend what is happening before me.

"No!" I am powerless, I am stuck, I am going to be forced to watch something that no child should ever have to endure. *Please no, please no.* The words beat within me like a heartbeat, taking control of my pulse, squeezing through my veins until there is nothing left except a single thought: *no no no no no no.* The sound of a gun firing comes to me from a far-off place, almost like I'm in a dream. It must be a dream, this can't be real.

"Behold, the consequences of your actions." Director Ellis stands triumphantly over my father's body, as I watch crimson red blood pool across the laboratory floor, like a river creeping toward me. I watch as it overtakes everything in its path, tiny droplets turning everything red. Leaving me indescribably and indefinitely alone.

I don't want to be strong anymore. Instead, I let my body sink down into the floor and I pray that somehow the ground will swallow me, and I can just disappear. Because I don't want to live in this world anymore. I just want to lie down. I just want to close my eyelids, let the sweet relief of darkness overtake me, and never open them again.

From the surface, I hear chatter over the radio, voices shouting and one of the guards saying, "We need to barricade the door, they've reached the white level." That must mean that the Rebel soldiers have made it into Paramus and into the Cortex building. Out of the corner of my eye I can see the last few seconds tick down on the central computer and when it gets to zero, the screen goes black.

We did it.

The nanobots have been disabled. I want to feel some sort of sense of accomplishment, some sort of victory, but I can't bring myself to feel anything. Arin is gone.

Someone yanks me up to my feet, I don't try to struggle. The fight inside me is finished. Too much sadness can break a person. I understand that now.

"You're coming with me," Eira growls in my ear and I can feel her slender fingers like talons wrapped tightly around my arm as she drags me away from the only people I've ever loved. I count the bodies as she pulls me through a door that I've never seen before: *Mom, Dad, Linc, Kace. Gone, gone, gone, gone.* Four artificial soldiers tightly surround us as we climb a dark and narrow staircase where the air that I pull into my lungs tastes damp and old, as if it hasn't seen daylight in a long time. I have no idea where we are or where we are going, but it hardly matters now. My hands and feet are still cuffed so my steps are slow and clumsy as Eira has to practically drag me upward. *Just kill me too,* I try to say the words, but nothing comes out. *I don't want to GO anywhere with anyone. I just want to die.* Eventually we stop outside of a heavy black door and I'm shoved inside. I blink slowly as my eyes adjust to the light, this room is even darker than the hidden corridor, lit only by a series of blinking dials and flashing little lights.

"Guard the door!" Eira commands the accompanying soldiers, and they place themselves in front of the room's entrances, both main and secret. Eira releases my arm and I sink to the floor, letting the cool white marble welcome me as I wait to die.

"Before we make our escape, I need to send one final broadcast," she explains. "I need the citizens of Paramus to know the truth about what I was trying to do, before these wretched Rebel soldiers try and defame my name." Her words set a kindling of a tiny fire in my chest, and I blink my eyes open from the daze I was in. I turn to watch Eira intently. How dare she, with so much blood on her hands, think that she deserves to give the city a charming farewell?

I know that the people out there must be scared, what with the Rebel soldiers flooding through the wall and the fighting happening all around us in the Cortex building. But if Eira goes out there and feeds them some kind of lie, making the Lost people out to be the enemy, then they might just believe her. And they might just fight back. And more Lost lives will be lost. No, the people of Paramus need to know who the true enemy is.

"Citizens of Paramus." Eira's usual greeting kick starts my heart with adrenaline as I fold myself in half and make myself small, out of the line of sight of the armed guards at each end of the room. Once I am sure that they cannot see me, I try to wriggle my handcuffed fingers down into my boot and, after a bit of careful maneuvering, I can feel the cold handle of the blade between my fingers. I slowly wriggle it along my body, working quickly to get it up to my mouth, checking every few seconds to make sure that neither guard has noticed me. With the handle firmly clasped beneath my teeth, I make careful work of the fasteners holding my electro-cuffs together. After what feels like a million rotations of my knife, the smallest screws pop away and the electric current goes out. From there, it's easy to remove the cuff and turn my attention to my second hand and then the cuffs around my ankles.

"In these unprecedented times, there are so little things that we as a city can be truly certain of. I thought it my duty to remind you of those truths as we impede this attack on our great city and show the resilience that we are known for as Gifted people." I try to ignore the burning indignation that flares up in my chest as Eira continues to lie to the people of Paramus and instead turn my attention to the guards left in the room. One has been stationed outside of the broadcasting room door, and one inside. The same with the secret entrance, one inside and one out. Two armed AI guards in the room to one Arin, not the best of odds.

Thankfully, I do have the element of surprise in my favor. I watch as the closest soldier droid scans the room slowly, counting how long it takes for him to get from one end to the other. When he starts his rotation over again, I make my move. Belly pressed against the broadcasting room floor, I shimmy quickly, my elbows complaining as they grind against the ground to pull me forward. My vision is zeroed in on one single point as I keep to the shadows and I crawl toward my target as Eira drones on in the background.

"We must turn and fight these Lost scum. They want to see everything that we've built crumble, they want to drag us down to desolation with them because they can *never* be what we are."

I grit my teeth as I get closer to the robot's legs, painfully aware that the number of seconds that I have left to make my attack is now almost zero. My heart pounds loudly against my rib cage as I carefully reach for the stun cuffs tucked beneath my shirt and set them to arm. They give a little crackle of electricity that makes me flinch as they start up, but no one else seems to have heard it. With all of the speed that I can muster, I strike swiftly and true, lunging forward to lock the stun cuffs around the artificial soldier's ankles and giving it a strong shove from behind, sending it toppling. It barely has time to register what has happened before I'm on top of the droid, wrestling it's firearm away. As soon as I feel the stun gun securely in my hand, I send one blast through the droid's brain and the other goes across the room to the second droid, who has already started shooting. I see Eira's eyes widen as she realizes what is happening. She looks almost comical, frozen in place for the first time ever during a live broadcast, mouth open but no words coming out. *Not such a fearless leader after all.*

The other two droids burst into the room from their posts outside of the door and fill the room with zig-zagged bursts of fire power. Eira screams and drops to the ground as one stray shot hits an exposed wire in the broadcasting panel and the entire thing bursts into flames, quickly filling the room with smoke. I take cover behind a large cart full of broadcasting equipment, peeking out only when I think that I've got a clear shot. Thankfully, the droids are loud, and I use that and the direction of their shots to find them, even as the air grows thick with smoke. I double check my calculations in my head before squeezing the trigger. Thankfully, the next sound is the screech of hot corroding metal as the blast burns away at the droids' circuits, sending it crashing to the ground. I can hear the sound of Eira choking on the smoke as it reaches where she is still standing, frozen in front of the broadcast camera, although I'm not sure if it's still sending anything out since a lot of the equipment is currently on fire. Under normal circumstances, the building would have already dispatched safety droids to put out the blaze but now that the entire building is unplugged, there are no safety measures in place and no way to stop the flames. I glance at Eira, who seems to no longer be in shock and is now glancing back and forth between both doors. I bet that she is going to try and make a run for it.

I feel the weight of the stun gun in my hands as I roll out from behind my cover, sending an array of blasts in the direction of the last droid, not so calculated this time, hoping that at least one of them is successful. I don't have time for precision at the moment—I need to make sure that Eira doesn't get away. The return fire stops so that must mean that one of my shots landed where it was supposed to. I grin triumphantly. Now there is nothing that stands in between Eira and I.

The fire around us crackles, like a big, impenetrable wall, quickly closing in. The heat causes my eyes to sting and the black smoke of so many different burning objects assaults the inside of my nose and burns my throat as I close in. Both exits on either side of us have been engulfed in the angry flames. I grip the stun gun tightly in my hand. Eira is trapped. It's either me or the fire, and she knows it. When I lock eyes with her, she looks back at me with an emotion that I've never seen before in her eyes. Fear.

The flames lick across the ground around us and billow towards the ceiling, sending waves of heat that singe my skin as I keep the gun trained steadily on my enemy. My heart pounds in my chest as I try to work up the courage to pull the trigger. *Come on Arin, just pull it and leave her here for the flames. She just killed everyone that you've ever loved. She deserves this.* To her credit, Eira doesn't try to plead with me. After all, what could she possibly say?

As I stare at the frightened woman before me, her panicked eyes darting frantically to the wall of flames and then back to the barrel of my gun, I want to feel the burning fires of rage in my veins, calling for revenge, after all that she's done, but it doesn't come. Instead, I hear Maz's voice in my head. *We belong to each other, no one is better than the other. We are all human.*

Eira always said that she saw a lot of herself in me. That we were so much alike. But the truth is, I'm not anything like her. And that means that I can't leave her here to die.

"Aargh!" I growl with frustration and shove the stun gun into the waistband of my pants while the thickening cloud of smoke continues to grow between us. I need to leave while I still have the chance. "You're on your own, Eira!" I manage to yell through the cloud that threatens to choke me with my very next breath. "No more favors from me!" I warn as I turn to go, and if she replies, it's lost in the roar of the hungry flames and the crackling of burning walls nearly ready to collapse. I don't look back as I run away from the control room, putting as much distance between myself and that nightmare as possible, my lungs begging for clean air.

There's no need for hidden staircases now, I decide as I make my way to the nearest elevators. The rebel soldiers have infiltrated Cortex and are well on their way to an easy victory. The air around me is filled with ear splitting screeches of emergency alarms as I step into the elevator. As the ascent begins to the white level, the glass walls give me a bird's eye view of the pandemonium below. People are spilling out of dorms and out of labs, a sea of confusion in these early morning hours. I'm sure many of the employees were sleeping when the chaos erupted, Rebel soldiers bursting onto each level, guns blazing, making arrests right and left. I wonder how many of them saw Eira's last broadcast? I also wonder what they think about the fact that Cortex has been taken over? I wish that I could get a message to them, telling the truth. The next few hours are going to no doubt be complete pandemonium. Maybe even the next few days.

Just as I can start to make out the white level, I spot several council members being escorted by rebel soldiers with weapons drawn.

What a sight. My mind flashes back to my mother and father.

To Kace.

To Linc.

They would have loved to have seen this.

The world is changing.

The elevator doors open with a pleasant chime and I step out carefully. Broken glass and paper litter the ground underfoot, the crunching of my footsteps echoing in the empty halls. The halls of this level are swarming with rebel soldiers, and several of them acknowledge me as I pass but I don't have anything to say to them neither do I think that I could say anything if I wanted to. The lump in my throat grows bigger and bigger with every familiar step that takes me back to the lab. *I need to see them. I need to say goodbye.*

"Hey!" I hear Ret's familiar voice as I reach the part of the glossy white room where I lost everything. But I barely hear him. My eyes are glued to the shape, respectfully covered up with the Rebel's army green jackets. I blink. One of them is missing. Whose body isn't there? My mind replays the horrible events of my father's last few moments. The gun, the blood. It can't be him. I feel my whole body start to shake. "Are you okay?" *No. And I never will be.*

"Arin, I need to know if you need medical attention." Ret approaches me, his voice concerned. But what can I say? That unless he can bring my mother and father and Linc and Kace back that there is nothing that I will ever need ever again?

"I don't need medical attention," I answer, despite the parts of me that are singed from the fire and the stabbing pain in my side. It doesn't matter. Nothing matters. The words that I say come out sounding flat. Hollow. Out of the corner of my eye I see a glimpse of something that jolts me back to life. The flash of a white pantsuit.

"Kace!" I yell, practically tripping over my own feet as I run to the side of my beautiful friend, her arm in an intricate bandage and her torn pant suit stained with blood. She's alive. "You're okay!" She wraps me up in a tight embrace with her good arm and as I bury my face in her soft, strawberry curls, I feel hot, warm tears roll down my cheeks. "I thought I lost you."

"I thought so too," she says, "but Eira's weapon was just a stun gun. It only knocked me out temporarily. And when I came to, the soldiers were here." *Wait, if Eira's gun wasn't lethal ... does that mean, the missing body belongs to Linc?*

"Have you seen Linc?" I gulp, but she shakes her head sadly. "No, when I woke up, he was gone." She glances over to the spot where my father's body lies. "Arin, your dad. I'm so sorry." I give her a somber nod.

"I need to say goodbye," I say mournfully.

"I'm not sure that is a good idea ..." Ret starts to say as I take careful steps towards him, but I ignore his warning.

There is a buzz of activity going on all around me but it all fades into the background as I drop to my knees beside a small mound covered by an army green coat. With trembling hands, I slowly pull back the fabric. My eyes are immediately drawn to the fine lines around my father's eyes that would crinkle when he would smile. A sob racks through my chest as I reach out and trace the familiar creases with my fingers. I can't believe that he'll never smile again.

"I'm sorry," I tell him, voice breaking as the tears come cascading down. "I wish that I could have saved you," I whisper, dropping my head onto my father's chest but there is no steady heartbeat to greet me, no warm reassurance, only cold silence. And in that silence, I find myself singing, voice and fingers shaking as I lift my head and begin to smooth his hair and close his eyes, saying a final goodbye.

May our candles light your way and bring you safely home.
We sing for those who've gone before, we miss them, every one.
May their footsteps guide you, until your journey's done.
For I am you, and you are me, and we exist as one.

"For I am you, and you are me, and we exist as one," I repeat, unsure just how I am going to be able to carry on in this world without his warmth and their guidance. I would give anything in this moment to be out from under the curious eyes of this room full of Rebel soldiers, completely alone. I just need to find somewhere quiet and dark so that I can scream and scream and scream until I explode like a supernova star and there is nothing left.

"Arin?" a familiar voice crackles in my skin coms, pulling me from the deepest darkest depth of sorrow. My consciousness rushes to the surface and it's like I can breathe again.

"Linc?" I gasp, startling the nearest soldier because I jump to my feet so quickly. "Where are you?" I frantically search the room around me for his face. "I thought you were dead!"

"I'm sorry, Arin." His voice is full of remorse and I wonder if he has any idea what the past hour has been like for me. "I … I didn't know if something had happened to you either. I'm so glad you're okay." I can hear his relief through my earpiece. "Just hang on, I'm coming." My heart swells with gratitude and I can feel the sting of tears threatening to break free and tumble down my cheeks. *Linc is alive!*

I feel a hand on my shoulder and turn to see Ret, his eyes sincere. "We will make sure that your father has the best burial ceremony that our people have ever seen," he assures me, before bending down and carefully covering my father's face again. When he's finished, he turns to me and I can see the emotion in his eyes. "He gave so much so that our people could live." He pauses, offering me a gentle smile. "You both did."

Without thinking, I find myself reaching out to embrace him, and he wraps me up in a tight hug that feels warm and reassuring and kind all at once. And after we separate, I feel like a small piece of me maybe isn't so broken. Ret is right. The sacrifices made today were huge, but I can't forget that they were made for a very important reason.

The Lost are saved.

"Arin!" It's Linc! His voice, in person, sends a jolt of electricity through me. *He's here and he's alive!* I find myself running, blindly at first, almost in a panic, until I spot him across the room through a sea of people. As soon as our eyes lock, a magnetic pull yanks me forward and I'm pushing through the crowd, feeling like I won't be able to breathe again until I can reach out and touch him.

And suddenly he's there. Standing right in front of me, green eyes dancing.

He's alive.

"It's really you," I breathe, drinking him in. Strong arms wrap around me as he pulls me tightly against his chest in an embrace so firm, I don't think he will ever let me go. I feel as though I could weep as the familiar smell of him washes over me and when I look up to meet his gaze, they mirror the same feelings of relief that are swelling in my own chest. Before I can say another word his lips crash into mine, hands tangled in my hair, pulling me closer with an intensity that reminds me that we are very much alive. His kisses pull me out from under the waves of despair that had threatened to overtake me, and when our lips finally part, I can feel my feet once again standing on solid ground. We stay locked in each other's embrace for a moment, unable to let go or to look away. Kace comes squealing from across the room.

"Linc!" She nearly plows him over with her relieved embrace. "I was so worried!" He gives her a tight hug in return, and we all stand there, rejoicing at the fact that we are reunited once again.

"We did it," Linc says with a smile, squeezing both of my hands. "It's over." I smile back at him but deep down I know that it isn't over. There is a whole new world waiting outside of this building, thousands of people whose lives will never be the same now that the wall has come down and their leader is gone. Who will guide them into this new era?

"Linc, there's something that I would like to say, to everyone." There is determination in my voice as I make the decision to speak to the people about what has occurred here today. "The last thing that everyone heard this morning was Eira's message of hate about the Lost. We can't let that be the message of today. Paramus deserves to know the truth." He nods.

"The broadcasting systems are down but I bet we can figure out a way to get your message to everyone. I'm supposed to meet with Steele and Sol in the high chambers. Let's see if they have any ideas."

He turns to go but I hesitate. My dad is in this room. I don't want to leave him.

"It's okay," Linc murmurs as he follows my gaze to the place where soldiers are carefully lifting the army-green-clad figure onto a stretcher, faces somber. "He wouldn't want to stay here."

Of course, Linc is right. Neither of my parents ever felt at home in Paramus, because their people have always been the Lost. And the Lost are my people now too, along with Paramus and its citizens. *We belong to each other.*

"I'm ready," I announce and with one last whispered goodbye, follow Linc away from this room, with Kace's reassuring hand on my shoulder, away from the darkness that occurred here and hopefully forward, on to something brighter.

Steele and Sol are thrilled to see us when we meet with them in the high chambers, greeting Linc and I with warm embraces and enthusiastic claps on the back. Sol's greeting to Kace is a bit more intimate, I find myself looking away from the series of passionate kisses. When they break away, Sol's entire face is beaming as he exclaims, "The wonder girl does it again!"

"Well, she's not quite done yet," Linc interjects, and Steele watches him curiously. "Arin has something that she would like to say to the people. We can't let Eira's poisonous words be the start of this brave new world we are building." Steele nods, his expression somber.

"I agree. And once the people hear the truth, we can let them decide what to do with her."

I feel my stomach drop as my head whips over to look at him. "She's been captured?"

"Oh yes, we caught her trying to flee. She was suffering from a few minor burns but still very much alive. I don't know how she managed to even get as far as she did with as many Rebel soldiers that we had in the building. She must be pretty damn lucky." I feel a pang of guilt in my chest. Luck had nothing to do with it.

"We can worry about Director Ellis later." Linc glances at Sol. "How soon can we be ready to broadcast?"

"Give me ten minutes."

CHAPTER

"You cannot know where you are going unless you know the history of where you've been."

- Maz Figueroa

My palms are sweating as I stare at the makeshift setup that we threw together for the broadcast in the middle of the high chamber. It didn't look so intimidating until the lights were added and now, with the camera in place, it's all starting to feel a little too real. I take a deep breath and try to quiet my nerves. *So what if there are ten thousand people watching just on the other side of that camera?* I've faced far worse things today. *And so have they,* I remind myself. The people on the other side of that lens are scared and confused. Many of them are seeing things today for the first time and probably all of them are wondering, what's next?

What's next? A question that I find that I keep asking myself. *What will this new Era look like?* I look away from the intimidating broadcasting setup and catch a glimpse of Kace, who is now forever safe from Eira and her council. She gives me an encouraging smile, as if to say, *you can do this.* I feel a reassuring hand press against my lower back, and I don't even have to turn around to know Linc is there, his mere presence enveloping me like a warm hug. I know that he too, believes in me, and the message that I need to bring to the people.

On the other side of the lights, Sol is busy at work, prepping the signal to be spread all across Paramus and Steele sits quietly, observing us all, content that there is only this one last battle to win. The battle for the hearts of the Lost and the people of Paramus. What exactly can be said to bring such opposing groups of people together? How can you plant seeds of unity where there has only been division and hate? For once, I don't know how to solve this problem, but I'm willing to try.

I square my shoulders, standing up tall before stepping in front of the blinding broadcast lights, turning everything into a sea of white until it's just myself and the camera in front of me. What I say next will either divide the people or finally, after all of this time, bring them together. But every problem has a solution, and sometimes you just have to find the calm in the middle of the storm.

I take a deep breath and give a nod to Sol so that he knows that it's time.

"We're ready," he calls and then a heavy silence falls over the room. I stare into the round eye of the camera, imaging the sea of faces waiting, listening intently on the other side. A small smile creeps across my lips. I know just what to say.

"Sometimes, life requires you to be extremely brave. And you'll have a choice to make."

The End

EPILOGUE

I stand next to Linc, his hand is warm in mine, overlooking the unending sea of crumbling white debris scattered between what once was Paramus and what once was the Lost city. For the first time in my life, I can watch the golden sun emerge onto the horizon, and I firmly believe that this is only one of many firsts now that the wall has been torn down. The first few weeks of what we are calling the "new era" have been a combination of chaos and beauty. It's incredible how much people can change under new leadership. Maz is leading the two people groups beautifully, and I hope that although they can only see the differences between them for the time being, that they will one day see themselves as belonging to just the one people group, which has yet to be named.

That morning at dinner, Linc, Kace, Sol, Steele, Ret, and a Gifted girl named Ana toss around ideas for what we should call the new colony.

"What about Concord?" Linc proposes through a bite of his apple.

"That's too serious." Kace interjects from her seat next to Sol, her head resting on his shoulder. "It needs to be something beautiful."

"Like Kace." Sol adds and the entire table groans.

"How about New Haven?" Ret's voice is so quiet that we all have to still to hear him. "Because this new city is a place for all." There are murmurs of agreement around the table, and I watch as Steele nods his head in agreement.

"I like it. Let's propose it to Maz after we're finished here." Steele suggests and I watch Ret's smile grow wide, and I already know in my heart that this is what we should be called.

"How did you come up with that?" I'm still amazed what those who were once labeled "witless" are contributing to our new society every day.

"Well my daughter's name is Haven," he grins sheepishly, and I can't help but smile. Ret's daughter, like so many others, was saved when the nanobots went offline. In total, the lives lost were just under two dozen and Gifted lives less than ten. There is one name still missing from that list though, Eira Ellis. Unfortunately, she hadn't been seen or heard from since the day she escaped Cortex. We had scouts looking though. It was thought that perhaps she ventured beyond the Lost Colony, to the uncharted, outer lying wastelands that our forefathers had never been brave enough to explore. I wasn't sure what or who was out there. Until recently, I had believed that Paramus was the only civilized city in the world. I was wrong about that. Who knows what else I could be misinformed about.

"Sir," a soldier named Flek pokes his head through the canvas flaps of the meal tent and Steele rises from the table to speak with him. "Our patrols just apprehended someone on the outskirts of the former Lost territory." My ears tune in to the conversation with new interest, my heart skipping a beat in my chest. *Could it be?*

"Do you know who it is?" Steele presses, and the rest of the group waits with bated breath for the Scout's announcement. Flek's sunburnt cheeks flush red and I can tell that he isn't used to speaking in front of such a large group of people. He clears his throat.

"It's former Director Ellis, sir." My pulse quickens and there is an audible gasp from somewhere on the other side of the table, but I don't turn to look. My eyes are glued to the scout, eagerly awaiting any more information. Unfortunately, he has none, and Steele departs with him to assist with the capture of Paramus' former leader. My stomach churns in knots as I try to imagine what will happen to her now that she has been found.

There's one thing that I know for sure, the issue of what to do with Eira, my biological mother, could divide the two people groups if not handled correctly. Linc notices my uneasiness and gives my arm a reassuring squeeze.

"Things are different now, Arin. This is New Haven. Justice will be served." I nod my agreement, but in the bottom of my stomach I can't help but worry about what this group will consider justice. As much as I thought that I wanted it, I now realize that I don't want to watch Eira, or anyone, die. There has been enough death in recent months to last for the rest of my lifetime. Besides, New Haven is a place where all are welcome. Does that mean the former leader of Cortex as well?

Even though I have the highest Criterion score ever recorded, I certainly don't have the answers. A fresh, new world sounds exciting, but navigating the waters of justice and replacing outdated ideologies with new ones is not an easy task. As Linc and I emerge from the tent, hand in hand, we once again look out over the unique souls that make up New Haven, with all of their differences, and with even more similarities, I know one thing for certain.

Whatever we decide, we will all decide together. No more will there be a cruel sovereign leader with a corrupt council.

No, this time, I have hope that we will do better.

And I know we will.

Because hope is a powerful thing.

the story continues:

HUNTED

coming spring 2022

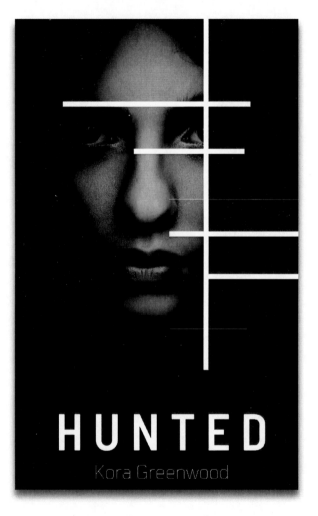

www.KoraGreenwood.com